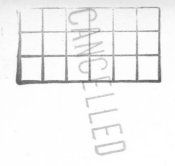

Prince

Also by Rory Clements

Martyr
Revenger

Prince

RORY CLEMENTS

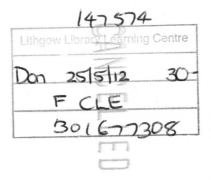

JOHN MURRAY

First published in Great Britain in 2011 by John Murray (Publishers)
An Hachette UK Company

1

© Rory Clements 2011

Map by Rosie Collins

A CIP catalogue record for this title is available from the British Library

Hardback ISBN 978-1-84854-425-3
Trade paperback ISBN 978-1-84854-426-0

Typeset in Adobe Garamond by Servis Filmsetting Ltd, Stockport, Cheshire

Printed and bound by Clays Ltd, St Ives plc

John Murray policy is to use papers that are natural, renewable and recyclable products and
made from wood grown in sustainable forests. The logging and manufacturing processes are
expected to conform to the environmental regulations of the country of origin.

John Murray (Publishers)
338 Euston Road
London NW1 3BH

www.johnmurray.co.uk

For Naomi,
my sweetheart and loving wife

Elizabet...

Gaynes Park Hall

City of London

Clerkenwell

Bromley-by-Bow

Three Mills Powdermill

Dutch Church

London Bridge

River Lea

Westminster

River

Southwark

Rotherhithe Powdermill

Isle of Dogs

Erith Marshes

Deptford

Greenwich

Hampton Court

Molesey

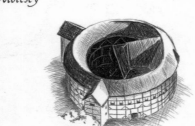

Godstone Powdermill

h's Thames

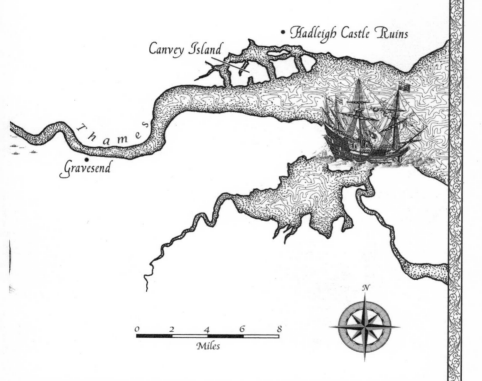

• Hadleigh Castle Ruins

Canvey Island

Thames

Gravesend

N

0   2   4   6   8
Miles

In Chambers, twenty in one house will lurke,
Raysing of rents, was never knowne before
   Living farre better then at native home
And our pore soules, are cleane thrust out of dore
   And to the warres are sent abroade to rome,
To fight it out for Fraunce & Belgia,
   And dy like dogges as sacrifice for you
Expect you therefore such a fatall day
   Shortly on you, & yours for to ensewe:
   as never was seene.
Since words nor threates nor any other thinge
   canne make you to avoyd this certaine ill
Weele cutt your throtes, in your temples praying
   Not paris massacre so much blood did spill
As we will doe iust vengeance on you all.

Chapter 1

FOUR MEN STARED down at the body of Christopher Marlowe. A last trickle of bright gore oozed from the deep wound over his right eye. His face and hair and upper torso were all thick with blood. One of the four men, Ingram Frizer, held the dripping dagger in his hand.

Frizer looked across at Robert Poley and grinned foolishly. 'He came at me.'

'Boar's balls, Mr Frizer, give me the dagger,' Poley said angrily.

Frizer held out the dagger. All the living eyes in the room followed the tentative movement of the blood-red blade. A sliver of brain hung like a grey-pink rat's tail from its tip. Poley took the weapon and wiped it on the dead poet's white hose. Suddenly, he struck out with the hilt and caught Frizer a hard blow on the side of his head. Frizer lurched backwards. Poley pushed him to the floor and jumped on him, knees on chest, hitting his head again, harder, pounding him until Nick Skeres tried to pull him away.

Poley stood back, shook off Skeres's hands and brushed down his doublet with sharp irritation. He was not a tall man, but he was strongly built and the veins in his muscled forearms and temples bulged out and pulsed. He kicked Frizer in the ribs. 'You were only supposed to gag him and apply the fingerscrew, you dung-witted dawcock. Not kill him.'

The afternoon sunlight of late May slanted in through the single, west-facing window. The presence of the men and the body made the room feel smaller than it really was. It was cleanly furnished; a well-turned settle made of fine-grained elm, a day bed where the body now lay, a table of polished walnut with benches either side and half-drunk jugs of ale atop it. The dusty floorboards were scuffed by the men's shoes; there was, too, a lot of blood and a few splashes of ale on the wood between the table and the day bed.

'And you . . .' Poley turned to Skeres. 'You were supposed to hold him. He was out of his mind with drink and you couldn't keep a grip.'

Ingram Frizer pulled himself painfully to his feet. He was doubled over, clutching his side where Poley's boot had connected.

Poley handed him the dagger. 'Here, take it. And listen well: it was *his* dagger – Marlowe's dagger. He came at you, pummelled your head with it. You fought back. In the struggle, the blade pierced his eye. You were defending yourself – it was an accident.'

Frizer took the dagger. He was slender with a lopsided face, the left eye half an inch higher than the right. The skin had been cut from the side of his head by Poley's beating. There was a livid gash, almost to the bone. His head and ribs throbbed, but he understood Poley's plan well enough. 'I liked this dagger,' he said, turning the weapon over in his hands and examining the ornate hilt and narrow, sharp-pointed blade. 'Cost me half a mark.' He tried to laugh.

'Well, it'll be Crown property now. Marlowe was always fighting. He was going to kill you. It's a simple story; remember it.' Poley turned to the third man, Skeres. 'And you, Mr Skeres.'

Skeres nodded. His bulbous face was sweating heavily. He mopped a kerchief across his brow. His gaze kept flicking towards the body, and then across to the fourth man, who stood close by the door. So far he had said nothing.

'No, let's change that,' Poley said, shaking his head slowly. 'Someone might recall that dagger. Say it was yours, Mr Frizer, but Marlowe snatched it off you, then you wrenched it away from him as he battered you. You struck backwards wildly, didn't know what you had done. Got that? And the knife didn't cost you half a mark, it cost you a shilling. The rest of the story holds.' Poley suddenly slammed his fist down on the table. 'Where's the screw?'

Ingram Frizer pointed to the floor beneath the window, to where a five-inch by four-inch vice of iron lay. It was designed to crush the fingers of a hand, slowly and painfully.

'Do I have to think for both of you? Pick it up!'

Frizer scurried across the room and brought the device back to Poley, who thrust it inside his doublet.

At last the fourth man spoke. He was heavy-set with a wispy beard. 'I'm going now. Wait two hours, drink some ale, then call the constable and the coroner. None of this comes back to me or my master. I was never here.'

'No,' Poley agreed. He understood well enough. There must only ever have been four men in this room, not five.

The man took one last look around the room and met the eyes of Poley, Skeres and Frizer. 'Not one word.' He lifted the latch and silently left the room.

The other three watched him go. A seagull landed on the sill of the open window, defecated, then flew off. 'There's a problem,' Skeres said, shaking the sweat out of his eyes.

'The only problem,' Poley said, 'is *you*. You're a flaccid prick of a man, Skeres.'

'We've got to say what they were fighting about, haven't we?'

'It was the bill, of course. The reckoning. Frizer said Marlowe had drunk more so should pay more. Mr Marlowe wanted to quarter the bill evenly.'

'The coroner will never believe it.'

Poley laughed. 'Pour the ale, Mr Skeres, then light me a pipe. How has a coney like you ever lived this long? Hear that, Mr Frizer? Mr Skeres says the coroner will never believe it.' Poley laughed again, louder this time, and Frizer and Skeres laughed nervously with him.

Chapter 2

JOHN SHAKESPEARE SPOKE briefly to the constable standing guard, before entering the room. He was a tall man, about six foot, and had to stoop to get through the door. He glanced around, taking in the furnishings, the window, the body. It was a fair-kept room. He stepped closer to the bloody remains of Christopher Marlowe and stared intently into his eyes. One was open and opaque, the other a black-brown scab of dried gore and brain. He remembered those clever eyes as they had been in the old days when he had performed certain secret tasks for Mr Secretary Walsingham. Marlowe had been clever and dangerous. Well, he'd met someone more dangerous.

The other three men in the room stood quietly by the table. Shakespeare caught Poley's gaze. They knew each other well. There had been times when they worked together, back in the mid eighties. It had never been a comfortable experience for Shakespeare. Now he lifted his chin in acknowledgement, if not exactly in greeting.

'Who did this, Poley? Who killed him?'

'Mr Frizer here. Ingram Frizer. It was self-defence. You know what Kit Marlowe was like.'

Indeed he did. Marlowe had been a fighter, a drinker, a poet, a character in the drama of his own life. He was Tamburlaine, Dr Faustus and any other number of Bedlam loons and

Shoreditch roarers, all rolled into one. He had been trouble; uncontrollable. Yes, self-defence seemed likely enough, knowing what Marlowe was like, with or without strong ale in his belly. The nagging doubt was the presence of Rob Poley. Very little was accidental when he was in the vicinity. Shakespeare turned to the others. 'Which one of you is Frizer?'

Frizer took two steps forward. He held the cleaned dagger in front of him, laid across both palms. Shakespeare did not take it from him; instead he gestured with his head to the table. 'Put it down over there.'

From outside, the bellman called nine of the clock. The room was still light. 'When did this happen?' Shakespeare demanded.

'Six,' Poley said. 'He was cup-shotten from a surfeit of ale. Wouldn't pay his portion of the bill. Attacked Mr Frizer here – and Mr Frizer defended himself.'

Shakespeare nodded. It sounded reasonable enough. But he didn't believe a word of it. 'What were you doing here?' He addressed the question to Ingram Frizer.

'Playing at cards,' Poley said. 'Smoking sotweed and drinking good ale.' He nodded towards the now empty ale jugs. 'Eating, too. Ellie Bull roasts a fine head of young pig and most excellent sweetmeats.'

'Do you speak for all, Mr Poley? The question was for Mr Frizer.'

'We were all here – I was just answering your question.'

'Well, don't, unless a question is asked of you.' He turned once more to Frizer. 'So where, pray, are the playing cards?'

Frizer looked blankly at Shakespeare, then nervously towards Poley. 'I – they—'

'I have them here,' Poley said, fetching a pack from his doublet. 'If I am permitted to speak, that is.'

'Put them over there, by the dagger.'

Poley ambled over to the table and fanned the cards out with a final, crisp flick for the last one. He smiled at Shakespeare. 'Might I know your interest in this sorry affair, Mr Shakespeare? It is naught but an everyday manslaughter and we were told to wait for coroner Danby. We have all stayed here in the proper way of things; none has attempted flight. What possible interest can this occurrence, tragical though it be, have for such an eminent a servant of the Crown as Mr John Shakespeare, senior secretary to Sir Robert Cecil?'

Shakespeare ignored the question. He was here because this was most decidedly his business. He had been investigating Marlowe on the orders of Cecil and a special Privy Council commission of inquiry. Marlowe had been suspected of involvement in an unsavoury episode – a vicious written attack on the many foreigners now living in London. A placard posted outside the Dutch church in Broad Street insulted England's Protestant friends from the Low Countries and France who had sought refuge here. Marlowe's style seemed to be writ all over the poster: fifty-three lines of seditious doggerel – and not just insults and threats to slit the incomers' throats, but strong criticism of the Queen and her government for allowing them to come here.

And why, specifically, was Marlowe a suspect? Because the placard was signed *Tamburlaine* – the heathen warrior king of his most celebrated play.

Yes, thought Shakespeare, this death was most certainly of interest.

'You,' he said brusquely, turning to Skeres. 'Who else was here?'

Unlike Frizer, Skeres had enough presence of mind not to glance towards Poley for guidance. But he was sweating heavily, even though the warmth of the day was long since turned to evening chill. 'Us three and Marlowe. That's all.'

'What is your name?'

'Skeres. Nick Skeres.'

'Who is your master?'

'I am my own man. I have property. My family is in the cloth trade – drapers, tailors.'

Shakespeare had heard the name Skeres before. Like Poley, he had worked for Walsingham occasionally. His presence in this room stank of rancid fat.

'Sweat pours from you like a heavy rainfall, Mr Skeres. Are you afraid of something?'

'A man has died here. What Christian would not be shaken, sir?'

'Indeed.'

'Would you like me to tell you exactly what happened, Mr Shakespeare?' Poley asked, his face a guileless mask.

'Save it for the coroner, Mr Poley. I am sure you have it well rehearsed . . .'

The door creaked open. All eyes turned to see the slim figure of Joshua Peace entering the room. Shakespeare smiled in greeting and stepped forward to clasp his hand. 'Thank you for coming, Joshua. It is good to see you.'

'What's *he* doing here?' Poley burst out.

'Mr Peace? He is here to examine the body and the scene of the crime – if there was a crime, of course. We must not pre-judge these matters, Mr Poley.' Shakespeare studied Poley's face, but the man had recovered himself.

Peace strode towards the corpse, barely acknowledging the three witnesses. For a few moments he stood and stared at the dead face. 'Marlowe, eh? A fair playmaker in his day. Smells like a taproom in here.' Peace, the Searcher of the Dead, was a man in his mid to late thirties. His eyes shone with wit and humour, yet you would pass him in the street and not note him. He was almost bald save for a thin circle of brown hair that always reminded Shakespeare of a monk's tonsure.

The Searcher rolled back his sleeve, then slid his right hand and forearm inside Marlowe's bloody doublet. He held it there against the dead man's still chest, the tips of his fingers in the armpit, for a full minute. At last he withdrew his hand. 'How long do you think he's been dead, John?'

'This crew of villains say he died at six — so that's three hours.'

Peace shook his head. 'No, five at least. Perhaps even six hours gone. He died between three and four of the clock.'

'Well, Mr Skeres, what do you say to that?'

'It's all lies—' Poley broke in.

Shakespeare thrust the palm of his hand into Poley's face, smacking his head against the wall to stop his mouth. 'Learn some manners, Mr Poley. Speak when you are spoken to.' He held Poley there, pinioned. 'Now, Mr Skeres, if you please.'

'Six of the clock. He died at six hours.'

Peace picked up the dagger and examined it. He held its tip to the wound over the eye, then slipped it slowly through the gore, four inches into the depths of Marlowe's head without resistance. 'Well, this is most certainly the weapon that inflicted the wound. A common enough assassin's strike, I would say.'

'It was an accident!' Poley shouted, wrenching his mouth from Shakespeare's grasp. 'It was a brabble. God's wounds, look at Mr Frizer's head. Look what Marlowe did to him first.'

Shakespeare pushed Poley's head back against the wall. 'Speak again unbidden and I will relieve you of your teeth, Mr Poley,' he said, then released his grip. Poley wiped his sleeve across his mouth.

For the next ten minutes the Searcher examined the body in silence, looking for other wounds or evidence of poisoning. He opened Marlowe's mouth and peered inside, then spent some time over his right hand, which was clearly injured. After his examination of the corpse he turned his attention to the living men. He made Frizer stand still while he looked at the wounds on his head. He took notes on the spread of blood across the body of the corpse and the killer. He also examined the garments and heads of the other two men for signs of injury or blood drops. At last he stood back from his work and gazed at Shakespeare.

'Well, Joshua?'

'I have no doubt that the stab to the eye killed him, though from the stench of him you might surmise he had drowned in ale. The blade penetrated the brain and brought forth a great rush of blood. There is no evidence of any other lethal injury, nor poison. The blood on that man —' he nodded towards Frizer — 'makes it quite clear that he wielded the knife.'

'Could it have been self-defence?'

'Yes.'

'And could the injuries inflicted on the knifeman, Frizer, have been caused by an attack by Marlowe?'

'Again, yes. Or by anyone else who happened to be in the room. I would add, John, that Marlowe's finger is interesting. The middle one of the right hand has been injured in some way. The knuckle was torn at about the time of death.'

'From landing a punch, Joshua?'

Peace hesitated. 'Most likely, yes. Although . . .'

'Although what?'

'No, nothing. It's pointless to surmise.'

'But I would be glad if you would anyway.'

'Well, the injury is really quite severe. The bone is visible. One might think the knuckle and the forejoint of the finger had been scraped by a rough edge of iron. More than that I cannot say.'

Shakespeare stepped forward and examined Marlowe's fingers himself, then turned back. He held up the limp hand. 'Well, Mr Poley – how do you explain this injury?'

'Take a look at Mr Frizer's head. That's how Marlowe hurt himself.'

Shakespeare turned away and clapped Peace about the shoulder. 'I want you here at the inquest, Joshua.'

He shook his head. 'No. I'll write you a report. That'll be enough for Danby. It's straightforward.'

'Put in the time of death as you estimate it.'

'Oh yes, I'll do that. But Danby will pay it no heed.'

The witnesses did not leave the premises for a day and two nights. An obliging Mrs Bull, owner of the house, bustled about bringing them food and ale, and provided a bed for them in another room. Two of the men slept on the outer sides of the bed, heads against the wall, while the third, Skeres, slept in between them, his booted feet against their ears, his farting, snoring bulk hogging much of the mattress.

The body of Marlowe was as cold as earth by the time the sixteen-man jury of local Deptford yeomen was assembled in the room where he had died. The jurors stood along one wall, heads bowed and fearful, clutching their caps and looking anywhere but at the body. Then the coroner appeared, a dark and formal cape about his shoulders and a fur hat under his arm. He sat at the table and called the room to order for the Lord's Prayer. At the coroner's side, Richard Topcliffe, the Queen's servant, took a seat, his white hair and dread face caught in the morning light from the little window.

John Shakespeare stood close to the doorway. He glared at Topcliffe, who smirked back. What was Topcliffe doing here, close-coupled with the coroner? This inquest could be none of his concern.

The proceedings were as Shakespeare expected; there was no one to gainsay the testimony of Poley, Skeres and Frizer, who all knew their lines well. William Danby, coroner to the royal court, then attending on the Queen less than a mile away in Greenwich, listened impassively. His manner was grave. He read Joshua Peace's report, which had been placed on the table in front of him, then set it aside without commenting on it to the jury.

For a moment, Shakespeare considered interrupting the inquest to point out the discrepancy over the time of the killing. But it would have been a waste of breath. Danby would merely have instructed the jurors to discount the testimony of Mr Peace, as he himself had done, and might well have thrown Shakespeare out of the hearing. And anyway, the hour of death, in itself, proved nothing. It was the *manner* of the killing that counted for all in this room.

The verdict was a foregone conclusion: self-defence. The jurors – each of whom had been required to step forward in turn to view the body and the fatal wound at close quarters – had done the job required of them. Ingram Frizer was to be taken to the Marshalsea prison to see whether he should be charged or no. That was the prerogative of the Queen and her ministers.

It was not the verdict which caused Shakespeare most consternation, it was the presence of the man who had sat at the coroner's side: Richard Topcliffe – killer, torturer, rapist, blood-lusting dog with the ear of the Queen.

The loathing between Shakespeare and Topcliffe ran deep. Their paths had crossed too many times over the years. Shakespeare had married a Catholic and Topcliffe wanted his blood. He wanted the blood of every Catholic in England. And who was to stop him when he had Elizabeth's licence to act as priest hunter and persecutor? No man could oppose him, not even the Privy Council, because he was answerable only to her.

As the jury shuffled out, Shakespeare approached the table. Danby was collecting up his papers.

'You know, of course, Mr Danby, that they were all lying.'

The coroner looked up, eyes wide, as if he had not seen Shakespeare before. 'Mr Shakespeare?'

'Frizer, Poley, Skeres. They concocted that story. And the time of the killing. You had Mr Peace's note in front of you, yet you paid it no heed.'

Danby bridled, though his indignation would not have alarmed a mole. Indeed, he was much like a burrowing creature with his dark cape, nervous eyes and twitching whiskers. 'You presume much to speak to a royal officer so, Mr Shakespeare. In truth I would go further, sir; you presume a great deal to call in the Searcher of the Dead without my authority.'

'If I had waited on your pleasure, Mr Danby, it might have been too late. The body would have been as cold as winter. Mr Peace might not have been able to determine the time of death with such accuracy.'

'It is for me to say how accurate Mr Peace's conclusions are. And I say that he is a diabolical dabbler. He plays with dead bodies in a most unchristian way. I will have none of Mr Peace.' Danby swept past Shakespeare, then paused at the door. 'And mark me well: I will have words with my lord Burghley regarding your part in this.' With a final, puffed-up flourish, he departed.

Topcliffe bared his yellow teeth and chuckled. He prodded Shakespeare's chest with his silver-tipped blackthorn stick. 'That's told you, Shakespeare.'

Shakespeare brushed the stick aside with a sweep of his arm and glared into Topcliffe's gloating face. 'God blind you,' he said. 'You are a malign presence.' This whole business was putting Shakespeare in an ill humour. He had not liked it from the start, when Cecil had ordered him to inquire into Marlowe's dealings. Anyone could have written those placards. And if it *had* been Marlowe, why would he have signed it *Tamburlaine*? Only a fool would draw attention to himself in such a way – and Marlowe, however hot-blooded and wild, had never been a fool.

'Now, now, Mr Shakespeare,' Topcliffe said, putting up his stick as if it were a rapier. 'Hear me out.'

'I want to hear nothing from you, Topcliffe. Have you not women or children to torment somewhere?'

'Wait, Shakespeare. I know we do not see eye to eye on much, but I have to tell you that I am with you on this. Marlowe was a dunghill of iniquity, but he had his fair parts. The verdict was wrong, I am certain. He was murdered.'

'Then why did you say nothing?'

'I had no evidence, Mr Shakespeare. Why did *you* say nothing?'

Shakespeare ignored the question. 'And what was Marlowe to you, anyway? Why are you here?'

Topcliffe took a smouldering pipe from the pocket of his fine doublet and thrust it in his mouth. He sucked hard and blew out two thin streams of smoke from his nostrils. 'Marlowe? I would happily have drawn out his entrails and hacked off his pizzle like a Papist girl-boy for his godless ways and playmaking. And yet –' Topcliffe's menacing growl almost softened for a moment. 'And yet I will admit, in other things his heart was right. His denunciation of the foreign incomers was something that should gladden all English hearts, for who can stomach these strangers overrunning our land, taking bread from stout English tables? Five years ago, Drake sank the strangers who tried to invade our shores. Now the Council welcomes so many ragtag beggars from France and the Low Countries that you scarce hear an English voice in London. Marlowe was right and I am with him. I would push every last one of them back into the narrow seas and cheer their drowning.'

The pall-bearers entered the room and lifted the body of Christopher Marlowe from the day bed to carry him away for burial.

Shakespeare turned away. Topcliffe understood nothing. This was not about Marlowe's views, this was about murder. The trouble was that in these days of famine and rising prices, when many men could not find a day's work, there were plenty who thought like Topcliffe, plenty who would do evil to the incomers and their wives and children, Catholic or Protestant. Their only crime? Not being English.

Chapter 3

OUTSIDE MRS BULL's house on Deptford Strand a small crowd had gathered, perhaps fifteen strong. Shakespeare was taken aback to see his brother Will among them, with a group of familiar faces from the playhouses. Henslowe was there, Alleyn and Burbage, an uncommonly doleful Will Kempe, his customary jest and smile absent today. Marlowe's patron, the poetry-loving Thomas Walsingham, stood tall and stiff with the little group. Nephew to Shakespeare's late employer, Sir Francis Walsingham, Thomas cut an elegant, mournful figure. He smiled wanly at Shakespeare. George Peele, the poet and playmaker, cut an equally desolate figure in an outrageously costly doublet and hose of green and gold satin that would not have been out of place at court.

Shakespeare took his brother by the hand, then drew him close in an embrace. 'This is a fine place to meet, Will.'

'Self-defence, they say. Do you believe it, John?'

'No, of course not. If Rob Poley said the sun was yellow I would believe it blue.'

'First Thomas Kyd is tortured within an inch of his life, now Kit is dead. Which of us will be next?'

Shakespeare frowned. He had not thought of this killing in the context of a threat to London's players and poets. Yet when he looked again at the group of men mourning Marlowe he saw anxiety as well as grief in their eyes. Also, despite the death and the arrest and hard questioning of playmaker Thomas Kyd for supposed heresy, he saw defiance in the crowd. He felt sick to the depths of his soul.

'Come, John,' Will Shakespeare said. 'Come with us to St Nicholas and see Kit interred at least. And then I shall head home to Stratford. This city has become unhealthy.'

A small cart clattered westwards from Aldgate through the mid-morning streets of London. It was a Friday and the roads were busy with heavy drays nose to tail, drovers with flocks of geese and sheep at every turn.

The little cart pushed on regardless. The two men at the front drove their reluctant horse through the dung-thick streets with a lash. Every now and then one of them glanced over his shoulder at the barrel that bounced and jostled in the back. It looked innocent enough; onlookers, had they been interested, might have guessed that it contained biscuit or salt pork. They would have been wrong. It was packed tight with fine corns of gunpowder.

'The city is like a farmyard today, Mr Curl.' Luke Laveroke spoke in an accent that seemed to have no home, though there was certainly a little Scottish in there somewhere. Easily the taller of the two men, perhaps a foot above his companion, Laveroke was a good-looking man, but his face was in shadow today beneath a close-fitting leather workman's cap. His greying hair, usually shoulder-length and well groomed, was neatly tied away from view. If anyone had cared to look closely, they might have noted his well-trimmed spade beard and fine features. But none would look at him today, for he wore the attire of a working man – a wool jerkin and knee-length brown hose – and had nothing to distinguish him from the common horde that cluttered these streets.

'Indeed, Mr Laveroke. One cannot think for the cackle of geese and the lowing of the great beasts heading for slaughter. If only the nobility and their Dutch friends were accompanying them.' Holy Trinity Curl was of an altogether different cut to Laveroke. His eyes were amber and piercing; so, too, his hair, almost concealed beneath a leather cap.

The cart arrived at Broad Street, its destination. Laveroke, who had the reins, pulled the unwilling horse to a halt.

'Well, Mr Curl, here we are. The Dutch church.'

'Not by right, Mr Laveroke. Not by right is it a Dutch church. A sad lapse by the poor young king, may God rest his soul. No part of England should *ever* belong to a scurvy foreign nation.'

'Quite so, Mr Curl. So let us give the Council something to consider in the matter of strangers – following the recent sad events at Deptford.'

'Sad events, Mr Laveroke, sad events.'

They drove the cart on a little further and stopped outside the colossal church, once the home of the Augustine friars but given to the Dutch nation by the boy king Edward VI in 1550. From inside, as they unloaded their deadly cask from the cart, they could hear the drone of prayers. The road and yard were busy; no one paid the two gunpowder men heed.

Together, they hauled and rolled the barrel along its bottom rim through the churchyard towards the north transept of the old building, which was well away from the road where their horse and cart waited.

'I have the beetle and the peg, Mr Curl. Shall we begin?'

'Why, yes, Mr Laveroke.'

With his mallet, Laveroke struck the strong wooden peg hard into the lower portion of the barrel. One hit was enough; the black powder spilled out of the small hole. Curl took a saltpetre-impregnated cord from inside his grubby leather jerkin. He ruffled up one end so that the strands separated, then thrust the other end into the hole. A small brown and white mongrel dog trotted over and stood sniffing his legs as he worked. Curl kicked out at it, but it would not go away. At last, the two men stood back and admired their efforts.

'Do you have a tinderbox, Mr Laveroke?'

'Indeed, I do, Mr Curl. It was a gift from a very great gentleman who wishes success to our endeavours.'

'Then let us blow an arsehole in this maggoty den.'

The praying from inside the church was barely audible at this part of the transept, little more than a low hum. Laveroke struck flint against steel and lit a taper with his ornate tinderbox. 'This should bring them a little closer to heaven, Mr Curl,' he said as he knelt down and touched the glowing taper to the saltpetre-soaked fuse. It immediately sparked up and the two men watched for a moment with satisfaction.

'Or hell, Mr Laveroke. Or hell, where they do belong.'

As the flame smouldered along the length of the fuse towards the barrel, the tall and handsome Mr Luke Laveroke and the amber-eyed Mr Holy Trinity Curl walked nonchalantly back towards their horse and cart.

The high-ceilinged meeting room in Sir Robert Cecil's small mansion close to his father's great house on the Strand was weakly lit. A tall window looked out over a central courtyard where the sun only ventured in high summer afternoons. Despite this, the room was not gloomy and had a pleasing air of intimacy and privacy. John Shakespeare sat opposite Francis Mills, his colleague in the service of Cecil. At one end of the table sat the stiff-necked Sir Henry Lee; at his side, the quiet, intense Thomas Bedwell.

The fifth man, Cecil, paced the room slowly and silently, his feet clad in pantoufles of rich blue velvet, his monogram *RC* braided in gold on each of them. 'One dog you say?' He addressed the question to Shakespeare.

'One dog dead. No other injuries. It was good fortune that the wall held or there might have been carnage. There is a deep hole and a great deal of rubble around the north transept of the church.'

Cecil turned to Lee. 'Perhaps, Sir Henry, you would explain to Mr Shakespeare and Mr Mills your role in this inquiry.'

Lee did not smile. The downward trajectory of his sandy moustache and beard might have conveyed the impression that this was a man rarely given to expressions of humour, yet his friends knew of his generosity and those who had served under him revered his courage on the field. 'I am commanded to convey from Her Royal Majesty the urgency of this affair,' he said in a curt voice accustomed to giving orders, 'lest you had thought otherwise.'

'I think we already understood the urgency of the threat,' Cecil said.

'She summoned me like a boy to her presence. She demanded to know what I, as Master-General of the Ordnance, was doing allowing villains and traitors access to gunpowder. Such was her fury, I would have rather faced a culverin's roar. She wants these men eviscerated and soon. They must be alive when bowelled and crying for mercy even as their hearts are torn from their bodies and held before their eyes. No one in this realm must be allowed to imagine that they can acquire powder and use it for such a purpose without suffering a similar fate.'

'You have made your point well, Sir Henry,' Cecil said. 'Which brings us on to the questions that must be answered. The powder. Where did it come from – and who ignited it?'

'Saltpetre, brimstone, charcoal. In parts seventy-five, ten, fifteen. Is that not correct, Mr Bedwell?' Lee demanded. 'How in the name of God would I know where it comes from? I am retired. The master-generalship is an honorarium; it is a pension for my years of service in the field. Ask Mr Bedwell where the damned powder came from.'

All eyes turned to Thomas Bedwell, Storekeeper of the Ordnance. He had a pair of spectacles on the table in front of him, which he now picked up and placed on the bridge of his nose. Bedwell was in his mid fifties, a few years younger than Lee though he looked a fair bit older. As an engineer, he had applied new technologies in the building of the defensive walls of Dover harbour and Portsmouth and along the Thames. He had modernised gunnery with his rules for elevation of cannon to establish the distance a ball would travel. More than that, he claimed to have devised a method of establishing longitude at sea. Now his primary task was ensuring the care and safekeeping of the ordnance and munitions held in the White Tower armoury and the nearby storehouses in the Minories, once home to nuns from the Order of St Clare.

'Well, Mr Bedwell?' Cecil said, an edge of impatience in his tone. 'Where did the powder come from?'

'Not the Tower. I am certain of that. But nor was it made in someone's backyard, for the quantity used was too great. I visited the site of the explosion and from the extent of the blast, I would say the barrel contained one hundredweight or more of fair quality powder.'

'So where?'

'From one of the mills. The powder is supposed to be kept secure in locked vaults, but some of the mill owners fall short. Powder is left lying about. Though the mills are supposed to be strictly guarded and are inspected regularly, it is entirely possible that an amount has been stolen or sold illegally.'

'Could it not have been stolen in transit?' Shakespeare asked.

'Yes, that is possible, but less likely. Had a highway robbery occurred, I would have been informed straightway, and I have had no such reports in recent months. The other places powder might have been acquired is from county stores or from the hold of a ship-of-war. County stores do not hold great quantities, but a ship is a distinct possibility. However, powder is usually not loaded until shortly before a ship weighs anchor, to reduce the risk of mishaps. My firm opinion is that a powdermill is the source.'

'Where are they, Mr Bedwell?'

'The nearest to London is Rotherhithe. It is powered by a watermill on a small tributary of the Thames. A little further afield, in Essex, you will find the Three Mills site on the river Lea at Bromley-by-Bow, which has recently been converted to powder production. There are also established mills at Faversham in Kent and Godstone in Surrey, and we have lately licensed a saltpetre works east of London in Suffolk.'

Cecil approached the table. He had heard all he needed from the ordnance men. 'Thank you, Mr Bedwell. I know you have brought papers with further details of the positioning of these mills, their keepers and production details. I would ask you to leave those with Mr Shakespeare. And Sir Henry, if you see Her Majesty before I do, please assure her of our most rigorous efforts in this matter.'

'Quite so, Sir Robert.' Sir Henry Lee rose from his seat, followed by Bedwell. 'I bid you all good day, leaving you with this thought. All spring, the Queen has talked of nothing else but her racehorse, Great Henry. She is convinced he will win the Golden Spur for the third year; but this news has quite distracted her. She considers the attack a personal affront to her authority. I would have her talking horses again, gentlemen, not raging like a North Sea tempest about gunpowder. That way we may all sleep a little better. So I urge you to put an end to this nonsense in short order. Until you do so, Her Majesty is expecting regular reports.'

After Lee and Bedwell had departed, Cecil turned to Mills. 'What are your thoughts, Frank?'

'Well, it clearly wasn't Marlowe.'

Cecil sighed. Wearily, he rubbed the hunch of his shoulder that had earned him the epithet Robin Crookback. He was a small man, neat and self-contained. Always in control – in control of himself, of others, of his surroundings. 'Yes,' he said impatiently. 'I think that is clear enough. It wasn't Marlowe. So who was it?'

Mills lowered his pinpoint eyes, chastened. He was a tall man, about Shakespeare's height, but thinner and older. He was becoming more and more stooped, as if he had invisible weights pressing down on him. Perhaps it was the burden of his sins, or the adulteries of his wife, that pulled him down.

He and Shakespeare had worked together for years, first for Walsingham and now under Cecil. Though their relationship had been reasonably cordial in recent months, Shakespeare could never forget that Mills had once betrayed him. Yes, he would work with him, but he would never trust him.

Mills's great talent was in drawing information from suspects. His presence alone could often produce results as quickly as Topcliffe's rack. At times the two interrogators had worked together – Topcliffe applying the engines of despair, Mills coaxing the confession or required information with soft words. He understood that the anticipation of agony and mutilation could often be as bad, worse even, than the pain itself.

Shakespeare disliked this in Mills, this resort to fear. Yet he had to concede that there was more to the man than this. Mills had a sharp, political mind that understood better than anyone the significance of intercepted correspondence between the courts of Europe – what to dismiss as tittle-tattle or disinformation, and what needed acting upon.

'A witness speaks of seeing two men rolling a barrel from a small cart,' Shakespeare said. 'One man was tall, the other not so tall. Other than that the witness could describe nothing remarkable about them and paid them no heed. Their features were concealed by caps or hoods.'

Silence descended on the room. Sir Robert Cecil, privy councillor, chief minister in all but name, did not expect Shakespeare and Mills to speak unless they had something noteworthy to say. In many ways he was like his predecessor, Walsingham; that fastidious attention to detail, that utter belief in the power of secret knowledge. Yet Cecil was *not* Walsingham. He was too worldly for that. Cecil's father had brought him up to understand the mechanics of power – and how to acquire it – without ever asking himself why he should want it. It was power for duty's sake and it was as natural as eating, breathing or pissing to Robert Cecil. Walsingham, on the other hand, had acquired power for a purpose. It was for his sovereign, his religion and his country. He had beggared himself getting it and holding it, and had died in penury because of it.

The seconds passed in the meeting room, hidden deep in the somewhat anonymous house. Cecil's father, Lord Burghley, Elizabeth's longest-serving and most faithful minister, had bought it for his second son so that he should have a town place of his own; his other, greater mansion on the Strand, would go to Robert's older half-brother, Thomas, along with the title Burghley. Robert knew, however, that he was his father's chosen son and that he would inherit the jewel of his father's holdings, the great palace of Theobalds in Hertfordshire.

'And yet we cannot ignore the Marlowe connection,' Shakespeare said, breaking the silence at last, glancing towards Mills for support. 'Anything that involves Rob Poley must always raise suspicion. And what is Topcliffe's interest?'

Shakespeare noticed the tightening of Cecil's little fist, the stretching of the short and slender neck away from the hunch; most would not. Was it the name Poley or Topcliffe that brought a chill to this room?

'Frank?' Cecil demanded, as if Shakespeare had not spoken.

Mills studiously avoided the question of Marlowe. 'There are many in this city who would wish harm to our Dutch friends, Sir Robert—'

Shakespeare recoiled slightly as Mills spoke. The man had midden breath and it wafted across the table at him. Before Mills could expound further, he interrupted. 'If Marlowe was in any way involved in the intimidating placards posted outside the Dutch church, then we *must* wonder about a possible connection to the men who laid powder in that very place. Their method was more extreme, yet their target was the same. The Council – and you Sir Robert – thought Marlowe a fit subject for investigation alive. Has so much changed now he is dead?'

Once more, Cecil ignored Shakespeare and addressed Mills. 'Who, Frank? Who in this city – Marlowe apart – would harm those who have sought refuge here? You called these strangers "our friends" – and they *are* friends of England. They bring skills and wealth with them at a time of great need. They help us open new trade routes. They help fill the war chest. And, above all, they abhor the Pope.'

Mills consulted a paper on the table in front of him. He smoothed it flat with the palm of his hand. 'The welcome offered by the Crown and Council is easily understood, but it is worth looking at this from the perspective of the merchants and the common man. Consider this,' he said, indicating the paper. 'It is a summary of the recent Return of Strangers, dated May the fourth – four weeks ago. The aldermen and constables of each of the twenty-six wards have been diligent in their searches and have noted the names of more than seven thousand refugees and their children. We must assume, however, that the true figure is considerably higher. Many strangers keep others illegally about their houses as servants and apprentices. They hide when the word gets about that searchers are in the area. It would not be unreasonable to suggest that a true figure of fifteen or even twenty thousand incomers now live here.'

'Out of perhaps two hundred thousand . . . possibly one in ten.'

'Indeed, Sir Robert. And they make their presence felt, for they have a wide variety of trades and crafts. They bring skills to produce fine lace, glass, shoes, starch, hats and many more items. Their produce is much admired and desired by the English – yet they resent them, too. It cannot be denied that in some cases they *do* take trade away from their English neighbours. And it is true that they often keep themselves aloof and do not learn to speak English. Many English merchants, shopkeepers and craftsmen hate them. They fear their livelihoods are threatened and feel that parts of the city – Blackfriars, Billingsgate, St Martin le Grand and, further afield, Southwark – are become strange lands where a very Babel of languages is spoken.'

Cecil stopped pacing. He drew up the chair at the head of the table where Lee had recently been positioned, and sat down. He leaned forward purposefully. 'Is there any evidence that Englishmen are joining together against the refugees?' he demanded. 'Have there been illegal gatherings? Will there be mobs in the street or insurrection?' Cecil took a draught of ale and wiped a finger across his thin lip.

Mills hesitated.

'Well?'

'I cannot give assurances that there will be no riots; no man could. We know that the apprentices, when they are in drink, often cast stones at those they take to be refugees. But I would say this: there is no evidence that such events are organised.'

'Somebody is organising gunpowder, however. It is a short step from there to insurrection.'

'As yet we have no suspects,' Mills said dolefully. 'Nowhere to start.'

Shakespeare sat in irritated silence. Cecil turned to him. 'John?'

'You know my feelings, Sir Robert.'

'Yes, I do. And I am mighty confused by them. You do not believe Marlowe wrote the outrage – and yet you think you should waste time and effort inquiring further into his death. I am surprised a man of your wit does not see the contradiction here. Furthermore, you talk of Poley: are you suggesting Robert Poley was somehow involved in this gunpowder incident? My understanding is that it occurred within a short time of Marlowe's inquest. Poley was there as a witness, was he not? And Topcliffe was there to report back to Her Majesty. How could either man have been in two places at once?'

Cecil's words were sharp, but Shakespeare would not roll over so easily. 'No,' he said, shaking his head, 'that is not it. I have not accused Poley or Topcliffe of complicity in the gunpowder intrigue. My point is that Marlowe's death was not straightforward. For one thing, there was the time discrepancy . . .'

For a moment, he wondered whether he had gone too far to speak to a senior minister thus. The moment passed. Nothing he could say would ever shock or dismay Cecil; that was why he worked for him – because he *could* talk to him man to man, he could disagree with him where others in power would expect to be fawned upon by obsequious underlings.

Cecil sat back from the table. 'Mr Shakespeare,' he said, his voice quieter, more intense. 'John . . . the discrepancy over the time of Christopher Marlowe's death is irrelevant. He still died from a blow of a dagger struck by Ingram Frizer. Even Searcher Peace agrees with that. And who are Poley, Frizer and Skeres anyway? Just the sort of low company that Marlowe always kept. There is no mystery here. He is buried. That is the end of it.' Cecil turned back to Mills. 'Now then, Frank, let us talk of the *other* faction that might have ignited the powder, if you please.'

Mills affected a solemn countenance. 'The Spanish, Sir Robert. They are the ones who stand to gain most from unrest in London. Even now they are building up the war fleet that God and the weather saved us from last year. Philip and his Romish toad-eater in the Vatican are the ones that would happily wreak bloodshed upon our Protestant refugee friends here in London . . .'

'John, the intelligence from Spain, if you will.'

Shakespeare smiled grimly. Cecil would not be moved on this. Marlowe was dead and that was it. He unfurled the paper on the table. 'This is from Anthony Standen, sent as he travelled back from Spain through France. He writes, "The fleets in Cadiz and Lisbon are fitted for a surprise attack given fair weather and an opportunity. They plan to have Brest soon. They will not wallow as in '88." ' Shakespeare did not mention the intended recipient of the message, the Earl of Essex – Cecil's great rival. The message had been intercepted from Essex's messenger by Cecil's searchers at Dover.

'Given an opportunity,' Cecil echoed. 'That is just what we must not give them. There are threats enough.'

Indeed, Cecil had rehearsed the perils recently for the House of Commons. There were, he declared in a speech of eloquence and drama, dangers on all fronts.

Shakespeare had heard the speech – and the plea for tax revenues – and had been impressed. The way Cecil spoke, he made it sound as if Spain was closing a net around England. His words, calm and precise, instilled in every member of the House both fury and fear, so that none should doubt the need to dig deep into their own coffers. He itemised the threats from west, east, north and south.

In the west, Sir John Norris's expeditionary force to Brittany was hard-pressed against the Spanish army of General Don Juan d'Aguila. Money, men and supplies were needed if Norris was to prevent the enemy taking the deep-water port of Brest on the western tip of that nose of land. Brest was a harbour so large it could safely have concealed the whole armada of 1588. If it should fall, Cecil proclaimed ominously, the Channel would be exposed to a new Spanish fleet, complete with invasion barges. Striking from Brittany, the whole of southern England would be at Spain's mercy. Such an armada would start with fresh supplies and could be resupplied with victuals and ammunition as it drove eastwards towards Kent and London. In two years of campaigning in Brittany, Norris's situation had become increasingly parlous. His poor band of troops was heavily depleted by disease, desertions, the wounding defeat at Craon and a devastating ambush at Ambrières. Now there was hard and bloody fighting at Laval. Norris needed help, and that cost money.

In the east, the Catholic king of Poland, Sigismund, had done a deal with Spain to disrupt English trade. If this was carried through, there was a real risk that some vessels of the Navy Royal would have to be diverted from their crucial role of protecting the western approaches and the narrow seas.

In the north there was subversive action among the Scots: the Catholic noblemen Erroll and Angus had corresponded secretly with the Escorial Palace with the aim of bringing Spanish troops to Scotland against James VI, and from there to march on England.

In the south, the Spanish fleet harried England's merchant ships in the Mediterranean; in France, the Catholic League promised towns and ports to Spain. Worse, the Protestant king, Henri IV, had announced he would receive instruction in the Catholic faith. It seemed he would convert to Catholicism to unite his country – but what would that mean for England? Elizabeth was grievously put out.

Cecil's words had been concise and they had hit home, for he had had his way with a huge triple subsidy to raise a hoped-for three hundred thousand pounds for the Treasury.

Shakespeare recalled one other thing Cecil said that day: 'Her Majesty, to her great renown, made this little land to be a sanctuary for all the persecuted saints of God.'

It was true. England had been a sanctuary for many thousands who had lost their homes and families to the Spanish onslaught on the mainland. Many Englishmen were unhappy, however; one member of parliament, Walter Ralegh, had gone so far as to protest that 'the nature of the Dutchman is to fly to no man but for his profit'. So what sort of a sanctuary did it seem now, with such hostile words bandied about and with gunpowder exploding outside church doors?

This unrest at home was the last thing England needed as the net drew tighter from outside.

'And so,' Cecil concluded, rising once more from his chair at the end of the table in his quiet room, 'we will find these gunpowder men without delay, and we must show them no mercy. The Queen is clear on that, and I echo her sentiments. John, this is your task. Nothing else. No Marlowe, no Poley – it is the powdermen I want. If you need manpower or funds, they are yours. Frank, you will summon every intelligencer in London and find out what they know. Report everything to Mr Shakespeare, however insignificant it might seem. Good day, gentlemen.'

As Shakespeare and Mills stood from their chairs, Cecil walked with businesslike little steps towards the door. Then he stopped and turned to Shakespeare. 'But tread lightly, John. You can offend Coroner Danby all you want, but do not walk roughshod over *English* sensibilities in this matter. We must protect our foreign friends for they have brought great honour to our realm, yet our charity to them must not hinder or injure ourselves.'

Chapter 4

AFTER A SUPPER of pike fried in butter, the juices soaked up with fresh bread, Shakespeare and his wife sat at the table drinking Gascon wine and picking at a piece of hard cheese.

'I think I am getting old, Catherine.'

'You are thirty-four, John. You are not old, you are angry.'

He poured them both more wine from the pitcher and he drank it quickly. It was true enough; he *was* angry. But he wasn't sure why. He had been angry before the meeting with Cecil, even before he saw Topcliffe at the inquest.

'Be wary with your loyalty, John.'

Shakespeare looked at his wife.

'I mean a man can be *too* loyal. A man can offer loyalty to a captain-general and receive no loyalty in return. Many have died for their sovereign. How many sovereigns have died for their subjects?'

Shakespeare laughed and shook his head. 'Your tongue, mistress. I thank the Lord these walls do not have ears . . .'

Catherine rose from the table. 'Wait, I have something to make you yet more discomfited.' She went through to the hall while he sat with his wine.

The Shakespeares lived in a great wood-frame house by the river Thames in Dowgate. They had turned the house into a school for the poor boys of London, but it was still closed as a result of the pestilence that had taken hold last summer. The city's mort-bills for the year of 1592 recorded that more than ten thousand souls had been claimed by the plague; this year the city fathers feared it would be as bad or worse. Shakespeare took another sip of wine. Perhaps it was just this decline of England that was getting to him: the rising prices, the unrest, the endless war with Spain, the worry that the school would never reopen, his fears for the future of their daughter, Mary, and for their adopted children, Andrew and Grace.

Catherine returned with a tattered broadsheet for her husband. As she leant over him to place it on the table, he reached out and clasped her breast in his hand. She laughed lightly, let her long dark hair fall about her face and moved her slender body towards him to close her mouth on his.

'Stirring again, Mr Shakespeare?' she said as their mouths parted and her own hand came to rest in his lap. 'Time for bed, I think.'

He tried to smile at her, but it was difficult to shut out the darkness that seemed to envelop him. Her blue eyes held his brown eyes for a moment, then she kissed him quickly once more before pulling away from his clasping hand. 'Read that, then bed.'

Shakespeare turned to the paper. It bore the title *The London Informer* and comprised one sheet, written in poor verse. He went cold as he read it. 'Where did you get this, Catherine?' he asked at last.

'Close by the Dutch market, John. I was visiting Berthe. There were two sellers. I thought their proximity to the market deliberate.'

'This is bad. Cecil will not be happy.'

The broadsheet was a noxious attack on the Dutch and German refugees in London. It accused them of working secretly for Spain, of taking English trade and English work, of seeking to invade and occupy the country by stealth. Worse, it spoke in gloating terms of the explosion outside the Dutch church and said there would be more such attacks – 'and next time the real dogs will die'. It was signed *Tamburlaine's Apostle*.

'This is Glebe's work,' Shakespeare muttered. 'Have I told you of Walstan Glebe? He is a most villainous purveyor of filth. I thought we had broken up his *London Informer* press – we should have broken him instead.'

'I recall you speaking of him.'

'He has a brand on his forehead – an *L* for *Liar*. I had hoped he was dead by now.' He sighed. 'But then again, it gives me a start. He knows something. I'll find him and bring him in.'

Shakespeare had been thinking hard about how to tackle the investigation. The first thing he had done was call his assistant Boltfoot Cooper to the library on the first floor.

As usual, Cooper had looked out of place as he shuffled into the fine room, dragging his deformed left foot. He seemed to be growing shorter and more knotted as he approached forty.

'Master?'

'I have a mission for you, Boltfoot. I want you to go to the powdermills.'

Boltfoot was silent. He and Jane had a child, a boy of eight months. He did not like leaving them.

'I know what you are thinking, Boltfoot. And you are right. This will take you from your family. You will need several days, perhaps a week or more. It is vital work. You know of the powder explosion at the Dutch church? Your task is to discover the source of the powder. It was almost certainly bought or stolen from a mill. Question the mill-keepers and workers. They will not admit selling powder illegally and will be reluc-tant to admit their safeguarding is so lax that a thief could gain access to it. Start with Rotherhithe. If you do not discover inconsistencies there, head for Bromley-by-Bow and the others. You will not be alone. The Royal Armoury is arranging assistance; a powder expert named William Sarjent. I am told he is a good man. He will meet you at Rotherhithe. I have full details here.' He handed over the paper Bedwell had passed to him. 'Ask them this, too: have cargoes gone missing en route by road or river? Has any man been dismissed or charged for dishonesty? Demand assistance on pain of arrest.'

Boltfoot grunted. 'What of the Royal Armoury itself, master? There is gunpowder aplenty there.'

'I am assured from the highest level that it is not the source. If all else fails I will go there. But in the meantime I have other inquiries to make. Set forth at dawn – and go armed.'

In bed, Catherine was tender. She enticed him in with soft words and practised movements of her belly and thighs, but tonight Shakespeare was a different animal to her, frenzied and ungiving, hard and dispassionate.

They made love twice. Her yielding warmth soothed him and her fondling words and whispered kisses drew much of the anger out of him. Yet there was still tension there, and she sensed it.

He lay back, sated, on the downy cushions and gazed into the black night. Their breathing subsided.

'I keep thinking of Poley,' he said. 'I know him too well. Marlowe's death smells like six-day fish.'

'Tell me of him, John.'

'No. You need sleep.'

They lay there a minute. Neither of them would sleep soon.

'Death and deceit follow him like a pair of hungry dogs,' Shakespeare said quietly. 'Walsingham used him to incriminate the Babington plotters in their conspiracy to murder the

Queen and free Mary of Scots. But whose side was he really on? I never knew. I don't think Mr Secretary was certain either. Even when Poley was imprisoned in the Tower, it is said he was employed to kill a bishop with poisoned cheese. But who was the paymaster?'

Catherine curled up against him, her dark hair across his chest. Shakespeare stroked her head.

'Is he Catholic or Protestant, or neither?' he went on, as much to himself as to her. 'He was poor but now he lives in splendour, though he has no honest trade. I think he has won gold from all sides. What is his connection to Marlowe – a shared interest in intelligencing or the common bond of coining?'

'Coining, John?'

'Marlowe had already been implicated in forging coin in the Low Countries; is Poley in the same line? Is that what this is about? Was the widow Bull's room a den of counterfeiters? Was the death nothing but a falling-out among thieves? A brabble and brawl about the proceeds of some crime? Or something yet more sinister . . .'

He knew Catherine was happy to hear him out. She would employ her wit and learning to make some sense of all he said. These were the times when they were at their closest, when they worked as confederates to solve a puzzle.

Yet not this night. A sudden noise shattered their peace. It came from the street outside their chamber. A splintering of wood, then shouting and hammering.

Shakespeare was up from the bed in a second and throwing open the shutters to look out of the window down on to the road. There were men there with pitch torches, storming through the broken front door of his neighbour's house.

Catherine was up, too, at his side. 'What is it, John?'

'Pursuivants.'

Quickly, he threw on his doublet over his bare chest and pulled on breeches. 'Stay here, Catherine.'

Barefoot, he ran down the oaken stairs, through the hall, into the courtyard and out into Dowgate. Two armed men with torches were now standing guard outside the neighbouring house. The building was older than the Shakespeares' home and almost as large. It was a stone-built city home for merchants and dated back a hundred years or so. Most recently, it had come into the possession of a wool merchant from Antwerp. They seemed good people who doffed their hats in the street and said good day in strongly accented English, and yet he did not know their names nor anything about them, save that they seemed wealthy and respectable.

There was shouting from within the house. Shakespeare marched up to the front door and saw that it had been stove in by a battering log, for it was lying flat in the hallway.

'What is this? What has happened here?' he demanded of the guards as he tried to peer inside.

'Hunting for rats,' one of the men said, dourly. He held a drawn sword. 'What's it to you?'

Shakespeare noted the Queen's escutcheon emblazoned on the man's jerkin. 'I am an officer to Sir Robert Cecil and these people are my neighbours, that is what it is to me. Now let me pass.' He stepped forward. As he did so, out of the corner of his eye, he noticed a figure a little way down the street, sheltering in the shadow cast by the wall of the house.

The two men moved across Shakespeare's path to bar his way. He elbowed them aside and pushed on through the front door. They laughed, but did not try too hard to stop him. Inside, the hall was ablaze with the flickering light of pitch torches and candles. Richard Topcliffe was sitting in the centre of the room on a coffer of polished elm, one leg swinging, his pipe stuck in his mouth, belching out smoke.

To one side of the room, Shakespeare saw the family who lived here. Father, mother and six children aged from about five to fifteen. They were all in their nightclothes and stood rigidly to attention, frightened witless.

'Well, well, Mr Shakespeare. What a pleasure to see you here,' Topcliffe growled like an undomesticated cat. He had a sheaf of papers in his hand. 'Come to help me flush out vermin, have you?'

On the other side of the room stood a line of serving men and women, half a dozen in all. Two were in livery, the others in nightclothes like their master's family.

'What are you talking about, Topcliffe?'

'This is Mr Sluyterman, according to the Return of Strangers here.' Topcliffe ran his finger down a list of names. 'Mr Jan Sluyterman. Says he has a wife, Gertrude, which I take to be that ugly oyster-wench at his side, and six children – Cornelius, another Jan, Pieter, Willem, Marthe and Jacob. Says, too, that he has six servants, three of them English and three Dutch.' Topcliffe turned to the master of the house. 'Is that all correct, Mr Sluyterman?'

Topcliffe had two heavily armed pursuivants at his side. These agents of the state, with powers of search and arrest, brandished swords and wheel-lock pistols. From other rooms came the sound of stamping boots and smashing panels. Obviously, there was a cohort of other men spread around the house, searching for someone – or something.

'*Ja* – yes, sir. It is correct. But—'

'Shut your filthy Dutch mouth, Mr Sluyterman. I will tell you when I wish you to speak.'

'But I thought you asked—'

'I don't like your Dutch voice, I don't like your Dutch whore of a wife and I don't like you, Sluyterman, so stow you before I force my blackthorn down your miserable gullet. Are you Calvinists? Her Majesty the Queen does not like Calvinists and nor do I.'

Shakespeare could tell from Sluyterman's eyes that he was concealing something. The Dutchman looked at Topcliffe with a steady, nervous gaze as if afraid that averting his eyes would confirm his guilt. He was a well-fed man in his forties. He looked as though he had never done anything more physical than lift a quill, write in a ledger and count coin. His wife was attractive in a homely, plump way, with a white lawn coif about her hair. Her children, all standing like statues with their arms at their sides, wore white linen nightcaps and long linen gowns.

'You question the servants, Shakespeare. You see if they're English or Dutch.'

'Do your own dirty work, Topcliffe. These are human beings, not vermin.'

'As you wish.' Topcliffe jumped from the coffer with a nimbleness that belied his sixty years. Clenching his pipe in his teeth, he approached the line of servants, swinging his silver-tipped blackthorn. One by one, he prodded them in the belly and demanded, 'Name, position, place of birth?' One by one, in quivering voices, they told him their names, outlined their duties and told him where they came from. It seemed they all knew Topcliffe by repute, for they looked at him as a rabbit might view a fox that had it cornered. All but one, Shakespeare noted. One of the English servants, a man of about thirty in nightclothes, seemed not so afraid. He and two others spoke clear English devoid of any foreign accent. The other three spoke enough English, but were obviously from the Low Countries.

'I will tell you what I like best, Shakespeare. I like to see the fear in their eyes, close up. When a man dare not look away from my eyes, though he cannot abide what he sees there, for it is his own pain and death reflected.'

'And what do you see in the looking-glass?'

Topcliffe hesitated, as if pondering the question. Against one wall of the room was a tall glass, darkly mottled by age. He walked to it and smashed it with the heavy, cudgel head of his blackthorn. The glass splintered into countless shards. 'Now then,' he said, standing back from the glass and addressing the whole hall. 'That all seems in order. Except that I have counted one servant missing.' His humour darkened considerably and he hammered his blackthorn against the floor. 'We have information that there is a Dutch serving girl here who was hidden from the Return. You know the law, Mr Sluyterman – for every stranger employed, you must employ one English servant. I tell you this, if you fail to tell me where she is hiding, you will *all* be considered accessories to treason, secretly harbouring an agent of a foreign power – and you will suffer the might of the law. Your children will be taken to Bridewell and broken like horses on the treadmill. You and your wife will be detained until such time as you are flung out of the country or worse. Do you have enough English to understand what that all means?'

Shakespeare had had enough. He strode forward. 'Call off your pack, Topcliffe. You have clearly been misinformed. Let these people go back to bed. You will find no one here. Any more of this, and I will hand a full report on your egregious deeds to my lord Burghley.'

Topcliffe spat on the floor. 'Burghley! Do you think I fear that gout-ridden shipwreck? There is a Dutch serving girl here, Shakespeare, brought in from Flushing not six weeks since. I know it. There is more – I know this Sluyterman to have a secret chamber for the making of fine leather stuffs, where none but prentices work. He cares not a sheep's cut bollock that English journeymen do starve. He is a usurer and a deceit and I will have him in Bridewell.'

Shakespeare was standing directly in front of a pursuivant. In one swift movement, he stepped backwards hard on to his foot, turning and thrusting his left elbow high into the man's face. As the pursuivant grunted and fell back, Shakespeare wrenched the pistol from his grasp and put it to Topcliffe's head.

'I do not know about this family's understanding of the English language, Topcliffe, but it is you that does not seem to comprehend your mother tongue well. I said you have done enough here. Even if what you claim about the maid *is* true, it is a matter so trivial that Her Majesty would be enraged to hear of your actions. Does she not employ many strangers herself – including her personal physician? As for the leather work, it is a matter for the Worshipful Company of Cordwainers, not you. Now go, Mr Topcliffe and take your vile dogs with you, before I do England a favour and blow off your head.'

Topcliffe laughed out loud.

Shakespeare moved closer to him, so that his mouth was at his temple. All the anger of the day was ready to explode in one little press of his trigger finger. 'Do you think I don't know what this is about?' he whispered harshly in the torturer's wizened ear. 'Now walk, or I will happily do for you, and trust in the rightness of my action and the protection of Sir Robert Cecil.'

Topcliffe laughed again. Five pursuivants had arrived in the hall from various parts of the house. Shakespeare was surrounded.

Sluyterman stepped forward. He had removed his nightcap and was clutching it in front of him. His head was bowed. He was shaking. He went down on his knees in supplication to both Topcliffe and Shakespeare. 'Please, I beg of you, do not let there be bloodshed . . .'

'Oh, there will be blood shed, Mr Sluyterman,' Topcliffe

snarled. 'You can be certain of that. There will be Dutch blood aplenty.'

Shakespeare thrust his hand into Topcliffe's thick white hair and pushed him down. He was stronger than Shakespeare expected and did not fall to his knees, but took a faltering step forward, then turned with a vicious wrench of his shoulders and pulled himself clear. But the primed gun was still trained on him, pointing full in his face.

'Get up, sir,' Shakespeare said to the Dutchman. 'This is nothing to do with you. It is about me. I am afraid you and your family were simply in the wrong place, living so close to me.'

An explosion rent the air. Topcliffe's men shied backwards like startled horses. One or two dropped flat to the floor and scrabbled for safety. Someone screamed.

As the smoke cleared, all eyes turned to the front doorway. Boltfoot Cooper stood there, a smoking wheel-lock pistol hanging from his hand. He dropped it to the floor, kicked it away and, with practised ease, unslung his ornate caliver from his back and cradled it in his arms, the octagonal muzzle pointing this way and that. He had another loaded wheel-lock thrust into his belt and his cutlass hung menacingly at his thigh.

'Very good to see you, Boltfoot,' Shakespeare said. 'Very good, indeed.'

Chapter 5

Topcliffe might not have been certain whether John Shakespeare would blow his head apart, but he had no doubt that Boltfoot Cooper would. He was not going to put his life on the line for a matter as insignificant as this.

Reluctantly he ordered his pursuivants out and as he himself turned at the door, he tarried a few seconds, cursing Shakespeare and Cooper to hell and threatening to spill the last drop of Sluyterman's blood, and that of his family. Boltfoot pushed the hoary old rackmaster in the chest with the muzzle of his primed caliver, until he had forced him out and away from the house. Topcliffe shook himself angrily and strode off towards his fellow pursuivants and their tethered mounts, spitting a vow of vengeance into the night.

Shakespeare made sure he had gone, then watched as the Sluyterman family fell into one another's arms, sobbing and shaking. He wondered briefly what this family had endured in the Low Countries at the hands of the Spanish. Many souls had lost their lives there, and many more had been thrown out of their homes into exile by the Duke of Parma and his steel-clad horde. All that, and then to come to this.

He walked across to the line of servants. They still stood in line and some were trembling. He avoided the gaze of the one who had shown no fear, though his instinct was to grasp him by the nape of the neck, pull him to the door and kick him out after Topcliffe, with whom he was doubtless in league. No, better to observe him; he might be made use of yet.

Sluyterman thanked the servants and dismissed them to their quarters. He kissed his children and asked his wife to take them to their beds.

'I must thank you, sir,' he said to Shakespeare when they were alone.

'I told you, Mr Sluyterman, this is about me. It can be no coincidence that he chose your home. I would say, however, that you have a treacherous servant in this house. The Englishman with black hair and a downturned mouth . . .'

'His name is Oliver Kettle. I have not felt happy about him. We had some argument. He spoke to my daughter Marthe without respect. I think he had unhealthy interests in her. Also, my wife caught him most importunely with one of the serving girls, his hands on her . . . I do not like to say more.' Sluyterman shook his head, his eyes drifting around the destruction wrought by the intruders on his comfortable home.

'Well, do not dismiss him, but watch him. I may have a purpose for him. Be careful. If you have more problems, I will have him consigned to Newgate. As for the serving girl that Mr Topcliffe sought . . .' Shakespeare paused to see the effect of his words and saw something akin to shame in the Dutchman's eyes. 'I believe she is safe. I saw a figure in the shadows outside.'

'Thank you, sir. Thank you.'

Shakespeare shook his hand. 'It is good to meet you properly, Mijnheer Sluyterman – even though these are not the happiest of circumstances. If I were you, I would adhere strictly to the law from now on and keep your head down. Mr Topcliffe is dangerous and relentless.'

*

Catherine found the servant girl shivering in a corner of their courtyard, half concealed behind an old wagon wheel awaiting repair by Boltfoot. The girl was on her haunches, her arms tight around her tall, slender body, still in her thin nightdress. She hid her face from the light of Catherine's lantern. Gently, Catherine put a comforting arm around her and whispered soft words. The girl, who looked no more than twelve and wore her hair in two shoulder-length plaits, had the height of an adult woman. She spoke no English, but quickly understood that this was a friend and said her name was Susanna.

'She can stay with us tonight, Mr Sluyterman,' Shakespeare said a short while later. 'And on the morrow you must move her to a safer place. You surely have friends who could take her in.'

Sluyterman bowed his head in thanks and relief. 'I will do that, Mr Shakespeare, sir. Thank you. You are a good neighbour.'

The Dutchman explained to Susanna what was happening and assured her she would be safe now. The girl nodded nervously but said nothing. Then the Shakespeares bade Sluyterman goodnight and brought her up to the room where their own five-year-old daughter, Mary, lay asleep. Catherine put down some blankets and cushions for the girl and left, quietly closing the door behind her.

Shakespeare and his wife were further from sleep than ever. As they sat together, he sipped at a beaker of rich milk, cool from the larder. 'This was about me, Catherine,' he said. 'I know it. Topcliffe was trying to intimidate me. He wasn't interested in that girl. It was a warning shot to *me*.'

'Something to do with the Marlowe killing and inquest?'

It was well after midnight and his blood was still pumping hard. 'Yes. But what? At the inquest Topcliffe seemed to suggest he was in agreement with me – that Marlowe had been murdered and that the jury had reached the wrong verdict.'

'Did he not also make it plain that he thought Marlowe was right to abuse and intimidate the refugees? If so, then that accords with what happened this night. It was said Marlowe did not like refugees. Now Topcliffe has shown himself of similar mind. And so he uses the Return of Strangers and information from a hateful servant to seek out one he thought he could harass. It is his way, John. It has always been his way. Catholics, foreigners, gypsies, all are vermin in Topcliffe's twisted mind.'

'True.' Shakespeare's deep, hooded eyes shone in the warm light of the single candle on the table between them. 'But there is something else here. He knew this was my neighbour. This was for *my* benefit. He targeted Sluyterman because he spotted on the Return that he lived next door to us. But why, Catherine? What game is Topcliffe playing with me?'

In the morning, shortly after dawn, Shakespeare slapped the flank of Boltfoot's horse and bade him farewell. He watched for a few moments as his assistant rode off at a trot towards the bridge on the first part of the journey to the powdermills. A little later, Shakespeare went back indoors and joined Catherine and the children for a breakfast of bread, eggs, cheese and ale, all served by Jane Cooper. The Dutch girl, Susanna, stayed in Mary's room and Jane took her some food and drink. Shakespeare had ordered that she be kept out of sight. The servant Oliver Kettle would be waiting for her return to the Sluyterman household; if she came back, he would hasten to Westminster to inform Topcliffe again. Nor would it surprise Shakespeare if Topcliffe had another watcher in Dowgate keeping an eye on both their houses.

At eight of the clock, Shakespeare eased himself into the

saddle of his grey mare in the mews stables and headed north and west through the narrow, hurried streets of the city.

He found Nicholas Henbird in a fine house on St Nicholas Shambles, not more than fifty yards from the enormous ancient priory of Christ's Church.

Henbird's house stood a little way beyond Stinking Lane. It was one of a number of fair wood-frames built around a pleasant central court with a well. A clerk opened the door and Shakespeare was soon shown through to Henbird's splendid solar, now filled with the morning sun. The cool, bright aspect lightened Shakespeare's spirits. He gazed upon Henbird's girth with wonder and smiled. He had changed a lot since winning the coveted post of Royal Purveyor of Poultry, a good reward for his secret work on behalf of Walsingham over many years. Shakespeare shook his old colleague by the hand. He guessed Henbird must be about fifty. He certainly looked it. He had gained the portly belly and rosy round face that so often came with the fine living of ermine-clad merchants. Yet Shakespeare was not deceived. Those kindly pink cheeks and convivial manner lied; the well-fed body housed a cold heart and dagger-sharp mind.

'Nick, I had not thought to see you so prosperous.'

Henbird's face broke into a satisfied beam, like a churchman at the thought of a Sunday sirloin and a quart of beer. 'The court cannot get enough poultry, John. Swan, geese, chickens, duck. My clerks do it all and the money comes in faster than I can spend it on buxom whores, fine foods and sweet wines. Look at this wondrous belly!' He patted his middle with pleasure. 'Has not Mr Secretary done me well? My clerks buy from the shires and arrange the sales and the neck-wringing. All I have to do is pluck the money. Why, the clerks even count my silver for me. Are you acquainted with turkey-cock? I shall arrange one to be killed and roasted for your supper tonight. A succulent white-fleshed bird – I hope you will agree it flavoursome.'

'Thank you, Nick. But I have come for something else.'

'You do not surprise me. I would have wagered a month of my warrant on it. So, John, let us talk of secrets. I have heard whispered gossip that you are engaged in that dark and bloody world once more. For little Robert Cecil, I do believe.'

Shakespeare took a seat at Henbird's intricately carved table. 'I do indeed work for Sir Robert, a man who has the best interests of his sovereign and his country at heart. Unlike *some* at court,' he added wryly.

Henbird laughed and his belly shook like a subtlety of milk jelly. 'Yes, there are those whose own interests do not always coincide with those of Her Most Royal Majesty.' He rubbed his ear. 'Did I not hear in the past year that you had fallen foul of my lord of Essex? A most grievous falling out, I am told.'

Shakespeare said nothing. It seemed that Henbird's ears were as close to the ground as ever, and his hearing as acute. The memory of the conflict with Essex was not one Shakespeare relished, but nor could he regret discovering the sly and treacherous heart of the Queen's favourite. One day, he and Cecil would doubtless need such information. In the meantime, he would never be a welcome guest at Essex House again. Nor would he wish to be. He had chosen the path of peace, tied to Cecil's star; let those who wished war join the Essex camp.

'Come now, John. Do not deny it.'

'I am not here for such talk, Nick. But I am glad that you have not lost your talent for discovering men's secrets, for I would make use of it.'

Henbird clapped his hands and a livery-clad serving man hurried in and bowed low. 'What will you have, John, honest English ale or good Burgundian wine?'

'Ale.'

Henbird nodded to the servant. 'A pitcher of ale. And make haste, man, before we die of thirst. Now, John . . .'

Shakespeare waited until the servant had closed the door behind him, then spoke. 'I want to find Glebe. Walstan Glebe. I recall you made use of him from time to time. Is there a way to seek him out?'

Henbird's eyes widened. He was enjoying this. 'Walstan Glebe? Have you looked in limbo or the pit? That's where I would put him and let him rot like kitchen waste. I would happily cut away his ears and nose to make him prettier. And I would sever his hands at the wrist to make my purse feel safer.'

'So you don't know where he is?'

Henbird put up a hand. 'Now, I didn't say that, John. I didn't say that at all. Permit me to guess: could this be something to do with the late issue of his *Informer*, in which he signs himself *Tamburlaine's Disciple*?'

'*Apostle.*'

'I begin to understand. A most sensitive subject, I am sure. Not one that Sir Robert or the court would care to dwell on for too long. They will want you to solve this and have the powdermen strung up in short order, John. They need the coin from these Dutch goldsmiths and wool merchants to fill the war coffer. Can't be upsetting the refugees and scaring them back to the Low Countries with their gold and silver.'

'And Glebe?'

'Yes, I think I know a way to him. What favour will you do me in return?'

'What do you want?' Shakespeare glanced around the room with its exquisite plasterwork, carved oak furnishings and delicate tapestries. 'You have gold aplenty.'

The ale arrived and they both drank deeply. At last Henbird wiped his gold-threaded sleeve across his mouth. 'I want to be part of it, John. I want to be part of your world once more.

This chicken warrant is most lucrative, but it wearies me to distraction. I would gladly not see another ledger or profit sheet in my life.'

Shakespeare looked Henbird in the eye and saw that he was being utterly serious. Suddenly he leaned forward, reached out his hand across the table and shook Henbird's firmly. 'Call it a trade, Nick. I need help and I can think of no one I would rather employ than you. You are well placed and I have a task for you, if you will take it.'

'Anything, John, anything to get me away from talk of fowl.'

'But first tell me a way to Glebe.'

'As you will. I believe I do have a way. Have you heard of Black Lucy?'

'Why, yes.'

'Glebe has long had an obsession with the whore. She is succubus to him. He worships her glistening black hide – can't get enough of it.'

'From what I have heard, he is not alone in that.'

'Indeed, John, she is a most wondrous exotic creature. Pope, saint or archbishop would be sore tempted by that one. I confess I have partaken of the fruit myself on occasion. A man could spend his family's fortune on Luce and not rue the day he first saw her. I know and like her well. When once you see her in *puris naturalibus*, you will desire no other.'

'Will she help me find him?'

Henbird spread out the plump palms of his hands. 'If she likes you, if you pay her enough, if she wants to do Glebe a bad turn – any one of those may bring you to him. But tread carefully and treat her well, for she is a greater gift to London than all the beasts in the menagerie.'

'One more question, Nick: you worked with Poley in the Babington inquiry of '86. Who does he work for now?'

'The same man he always worked for – himself. Other than that, I have heard tell that he has connections to Essex House and to Thomas Walsingham. They all do – Poley, Frizer and Skeres. Frizer has been Walsingham's servant. Poley and Skeres worked with him against the Babington plot. But Thomas Walsingham has no interest in such things now. He is a country gentleman, tending his estates in Kent, dabbling with poetry.'

Shakespeare thought of Thomas Walsingham. Was any man more different from his kin? He was a warm, good-natured man, as far removed from his uncle Francis, the Queen's late principal secretary, as it was possible to be. He could not see him as the puppet master pulling these strings. Yet nothing could be ruled out in such affairs.

'Give me your opinion. Who was behind the Marlowe killing? Who was the paymaster and what was the motive?'

Henbird was a man who had stayed alive in the lethal underworld of spies, assassins and traitors by knowing when to talk and when not. 'That would be an opinion too far, John. My neck might be thicker than a chicken's, yet it is equally susceptible to the farm-wife's blade.'

'You said you wished to go intelligencing again, Nick. I had not thought you afraid of farm-wives.'

'Do not underestimate farm-wives, nor Queen's servants . . .'

Shakespeare nodded. He understood. Queen's servants. 'Topcliffe?'

'You said the name, not I.'

'But why?'

'That is for *you* to discover. And there is the one that said most recently that Marlowe should be silenced . . .'

'Baines. Richard Baines.' Shakespeare frowned. It was a name that had cropped up in his investigations, even before Marlowe's death. Baines, another sometime spy for

Walsingham, had written a tract against Marlowe within the past month in which he said that all Christians should 'endeavour that the mouth of so dangerous a member be stopped'.

'Again, John, you said the name. I believe he complained of Kit Marlowe's irreverence. But that did not sit well with me, for I do not recall Rick Baines having much in the way of religion. Anyway, his wish came true, for Marlowe's mouth was indeed stopped. Does that mean he did it, though?'

'It would not be the first man he had killed in cold blood.' Topcliffe and Baines. Shakespeare tried to find a connection between the two men. What an unholy alliance. 'You have said enough, Nick. Now, my small task for you: I wish you to discover what you may about a man named Oliver Kettle, presently a servant in the house of a Dutch wool merchant named Jan Sluyterman, of Dowgate. I have a notion about him. But be careful.'

'As always, John. And the fee?'

'First find me some information, then ask that.'

'Ah yes, I had forgot, you learned thrift from Mr Secretary . . .'

Chapter 6

BOLTFOOT COOPER RODE across London Bridge, beneath the severed heads of traitors. He did not look up; he knew they were there, parboiled and pecked at by the kites, and he had no wish to see them.

Once away from the bridge, he turned east and followed the river along the Deptford road, a track of dust and holes. The road was heavy with an endless train of long open-sided carts, laden with felled oaks and casks of provisions for the shipyards. He passed a line of six great wagons – each pulled by six oxen – that bore mighty guns to arm the Navy Royal. Boltfoot glanced at them: culverin, demi-culverin, saker, minion, falconet. This was ordnance to stir the blood and strike fear into enemy hearts: the culverin, two tons of bronze that could fire seventeen-pound iron balls into the bulwarks and gunwales of King Philip's galleons; the cannon-perier, a stumpy gun that hurled round stones at ships, shattering into deadly shards as they hit a deck or mast.

Boltfoot was not stirred. The sea and its battles had long since lost their hold over him; three years under the command of Drake as he sailed the globe had seen to that.

After a mile and a half he turned left, on to the spit of land that bulged into the Thames. There were docks and industry, and bustling villages housing the lightermen and those who worked at loading and unloading the carracks heading for the Indies. In clearings beside the road he began to see charcoal burners at work, the smoke rising from their stacks of willow, and then he came to a wooded area close to the water's edge and saw the stockade protecting the Rotherhithe powdermill.

There were several buildings, scattered over two or three acres and sheltered by trees. Boltfoot understood the need for such a siting: if the powder store exploded, the canopy of trees would muffle the explosion and protect the nearby shipping and dockyards.

Reining in to a slow walk, he rode around the perimeter of the stockaded area. The enclosure was between eight and nine feet high, built of stakes driven into the ground close together to form a palisade. It would be possible to scale with a ladder, unwatched at night. But how good were the guards on the other side?

He approached the front gate, but as he tried to ride on through he was immediately stopped by a pair of sentries. They stepped out in front of him. Both had crossbows at their shoulders, drawn taut, bolts loaded and aimed directly at his chest. Behind them, three ban-dogs in studded collars were leashed to the small guardhouse, slavering and growling.

Boltfoot dropped the reins and put his hands in the air to show he was no threat.

'I am here on Queen's business,' he said. 'I am to see the keeper.'

The sentries looked like military men to Boltfoot. They were both powerfully built and wore jerkins of hide. They had neat-trimmed beards and bold faces, the sort of men any captain-general would have been happy to have at his disposal. 'Dismount,' said one of them, who was slightly taller and more imposing than the other. 'No sudden movements.'

Boltfoot slowly slid from his horse. He sniffed the air. It was thick with the scent of raw gunpowder.

'Now the gun. Unsling it. Put it on the ground, gently.'

Again, he did what was required of him, carefully laying the caliver across his arms, his finger well away from the trigger. He bent at the knees and lowered the weapon safely to the turf beneath his feet.

'Your sword, too, and daggers. All things metal, be they steel or iron. Deposit them by the caliver. Tinderbox, pipe and tobacco, too.'

With an exaggerated lack of haste, Boltfoot obeyed the man.

'The horse is shod. It'll have to stay tethered out here. No metal inside.'

The second sentry lowered his crossbow. Boltfoot noticed it was made entirely of wood, apart from the string of gut; even the bolt had a charred and sharpened point, rather than a steel tip. But it was deadly enough, all the same, and would pierce him through if unleashed at that distance. The sentry took the horse's reins.

'I understand,' Boltfoot said.

'One little spark from a piece of metal on flint. One shod hoof sparking on stone, that's all it takes and this place will go straight to the heavens and take good men with it. Now then, who are you?'

'Boltfoot Cooper. My master is John Shakespeare, intelligence secretary to Sir Robert Cecil.'

'This will be about the Dutch church.'

'Yes.'

'Well, we are all a little more wary than usual here.'

'Are you not always so wary, then?'

The sentry's blood rose and he pushed forward his crossbow so it was less than a foot from Boltfoot's heart. 'Don't come the cunning man with me, Mr Cooper.'

Boltfoot did not back off, but decided there was nothing to be gained from provoking the sentry further. 'I have orders to see the mill-keeper, Jeremiah Quincesmith.'

'Do you have papers?'

Boltfoot put his hand in his jerkin and brought out the letter-patent signed by Shakespeare and Bedwell, warranting him to be received by the keepers of the mills he was to visit and have his questions answered.

The first sentry studied it. 'Wait here,' he said, then walked off with the paper, leaving the other guard with Boltfoot. In a few minutes he returned. 'Follow me.'

Boltfoot looked down at his caliver and cutlass.

'Don't worry about that. Mr Willis will look out for your horse and arms.'

'If they are safe when I return, you will have a groat from me,' Boltfoot told the second sentry. Reluctantly he turned away from his precious belongings and walked away, dragging his left foot through the dust.

He followed the first sentry to the nearest building, the most substantial of the five. It was constructed of brick and was attached to the great wheel that was turned day and night by the flow of water in a short canal spur carved across the land from the river Thames. The other mill houses were made of timber, daub and wattle with heavy thatching on the roof to keep the contents dry. He knew enough to realise that those buildings would be used for storing the raw ingredients – the grough or crude saltpetre, the charcoal produced by the burners outside the stockade, the sulfur imported from the lands of Italy and elsewhere. The process involved refining and mixing these three components in the correct ratio. The buildings were deliberately flimsy; they would be no loss if the place exploded – and the damage caused by flying twigs and staves would be considerably less than an explosion involving stone or brick.

Boltfoot was taken through to the mill room where he could see the great wheels turning and charcoal and sulfur being crushed by edge-runners of stone.

'Mr Quincesmith,' the sentry said. 'This is Mr Cooper.'

'Thank you, Mr Amos. You may go.'

Jeremiah Quincesmith was a bull of a man. His chest had the dimensions of a cask and threatened to burst from his drab worsted doublet. The muscles of his arms bulged in his sleeves. He had been talking to the men minding the crushing equipment, but now he looked Boltfoot up and down critically like a muster-master appraising a new soldier and finding him wanting. He brushed his hands together and a dusting of black powder sprinkled to the sawdust floor. He then perused the letter-patent from Shakespeare.

'Well, Mr Cooper,' he said. 'I can understand why your master has sent you here, but you can assure him that we have no leaks. You saw the stockade. Day and night, we have six guardsmen on duty with fighting mastiffs. And all the powder is transported direct to the storehouse in the White Tower by barge under red flag. The powder is weighed out and weighed in. It is a short trip and none has gone missing. This is a well-run establishment, inspected twice a year by officers of the Ordnance Storekeeper. On one occasion last year Mr Bedwell came here himself and complimented us. Does that answer all your questions? I am a busy man. And Mr Sarjent here knows us well.'

Boltfoot suddenly realised there was another man in the room. He was tall and martial, like the guards, with a bristling black beard and eyes that seemed no more than slits. So this was the man who was to accompany him. The man nodded to him in acknowledgement, but Boltfoot did not reciprocate. He turned back to Quincesmith. 'Where is the vault?'

'I'll show you. It's through here.' He led Boltfoot out to a thick-walled outhouse, followed by Sarjent. A sentry with a wooden pike and leashed mastiff stood guard. The vault had a heavy oaken door and a series of black-painted bolts, all of which were on the outside so that no metal was on the inside, close to the powder.

'If not from here, Mr Quincesmith, whence did the Dutch church powder come?' Boltfoot asked after looking inside the room at the pile of black powder awaiting casking.

Quincesmith smiled as he relocked the door. 'Have you been a soldier, Mr Cooper? You are a poor sort of man with your crippled foot, but you look strong enough otherwise. And at least you stand as straight as you can, not scratching your balls like the levies of thieves and rogues that captains must accept as foot soldiers in these wars. I like the look of you.'

'I was at sea.'

'Against the Armada? Are you a cooper, as your name implies? We need good coopers here. You'd have to learn to hoop the kegs with osier, like water butts, not steel. Copper's safe, too. Do you work with copper? The pay is good.'

'No, Mr Quincesmith. I ask again. How did these men get their gunpowder?'

Quincesmith shrugged his broad shoulders. 'Does your Mr Shakespeare think we are all fools here? We know the threat from Spain. Their agents would dearly love to put a spark in the powder store. That is why we are so tight. That is why our guards – men like Mr Amos and Mr Willis, whom you have met – are all veterans of the Low Countries campaign under Norris. Hard, disciplined men. And nor are we complacent, Mr Cooper. Our guards are out with the trainbands every week to hone their fighting skills. They will not hesitate to kill.'

'You have not answered my question.'

'Where did the powder come from? I might guess a carrack's

hold. Once the powder is aboard ship, no one will notice a portion vanishing.'

Boltfoot said nothing. Of course, that was possible – but improbable. Before a merchantman set sail, the vessel would be full of men and the powder would be secured in the hold. It would be no easy matter spiriting it away unseen.

'Or,' Quincesmith continued, 'it might be another powder-mill. There are those that say Three Mills at Bromley-by-Bow is not kept as well as it should be.'

'Who told you that?'

'I hear things, Mr Cooper. The lads at the Royal Armoury . . .'

'But who? Give me a name.'

Quincesmith smiled and tilted his chin towards the third man in the room. 'Mr Sarjent here for one. He knows Three Mills well and will not say a good word for it. Go and look at the place yourself if you want to know more.'

'I need more than that. You have made accusations against another powdermill. Tell me the detail.'

Quincesmith stepped forward and took Boltfoot's hand. 'Let me shake you by the hand, Mr Cooper, for you are a stub-born stump of man and I want to help you. Others might wish to shake you by the throat, but, in truth, I think I would have been pleased to have had you as a soldier. Here, look at this before you go seeking out warrants.' He produced a paper. 'I received this not an hour since from Mr Bedwell at the Tower, brought with Mr William Sarjent here. It says I am to do all in my power to assist you with what knowledge I have – and that I am to show you the inner workings of my fine mill. It says, too, that Mr Sarjent is to accompany you during your investigations.'

'I know that,' Boltfoot said, declining to look at the paper.

Quincesmith grinned and revealed his teeth, a few of which were missing. He put the paper aside. 'Now then, Mr Cooper, what more can I tell you? Allow me to explain the making and storing of gunpowder to you in small detail, as if I was talking to a simpleton or a child. Then Mr Sarjent will take you on your way. You will find him a stern companion, I have no doubt, but he is a brave fighting man and knows as much about the safekeeping of gunpowder as any man in the realm. I pray you find the source of this powder without delay, for it does none of us any good to have such things happening . . .'

Chapter 7

As John Shakespeare approached the ancient nunnery of St Mary at Clerkenwell, the birdsong was suddenly silenced by the crack of a gunshot. Shakespeare reined in his grey mare. A pair of boys in ragged clothes wrestled furiously on the dusty path in front of him, oblivious to everything but their fight.

He looked about. It seemed the firing had come from within the former convent. Kicking on again, he stepped the mare around the boys and walked on past the well where the parish clerks once performed mystery plays. Ahead of him was the great entrance door to St Mary's. The spring sun streaming through the leaves of a pair of silver birches dappled the grassy verge with light.

Shakespeare tethered the mare to a post, then strode on foot to the convent entrance. The great arched gateway was open and untended. He called out, but no one came. He walked in towards the central courtyard, from where he heard voices, then another volley of gunfire and cackling laughter.

Through clouds of powder smoke, he saw that the courtyard was a wide open, arid place, uncared for and thick with weeds. Had the Benedictine sisters still been here, they would surely have been aghast at the vision they beheld. Or perhaps they wouldn't, he thought wryly; it depended whose version you accepted of what went on in the Catholic monasteries.

Three women were at one end of the yard. Two of them sat against the wall, flagons of some liquor or ale in their hands. The third one, a fair-haired woman in her forties who must once have been pretty, was on her feet, a smoking wheel-lock pistol hanging loosely from her fingers. Her top was bare, her breasts pendulous over a belly of loose skin and fat. The two sitting women were scarcely more decent, sitting with their legs apart and their cheap kirtles hitched up to reveal their thighs and more. Their hair was awry and their chemises open. One scratched at a pustule on her haggard face. The other, a dark-haired girl no older than seventeen, would have been comely if she had combed her hair – and if she had looked less hard and villainous. She had unmarked skin, like a milkmaid, and puffed at a clay pipe.

At the far end of the yard, tied by a cord to a hook in the wall, was a small dog, lying in a pool of its own blood. It was moving, but slowly, close to death from the pistol balls that had pierced it.

The women turned as Shakespeare entered. The bare-breasted woman raised the pistol and pointed it at him. Her friends burst out laughing once again.

Without hesitation, Shakespeare walked forward and wrenched the spent firearm from the woman's grasp. She seemed unconcerned. 'A sovereign and I'll fire your pistol, dove. I know how to fire a man's pistol . . .'

Shakespeare ignored her and went to the listless dog. He removed his dagger and cut its throat as an act of mercy, then returned to the women.

'I am looking for Black Lucy. I believe she has premises here. Do you work for her?'

'Work for Luce? The maggoty Moor wouldn't look at us. And nor would we work for such a greasy drab.'

'But you know where she is?'

'What's it to you – and what's it worth?' She grasped hold of one of her breasts and tried to push it into Shakespeare's face. But she was unsteady from the drink and her knees buckled, sending her toppling forward. Shakespeare could have reached out and held her up, but he stepped back and let her fall to the cobble-stone ground. Her friends laughed. Shakespeare turned to them.

'Do either of you know where she is? I'll give you threepence.'

'You done for our dog, mister,' the young one said, blowing out smoke. 'That little bitch was worth a lot to us. We saved her from the plague men and loved her like she was our kin.' The woman began coughing.

Shakespeare knelt down and took the flagons from them. They were both about half full of strong ale. He started pouring one away. The women bridled and reached out their hands as if they were birds' talons, but he easily evaded their grasp. 'Well?' he demanded as the last drop fell to the ground.

'Sixpence,' the young, hard-faced one said.

Shakespeare took out three pennies and held them up. 'One each and you can have the rest of the ale back.'

'Give them to us, then we'll tell you.'

'Tell me first.'

She threw back her knotted hair and gestured vaguely to a small passageway leading from the courtyard to the northern precinct of the old nunnery. 'Back there. But you'd do better with us. Swive the three of us for a crown and we'll use alum to make us virgins. She'll charge you three sovereigns for just one of her loose-cunnied whores.' The girl pulled her kirtle up past her bare belly and thighs and displayed herself to him.

Shakespeare put the flagon down, tossed them the three pennies and walked away.

'Here,' one of them called. 'That's our pistol you got there.'

'It's safer with me.'

A sign hung over the doorway of the old dorter where once the nuns had their plain beds and sparse living quarters. The sign was painted in gold on a black background and said simply *Vespers*.

Unlike the dust-strewn courtyard, the area here was well kept; the ground swept, the mortar and woodwork maintained in good repair. The door beneath the sign was newly crafted from oak and inviting.

Shakespeare saw that it was ajar and pushed it open. It gave on to an open hall with wood panelling. On the far wall, beneath a gallery, hung a long, brightly coloured tapestry. Shakespeare glanced at it, expecting its subject to be religious, perhaps the Virgin Mary, or some hunting scene. But then he saw that it was an exquisite needlework respresentation of a naked woman, dark-skinned, with chains of gold about her throat, her slender waist, her wrists and her ankles.

'Good day to you, sir.'

Shakespeare turned. He frowned. She was a fair-faced woman in her early thirties, with a warm smile. The voice and face were vaguely familiar, but he couldn't place them. She seemed to have a clearer idea, for she stiffened, as if she recognised him.

'I am seeking Lucy, whom I believe to be the mistress of this establishment.'

The woman, who wore good clothes, though bordering on the immodest with a low-cut bodice, regained her composure and bowed to him. 'Please wait here, sir. There is a settle in the hall. Would you like the maid to bring you beer or wine?'

'Beer would suit me well.'

'It will be with you straightway.' She began to walk off.

'Do you not wish to know my name?'

The woman looked back and smiled conspiratorially. 'We do not often deal with names at Vespers, sir, though you may invent one if you desire.'

Shakespeare laughed; it seemed he was taken for a client. The woman disappeared and he looked around the hall. It was beautifully furnished with cushion-laden settles, a polished table and coffers, and drapes about the high windows. He sat down and waited. After a minute a maid appeared, bowed and handed him a pewter pot of beer. He took a deep quaff, enjoying the tang of hops on his parched throat. He noticed some books on the table and picked one up, quickly looking through the pages. He smiled again; they were amatory sonnets. It occurred to him that the fine nature of the room might have led the casual visitor to believe this was a respectable house, but the book gave the lie to that. This was a whorehouse, however it might present itself. He sipped again at the beer and waited.

At the soft whisper of footsteps he looked towards the staircase that curved down from the gallery. A tall and elegant woman was gliding down. Her skin was of the darkest hue that Shakespeare had ever seen, her features exquisite and her bearing regal. As she approached him, with the woman from the door trailing in her wake, she seemed to curtsy, but it wasn't really that, nothing more in truth than a gracious acknowledgement of his presence.

'Good day, Mr Shakespeare. It is a great pleasure to meet you. I am Lucy.'

'How do you know my name?' He could not take his eyes from her skin, exposed at her neck and face and wrists, vanishing into a gown of gold.

She glanced at the woman at her side. 'Beth knows you. Think back, Mr Shakespeare. Do you not remember your first love, Beth Evans?'

His brow creased in puzzlement and wonder. Beth Evans? Here, in a whorehouse? Could this be true? He stared at her and his eyes widened in recognition.

'Beth?' he said quietly.

'Yes, it is me, John.' Her eyes smiled back at him. 'You really didn't know me, did you?'

He shook his head.

'I think you always had your nose in a book when you should have been looking at me.' Her dark brown eyes and full lips creased in good humour. 'I have watched your progress from afar, John. You have come a great distance from the Warwickshire meadows where we ran together.'

They had been but sixteen, sweethearts for one summer, or so it seemed. Perhaps five weeks, hardly more, and then she had taken up with the smithy's son and left Shakespeare heartbroken. He felt a pang at the memory of it; he had sworn to be hers forever and now, when he met her again, he had not known her. How their paths had diverged: he had gone to Gray's Inn, entered the service of Sir Francis Walsingham and later that of Sir Robert Cecil, and was believed, by some, to be destined for great things. Beth had become a common whore. Well, not so common by the look of her and this sumptuous establishment.

Lucy touched his arm. 'I am sure there will be time aplenty for you to talk of times past. Come, Mr Shakespeare, how can I help you? I am sure it is not swiving you are after, for Beth assures me you are above the lewd sportings we habitually offer our clients.'

It was true enough, but somehow, in this place, it made him sound a very dull man.

'I think I know you, John,' Beth said, 'even after all these years.'

Of course. He had been slow off the mark that summer of '75. He had treated her like a lady and talked of Socrates and Bosworth Field, of Chaucer and his great ambitions for himself and England, when all she wanted was to be rolled in the hay like all her friends. 'It is true,' he said, nodding with a resigned sigh. 'You do know me.' He turned to Lucy. 'No, I am not here for your services, mistress. I am here on Queen's business with one question. Do you know the whereabouts of Walstan Glebe?'

Lucy furrowed her brow as if she did not quite understand the question, but he was certain he saw a sparkle in her dark brown eyes. 'Walstan Glebe?'

'Come, come, mistress, you know him well. *L* for *Liar* burned on to his forehead. You must know, too, that I could have this establishment closed down before nightfall and you and all the whores –' he caught the accusing stare of Beth Evans – 'all the *occupants* interned at Bridewell.'

'Mr Shakespeare, you do not need to threaten me. I will answer you straight. Of course I know Wally Glebe. But I will not tell you where he is, for that would be a breach of trust. I will, if you wish, get a message to him saying that you would talk with him.'

'I cannot overemphasise the seriousness of this business. We have reason to believe that Glebe has knowledge of the recent gunpowder atrocity at the Dutch church. If he is in any way involved, then he is guilty of high treason. Anyone withholding evidence of any kind – including knowledge of his whereabouts – will be considered an accessory.'

Lucy folded her arms across her chest. 'Mr Shakespeare, I wish the culprits caught as much as you. A great many of my clients are strangers from France and the Low Countries. I am, myself, of foreign birth and I do not like this present fervour against strangers. I have said I will go to Glebe – and I will.'

'No, that is not enough. If you did so he would simply disappear, as he has done before. I have no wish to harm you, mistress, and I care not a jot how you earn your living, but if you do not give me the information I require, pursuivants will take you to the Tower, where you will be subjected to hard questioning none can resist. I must tell you that the Council has authorised the use of torture in this matter.'

'Then you will have to torture me.'

Shakespeare was bemused. He had always hesitated to use such threats, but when he did they inevitably had an instant and dramatic effect. Not so here; she had not lost her charm, nor her equanimity. Her eyes still looked at him with humour. If she was afraid, there was no sign of it.

'I will take you to him,' Beth Evans said.

Shakespeare looked at her, then back to Lucy. Lucy said nothing, but the glimmer of a smile played around her full lips.

'Will that do?'

'You know where he is?'

She nodded. 'Yes, he likes me, too. Return here at seven of the clock and I will take you. I know where he will be at that time, for I have been summoned to him.'

Chapter 8

'MARINER WERE YOU, Mr Cooper?' William Sarjent said, his voice booming across the riverbank as they awaited the ferry. 'A sea battle don't compare to the stench of powder and the clash of steel on land. When two regiments of foot meet on the field there is no hold to escape to; a captain of infantry cannot just turn with the wind and sail away, Mr Cooper. At the Maas river, in the mud and rain with every man's powder wet and useless, I was at Norris's side fighting pike to pike when he received a bloody wound to his chest that brought blood to his mouth, yet still we won the day.'

Boltfoot stood beside his horse in silence. In his ear there was the drum of a man's voice, but he did not hear the words.

'I was at Sidney's side, too, when he received his fatal wound in the Low Countries. Place called Zutphen. We had two hundred foot and three hundred horse. Suddenly the fog lifted and three thousand Spaniards appeared. But we did not turn. No man under Norris's command ever turned from a fight without express order. Never did you see a more gallant gentleman than Sir Philip Sidney. And Norris is the boldest of them all. You can keep your Drakes and Frobishers, Mr Cooper. They are ducks upon the water, not true fighting men. Norris — there's a man's man. Mr Quincesmith was his powder-master and took me as his prentice.'

At last the Woolwich ferry arrived and they walked their horses carefully aboard, amidst a packed group of wagons and a host of foot passengers. The rocking of the tide as the low barge pulled away from its moorings spooked one of the harnessed horses and it had to be restrained from pulling its wagon and several men into the dark grey flood.

On the north side of the Thames, deep in the dockyards that brought the wealth of the world to London, they disembarked from the ferry and mounted up once more. Turning westwards, they quickly joined the river Lea at its mouth and rode inland along its course. The landscape was low and fertile either side of the slow, winding stream. Water meadows and copses bounded the banks. Boltfoot reined in to get his bearings. Three Mills should be close now.

At his left side, Sarjent was running his hand through his black hair and saying something about the thunder of cannon and the taste of hot blood, words that every farm boy and villager for a mile about must have heard, so loud was the man. Boltfoot dug his heels sharply into the side of his long-suffering steed and rode ahead, wishing himself rid of this infernal braggart with his hunting-horn voice. He was not certain he could stand another day of this ceaseless roaring in his ear.

As he rode back towards the city, Shakespeare knew he was being watched. He knew well enough how to lose a following horseman, but instead he slowed down.

The day was dull and windless. He thought again about Henbird; had he misunderstood him or had he, indeed, been suggesting that Topcliffe was linked to Robert Poley and to the death of Marlowe? *Do not underestimate Queen's servants.*

But why would Topcliffe and Poley have conspired to kill Marlowe? Topcliffe said he shared the playwright's antipathy towards London's population of foreigners – so why kill him? And why tell Shakespeare he believed Marlowe was murdered? Shakespeare rode his grey mare across the busy six acres of Smith Field, then into the broad sweep of Little Britain, cutting in towards the city. He casually reined the horse to the right and into the labyrinth of narrow streets close by City Ditch. He walked on down a lane of overhanging houses, then turned left. Seeing that no one was about, he quickly dismounted and waited. He heard the follower before he saw him; the soft clip-clop of hooves on cobbles.

As his pursuer rode into the street, Shakespeare reached up and grasped at his arm and leg, wrenching him clean from the saddle. The man grunted in shock as he flew sideways and fell heavily to the ground. As he landed, he let out a cry of pain, his elbow and the side of his head cracking against the flagstones. Shakespeare was on him in an instant. In his hand he had the wheel-lock pistol he had taken from the three trugs close to Black Lucy's bawdy-house. He sat astride the man and held the muzzle of the unloaded gun to his face.

'One wrong move and you die here.'

'Please – wait.'

'Who are you?'

'You know me.'

Shakespeare did, indeed, know him. He knew that soft, oily voice. He knew that slender, serpentine frame with the shoulders that were almost as one with the neck and he knew that contemptible, self-satisfied expression. It did not seem so smug now.

'Morley . . .'

'Mr Shakespeare, I must talk with you.'

Shakespeare held the gun back a few inches but it was still trained on Morley's face. 'If you want to talk to me, come to my door. Follow me like an assassin and you are like to die.'

'I could not approach you at your house. I might have been seen.'

'Well, you are seen now, and will pay for it.'

'Please, Mr Shakespeare. I have followed you to Clerkenwell and now here. Had I wished to harm you, I could have done so before now. Will you not hear my story?'

Morley. Christopher Morley. One-time tutor to the Lady Arbella Stuart, claimant to the throne of England, in the household of Bess of Hardwick; one-time spy for Walsingham, but not to be trusted by any man; one-time confederate of the Earl of Essex in a high treason that had nearly cost both men – and others – their heads. Morley had crossed Shakespeare's path once before – and that had been one time too many. He had hoped never to see the man again.

'I should kill you here, in this street, like a plague dog.'

'Then you would never hear the intelligence I have for you.'

'Five seconds, Morley. Five, four—'

'I know the name of the powderman . . .'

He was still in the scarlet velvet doublet and breeches he had worn when last they met, little more than half a year ago. Now the once fine velvet was dirt-stained, torn and threadbare, as if he had been living wild. His hair was uncombed and had grown longer; his wispy, dark moustache and the few strands of hair that constituted his beard had not been trimmed in weeks. He looked like a vagrant.

'Indeed. Then tell me before I fire.'

'I cannot – yet. But I *will* tell you.'

Shakespeare looked into his eyes, then withdrew the gun and stood up. Roughly, he pulled Morley up by the front of his filthy doublet. From his own saddlepack he took a length of cord, then thrust the wheel-lock under his arm, seized Morley's arms and lashed his wrists together in front of him, knotting them tightly. He left a lead of about six feet, which he secured to the stirrup of the mare. It all happened so fast, Morley scarce had time to protest. Shakespeare clambered aboard the grey mare, leant across to take the reins of Morley's horse and prepared to ride, dragging Morley behind.

'Wait, there is more,' his captive managed to say at last. 'This is to do with Marlowe. They meant to kill me, not Kit. They are after me, Mr Shakespeare.'

Shakespeare looked down at him with disdain. 'This street is not the place to discuss such things. We are going to Newgate. You will be very comfortable there, I am sure.'

'Not Newgate . . .'

Shakespeare ignored him and slapped the grey mare's flank.

Morley pulled back on the cord, his heels trying to dig into the ground. 'No, not Newgate – your home – anywhere but Newgate. I will be known there and killed.'

'Look at the place, Mr Cooper. It is a disgrace.'

Boltfoot surveyed the Three Mills. The palisade was too low and, in places, the stakes had fallen. A man could get in there with ease. No, he thought, a *squadron* of men could enter undetected.

In the distance he saw a group of idlers leaning against the side of the main mill building. They were dressed in jerkins and hose like workmen, but they were drinking, not working, and seemed engaged in chatter like denizens of the taproom.

Boltfoot shook his head in dismay. Sarjent's verdict was true enough. It was easy to imagine powder disappearing from this place; from this distance, on a bridge over the Lea some six hundred yards away, it looked as watertight as a malkin's colander.

'They should have stayed with flour milling,' Sarjent said.

Boltfoot looked at his companion curiously. 'What do you know of this place, Mr Sarjent?'

'It was a flour mill. There were three of them here, hence the name. Then two. Now one of those two is a gunpowder mill, founded five years since at the time of the Spanish Armada. See how she straddles the Lea? The river is tidal here, and it is the ebb that drives the wheels.'

'Have you been here before?'

'Aye,' Sarjent said, his voice quieter now. 'I was deputed here in '88 when it was converted by the Knaggs. That's Thomas Knagg and his father, who is now dead. But we fell out. I did not like their methods. They were not military men and seemed unaware – uncaring – about the dangers of powder.'

Boltfoot said nothing. He shook the reins of his mount.

Sarjent kicked on after him. 'Come, Mr Cooper, let us go and pummel a few skulls.'

The keeper of the Counter prison in Wood Street was pleased to accept two shillings in his hand from Shakespeare. 'Don't you worry, sir,' he said. 'Mr Morley will not escape from here.'

'Leave us now, master keeper. Send a turnkey with ale.'

The keeper, a bony-handed ancient with a long, ash-grey beard, bowed and backed out of the small cell. Morley sat hunched on a pile of clean straw, his back to the damp wall. He had the cell to himself, but there were no comforts other than this straw and the weak light that slanted in through a barred window high up in the thick stone.

Shakespeare stood by the door and eyed his miserable captive. He was surprised to see real fear in his face; he was used to the curled lip of sneering contempt from this man. 'Well, Mr Morley,' he said at last. 'You are a shambles of a human being. Not one of the creator's finest works, that is certain.'

'I am brought to penury, Mr Shakespeare. I cannot work as a tutor without a recommendation from the Countess of

Shrewsbury, and she will not give me one. Nor can I sell my odes, for no one has coin in these straitened times.'

'What do you bring me? If you wish to stay out of Newgate, you had best tell the whole truth, and soon.'

'I will tell you nothing without assurances of freedom – and silver. You have to protect me.'

Shakespeare cupped his hand on the hilt of his sword. 'Protect you, Morley? All you will get is iron, fire and the Tyburn halter if you do *not* tell me everything I wish to know.'

'Tyburn!' the prisoner attempted to laugh at the dread word, but it came out as a sour bark. 'Tyburn holds no terrors. It would be a blessed release from my woes. Nothing you threaten can make me more afraid than I am already, Mr Shakespeare. The men I talk of have forgot more about inflicting pain than the Spanish Inquisition ever learned.'

'Why have you come to me?'

'I told you: I need your protection. There is no one I can trust and I took you for an honourable man. You must give me the means to get to a place of sanctuary, as far from this rotten town as a man may go. Give me that and you shall have all the information you require.'

'How much do you think you need?'

'A hundred sovereigns. No less than that. I must have money to leave here and start life anew.'

'I could not find such a sum and you know it, Mr Morley.'

'Cecil could.'

'Then give me something worth taking him. He would laugh and order in Topcliffe if I brought what you have told me thus far.'

The turnkey returned with ale. He was a gnat of a man, no more than four and a half foot tall, but square built. His keys rattled at his belt. In one hand he carried two beakers of musty ale. He picked a large lump of something unpleasant from his nose and scraped it into one of the beakers, which he handed to Morley before exiting with a smirk.

Morley hurled the defiled beaker of ale to the ground.

'This is your life now, Morley, or what is left of it,' Shakespeare said, handing him his own stale liquor. 'If you do not cooperate with me you will live with rats and taste London's prison holes until the hurdle draws you to your death.'

'I will tell you what I know. But you will have no names from me until you return with one hundred sovereigns.'

'Speak, then.'

Morley supped from Shakespeare's ale and immediately spat it out with a retching noise.

'Start with Marlowe. You said you were the intended victim, but that cannot be – Poley knew Marlowe well. There could have been no error there.'

'This is poison, not ale!'

'Marlowe . . .'

Morley wiped his grubby, threadbare velvet sleeve across his mouth and tangled beard. 'I have oftentimes being confused with Marlowe. Our names can sometimes sound the same and we were both university wits and poets from Cambridge. But that is by the by. The one who ordered the killing was befuddled. He believed Marlowe wrote the placards by the Dutch church. An easy mistake to make – why, even the Council was deceived, so I am told.'

'But it was you?'

He shook his head. 'Not me alone. A group of us. But the one who paid for Marlowe's death believed I was a threat to him, for I recognised him and realised he was not what he seemed. He will know soon enough, though, that he has had the wrong man killed.'

'Was he one of your confederates?'

'I cannot tell you. But I do now believe they want me dead, for they are convinced that I have betrayed them.'

'But who are they?'

'Bring me the sovereigns.'

'Tell me – without names, if you must – what manner of people are they?'

Morley hesitated, as if wondering how much information he could afford to divulge.

'I must have at least this, Morley.' Shakespeare's voice was less harsh. 'The ones who wrote the placards must be the powdermen, yes?

'Do not ask too much, or we will both die.'

'Well?'

'Mr Shakespeare, I will help you all I can. But I beg you to be circumspect. We – this group and I – wish to see the strangers sent home from our midst. There are many others. More than the Council could ever imagine: apprentices, merchants, even noblemen . . . men who do not like the strangers' ways. They take our business. Why, I do believe the Countess of Shrewsbury herself has replaced me with a German or some such. They are like leeches or some canker on the body of England.'

'But among these many opponents of the strangers, there is this smaller group? A core of men prepared to use force of arms and powder to achieve their ends?'

'Yes.'

'How many?'

'Six . . . ten sometimes. They used me for the poster-writing, for I have some small skill with words, but I think they never intended I should live. Not once *he* had seen me and realised I recognised him . . .'

'He?'

Morley said nothing.

'Was Glebe among them? Walstan Glebe?'

Morley seemed to think a moment, then shook his head slowly. 'I know no one of that name.'

'And Poley – Robert Poley – how was he connected to this band of malcontents?'

'He was not. Poley is nothing but a hireling. A killer for money, a mercenary. Had he been one of these men, there would have been no confusion.'

Shakespeare was silent a moment; that was just how he saw Poley. But he also knew that Poley had connections. He insinuated himself with those on whom he would prey. 'This core group – they are the ones who wrote the libels and placed the powder?'

Morley sighed heavily, his narrow shoulders rising and falling as his mouth opened and fell closed. 'We all did write the words – though I confess it was I who put it into verse – but there was but one powderman, I believe.'

Shakespeare moved forward, drawing his dagger seamlessly and putting its point to Morley's naked throat. 'Give me his name, Morley.' His voice now was a rasp. 'Give me the name, for you have already told me enough to order you racked till every bone in your body crack asunder. And I will do it, for the Council would demand it of me.'

Morley recoiled from the sharp tip. A spot of blood dripped from his Adam's apple on to the stained falling band about his neck. Shakespeare saw that he was shaking.

'Fifty, Mr Shakespeare. I beg you. Find me fifty sovereigns and you shall have it all.'

'The name!'

'I will not. It is the one thing that can save me. I will give it to no man without having the silver and freedom that I must have. Elsewise I am dead, whether racked or no.'

Chapter 9

Sir Robert Cecil sat in a straight-backed chair and remained perfectly still as a barber shaved his whiskers from his cheeks, leaving moustaches and a neat beard, which he trimmed into a point. As Shakespeare entered the room, the privy councillor snatched a towel and dabbed at his face. 'John, I am glad you have come to me. I was about to send for you. There is a change of plan.'

The barber did not wait to be dismissed, but immediately bowed and left the room, carrying his razor, strop and basin.

Shakespeare had been shown straight through to Cecil's coolly efficient rooms at Greenwich Palace. There were dark, polished shelves here, a plain walnut table, two straight-backed chairs, an inkpot and quills; nothing superfluous to his needs as privy councillor with responsibility for the day-to-day management and security of the realm. He was not a man to clutter his desk with books and scrolls. Business was attended to, then filed away. The room was a reflection of Cecil's own unflustered demeanour, yet today he seemed strangely agitated.

'Sir Robert, I have an important development to report,' Shakespeare said, bowing lightly in deference to his master.

Cecil did not meet Shakespeare's gaze. Rising to his feet, he put down the towel and reached across to his shelves and took a paper from a file of records. 'I am removing you from the powder inquiry, John. You are to travel to Gaynes Park Hall in Essex without delay.' He did not wait for Shakespeare to register his surprise, but ploughed on. 'You will there meet Antonio Perez and work your charm to secure certain intelligence from him. You will be gone from here within the hour and will ride overnight so that you arrive by dawn at the latest. Mr Mills, in the meantime, will take charge of the Dutch church inquiries. Pass on all your information to him. Here —' he handed Shakespeare the sheet '— everything you need is in that paper. Clarkson has already drawn up letters-patent for you to present to Perez. He will organise a messenger to inform your wife that you will not be home tonight and perhaps not for days to come, until your work is completed.'

Shakespeare took the paper from Cecil's taut little hand. For a moment he had no words; this change of mission was sudden, unexpected and disturbing. He had to speak. 'Sir Robert, if you would give me a hearing before you take this further. Can no one else go to Perez?'

'No.'

'My inquiries are at a critical stage. I have a man in custody who says he has the name of the powderman. He is scared for his life and is begging fifty sovereigns to effect his escape. In return he will give us the name. Can there be anything more important than this?'

'Get Topcliffe on to him. That will loosen his tongue.'

'The man came to me because he trusted me. He deserves better.'

'Frank Mills then.'

'He will bring in Topcliffe. They have interrogated prisoners together in the past.'

'I will talk to Mills. There will be no torture. But nor will there be fifty sovereigns. Mills will give the man ten marks if his intelligence is sound. Does that satisfy you, John? Well done in finding this man, but you must set him aside for others to deal with. I need you for this Perez assignment, for reasons that I shall explain.'

Shakespeare was stunned into silence. How could he bring up the other line of inquiry – Beth Evans was supposed to be taking him to Walstan Glebe this evening; he could not hand over Beth to the dubious care of Francis Mills.

'You know a great deal about Perez, I believe, John?'

He nodded. 'Yes.' He probably knew more about the Spaniard than any man in England, having followed his career – and downfall – closely over many years, both in his time with Walsingham and now with Cecil. In recent weeks he had read the intelligence reports assiduously since hearing Perez was coming to England. Calais swarmed with English spies and Spanish assassins, some of them intent on killing the Spaniard and claiming the reward of twenty thousand ducats offered by King Philip. Enough to make any man rich. Mentally, Shakespeare rehearsed all he knew about Perez. At one time he had been Philip's most trusted minister; as powerful as a Wolsey or a Cromwell. More powerful, perhaps, for his master always followed his advice and was less capricious than Great Henry. Now Perez was a fugitive, having sought refuge in France to escape a death sentence for a lurid variety of alleged crimes, including the murder of Juan de Escobedo, another of Philip's senior government officials.

As Shakespeare recalled it, Perez had installed Escobedo as secretary to King Philip's half-brother, Don John of Austria, with orders to spy on him. Philip did not trust Don John and wanted him closely observed.

But Escobedo had not kept his side of the bargain – he had, in fact, fomented Don John's subversive ambitions – so Perez had decided that Escobedo must die. Perez had tried to poison Escobedo. When that failed, he hired assassins to hack him to death with swords in a dark back street of Madrid. That was not the end of the matter, for there were those who said Philip had colluded in the murder.

Philip had never been averse to political assassination, but he did not like to have his name associated with a case such as this, so he determined to bring about the ruin and the death of Perez. The minister was arrested, but escaped and fled to Aragon where internal politics had stayed Philip's hand. By the time Philip was eventually able to move against Perez, he had fled again, this time to France where, in recent months, he had been a guest of Henri IV, earning a precarious living selling Spanish secrets to the highest bidder.

Perez's former partner in crime, the beautiful Princess of Eboli, had not been so fortunate. She had died in prison. Her relationship with Perez, and indeed King Philip, had never been clear. Some said she was the lover of both men, and that that had been the real argument between them, rather than the murder of Escobedo.

For the past few weeks Perez had been here in England, under the patronage of the Earl of Essex. Thus far the Queen had refused to receive him, fearing that to do so would unnerve her Dutch allies and provoke Philip unnecessarily. Anyway, it was not wise to show favour to traitors, even foreign traitors.

All this was known; what more could Cecil want?

As if hearing Shakespeare's thoughts, Cecil said, 'He has a secret to sell. You speak enough Spanish. You will negotiate a price, then bring him to me.'

Shakespeare felt distinctly uneasy; the word from intelligencers in France was that Perez's secrets were rarely of any real value. He had been away from the Escorial court too long. And there was another problem here – Essex. 'Sir Robert, you know my history with the earl. He is Don Antonio's host – he will not allow me into his presence.'

'Essex is here at court, attending on Her Majesty. You have the field to yourself. Perez is in the country clutching his confounded box of potions and amusing himself with his little group of friends. There will be no better time. It is a difficult mission, John, and it will require your most delicate touch. He will try to extort a high price. I must tell you, too, that you are unlikely to enjoy these people's company. One of them is Prégent de la Fin, son of the French ambassador. Be wary of him, yet do not make a foe of him, for we need to keep peace with France in these hard days. I fear you may not enjoy the stench of debauchery among this Spaniard and his train, but stop up your nose for the sake of England. Perez has got word to me that he wishes to sell me his secret, otherwise, he will dispense it elsewhere. I cannot allow that.'

Shakespeare wanted to ask why this was considered more important than the gunpowder inquiry. But he knew the answer. This might be no more than some inconsequential and ancient piece of tittle-tattle from the Spanish court, but it would be Cecil's tittle-tattle, not Essex's.

Cecil shook his head briskly, a short, sharp move from left to right and back as if fending off a wasp. 'I know what you are thinking. That this will amount to nothing – a scraping of horse dung upon the road. But I am sure there *is* something here and it pertains to the succession. Nothing in this realm is more important than that. I pray I am wrong, but I very much fear that he will disclose something bad, some rotten stink. It is something we must know. Find out what it is. Bring it to me.'

Shakespeare bowed in deference. 'Very well, Sir Robert. I shall do as you command. What may I offer to seal the secret?'

'He will demand an impossible sum. It is his way. He has been accustomed to a life of immense wealth and great extravagance and is reduced to living off the charity of Essex and other noblemen. He will want many thousands of pounds. But I wish to pay no more than five hundred, less if possible. Above all, you must ensure that we do not pay a preposterous amount for intelligence that is without worth. There must be a proviso that the secret is both significant and true. Otherwise, let him know, we will have our gold back by any means. Now go.'

Shakespeare bowed again and turned to leave.

'And remember,' Cecil added. 'Perez is hid away because Philip of Spain wants him dead.'

Mills stooped his crowlike frame over the table and scratched a note of everything Christopher Morley had told Shakespeare. 'And you say he is in the Wood Street Counter?'

'And most unhappy about it. He is in mortal dread.'

'Good. He is a fly to be squashed.'

'He came to me in good faith. I have as little time for him as you, Frank, but do not apply torture. Sir Robert has agreed there will be no racking, no Topcliffe. Offer Morley ten marks for the powderman's name. Tell him the alternative is a charge of treason if he withholds it.'

'As you wish,' Mills said without conviction.

Shakespeare looked closely into Mills's eyes and knew he was lying. He would have Morley racked as a first rather than a last option. 'This is no jest, Frank. You have crossed me before – do not betray me on this. I will not forgive you twice.'

'This is a matter of state, John. Bishops may fuck their fill and not be married. Secretaries of state may tighten your body with ropes and not be crossed. I will be guided by the wishes of Sir Robert. If, as you say, he forbids torture, then there will be no torture.'

There was no more to be said. The question left hanging was whether Cecil would change his mind. Shakespeare knew that Cecil did not like the use of torture, but he knew, too, that if it was the only way, he would authorise it. The only hope now was that Morley would take the ten marks and provide the name – or that Shakespeare's mission would be completed in short order, allowing him a quick return to the Dutch church investigation.

Boltfoot Cooper was with Thomas Knagg in the powder-mixing room. William Sarjent was at the vault, inspecting the stores.

'Happy, Mr Cooper?' Knagg said. He was a stone-faced young man, not more than thirty years of age, and wore a pair of wire-framed spectacles perched at the end of his nose.

'The stockade is very poor.'

Knagg was sitting on a three-legged stool with his booted feet upon a workbench. 'The palisade is under bloody repair. And at least we have one. Look at Faversham. They have no stockade. And Godstone is so full of holes that a Roman general might march an elephant in unseen.'

'Your guards stand idle. Who looks after this place?'

'Those men are carpenters, not guards. They are repairing and improving our defences. Even carpenters must be allowed ten minutes now and then for a pint of ale and nourishment. And there are guards enough. You were stopped as you came in, were you not?'

Boltfoot murmured. Yes, they had been stopped – and Sarjent had straightway got into a dispute with the guard, a broad-shouldered bull of a man with an agitated, slightly timorous look that belied his great size and seeming strength. Boltfoot had had to pull Sarjent off the man.

'He's a bad lot that William Sarjent,' Knagg said. 'I did not like him when he was here in '88 and I still do not. Sniff him next to a turd and you would not tell them apart.'

'He says much the same about you.'

'Aye, he would.'

'What came between you?'

'His manner and his opinions. His soldiering gave him ideas above his rank. I was his master, yet he believed he could command me through his knowledge of powder, which was no more than mine.'

The door opened. Sarjent strode in. His gaze was piercing, aimed directly at Knagg, who pushed his spectacles up closer to his eyes, tilted his head and gazed back with ill humour. Sarjent turned to Boltfoot. 'We must close down this mill, Mr Cooper. Powder has gone missing. Knagg has been engaged in illegal trades. The place is a midden of villainy and rotten practice. One man had a tinderbox in his pocket.' He held up the offending object. 'We will take Knagg into custody and send pursuivants to take the place under proper control.'

Boltfoot looked at Knagg. 'What do you say, Mr Knagg?'

Knagg shook his head slowly. 'I say you should bring the man who supposedly had that tinderbox, for I do not believe any of my men has been so foolish. And I would ask Mr Sarjent for the poxy so-called evidence of missing powder, Mr Cooper. For I pledge on my word as a Christian gentleman that none is gone from Three Mills unaccounted for.'

'The devil you do!' Sarjent said, his body stiff with rage. 'Let us show you the rack, then we shall hear the truth – and we shall have the powderman's name from your dissembling lips.'

Catherine Shakespeare answered the door. There had already been two callers this evening – one a messenger from Cecil, the other a servant from someone called Henbird with a roasted turkey cock. Well, John was not here to share it, so it would have to wait.

Now, Jan Sluyterman was on the doorstep. He looked distressed. 'Mistress Shakespeare,' he said, a pleading note in his heavily accented voice. 'Is your husband at home?'

'No. He will not be here this night.'

She saw that Sluyterman seemed undecided what to do or say next.

'Please, come in, Mr Sluyterman,' she offered, opening the door wider. She glanced up and down Dowgate. The street was empty save for a pair of tethered horses along the way towards the stable block. She smiled at her Dutch neighbour. 'Perhaps I can help in some way.'

He nodded gratefully and stepped inside. They went through to the refectory. She offered him refreshment, but he declined. His hands were clenched into pink fists. His face was flushed, the colour of raw pork belly.

'Please,' he said. 'Let me speak plain to you, mistress. I have tried to find lodging for Susanna, but no one is willing to help. The recent Return of Strangers, the placards, the gunpowder, our midnight call from Mr Topcliffe . . . all are scared.'

'I understand.'

He looked around as if suddenly wondering where his servant girl was. 'Is Susanna—'

Catherine shook her head. 'You have nothing to worry about. She is well. She is in the kitchen with Jane, my house-keeper. I believe she is learning a few words of English.'

'You are good people. Thank you.'

'How did Susanna arrive here in England?'

'It is a terrible story. She is the daughter of my clerk in Antwerp. He was taken prisoner by the Spanish. His throat was cut while he was bound. His wife – Susanna's mother – has disappeared. No one knows where she is, but we fear the worst. Susanna escaped to Flushing, but she has suffered most griev-ously, mistress. She must not be sent back to the Low Countries. I fear she would throw herself overboard if they forced her on to a boat.'

'We won't let that happen to her.'

'But she cannot stay here?'

Catherine shrank from the question. 'No,' she said quietly. 'No, Mr Sluyterman, she cannot stay here. That would be too dangerous for all of us.'

'What are we to do, then?'

She reached out and touched his hand reassuringly. 'Fear not, I believe I know where she may go and remain in safety.'

Shakespeare understood well what this Perez mission was all about. One word: Essex. It was said the earl had changed from an exuberant, hot-blooded youth into a mature statesman within the past year. That, at least, was the image he wished to cultivate. Since being appointed a privy councillor just three months previously, he had been affecting the ways of an administrator, attending the House of Lords every morning and sitting in committees during the afternoon. The field of battle was now in his past; he fought instead for high office. He had certainly cozened those close to him. Shakespeare laughed bitterly at the words of the earl's steward, Anthony Bagot, reported to him with glee by one of his intelligencers: 'His lordship has become a new man, clean forsaking all his former youthful tricks, carrying himself with honourable gravity.' *A new man?* New tricks, perchance, but there was nothing new about the man, nor his dark desires. Shakespeare knew from sharp experience that Essex had but one ambition – his own advancement. Nobleman, workman, priest, sovereign – all could hang if they stood in his way.

The rivalry between Robert Cecil and Robert Devereux, second Earl of Essex, was well known now. This was as open as the warfare between England and Spain. So if Essex had access to the secrets of a Spanish defector, then Cecil would pay almost any sum to have them first. Achieving that was John Shakespeare's task, and he did not relish it.

He rode through the long evening hours. It was not an easy journey, for the road was poor and deeply holed and soon turned from open farmland to dense woodland. A drizzle came towards midnight, as he walked his mare through the dark acres of Epping Forest. A steady, slow rain dripped from the high, broad-leaf trees. The darkness was all-consuming and he became slower and slower. After he passed the village of Loughton, the tracks became thinner and more difficult to follow, with no milestones evident. His progress was painful. He had to pick his way like a blind man, continually ducking below low branches and over trees fallen across the muddy, neglected path. He was making not more than one mile to the hour. Finally, in the early morning, in the still twilight before dawn, he arrived at the hamlet of Epping. The rain had stopped. The village was nothing but a collection of farm buildings, a church, a pit of water for the passing livestock to drink their fill, and a wayside inn. He was pleased to see human movement in the yard.

A plump goodwife in kirtle and smock was feeding chickens. She looked up at him wide-eyed, startled to see a traveller at this hour. Shakespeare doffed his sodden cap to her and slid wearily from the grey mare. He and the horse needed victuals and drying out before he could call at Gaynes Park.

Twenty minutes later, wrapped in blankets, he sat in the inn's kitchens. He had a mug of ale, some bread and butter. The landlord's wife stoked up the cooking fire and hung his clothes across the mantel to dry. She put on three eggs to boil and laid out cold meats on a trencher.

'How far to Gaynes Park, mistress?'

'Two miles across the fields, master.'

'Have you seen the people presently living there?'

'Them?' She hesitated as if the sharpness of her voice already told too much, then dismissed her caution. 'Aye, they came here while riding out after deer one day last week. They stopped for ale. Two foreign gentlemen, sir, and a lady, with their retainers.'

'What manner of people were they?'

'That depends whom I'm talking to, master. I might say something different to my husbandman than I would say to you . . .'

'I am no friend of theirs, but an officer of the Crown. You may speak plain to me in safety.'

'Well, master, I will tell you this: they took ale and pie, then did ride off without paying, laughing all the while. We told the headborough, but he said he could do nothing, that they were the Earl of Essex's guests.'

Chapter 10

'How many barrels of gunpowder do you think this time, Mr Laveroke?'

'Six at the most. Waste not, want not. A quarter of a last will make a pleasant enough bang this fine June day, Mr Curl.'

Luke Laveroke and Holy Trinity Curl were in their rented warehouse close to the glassworks in Crutched Friars, just inside the walls to the east of the city. Shafts of sunlight from the gaps in the barnlike door caught the motes in the air and the dust of the powder, making a series of heavenly beams that seemed to illuminate the two men's work. By the closed doors lay a heap of dung bought from the gong farmers. Its stench overpowered the distinctive smell of gunpowder so that passers-by would not wonder about the true contents of the building.

An old, rotting wagon that no one would miss when it had been blown to splinterwood stood backed up to the banks of barrels that filled half the dusty floor space of this ancient barn.

'With God's help, Mr Laveroke, it will make a very pretty bang and turn our enemies to offal. With God's *bountiful* help. And we must pray that its ripples spread far, and serve to drive these venal Flemings and Walloons back to their own benighted land, and leave this fair city to us, the common people of England, to whom it rightly belongs. I think we shall have earned the gratitude of all true patriots for the work we do this day.' Curl's amber eyes met Laveroke's and sought his approbation.

In reply, Luke Laveroke smiled a handsome smile as he idly cut his fingernails with the razor edge of his poniard. His teeth were good and his hair shone in the light. All true Englishmen might well be pleased by this day's work, he thought, but even more so would true Spanish men. But that was not something he would say to Holy Trinity Curl. 'Indeed,' was all he said, thrusting his poniard back into his belt, then hoisting a barrel on to the wagon. 'We shall earn a great deal of gratitude this day. Now haul away, Mr Curl. Our target awaits us.'

'There is much work to be done.'

'And we shall need much powder to carry it out to our satisfaction. After this, we shall want a hundred and twenty barrels for our next little turn, all of which must be brought forth and sieved . . .'

Curl stopped abruptly as he was about to haul up the next barrel. 'Did you say a *hundred and twenty*, Mr Laveroke?'

'I did, Mr Curl.'

'Why, that is enough to blow up a small town!'

'I hope so. I do hope so.'

Shakespeare raised his hand to hammer at the great door of the Gaynes Park Hall. Set in parkland amid tall trees, this was a house belonging to an aunt of the Earl of Essex's wife, Frances Walsingham, through her first marriage to the heroic Philip Sidney. The old manor-house was far from palatial, but it would do well enough as a hideaway for a Spanish fugitive and his small train. Before his fist came down against the wood, a hand grasped his wrist in a grip of iron. Shakespeare turned. The hand belonged to one of three burly, heavily armed men who appeared beside him, seemingly from nowhere.

'Yes?' the one who held him said. He was wearing the tangerine tabard of the Earl of Essex's retinue, above military mail, as were his two comrades. They were clearly bodyguards.

'My name is John Shakespeare. I am here on Queen's business to see Don Antonio.'

'Well I am Edward Wilton, chief of the guard, so I shall require your letters-patent and ask you to disarm.' He released his grip on Shakespeare's wrist.

Shakespeare had brought no firearm. He handed over his sword and dagger and the paper Cecil had given him. Wilton studied it, then ran his strong-fingered hands across Shakespeare's clothing, searching for secreted weapons. When he found none, he stood back. 'Thank you, sir. That is in order.' He opened the door. A footman in a yet finer tangerine and black livery answered the door. He looked nervous and tired, as if he would rather be anywhere else in the world than here.

The footman bowed and retreated into the darkness of the hall without a word.

'Collect the sword on your way out, Mr Shakespeare,' Wilton said.

Shakespeare did not wait to be invited in, but stepped into the hallway and shut the door behind him. He looked about at his surroundings. The place appeared as fatigued as the footman. Above the wainscot, the plasterwork was rent and falling away in places and much of it seemed disfigured by damp and dark yellow and brown blots. There were no portraits, nor any hangings. There was a strong smell of rot. Shakespeare guessed that the house had been unoccupied for years and opened up only recently to accommodate Antonio Perez and his entourage.

'How may we help you, Mr Shakespeare?'

Shakespeare turned around at the sound of the heavily

accented voice; a Spanish accent – something to chill the heart of any Englishmen in these long days of warfare between the two countries. He was face to face with a tall young man, perhaps half an inch above his own six feet. The man was well dressed, in a doublet of silver and black brocaded velvet and slashed silver sleeves. His hair was long, black and combed back. His skin was copper-dark with a sheen of robust health.

'Don Antonio?' Even as he said the words, Shakespeare realised it was a foolish question. This man was half Perez's age.

The man smiled with something akin to condescension. 'I am his personal secretary, Mr Shakespeare.'

'I am sent by Sir Robert Cecil. I am told Don Antonio would talk with me.'

'We were expecting you. But it is very early in the morning. Don Antonio has been unwell and tends to sleep in until midday. Perhaps you will come back later – or would you care to wait?'

'I will wait. But I would be grateful if he could be woken a little earlier. I have pressing business.'

'I understand, sir. Let me show you to the parlour and I will alert Don Antonio to your presence as soon as I dare. Would you care for something to eat or drink?'

Shakespeare declined and followed the Spaniard through to a slightly more comfortable room with a settle, a card table and a few books. A tall cedar of Lebanon dominated the gardens outside the window and took most of the light from the room.

The secretary bowed without a great deal of deference and said he would have the servants light a fire, then disappeared. A plain young rustic girl came in, nodded quickly and fearfully to him, then attended to the fireplace. It occurred to Shakespeare that a fire was the last thing he needed on so fine a day, but he suspected the house needed as much warmth as it could get and, anyway, watching her passed the time. Soon the sound of crackling logs and the joyful light of a blazing fire brought some cheer to the room.

Shakespeare sat back and skimmed through the books. They were all Spanish poetry, which did little for him except test his command of the language, which was not, he realised, what it had once been. There were few Spaniards to talk to in London these days, and had not been, in fact, in the nine years since Ambassador Mendoza was expelled from England. The only Spanish that Shakespeare read now was in decoded intercepts of letters criss-crossing between the courts of Europe.

He was just grappling with Herrera's *Rimas Juventiles* – youthful rhymes – when a woman swept into the room unannounced. Shakespeare turned at the creak of the door and the rustle of her gown. She was dressed for riding in a long velvet cape, a simple dress of fine brown worsted with a safe-guard to protect it, a white linen partlet about her breast and a cap adorned with a feather. Most striking of all, she wore a black patch over her left eye. The only time Shakespeare had ever seen a woman affect such a decoration was in a portrait of the notorious Princess of Eboli, said to have been lover and co-conspirator to Perez. Who was this woman who looked so like his former love?

She carried a hunting-crop in her small white-gloved hand. She stopped and gazed with her one seeing eye at Shakespeare, looking him up and down as a horse trader might appraise a prize stallion. Even in her respectable riding attire, a man could not help but notice the voluptuousness of her body, which shimmered even as she stood still.

'I had heard that we had a visitor,' she said in slightly stilted English. Her voice was husky and warm, with the mellow, sing-song timbre of her native Spanish. 'I must say, you do not *look* like one of King Philip's assassins. But who can tell? Everyone I meet these days seems to be a spy or a mercenary.'

'I am no assassin, señora.'

'My name is Ana Cabral,' she replied, holding out her delicate hand to Shakespeare. 'Doña Ana. And if you were an assassin, sir, I assure you that you would not get very far. My lord of Essex has the place swarming with his men-at-arms.'

Shakespeare took the gloved hand and bent to kiss it. It remained in his hand a few beats too long.

'I am with Don Antonio's party, his travelling companion . . .'

He did not need to ask in what capacity she accompanied Perez. Something about her manner told him she was his *cortisane.* He guessed her age at twenty-four or twenty-five. She was fair-haired with a streak of silver through one side of her well-coiffed locks. Her English, though accented, was clear-spoken and accurate. She had about her the sensuous demeanour of courtesans everywhere. Perhaps she was born with it. No man could look at her and fail to wonder how she would move beneath the sheets. She was not beautiful, nor even pretty, but she did not need to be, for she dazzled like a rare jewelstone. She would know, Shakespeare thought, all the sexual wiles necessary to keep a man beguiled in bed for as long as she desired, or as long as he had gold enough. She was *worldly*.

'And you, sir, who are you?'

'John Shakespeare. I have orders to talk with Antonio Perez.'

'I imagine you are here to grant him access to the Queen. He has waited nearly two months now and is becoming impatient. And so am I, for I wish to dance at court. Well, come with me. I will take you to his chamber before I go for my ride. You do not have a Spanish wheel-lock secreted up your sleeve, I presume?'

Shakespeare smiled. 'No wheel-lock. But I had heard Don Antonio was asleep.'

'That is just his secretary. Pay him no heed. He plays his

little games. Very proud and insolent for a mere servant, do you not think?'

Indeed, Shakespeare did think so, but he said nothing. He followed the woman through to the hall and up the stairway to the first floor.

'Look at this place, Mr Shakespeare,' she said brushing a cobweb from the corner of a cracked window in the gallery. 'Henri of Navarre would not treat an honoured guest to his country so.' She threw open the door to a chamber and pushed on in. A four-poster bed hung with rich drapes stood in the centre of the dimly lit room. The floor was littered with clothing – farm clothes of wool and linsey-kersey, smocks and breeches and a hide jerkin that looked and smelled a hundred years old. Ana Cabral drew the bed curtains apart.

Shakespeare saw what appeared to be a mass of bodies on the bed. He counted limbs and reckoned there to be four people. Two men and two women. All were asleep, softly snoring, though they stirred at the noise and sudden admission of light to their little world. He was assailed by the stench of sweat, stale alcohol, farting and copulation.

'Don Antonio, you have a visitor,' Ana said in Spanish, idly stroking one of the limbs with her gloved hand. 'Mr Shakespeare from the office of Sir Robert Cecil.'

The elder of the two men grunted from the depths of the bedding. Ana leant over and kissed him on the mouth. Shakespeare saw that he had a beet-swarthy face of broken veins, a stubble of beard and a straggle of dyed black hair. He opened his eyes, blinking. Was this the face that had won the love of the tragic Princess of Eboli? Shakespeare shuddered. Carelessly elbowing one of the women in the face, Perez raised himself up against the bed cushions.

'Shakespeare?'

'At your service, Don Antonio.'

'Ana, pay these peasants and send them away. Give more to the little fair one and tell her to return this night. And bring her sister – or brother – if she has one.'

Without a word, Ana began to lay about Perez's young bed-mates with her crop, lashing them hard across legs, buttocks and heads until they leapt up and ran naked from the room, dragging their garments behind them. She laughed at their going, then stretched over the bed once more and kissed Perez. 'I shall go and give them their dues now. I will have wine and meats brought to you and Mr Shakespeare.'

After she had gone, Perez patted the bed at his side with a gloved hand. 'Come, sit with me, Mr Shakespeare. Tell me what treasure Sir Robert has to offer.'

Shakespeare lowered his eyes respectfully. Whatever this man had become, he had once been a minister to the crown of the most powerful land in the world and had led an extraordinary life. His relationship with the Princess of Eboli was the stuff of legend. If Perez felt grief for her loss, he showed no signs of it here, in this shabby room with these sweaty farm youths.

Shakespeare sat on the bed beside the grizzled old courtier. He was grateful, at least, that the Spaniard spoke passable English.

'Look what I am reduced to, Mr Shakespeare.' Don Antonio waved his hand in an extravagant gesture of displeasure at his surroundings. 'Forty years ago, my father came to England in honour as secretary to Philip on his marriage to your Queen Mary. And was I not his equal in every way? Once my homes were the most gracious palaces of Aragon and Castile. In my *casilla* outside Madrid I sported and dallied with princesses in courtyards of marble, to the sound of cool-flowing fountains, the scent of lemons and the colours of oleander. Even the horse I rode was scented. Now I make do with toothless country girls who stink of the stables and believe themselves well paid at half a ducat a night. Does no one in this country wash?'

Shakespeare could not contain a light laugh. Even on a summer's day, this house was no palace and the scent of an English farmyard could be no substitute for fresh Spanish lemons. And it was true; few enough people in England had discovered the joys and profits of bathing.

'Why do you think I am here, Mr Shakespeare?'

'I believe you are a guest of my lord of Essex.'

'True. But that is not why I have come here. I come here as an envoy with my good friend the Vidame de Chartres. We have an important message from Henri of France to Her Majesty Queen Elizabeth.'

'Concerning the possibility of a conversion?'

'He is, indeed, taking instructions in the Catholic faith and will soon embrace it. Then Paris will be his and France will be one for the first time in many years. But he wishes to reassure the Basilisk – I apologise, Elizabeth Tudor – whom he esteems, that he will not be a friend to Spain nor an enemy to England. The vidame and I must be admitted to her presence so that we can deliver this vital message to her personally. There are letters . . .'

'And I am sure that Her Majesty will, in due course, receive you and take pleasure in your gracious company. I know she will be glad to receive assurances regarding the intentions of *le roi* Henri.'

Perez removed his gloves and covered Shakespeare's hand with his own on the rumpled bedding. 'But *you* are here on another matter . . .'

Shakespeare was struck by the delicate smoothness of the hand. He had heard it said that Spanish courtiers wore oiled gloves at night to give their hands a feminine softness and to keep them unnaturally white, but when he looked down he saw that Perez's hand was blotched and clawlike with age. He did not enjoy its touch and recoiled at the thought of the hand upon the fresh young bodies of the peasant girls and boy who had been in his bed. He found himself thinking, too, of its caresses upon the fine body of Ana Cabral.

'Indeed, Don Antonio,' he said, removing his hand from Perez's and reaching into his doublet for his letter-patent from Cecil. 'Sir Robert has commanded me to negotiate with you for important information, some secret you possess.'

'Let us not be maidenly, then, Mr Shakespeare. I have something to sell. You wish to buy it. What are you prepared to offer?'

'Two hundred.'

Perez cupped his hand about his ear like a scallop shell. 'I believe I misheard you. I thought for a moment you said two hundred. I am sure you meant twenty thousand, Mr Shakespeare. Sovereigns of gold. As a point at which to start . . .'

'It seems we are a world apart.'

'I call myself *El Peregrino*, for like a desert nomad, I am doomed to travel the world forever. I am sure your Robertus Diabolus can travel a long way, too. How far is it from two hundred to twenty thousand? Not such a great distance.'

'To me, it seems like the distance from London to Peru,' Shakespeare replied. 'May I ask you, Don Antonio, why do you offer this information to Sir Robert rather than to my lord of Essex? He is your host; he would welcome such intelligence.'

Perez's head was too large for his small body and when he put it to one side quizzically, as if considering the question, it almost seemed as if it might roll away. 'I am sure you know why, Mr Shakespeare. You, better than anyone, must know who holds the purse strings in this country. The Cecils. The father is Lord Treasurer, the son is as good as Principal

Secretary. I do not think for a moment that the Earl of Essex could secure the necessary funds. Do you?'

'No, not the sums you talk of. So that means there is no other bidder. Which must weaken your position.'

Perez suddenly became agitated and rose, naked, from the bed. Shakespeare was surprised to see how short he was, perhaps five foot at the most. His head atop his distended and ageing body looked like a purple-brown watermelon thrust on a short-hafted hoe. Yet somewhere in that grotesque figure was the distant memory of a handsome young man who had made love to half the court of Spain, men as well as women, if spies like Standen were to be believed. The years of excess had wrought much damage.

The Spaniard scrabbled about on the floor then rose triumphantly, clutching a small golden box. He lifted the lid. Inside, Shakespeare could see little glass vials – potions and preparations of some sort. Perez took the stopper from one of the vials, threw back his head and poured the contents into his gaping mouth. Then he sighed and closed his eyes.

He sat back down on the edge of the bed, his balls and prick hanging heavy and loose between his thin legs. 'I have much pain, Mr Shakespeare. My bones. My head. I had wanted food. Where is that food and ale Ana promised?'

'I am sure it will be here soon.'

'Do you know, Mr Shakespeare, I was once the most powerful man in the world. Do not sneer when you look at me now, for there was a time when I could make the King of Spain do my bidding. The King of Spain – emperor of half the world, an empire greater than that of Rome or Persia. The Pope himself had to treat with me if he wished anything of Spain. With a snap of my fingers I could have had you arrested by the Inquisition, or, if I liked you, I could have given you letters of introduction to my old friend Titian, who was the greatest painter that ever lived. So when you talk to me of money, do not offer me a carpenter's wage, for I have a secret worth a king's treasure chest.'

'Forgive me, Don Antonio. I can assure you I do not sneer at you. I hold you in the highest esteem and have the greatest admiration for your remarkable career. But I am here to discover a price which is acceptable to you and to Sir Robert. It is a matter of finding some middle way.'

Perez, still naked, went to the door and shouted in Spanish for his food. 'Do you want me to starve!' He returned to the room and found a crumpled chemise and netherstocks and pulled them on. 'Mr Shakespeare, if you want tittle-tattle about the Spanish court, I will give it you for nothing. I will tell you everything you wish about the mouselike king who whispers so quiet that his courtiers cannot hear him and who makes sure he takes the same number of mouthfuls of food at every meal and chews each morsel the exact same number of times – twelve. Yes, twelve chews for each bite; I have counted them a thousand times and thought I would go mad myself in doing so. I can spend all day with you and tell you ten times a hundred such titbits. Or I can tell you what you have come for: information that will rock this little realm to its foundations. And I promise you this, Mr Shakespeare, it were better you knew the secret now rather than later. For if you leave it much longer, it will be too late for you to act upon.'

Shakespeare believed him. He knew this man for a dissembling, cunning, murdering, degenerate poisoner. Yet he believed him on this. He had some information which Cecil *had* to know. And quickly. 'A thousand pounds,' he said, going way beyond his brief. 'But I would have to confirm that. I am not authorised to pay such a sum.'

'That is a long way from twenty thousand, Mr Shakespeare.'

There was a knock at the door. A serving man appeared with

a silver tray of food and drink, followed by Ana Cabral. Perez waved them away, then turned to Shakespeare. 'Go now. We will talk again later, when you have had time to reflect a little more. This talk has wearied me. I must sleep.'

Reluctantly, Shakespeare bowed and took his leave. There was a gulf here. He was not at all sure how he would build a bridge.

Outside the room, Ana was waiting for him. 'Did he take some tincture, Mr Shakespeare?'

'Yes, he drank from a vial.'

'It is a spirit of opium. He has much pain, you know. They used him ill in prison.'

'I understand.'

'He will drift into sleep now. Come, sir, why do you not ride with the vidame and me? We have fine horses. Unless you have other pleasures in mind . . .'

Chapter 11

CATHERINE SHAKESPEARE BUSIED herself preparing Susanna for their short journey across London. Her adoptive daughter, Grace Woode, fished a good summer dress from her clothes coffer and held it up to the Sluytermans' serving girl.

'Would this suit, Mama?' she asked Catherine. 'Do you not think it would fit her?'

Catherine laughed. The gown was far too small. Grace was ten and small for her age; Susanna was twelve and tall. 'I think one of my own would fit a little better, Grace. Let us see what we can find.'

They eventually found a serviceable outfit of light-brown linen that would not look out of place on a well-to-do townswoman's daughter. Catherine stood back and looked at the girl admiringly. '*Voelt dat goed aan*, Susanna?' She had learned a little Dutch from her friend, Berthe Haan.

Susanna smiled. '*Het past goed, Vrouw* Shakespeare. *Dank U.*'

Both carried baskets and wore respectable lawn pynners as they set off up Dowgate. Catherine wore her brightest summer dress, saffron and green. To avoid the suspicion of any watchers, they kept their eyes straight ahead or looked at each other and chatted as if they were merely a mother and daughter off to market on a fine summer's morning. By the time they were halfway up the road they had the confidence to look about them. On their right they gazed at the Erber, the great mansion where Vice-Admiral Sir Francis Drake lived when he was in London. Susanna asked about it and Catherine tried to explain in her faltering Dutch. The words 'Francis Drake' had the required effect.

Susanna smiled. 'Ah, Drake, *de geweldige zee kapitein. De veroveraar van de Spaanse Armada.*'

'Well done, Susanna. Remember, the English people are your friends, as is the Queen. Men like Topcliffe twist the law to their own ends. You will be safe now.'

The girl nodded uncertainly. They continued on due north, taking in the sights, smells and noises of the city. Susanna seemed to lose her nerves and became increasingly exhilarated by all she saw. Instinctively, she put her hand in Catherine's as they passed the stocks market. They then turned a little east-wards into the wide avenue of Threadneedle Street, before heading north again into Broad Street.

Catherine squeezed the girl's hand. She always liked to visit Berthe Haan. She had sent Jane to her last night with a written message about Susanna. The reply had been instant: yes, of course, they would be happy to take Susanna in. They were entitled to have a Dutch servant girl, so she would be safe there and legal.

As they turned across the street to the Dutch market, the place was alive with colour and noise. Susanna's eyes opened wide with pleasure at the sound of so many voices in her own language. Catherine decided there was enough time to look around; it was a good opportunity to buy some of the Dutch cheese that John enjoyed so much with his breakfast bread and ale.

*

'Well, Mr Curl, where shall we park our wagon?'

'We are spoilt for choice, Mr Laveroke. One cannot move for Dutch dogs in this market. I cannot abide their strange attire – the bonnets of lace, the clogs of wood. Let us see how many we can kill. It will be better than a show of fireworks organised by the Fire Master of England.'

'Indeed, Mr Curl. I do believe it will be. And who knows what fire may fly to the heart of this foul regime and scorch the Queen's treacherous pseudo-ministers. We need rioting. That is your task, Mr Curl. Rage from the pulpit and the street corner. Get the apprentices out; tell your followers to take to the streets. We need you to do your business, Mr Curl. England needs you.'

'I shall speak from the heart, Mr Laveroke.'

'Here, then, by this cheese stall. I shall set the clock now.' Laveroke climbed down from the front of the wagon and went around to the back. Hidden between two of the six barrels was a curious bronze and steel mechanism of gears and balances. He released the brake and set it in motion. In two minutes' time, if all went as planned, a shard of flint would fall against a plate of steel and send a shower of sparks into the pan of powder protruding from one of the kegs. 'Let us now walk away at a brisk pace. If we stand well back, we can enjoy the spectacle.'

John Shakespeare joined Ana Cabral and the Vidame de Chartres outside the postern door, close to the stables. Grooms were there with three horses, ready saddled. They were well-conformed animals, with quarters built for speed. Shakespeare noticed a pair of guards in the shadows of nearby trees.

'Mr Shakespeare, allow me to introduce you to Prégent de la Fin, Vidame de Chartres,' Ana said. 'Perhaps you know his father, Jean de la Fin, France's ambassador here in England.'

'Of course.' Shakespeare bowed to the man and noted that he had extended a slender hand to be kissed. Shakespeare ignored it. 'I have, indeed met your father, Monsieur le Vidame. It is an honour to meet you.'

'Do you race horses, Mr Shakespeare?'

'Not since boyhood.'

'But you will race against me, yes?'

Why not? If that was what they wanted. Shakespeare knew himself to be a good enough rider. If the horse was up to the task, so was he. And there was nothing else to do while he waited for Perez to wake from his opium slumber.

The vidame was in his thirties. He was exceedingly slim but, perhaps, strong, too. His dark hair was long, hanging loose about his shoulders. He wore doublet and hose of brilliant yellow, green and gold, beneath a green velvet hat. Shakespeare would have called him pretty rather than handsome, and yet he was not effeminate; too much steeliness in him for that.

'Let us ride, then. You see the church? It is two miles, Mr Shakespeare. The first to the large yew tree beside it. You choose: the black filly or the bay colt. Your best sword for mine – and mine has a hundred gemstones in its hilt. Ana, ride on ahead. You are the judge in this.'

Shakespeare examined the two animals. They both looked fine specimens, but the filly seemed to have a more intelligent eye. He gestured with a tilt of his chin. 'I will have her.'

'A fine choice. She is the better animal.'

With the help of a groom, Shakespeare mounted the black filly. She was nervy and had clearly never pulled a plough or wagon. Ana was trotting away into the distance.

'I will race you for the *honour*, Monsieur le Vidame, not the sword,' Shakespeare said. 'For all that I know,' he added disingenuously, 'this is a farm nag.'

'Does she *look* like a farm nag? You are sitting astride a

pure-bred Barb, sir, bred in Rome and brought with me from the finest stables in France. A three-year-old Barbary colt. That is a racehorse, not a nag. You may keep your English hobbies and your Spanish jennets. The Barb wins every time. I believe the Queen has a fine hobby named Great Henry. At the summer races, we will take pleasure in beating her with our filly.'

'In the meantime, we ride for honour.'

'No, there must be a prize. If not a sword, let us race for a favour.'

Shakespeare was not happy. 'A favour it is,' he said reluctantly. 'But a *legal* favour, and of small value. Doña Ana to be arbiter . . .'

'Very well. Now ride. I give you a ten-yard start.'

The vidame clapped his hands, Shakespeare shook the reins, and the horse set off like a ball from an arquebus. This was, indeed, a racehorse. Catching his breath, he settled down and gripped his thighs against the muscled barrel of the filly.

As the horse thundered across the parkland he sensed she was going too fast. This was no half-mile dash; she would never stay two miles at such a speed. He turned and saw that the Frenchman was a hundred yards behind him and losing ground. The vidame's pace was far more sensible. Gently, Shakespeare shortened the reins and brought her on the bit. The young filly fought the restraint, her head high and struggling to be let loose, but Shakespeare held her hard.

He crouched low in the saddle, as he had seen riders do at the royal races, almost lying along the horse's withers, his face close to her flying mane. He could hear the sound of the vidame close behind now; that was where he wanted him.

Shakespeare reckoned they had gone the best part of a mile. Time to keep his nerve. Let the vidame pass, go on a few yards if he wished. Beyond some cottages and to the left of a copse, they came to an incline. The vidame was with him. He was still hardly moving a muscle on his bay colt. Yet Shakespeare could feel that his own mount had plenty left to give. The race was on.

They came to a dip. The filly faltered on the downhill, as if untrained for inclines, but quickly regained her legs. The church was out of sight now. With a kick of his spurs the vidame shot his mount ahead as they came to the rise. Shakespeare had been caught unawares. The vidame knew this territory; this was no time to lose position. Within seconds the bay colt was five yards ahead. They came to the crest of the rise. The church was a furlong away and they were riding a well-trodden path.

Up ahead, Shakespeare saw Ana reining in beside a tree. He gave his filly the bridle, cracked her flank with his whip-stock and kicked hard with his unspurred heels. The horse surged forwards. Shakespeare had never felt such power beneath him. In a few strides he was once more up to the tail of the bay colt and closing. But the colt wasn't stopping. The filly inched closer and closer. Half a length now, a neck. Then they were past the tree.

The vidame had won, by no more than the length of his colt's powerful neck. Shakespeare cursed himself. His horse could have won, should have won, given a more clever ride. Slowly, he pulled up, then wheeled his dripping mount and trotted back to the yew. Ana was grinning at him.

'You rode a poor race, Mr Shakespeare. The filly is ten lengths better than the colt, a different class of animal. You should have slapped her earlier. What filly does not lengthen her stride when hit with a crop?'

'I confess it – the colt had the better rider. On the day.'

'Do not berate yourself. The vidame knows this path well. He knows both the horses. I think the filly can beat any horse in England in a fair race. We call her Conquistadora.'

'I am surprised you entrusted her to me.'

'Oh, I trust you, Mr Shakespeare. I know more about you than you might imagine.'

The vidame was now with them. 'Well, well, Mr Shakespeare. I do believe you owe me a favour. What shall it be?'

'You tell me, Monsieur le Vidame.'

Boltfoot Cooper parted company with Sarjent at Three Mills. Sarjent had insisted on going to fetch pursuivants to take over the mill, but Boltfoot would have none of it.

'I will stay here with Mr Knagg and ensure he does not leave. You can take him in when you return with your men.'

Sarjent seemed reluctant to go under such conditions but quickly realised he had no option. Boltfoot watched him ride off and felt only relief; he wished to move on alone.

'Well, Mr Knagg,' Boltfoot had said before leaving the powdermill. 'It appears you are soon to have a visit from the pursuivants.'

'This is an outrage,' Knagg had spluttered. 'You know there is no evidence of wrong-dealing here. No powder is missing and nor has any man brought in a tinderbox. Sarjent is a liar, a custrel, a bloody fabricator of evidence – and worse.'

Boltfoot had observed him closely. The man was distressed and afraid. But that did not make him guilty. 'Do you have lawyers, Mr Knagg? I know nothing of such things, but I think it were to your benefit to consult them.'

'You will speak for me in court, will you, Mr Cooper? You and Sir Robert Cecil? You will be gone like dust in the wind.'

Boltfoot had shifted uneasily. He must ride on. There was much to be done and little time.

'A lawyer, Mr Knagg,' he said. 'Either bring a lawyer here to defend you – or make haste to disappear. And take your family with you.'

'Are you suggesting I leave my post, Mr Cooper?'

'That is for you to decide. Good day, Mr Knagg.'

Boltfoot had ridden away with a heavy heart, heading south and west towards the county of Surrey. Now, twenty hours later, he reined in his horse and gazed across the fields towards the village of Godstone and saw the familiar spirals of smoke from the charcoal pyres in the coppiced woods of alder and willow. He was glad to be rid of Sarjent and his infernal bragging. He had had enough of such vanity under Drake, and wanted no more. But what of Knagg? Boltfoot's years of close-living with men in the confines of a square-rigger had taught him much, but in this case he felt distinctly uncertain. Sarjent insisted Knagg was guilty, but Boltfoot's instinct suggested otherwise.

Ana Cabral took Shakespeare to the withdrawing room. 'Wait here,' she said, touching his arm. 'Don Antonio will make himself available to you soon. Servants will attend on your requirements.' She kissed him lightly on the cheek. 'I would enjoy spending more time with you – but I have other matters that must be attended to.' As she walked from the room, her hips moving in a rhythm like dance, he could not take his eyes from her.

He was brought cold meats and ale, which he consumed. Irritably, he paced the room. He opened the door and looked out. A guard was there, watching him.

'I need the gong-house.'

The sentinel grunted and gestured with his head towards the far end of the hall. Shakespeare found the hole close by the eastern end of the building, by a boot-room. He had a much needed piss. Adjusting his breeches, he spotted a small, winding staircase. Without hesitation, he ascended to the first floor and found himself in an ill-lit passageway. For a few moments, he looked about him, then crept forward. The passageway led into another. He came to the gallery by the main staircase, near Perez's chamber. He hastened along it. Further down the passageway he came to the door of another chamber. He stopped; he could hear noises from within. The door was slightly ajar. He pushed it gently and it glided further open, soundlessly. He peered into the room. The curtains were drawn closed but enough light penetrated for him to see two naked figures on the bed: Ana Cabral and Perez's secretary.

Very proud and insolent for a mere secretary. Indeed, he was, if this was the way he served his master's mistress. And what of her, betraying her lord in the same building where he slept?

Ana lay back on the cushions. Her eyes were open, uncovered by the black patch, staring straight into Shakespeare's. So the patch was nothing but an affectation, perhaps for Don Antonio's pleasure, to remind him of his tragic princess. The secretary lay between Ana's legs, low down, moving slowly, unaware that he was being observed. Ana caressed her breast and smiled at Shakespeare, forming her lips into a kiss.

Shakespeare stepped back, pulling the door silently closed behind him. He stood a moment, his blood thudding from his heart to his yard. He wanted to look again, but he turned away. At the far end of the passageway, he thought he saw the stooped figure of an old woman coming his way, hobbling with a walking stick; then he felt the touch of a hand on his shoulder and turned to see the burly figure of Edward Wilton, the chief of guards.

'You're a long way from the house of easement, Mr Shakespeare. Got lost, did we? Let me show you back to the withdrawing room.'

Chapter 12

A TABLE HAD been set for five in the great hall.
'I believe you owe Monsieur le Vidame a favour, Mr Shakespeare,' Perez said. He was wide awake and full of vigour after his long hours of rest. 'I am a generous man. He has told me what favour he desires. So I say to you this: grant him his favour, arrange for me to be presented to the Queen at the royal court, and pay me some token sum – say ten thousand sovereigns – and you shall know my secret. This is information known to none but King Philip and his closest advisers. I promise you this: it is a secret that will drain the blood from those wizened faces on the Privy Council and shock even the Basilisk herself.'

Shakespeare balked at the insult to Elizabeth. 'Don Antonio, if you have a mind to go to court and to be presented to the Queen, you would do well to think on how you refer to Her Majesty.'

Perez smirked. 'My humble apologies. Old habits . . . it was always the way of King Philip to refer to his former sister-in-law thus. I never liked it. A basilisk is a foul-hissing serpent with a gaze that will strike you dead, whereas I believe your queen to be a soft-purring kitten with a gaze that casts golden balm on all she surveys.'

Shakespeare did not laugh, though the others in the room did.

'My secret comes from the distant past,' Perez continued. 'More than twenty years ago. And like good wine, it improves with age and the price must continually rise.'

Perez was at the head of the table. In the background – far enough away that they could not hear the conversation – a trio with viols played a soft, lilting ballad. Perez had been indisposed all day, rising only with the onset of evening. The small gold box from which he had taken the opium spirit lay on the table before him, under his watchful eye. The Vidame de Chartres sat to his right, Shakespeare to his left, with Ana at his own left side. The place beside the vidame was empty, but set with knife and napkin. Would Perez's secretary sit there? If not, then who?

Shakespeare felt the eyes of his fellow guests upon him. Amusement still played around Ana's unpatched eye; the vidame stared at him with bored curiosity, though his mouth had the semblance of a smile.

'In truth, of course,' Perez continued, 'it is Philip who is the basilisk. Less than a basilisk, for at least a hissing snake is a fearsome thing. Philip is timorous and cringing. By birth, he is a king, but by nature he is lower than a slurry-man in a pig yard. His mind is feeble.'

'Oh, *I* believe him to be a basilisk,' the vidame said. 'Do snakes not eat the dirt of the earth and slink into holes?'

'Hush now,' Ana said. 'Mr Shakespeare is here for a serious purpose. He must talk with Don Antonio about matters of state. Without his help, I fear we will be consigned to this pleasureless dungeon forever.'

Shakespeare felt hot and uncomfortable. This dining table was no place to talk with Perez. 'I would rather negotiate in private, Don Antonio,' he said brusquely, 'but I can tell you that the sum you request is too high. It will not be countenanced.'

Servants arrived with platters of roast venison, dainty curlew breasts, suckling pig and a peacock dressed in its feathers. The table was laden with fine Spanish wines rarely seen in England these days.

Perez waved his hand dismissively. 'We will talk in due course. But you must ensure, Mr Shakespeare, that we go to court without delay. We shall all die of tedium if we have to stay in this wretched backwater a week longer.'

Shakespeare smiled diplomatically. 'I know that this secret, should you divulge it, will smooth your path to the presence-chamber.'

Ana reached across and touched his hand. She no longer wore gloves and the sensation of her fingers surprised him with their sudden heat. 'You are a hard man, Mr Shakespeare. Don Antonio has come to you in good faith – a little faith from the Cecils in return would not go amiss. I am sure you will learn the secret soon.' Her hand lingered. And then her fingertips slid away.

Shakespeare bowed his head in apology. 'I had not meant to imply lack of trust.' And yet, in truth, he did not trust any person here in this house. His enforced leisure during the afternoon had been frustrating when there was so much to be pursued in the gunpowder inquiry. And what of the miserable Christopher Morley in the Wood Street Counter while he was idling away his time here?

'The actions of a quarter-century past reverberate down the years, Mr Shakespeare. You must bring me gold.'

Shakespeare sipped some wine. 'If I am to get close to your position, Don Antonio, you must tell me more. You must give me enough to commend you to Sir Robert with conviction.'

The broken veins on Perez's purple face creased into a smile. His hand rested on the small box of vials. 'Let us talk of the favour for Prégent first.'

'What could a poor officer of state such as myself offer a member of the nobility of France?'

'Why, what does any man want, Mr Shakespeare? We all wish the same – soft bright gold, hard red rubies and fine pink cunnies. Of the three, I believe Monsieur le Vidame wants a woman.'

Shakespeare's gaze fell upon the Frenchman. 'I am sure the vidame does not need my help in that regard.'

'But this is a most particular woman. She is a black Ethiop. He bought her and she is his. But she was stolen from him by one of Hawkins's pirate ships en route from Lisbon to Harfleur. She is now here in England. Monsieur le Vidame wishes to have her back.'

The vidame smiled and raised his fine chin in acknowledgement. Ana Cabral dipped her fingers into a plate of chicken and pulled a piece of crisp, golden skin from the flesh. She put the skin in her mouth and a trickle of juice ran from her lips. Slowly, her pink tongue descended and lapped all but the last drop back into her mouth.

Chapter 13

Black Lucy. There were few enough dark-skinned women in England, and fewer still of such extraordinary beauty that a man might search the world for her. Shakespeare did not venture her name, however. 'You will have to tell me a little more, sir,' he said. 'I have met one or two blackamoor women in London.'

'I call her Monique,' the vidame said languidly, as if it were an effort to talk at all. 'But she now goes under the name Lucy. Some call her the Black Abbess, for she has her bawdy-house in a former nunnery. You *must* know of her, Mr Shakespeare. She is much feted.'

'Yes, I have heard of Black Lucy. Is she indentured to you? I had no idea. Nor had I heard of Hawkins's part in her arrival on these shores. I had believed her a free woman and a Christian, though sinful.'

The vidame leaned back in his chair and examined his neat fingers with studied nonchalance. He looked up and met Shakespeare's eyes. 'In truth, sir, I care not whether she is a Christian or a mermaid. She is mine and I would like England to return her to me. She is stolen property. Sir Robert Cecil could have no objection. He wishes good relations with the new France of Henri IV, does he not? And I am sure you have enough whores in London that you could manage without Monique.'

As he spoke, the candles in the hall guttered at the opening of a door. Shakespeare turned his head and saw the sleek, copper-hued face of Perez's impertinent secretary. Then his sinews stiffened, for he was closely followed by another man – a man he had no wish to see.

The secretary bowed with a lazy half-flourish, then introduced the newcomer. 'Monsieur le Vidame, Don Antonio, Doña Ana, Mr Shakespeare, allow me to present Mr Richard Baines. He has ridden hard from London to attend upon you.'

'Aha,' Perez said. 'Our fifth guest. Take a seat, Mr Baines. You are just in time to dine with us.'

Shakespeare eyed him coldly. He knew Baines all too well. Like Robert Poley, he was an intelligencer from the days of Walsingham, yet there the similarity ended. While Poley fished in the murkier estuaries of intrigue for his prey, Baines flew in more elevated company, scavenging for information at court and in great houses, as a kestrel hunts mice. Shakespeare sniffed the air. The man smelled bad. And yet his clothes were expensively cut – a fine doublet of brown and gold brocade, a modest though modish ruff and riding breeches to the knee, cut from good fustian. Why, though, was he here – and why did his name keep surfacing? It had been Baines who wrote that Kit Marlowe's mouth should be stopped – just a few days before it was stopped forever. Baines the turncoat, betraying a former friend and partner in crime. He and Marlowe had lived together in the Low Countries and had been accused of counterfeiting coin together. But then their friendship had come apart in volcanic fashion, each accusing the other of planning to go over to the forces of Rome and Spain. The final knife jab had been the note delivered to the Privy Council just a few days before Marlowe's death. Shakespeare had seen this note during his investigations and he had been shocked to the core. The content itself was bad enough, but that a man should write such things about a one-time friend left him feeling sick to his stomach. The devastating note accused Marlowe of saying

That Moses was but a juggler.

That Christ was a bastard and his mother dishonest.

That Christ deserved better to die than Barabbas and that the Jews made a good choice, though Barabbas was both a thief and a murderer.

That the woman of Samaria and her sister were whores and that Christ knew them dishonestly.

That St John the Evangelist was bedfellow to Christ, that he used him as the sinners of Sodom.

That they who love not tobacco and boys are fools.

That all the apostles were base fellows neither of wit nor worth.

That he (Marlowe) had as good right to coin as the Queen of England.

That the Angel Gabriel was bawd to the Holy Ghost.

Shakespeare knew Baines – and yet he didn't really know him. He flitted and hunted but did not land long enough for any eye to catch his design. One day he was an ordained Roman Catholic priest, the next a spy for Protestant England. He might have been a player at the Rose, so consummate was his skill at trickery. In looks, he was handsome, tall and well formed. He wore his hair long, though not as long as the vidame's, and his beard was sharply trimmed. But the inner workings of his mind? That was harder to discern. And had Nicholas Henbird not hinted at some diabolical link between Baines and Topcliffe?

Baines greeted each in turn. He bowed and kissed Ana's proffered hand. She averted her face. 'Mr Baines, I must tell you that you stink like the bilge of a home-coming galleon.'

'I apologise. It is the hard ride from London. Sweat and dirt.

I shall bathe.' He moved on to Shakespeare, and allowed himself to be introduced as though they had never met.

Shakespeare was puzzled. 'I know you well, Mr Baines,' he said, refusing to play along with his strange and unnecessary deception. 'I am certain you must remember me, for we were both in the service of Mr Secretary.'

Baines's brown eyes widened as if in sudden recognition. 'Of course – Mr Shakespeare. I felt I recognised you from somewhere, but was not certain where. A thousand pardons, sir.'

'It is no matter. I see your wish came true in the case of Kit Marlowe. His mouth is, indeed, stopped. You must be exceeding pleased.'

Baines laughed. 'The world is well rid of him. He denied God. Well, he will know the truth by now, as he screams in the eternal fire.'

'Did *you* kill him?'

'I believe it was a Mr Frizer that killed him, Mr Shakespeare. Has an inquest not already concluded that?'

'Indeed, but who ordered the killing? Who was the motion-man?'

'Mr Shakespeare, I believe you seek something which is not there, a will-o'-the-wisp. The case is clear and closed. Marlowe had a careless hand; he should have thought more closely before he uttered his blasphemies. And do you think old Burghley enjoyed being depicted as the great overreacher Mortimer?' He turned and smiled at Perez. 'I fear we are showing poor manners to our hosts with such arcane talk.'

Shakespeare gazed at Baines with a questioning eye. Not for the first time, he tried to divine what lay in that cold, labyrinthine mind.

'Well, Mr Baines,' the vidame said languidly, as if the mere effort of speech was too much for him. 'Do you bring Don Antonio a fine offer of gold from my lord of Essex?'

'More importantly,' Perez put in. 'Have you brought us fresh whores? I swear I will leave England by the next packet if you serve me another milkmaid or taproom girl. We are in exile, Mr Baines. Can the earl really not take me to court where, I believe, there are clean-scrubbed ladies and maids aplenty?'

'My apologies, but it is the Queen's way to make envoys wait. She enjoys discomfiting those who would attend on her. I promise you it will not last much longer, for my lord of Essex is with her and he is certain you will be admitted before July.'

'And the sum, Mr Baines,' Perez demanded. 'What sum has he laid on the table?'

Shakespeare went cold. Was Essex bidding for this secret, after all? Had he some access to new wealth? This complicated matters considerably.

'I am sure you will be pleased with it, but I would prefer –' Baines looked now at Shakespeare – 'to talk of this in private. I do, however, bring you tidings of great moment. There has been another powder blast, an atrocity at the Dutch market, this very morning. I believe there are dead.'

Shakespeare half rose from his chair and leant forward. 'Do you know more, Mr Baines?'

Baines shook his head slowly. 'Very little. I was told it was a much larger explosion than the one at the church, and was in a busy place where wives traded with stallholders. Who is behind it?' He turned towards Perez. 'I fear the Spanish are suspected.'

'Most likely. Do not attempt to spare my feelings, Mr Baines, for I am as one with the English. In truth, I would petition the Bas—, Her Majesty to sponsor an invasion to liberate my home country. Dutch, Portuguese, French, English, even the Turks should join forces to oust this king whose empire has grown so great.'

Suddenly Shakespeare wanted more than anything to be

away from here. It felt wrong, negotiating for some elusive secret when powdermen were blowing up London and its people. He should be there, in the city, where he was needed. He said a silent prayer.

'It is a most heinous crime, Mr Baines,' Ana Cabral said. 'Which of us is safe if powder is ignited in public places?'

Perez banged his gnarled hand upon the table. 'Let us talk of pleasanter things,' he said angrily, reaching for his box of vials. 'Let us talk of gold – and of the glittering court of Elizabeth Tudor.'

Shakespeare lay on the bed, staring into the darkness. The bedclothes were damp and musty and the air was infused with an unpleasant smell of mould. He could not rest. His mind was in turmoil.

Before retiring to his chamber he had spoken briefly with Perez and demanded to know why he had lied over Essex's interest.

'Why are you surprised, Mr Shakespeare? Of course I would wish to discuss the matter of my great secret with my host.' Perez had shrugged his shoulders dismissively. 'Such things are my source of income these days. How else may an exile earn his keep?'

'I understand, but you said—'

'One says many things. I am sure that a man who has worked for Walsingham and who now represents Sir Robert Cecil must understand the way of the world. I vow to you, however, that I will not accept an offer from Essex until you have had a chance to better it. I say that as a man of honour.'

'Ride with me to Cecil on the morrow,' Shakespeare said suddenly. 'You will get a good price and Cecil will present you at court. We will seal this once and for all.'

'You wish to be away from here, I think.'

'I wish to have this settled.'

'I shall sleep on it.'

Now Shakespeare lay on this fetid bed, the candle snuffed on a small table at his side. Then he heard footfalls outside his chamber. He had no weapons – they were still in the possession of the guards – but he rose instantly to his feet and grasped the candlestick, holding it defensively as a club. The latch lifted and the door slowly opened, the light of a candle flickering shadows into the room.

'Mr Shakespeare . . .?'

The voice was a whisper, but he knew it straightway.

'Mr Shakespeare, are you awake? It is Ana.'

'I am here.' He still held the candlestick ready as a weapon.

'I must talk with you.'

'Step inside, slowly, and close the door.'

Ana held the candle in front of her, the flame illuminating her smooth, beautiful skin. She was, Shakespeare thought, like a horse-chestnut fresh removed from its husk and burnished by the autumn sun. She wore a nightgown, which scarce concealed her slender, sumptuous body.

'Well?'

'I am come to tell you Don Antonio's great secret.'

'And how would you know such a thing?'

'I know everything about Don Antonio. He has no secrets from me. I know the colour and consistency of his turds. I know when he has swived and with whom. What he eats, what he drinks.'

And you know the pizzle and balls of his secretary, thought Shakespeare, though he did not say so.

'Why are you here, Doña Ana?'

'Come with me.'

'Where?'

'Just come. If you would wish to know the secret, come with me now.'

'How much?'

'You have offered Don Antonio a thousand pounds. I ask only seven hundred and fifty and you shall have exactly the same information.'

'Why would you trust me to pay?'

'My whole life has been about learning who to trust and who not, Mr Shakespeare.'

'And why should I trust *you*?'

'Because you are in a hurry. You want this information before the Earl of Essex has it – and you wish to be away from this hellish place.'

'That is not enough.'

'Come with me, and then you will believe me.'

Shakespeare said nothing for a few moments. What did he have to lose? 'Very well,' he said quietly. 'I will come with you.'

'Then tread softly. There are many eyes in this house.'

Chapter 14

THE OLD WOMAN wore the coif, veil and black holy habit of a nun. Her shoulders were wrapped in a threadbare shawl of finely spun wool. She sat alone in her room, on a wooden chair beside her bed. Her stick was on the bed. Around her neck she wore a gold chain with the cross and body of Christ. She was still and silent, scarcely stirring at the entrance of Shakespeare and Cabral; no more than a slight inclining of her chin, like a deer that has heard something on the wind or caught a scent.

'Sister Madeleine, it is I, Ana Cabral.'

'I know who you are, Doña Ana. I may be ancient and my sight may be failing, but I have not lost my wits. Who is with you?'

They were in a small attic room with sloping ceilings and a single, curtained window. Cabral's candle was the only light, and it reflected off the black rosary beads that the old woman twisted through her bony fingers. Though her body looked frail and bent, her voice was strong for her years, which Shakespeare took to be approaching sixty. Her accent was instantly discernible as Scottish.

'His name is Mr Shakespeare, sister. John Shakespeare.'

'I do not know you. Come closer. Take my hand, Mr Shakespeare.'

Shakespeare stepped forward and allowed the *religieuse* to clasp his right hand. She held it in her own right hand and stroked it with her left, as though she would divine his character from it. The beads entwined in her fingers were cool on his knuckles. He saw that she wore a thick gold and diamond-encrusted band around the ring finger of her left hand.

'From your hand I take you to be a gentleman, sir. I can tell, too, that your sinews are drawn, as though you were fearful, but perhaps you are merely attentive and alert. We shall see. Have you come to hear my story? Doña Ana told me I would be asked to say it. It has been a secret so long. Almost twenty-six years. Too long. My little prince . . .'

'Indeed, that is why he is here, sister. It is time.'

'Mr Shakespeare, I have longed for this day. I must tell it before I die. The canker in my breast grows and grows.' She still held Shakespeare's hand and her movement guided him to sit on the bed at her side. 'My little prince must claim his inheritance. No one but me can bear witness. Sit here with me, sir. Do you feel this ring on my finger.'

'I do.'

'This ring was presented to me by the blessed martyr Mary Stuart, Queen of Scots – Queen Mary the Second of England in the eyes of God. She placed it on my finger in the November of 1567, and it has been there ever since. It was a day so cold I feel it in my bones still, and yet the ring burned me with its grace. The last day of November. It was the day she gave birth to her little prince and placed him in my arms.' The old nun turned to Ana Cabral. 'Give me the Holy Bible, Doña Ana, for what I am about to tell you is sacred to my heart . . .'

'I have thought often how I would tell this history, Mr Shakespeare. I shall try to make it short and as direct as I can, for it is important that you should understand it clearly and believe it. In June of the year '67, after the meeting of the armies at Carberry Hill, Queen Mary was taken prisoner by the rebel lords and imprisoned in the island castle of Lochleven, near Kinross, twenty miles north of Edinburgh. I was one of her two chamber servants, and I was taken there with her.'

Shakespeare watched her closely. The Holy Bible lay on her lap, her hand upon it with the ring finger prominent and slightly more crooked than the others. The diamonds sparkled in the candlelight.

'It was clear to all that she was with child. She had been vomiting and now she was putting on weight. Everyone knew that the Earl of Bothwell must be the father, but no one really knew how many months had passed since the conception. Her Majesty was scared. Though she had seen much in her twenty-five years – three marriages, war, murder and treachery – she was very lonely in those dreadful days. She wept in fits and tore her hair and oft-times threatened to throw herself from the castle battlements to her death. She told me she knew that the child would be killed. Her enemies – Moray, Morton, Lindsay, Kirkcaldy, Melville and the other lords – would never suffer a child conceived of Bothwell to survive.

'They were watching her as a hawk will watch a leveret. Their spies were all around us, not least of them William Douglas, the laird of Lochleven, who was her keeper. He was half-brother to Moray and a kinsman to Morton, and he had no love for his sovereign lady. In her small apartment in the round tower of the castle, she had always to have two ladies attending, day and night. They slept at her side. In all she had five ladies-in-waiting, who took these duties in turn. One of them was Mary Seton, her firm friend from childhood days when she and the three other Marys – Livingston, Fleming and Beaton – had accompanied the five-year-old Queen to France as her play-mates and companions. Mary Seton was distraught at the state to which her sovereign had been brought and begged to be allowed to dress her hair as she had always done. Mary Seton and I were the only ones at Lochleven that Her Majesty trusted. When we had the opportunity, we would whisper together about what we might do to save the baby.

'The best hope seemed to be to escape. But how? The island was half a mile into the loch and was always under guard. Perhaps she might go ashore disguised as one of her ladies or maids. At one time she tried that, wearing Mary Seton's garb, but she was recognised by the ferryman because of her uncommon height and was returned to her gaol. Then Mary Seton had another design to save her unborn child. It was a plan of such guile and deception that I still can scarce believe that it worked. But it did.

'I had a close cousin, Margaret Rule, not far from Kinross, one whom I loved and who loved me. She was a faithful Roman Catholic and a midwife of long standing in those parts and knew all the wives, so that whenever one suffered a miscarriage, she would be aware of it. Though it is a mortal sin, sir, I do know, too, that sometimes she did help to shift a pregnancy when a young girl was in trouble outside of marriage. I went to her with Mary Seton's plan and she agreed without hesitation to help us.

'In July of that year, my cousin sent a message for me to come to her. She had what we wanted. I went to her straightway, across the loch, and found her waiting for me with a bag, waterproofed and sealed with beeswax. It contained the dead foetuses of twins, miscarried just hours earlier, still attached to their navel strings, with the placenta, all immersed in pig's blood from the butcher.

'I kissed my cousin and offered her silver, which she would not accept. She was helping me for the love of our sovereign and for the love of God. The bag was easy to conceal in my gowns, and I returned with it across the water to the island of Lochleven. For the next few hours we waited our moment. We needed a time when the other ladies and servants were dining and I and the Lady Mary Seton were alone with the Queen. Our chance came in the late evening, just before darkness fell.'

Shakespeare listened intently. Sir Francis Walsingham had once told him that Mary had miscarried twins at Lochleven. There had never been any doubt that it had happened, for the Lord Lindsay and other rebels had come to her the next day on one of their regular visits and had seen her, weeping, still in her bloody clothes and bedding, and had lain their eyes on the dead foetuses before they were taken away for burial in unconsecrated ground. 'It was a good deed that God did that day,' Walsingham had said. 'For a claimant born to the adulterous Scots devil and her co-conspirator in murder would have shaken the very earth of Scotland and England.' Now this woman, this nun and one-time maidservant to Mary, Queen of Scots, seemed to be telling a different tale.

'We had to be quick, but we accomplished our task. The Queen lay on her bed and we spread the pig's blood all about her nether parts and on the sheets. Then we placed the foetuses and placenta in a bowl as if it were she that had miscarried twins. Finally, with much ado, we called for help. The other women came and saw what seemed to have happened and there was much sorrowing and wailing. Lady Mary Seton's design had worked, but the deception was far from complete. We still had to bring Her Majesty to term and protect her baby.

'Every month from then on, I would bring in pig's blood to soak in rags and sprinkle about her bedding to show that she had been brought to her flowers in normal kind, as any woman who is not with child. All this time, of course, she was putting on weight, but she wore loose gowns and her weight gain was attributed to her great sadness, an increased appetite and her lack of proper exercise, so that no one questioned it. And why should they have? For all were certain that she had lost her babies, as they thought.

'At last, on the thirtieth day of November, she was delivered of a healthy boy. Her throes were thankfully short, no more than two hours, and we stifled her groans and cries with cushions. We had been most fearful that the child would arrive when others less well disposed were about, but God smiled upon us. Apart from me, there were in attendance her other maidservant, who was a Frenchwoman, the Lady Mary Seton and Her Majesty's private physician, who had by then been brought to her prison household. He was afraid, but she swore him to secrecy, that he would tell no man what was happening on the hazard of his immortal soul.

'As soon as the child was born, there was no time to lose, for sooner or later the wails would be heard. I took the baby away that night by the ferry, all wrapped tight in swaddling and huddled inside my cloak. He had been well fed by his mother's milk to make him sleep, and I also gave him a sleeping draught of brandy and herbs so that he should not wake. At one point on the short ferry journey to Kinross the baby stirred, but I was talking loudly to the ferryman and offering him wine to keep his mind distracted, and he seemed to hear nothing of the bairn. And so we arrived safe and I handed the child to my cousin, who found him a wet nurse.

'The wet nurse never knew whose baby she fed for the next six months, but she fed him well and he grew strong and bonny. At last my sovereign lady escaped and fled to England, where she was to end her days, but I did not go with her. I took charge of the baby boy and, with the help of a certain gentleman, brought him across the sea to Spain, where he was raised to be a king and one day claim his inheritance. And that is my story, sir. Simply told, but true in every detail.'

The tale sounded true to Shakespeare. It had been so guilelessly told that none could doubt it. But what was the old nun's motive in telling it? Perez wanted money, so did Cabral – but what did the old woman want? He put the question to her.

'I told you, sir, I want the prince to claim his inheritance. If James the Sixth should die without issue, he must become king of Scotland and heir to the throne of England. It is what Queen Mary always wished and why she wished so desperately that the boy should survive.'

'Why did you say nothing before?'

Sister Madeleine smiled. 'Because Walsingham would have despatched an assassin to do away with him.'

'And now?'

'Now he is here in England ready to take his rightful place.'

'No one will believe this. There would need to be proof.'

'There is proof. And there are witnesses. For the time left to me, I will bear witness. My cousin still lives, as does the Queen's physician at Lochleven Castle. And though she is now frail and confined to her convent in Rheims, the Lady Mary Seton will tell her story. There are letters, too, in Queen Mary's hand, which mention her baby's birthmark. Fear not, Mr Shakespeare, there is no doubt. There will be no doubt in any man's mind when the Prince steps forward.'

'When will that be?'

'Soon enough.'

'Where exactly is he?'

'I cannot say.'

'Cannot – or will not?'

The old woman said nothing. Her dim eyes did not waver. Shakespeare turned to look at Ana, who stood as still as a rock and gave nothing away.

'What is this prince's name, Sister Madeleine?'

'Francis Philip Bothwell Stuart.'

'You must tell me his whereabouts,' Shakespeare commanded. 'It is treasonable not to.'

'I am not English, Mr Shakespeare. And you have no threats to frighten a dying woman. Truly, I would accept martyrdom as a blessing.'

Shakespeare rose from the bed. He turned once again to Ana Cabral. 'You shall have your gold, Doña Ana,' he said. 'Come to me in London. I must ride from here without delay.'

'Of course, Mr Shakespeare. I would not have expected it otherwise. But take care as you leave, for you are unarmed – and there are those here who do not wish you well.'

Chapter 15

For hours, as daylight turned to night, Boltfoot watched the stockade of Godstone powdermill from the woods. He observed the comings and goings of those who worked there and those who visited until, in the end, exhaustion took him and he slept beneath a blanket of leaves.

He was startled awake by a sound of cracking twigs and rustling leaves. He did not move but listened. There were whispers. In the thin light he could make out the shapes of two men carrying what looked like heavy staves. Were they charcoal-colliers? Unlikely. Honest workmen would not lower their voices so. They were ten yards from him, moving stealthily away, towards the powdermill. He allowed them to go on further, then followed, silently, as a bowman stalks a deer.

From their manner of walking he took one to be an older man and one a youth. Close by the stockade they stopped. The older one stood in the shelter of a tree. On the outside of the stockade there was a series of pitch lanterns, the flames safely enclosed in sides of thin, translucent horn so that no errant sparks should fly. Boltfoot could see now that the men did not carry staves but muskets. They were dressed in common countrymen's clothes; coarse wool breeches, frayed and torn jerkins of hide and felt caps about their heads and ears. The older man waited at the tree with both the muskets while the younger crawled forward on his belly. Boltfoot saw immediately that he was making his way towards a hole in the palisade. He disappeared through it like a fox going to earth.

Boltfoot watched them from cover fifteen yards away. After two or three minutes the younger man emerged from the stockade, scrabbling to his feet and hastening at a crouch to his comrade. He held something out to show him, then they melted back into the woods. Boltfoot stayed on their trail.

When the men thought they were safe away, they stopped again, sat on the ground and unslung their muskets and bags. The older man, grey-bearded and weathered, took out his tinderbox and sparked up a rushlight, which cast a weak glow on the scene. His young copesmate – Boltfoot thought it could have been his son, for their features were alike – took a flagon and bread from his bag and the two began to eat and drink.

'Hold still.' Boltfoot stood behind them with his caliver loaded and aimed at the back of the older man. 'I am armed.'

The men twisted around in alarm, rising to their feet, and found themselves looking into the octagonal muzzle of Boltfoot's fine-wrought weapon. The younger man, who had no more than a few wisps to warm his chin, reached to his belt for his dagger.

'Touch the knife and it will be the last thing you do,' Boltfoot said.

'Take a little bread and be on your way,' the greybeard growled. 'We have nothing for you.'

Boltfoot looked at their muskets. 'What about those?'

'They put rabbit and fowl on our table. I'll die before you have either of them.'

'I don't want them, nor your bread. I want information. What were you doing at the powdermill?' As he spoke, Boltfoot realised that the men were losing their fear of him, even though he had them at his mercy.

'Reckon it out for yourself. What would a man want at a powdermill?'

The younger one laughed at his father's drollness.

'Just enough powder corn to fire your hagbuts?'

'And a little left over to make a gunpowder pudding.' The older man was smirking now.

'So you just walk in and take it? Or does someone sell it to you?'

'What's it to you?'

'I need powder myself, that's what. I been watching the place, wondering how to get some. Can I slip in the way you did – or will I meet a mastiff on the other side?'

'How much do you want?'

'How much can you get me?' Boltfoot demanded.

'I didn't say I could get you any. I'm not a trader in gunpowder. Just a freeborn Englishman trying to keep my family alive in hard days.'

'A poacher.'

'And what are *you*? You don't look like no constable nor any honest man I've ever seen, with your dragging foot and your outlandish weapon in the forest at witching time. Is that a hagbut or a pistol? Ain't never seen its like.'

'Could you get me a hundredweight of powder?'

'A hundredweight!' the younger one exclaimed. He had been silent until then. 'What do you want a hundredweight for?'

'I do reckon he's a Spaniard mercenary, Jed. Come to blow up our queen.'

On an impulse, Boltfoot lowered the muzzle of his wheel-lock caliver. 'I don't want powder and I don't care a maggot for your poaching, but I do want your help. And I'll pay you for it.'

The greybeard grinned. 'We could do for you now you've dropped your weapon.'

'Aye, you could,' Boltfoot said. 'But you won't, will you? Because you're honest men. Honest poachers . . .'

The older man's grin turned into a laugh and he put out his bare hand. 'Well then, now you're talking like a civil man. No need for threats. Come break bread and take some ale with us and let's find out who you are.'

Boltfoot shook the hand. 'Fair enough,' he said. 'I'll tell you this, I am no Spanish mercenary but you may not be far out with your talk. And I will tell you that my name is Boltfoot Cooper.'

'And we're both called Jed Brooker, father and son, if you hadn't divined the similarity for yourself. Most folks do. Now then, Mr Cooper, talk on. Weave your tale of intrigue and tell us your business in Godstone woods.'

Boltfoot told them of the powder blast at the Dutch church and of his commission from Sir Robert Cecil's office to find the source of the gunpowder. 'And I'm thinking that if you and your son here manage to get in and out for powder for your poaching, another might be able to acquire a barrel of the stuff and use it for attacking Dutchmen.'

'If I talk to you, Mr Cooper, what assurance do I have that my name goes no further, that none of this comes back to me and my boy?' Jed the elder said.

'My word, Mr Brooker.'

'We're good huntsmen, Mr Cooper. We could track down and snare a man that had betrayed us as well as we could take duck or hare.'

'You'll have no need. My word is unbreakable.'

Jed the elder nodded slowly, as if he saw something of himself in Boltfoot Cooper, a rough honesty, perhaps, or a shared belief in the freedom of the spirit. 'Well then, I will tell you what I know. Jed, pass the flagon to Mr Cooper and let him sup more ale.'

The three men squatted in the darkness of the wood, lit only by the rushlight and a thin slice of moon that now and then pierced through the clouds and the canopy of trees.

'My daughter's husbandman, Tom Jackson, works there at the Godstone mill. He passes us a little fine-ground musket powder, just enough, but he'd never do more than that – never pass a keg of the stuff to no man. And I reckon the others as works there would be the same. They'd all pass a little to their kinfolk to powder their hagbuts, but no more.'

'So you're saying the place is secure. No leaks?'

'No leaks that I've heard of, Mr Cooper, but there is something you should know. Tom told me there was an attempt most recently to breach the stockade. Two men trying to force their way in by night. But they were spotted and driven away by the mastiffs. I did think at first that you must have been one of them, Mr Cooper.'

Boltfoot said nothing.

'I know different now, don't I. Unless I'm the biggest doddypoll in the whole county of Surrey.'

'I am sure you are not, Mr Brooker.'

'But what I can tell you is that the attempt on the mill was not the first. About a month ago, a stranger was hanging around the Mill Tavern buying drinks for the men, asking whether powder ever went missing, asking whether a man might acquire some for a good price. But he quickly disappeared when he saw Tom, for Tom knew him.'

'Who was this man?'

'I'm coming to that. Before Tom married my lass, he worked at another mill at Bromley-by-Bow, on the river Lea, east of London town. And this man worked there, too. He was a good powderman, Tom says, but he was a rabble-rouser and a hedge-priest. Believed that Christ intended all men to be equal and that the lands should be taken from the lords and shared out between God-fearing Englishmen whatever their birth. He would try to stir up the mill workers, get them along to his mad sermonising and meetings. But word got back to the miller, who dismissed him on the spot.'

'Had there been any suggestion that this man tried to obtain powder from the Bromley-by-Bow mill?'

'I couldn't say, but I can tell you the man's name if you like, for it is such a name as I could never forget. Holy Trinity Curl. That's what Tom called him. *Holy Trinity*! Now what sort of name is that for a man?'

Chapter 16

JOHN SHAKESPEARE FOUND the chief of guards, Edward Wilton, outside the main door of Gaynes Park Hall. 'I must take my leave, Mr Wilton. Please fetch my horse and weapons.'

'Leaving in the middle of the night, Mr Shakespeare? Only thieves and murderers sneak from houses at such a time . . .'

'Watch your tongue, Mr Wilton, lest you be relieved of it.'

'I know about you, Mr Shakespeare. Oh yes, sir, I know all about you and your spying for Robin Crookback.'

Shakespeare was tempted to strike the man. 'I am in the service of Her Majesty. Who do *you* serve, Mr Wilton? Now fetch my mare, sword and dagger or expect to find yourself arraigned before court. This is Queen's business and I will not be delayed.'

Wilton's face was suffused with scorn. 'I'll get your bloody horse. Hope it goes lame on you.'

Soon after dawn, Shakespeare arrived at Cecil's mansion near the Strand. The footman at the door looked at him with a strange mixture of horror and pity, as though he had some grotesque deformity, then hurried away into the house. He returned quickly and said Sir Robert would see him.

He followed the servant through the hallway to the meeting room. Cecil was already there, standing stiffly and unsmiling.

'John . . .'

Shakespeare bowed. 'Sir Robert, I believe I have what you require.'

'John, there has been another gunpowder blast.'

'I heard. The Dutch market. Rick Baines arrived at Gaynes Park with the news. I believe there were dead or wounded.'

'You have not heard then?'

Something in Cecil's normally unreadable face brought a rush of cold panic to Shakespeare's chest. He could not draw breath, nor speak. He shook his head.

'John, sit down. I have grave news. Your wife . . .'

No.

'She took the full force of the blast, John. She could have known nothing of it. I am so sorry.'

Shakespeare felt that his knees should buckle and he should slump to the ground, but his joints were rigid, immovable. Like a drowning man, he gasped for air but could not breathe. His body was closing down with his mind, which could not take this in.

'There was a young Dutch girl with her, who identified her. The girl is badly injured and is presently at St Bartholomew's Hospital.'

Catherine dead?

Cecil stepped towards him. He was a head shorter than Shakespeare, yet he put his arm about him; perhaps for the first time in his life, he felt moved to open himself to another.

The mother of his child. His bedmate, soulmate.

The footman who had brought him to this room reappeared at the doorway with a flask of brandy and two small silver cups. Cecil nodded to him and he poured out two measures.

'Drink this.'

Shakespeare obeyed. He downed the brandy in one gulp. Cecil did likewise.

'Now sit.' Cecil pushed him down into a chair. He signalled to the footman to refill the cups. 'Now drink again.'

Shakespeare drank the second dram. The spirit burned down his throat to his belly.

'*Catherine* . . .' he managed to say, at last, his breathing long and deep. 'Is this true, Sir Robert?'

'It is true, John. There is no doubt.'

'I should not have left her.'

'It was cruel chance, nothing else. The Dutch girl says they were there purely on a whim. They were walking by and saw the market. Mistress Shakespeare was one of five that died. Many others are injured. Mr Bedwell from the Tower Ordnance estimates a quarter-ton of powder was used.'

'Where is she?'

'The Dutch girl?'

'Catherine.'

'Her remains are with Mr Peace at St Paul's, with the other dead.'

'I must go to her.'

'Go then, John. But first, I beg you, steel yourself and tell me what you have discovered at Gaynes Park.'

In the St Paul's crypt Joshua Peace was at his work as Searcher of the Dead. He was examining the corpse of one of the Dutch market victims. He heard the door open and turned to see John Shakespeare. His face drained.

'John, I am so sorry.'

'Where is she, Joshua?'

'I do not want to show you the remains, John.'

'I need to see her.'

Peace shook his head. 'Please, do not ask me that.'

'I must.'

'I beg you, remember her as you last saw her. If you see her now that will always be your last memory. In all your dreams and in all your waking moments, it will be there. You will never wash it away.'

Shakespeare was silent a few moments, then his eyes drifted to the mutilated body on the slab. 'Like that?'

'Worse, John. Ripped apart. There is nothing recognisable. Without the Dutch girl we might never have identified her. One moment living, the next with God.'

'You must help me, Joshua. All your skill. I want to find this powderman and do to him as he has done.'

'There is something . . . a clue, perchance . . .'

'What?'

'How will you use this, John?'

'Justice. I want justice, not vengeance. Let the law take its course.'

Peace stepped to the side of the crypt and took a copper bowl from a shelf. He showed its contents to Shakespeare. There were pieces of metal – a toothed wheel, brass or bronze, and shards of steel. They were twisted and mangled, but it was clear that they had been parts from an unusual instrument. 'I believe these articles constituted some sort of timepiece. Even in this state, it is clear to me that they were fine-made. These parts were found . . .'

'In the bodies of the dead?'

'Yes.'

'What does it mean?'

'If I am correct, it means there was a time-delay mechanism. The powdermen set the clock, then made their escape. At the predetermined moment, the device released a flint against a steel plate, sending a shower of sparks into the powder.'

'Like a wheel-lock pistol.'

'Precisely.'

'Have you heard of such a thing before?'

'When I was in the Low Countries I heard of such a method being used at the siege of Antwerp. The town's defenders used the services of a skilled clockmaker to devise such a machine, which was then used with deadly purpose against the Spanish.'

'Then I must find this clockmaker.' Shakespeare stood there, irresolute. Even in his numbness, he could see the truth in what Peace said about remembering Catherine as she had been in life, not in death. His eyes caught a patch of colour close to the old, cold walls of the crypt. There were strips and shreds of material there in hues of green, saffron and rusty-blood. 'Her dress?'

Peace nodded helplessly.

'Thank you, Joshua.' Without another word, Shakespeare left the crypt; he had seen enough.

As he rode north-eastwards with lethal purpose, Shakespeare felt nothing. His heart was empty. He was hunting because it was his instinct so to do, nothing more. He could not examine himself thus, for that would open up the pain, and he had to keep it closed away. There was no time for grief.

The long-bearded keeper of the Counter gaol in Wood Street rubbed his bony old hands and looked at him with surprise. 'I had not expected you, Mr Shakespeare. Indeed, I had not. I had heard – there was word . . .' the ancient, tremulous voice trailed away.

'Has Mr Mills been to see Morley?'

'He came yesterday in the forenoon.'

'Alone?'

'Yes, Mr Shakespeare. He did stay no more than an hour.'

'Take me to Morley,' Shakespeare said flatly. He scarcely noted his surroundings, the bleak walls, the stench of human ordure, the bold rats playing about his feet.

'Of course, Mr Shakespeare, sir. Please, follow me.'

The gloomy entrails of the prison were lit by tallow sconces which threw out black smoke and burned in uneven flares, lighting the faces of prisoners in a hideous manner as they leered through their cage bars at the keeper and his visitor. They arrived at the cell where Shakespeare had left Morley. The keeper pushed open the door.

Shakespeare saw immediately that Morley was dead. He hung limply from a noose made of a thin cord tied to the bars of the room's single high window. Both men looked at the body in stunned silence for several seconds. Shakespeare turned to the keeper, dark fury in his eyes.

'Mr Shakespeare, sir, I did not know . . .' the old man spluttered helplessly.

'Cut him down.'

The keeper took a dagger from his belt and tried to reach up to cut the rope, but he was not tall enough. 'Here, give it to me,' Shakespeare ordered impatiently, snatching the blade from his hand. He sliced at the cord and the body fell to the ground. 'Who has been in here, master keeper?'

'No one . . . just the turnkey with victuals.'

Shakespeare recalled the small gnat-like creature who had brought foul ale when last he was here. 'Bring him to me. Now.'

The keeper hurried away, clearly panicked and trying to weigh up the implications; these men – Shakespeare and Mills – were important personages. They could bring him trouble.

Shakespeare examined the body. At first sight, there was no reason to believe this was other than a self-killing. Certainly Morley had been frightened enough to take his own life. Mills might well have scared him yet more, with threats of Topcliffe and torture. Yet, from what Morley had said, there were also those who badly wished him dead. He examined the hands and wrists. The wrists had raised weals as if they had been tied tight, but that was not surprising, for he himself had bound the man and dragged him behind his horse. His tongue was engorged and thrust obscenely from his mouth in a way that Shakespeare had noted on other hanged men, so it seemed probable that was the cause of death. But was it a voluntary death?

There was also a dribble of blood from the dead man's mouth, on his chin and throat. Had he bitten his tongue? Then Shakespeare noticed spots of blood on the stone floor on the other side of the cell, away from the body. They could not have come from the man while he was hanging. He kicked away the straw and saw more blood. Was it his imagining, or was the blood formed into letters? He looked closer. The blood was dried and difficult to discern, but he was almost certain there were two letters there, almost certainly described with a finger-tip. They seemed to be initials. There was definitely an *R*, but what was the second letter? It could be a *B* or a *P*. *RP*, *RB*. Two names came to mind: Rob Poley and Rick Baines. There were also two straight lines, hooked at the end. Was this a message from the dying Morley? The name of the man who killed him – if, indeed, he had been murdered – or the name of the powderman? With the side of his foot, Shakespeare brushed the straw back over the bloody letters.

On its own it was worthless. Not evidence, not really a clue. If only he had got to Morley. If only he had never left London. But he had gone to Gaynes Park and he had left his wife and family. He punched his fist into the wall and gasped with pain. But even pain was better than nothing; it meant he could still feel.

The keeper returned with the turnkey. Shakespeare towered over the little square-set gaoler by a foot and a half. He looked strong, his arms rippling beneath his filthy jerkin and shirt, but could such a small man have hoisted Morley to his death?

'What do you know about this, turnkey?'

The turnkey shrugged. 'Don't look well, does he, Mr Shakespeare. Nor does your hand, sir. Why, you have a nasty graze on your knuckles, I should say.'

'Where did he get the cord?'

The turnkey turned his head away impudently. The keeper looked on nervously.

'Has he had visitors other than Mr Mills?'

'Ask him yourself,' the turnkey said. 'I'm paid to feed prisoners and keep them locked away, not answer questions. If he wanted to top himself, that's his look-out. There's always ways to do it for those who are desperate, but who cares. Saves the hangman a task and leaves more victuals for the rest of us.'

Shakespeare turned to the keeper. 'I do not have time for this. Have this man put in fetters. Send me word when he wishes to answer my questions. He is to stay incarcerated until I say otherwise. And remove the corpse to the Searcher of the Dead at St Paul's.'

Shakespeare strode from the Counter prison into the air of London, and found it no more clean or wholesome than that of the gaol. There was a foulness in the city, a miasma of death and decay. He had to go home. He had a small daughter and two adopted children to look after. They would need him. And he needed time to himself, to think and to mourn.

Chapter 17

IN THE LAST light of evening, Boltfoot looked across the water meadows of the Lea towards the Three Mills site. He saw the place with new and questioning eyes. What secret did this powdermill hold if the man named Holy Trinity Curl had worked here? Why had the proprietor Knagg not mentioned him?

There had been no further information to glean from the poachers in the woods at Godstone, but the older man had agreed to bring his son-in-law, Tom Jackson, to meet Boltfoot and tell him what he knew of Curl. Jackson was suspicious and evasive; he was clearly scared of being involved in any way with officers of the state, even one as unimposing as Boltfoot. The meeting had achieved little beyond a vague comment about Curl being a small man with yellow-red hair and eyes of a similar hue. If Jackson knew more, he wasn't saying. 'Talk to them at Three Mills,' he said shortly. 'Thomas Knagg knows all about him. I never paid the man much heed.'

After that, Boltfoot went to the Godstone mill and met the miller, Mr Evelyn, who was open with his replies. Yes, there had been an attempt to breach the stockade and, yes, there had been attempts at bribery. The constable had been informed, and he had been to the county sheriff. There had been a full inquiry but the man they now knew as Curl (he had used an alias when insinuating himself with the powder-millers in the tavern) had disappeared and no one knew where he was. The inquiry had been dealt with in a thorough manner and there had been no repeat of the episode; there was nothing more to be done. As Boltfoot listened, he itched to be gone, certain that the answer to this investigation did not lie here. Though tired from a night with no more than one hour of sleep, he rode hard for Bromley-by-Bow, where this rabble-rousing hedge-priest had once been employed. They must know where he lived and more about him. So far, he had a description of him, nothing more.

Now he sat astride his horse, looking across at Three Mills, planning his next move. He shook the reins and rode up to the stockade gateway, where he dismounted.

The swag-belly guard recognised him and looked anxious. Boltfoot stood square in front of him and stared steadily up into his eyes.

'Where is Mr Knagg? Is he here or taken by Sarjent?'

'He has gone, Mr Cooper. No one knows where. The pursuivants came with Mr Sarjent but Mr Knagg had already departed with his family. Mr Sarjent and the pursuivants are in charge now.'

'How long have you worked here, guard?'

'Five years, sir, since Armada time when first it was changed from wheat flour to powder milling.'

'Do you remember a man called Curl – Holy Trinity Curl?'

The blood drained from the guard's face.

'Answer me.'

'Aye. I recall the man,' he replied, nodding slowly as he spoke. Boltfoot could see that he was frightened.

'Where can I find him?'

The guard glanced around nervously to see who might be listening.

Boltfoot's hand went to the hilt of his cutlass. 'Will you answer me?'

'Mr Cooper, please. There are pursuivants here. We have been told to talk to no man.'

'Shall I relieve you of your sweetbreads?'

The guard's eyes were wide, like those of a tethered goat that has caught the scent of a predator and has no escape. His shoulders slumped and his chest sagged to his belly. 'All I know is that he did sometimes preach at the churchyard at St Botolph without the wall at Aldgate.'

'You have seen him there?'

His great girth could do nothing for him here. 'No, but he did ask me to go there and hear him. Said I would find many like-minded men there.'

'What did he mean by that?'

'I do not know, Mr Cooper.'

'What do you *think* he meant?'

'Will this come back to me, Mr Cooper?'

'It will if you do not talk plain. Be certain of that. Better to talk to me now than be racked by others.'

'Please, sir, I have a wife. And I have nine children, all of them aged under ten years.'

'Then if you wish to remain with them, you will give me all the information I require.'

The guard was quivering. Boltfoot waited and watched him, absolutely still.

'Very well,' the guard said at last. 'I do believe he meant those who do not like the strangers coming to England, sir, for he knew those were my feelings. We had talked of it, as some others here do. He told me . . .'

'He told you what?'

'He told me there were many who thought like me, sir. That many men were organising themselves against the Low

Country foreigners who come here and take our trade. Why should we fight and beat the Spanish, he said, and then be invaded by Netherlanders and Frenchies? He said God would visit a terrible retribution upon the strangers and any who welcomed them.'

'And *did* you go to hear him?'

The guard was built like a plough-ox, twice the size of Boltfoot, yet he seemed like a schoolboy standing before his teacher awaiting the birch rod across his palm. His slowness to reply gave Boltfoot all the answer he needed.

'Who was there? How many? What did this Curl say?'

'I went but once, Mr Cooper.'

'Did you know that the Privy Council has authorised torture for those suspected of defaming strangers?'

'I would say there were fifty there. Apprentices and journey-men mostly, a few masterless men, too. Mr Curl did speak and sermonise. He told us that breaking and burning the Antichrist's idols and relics was but the start. He said Christ had decreed that all men were the same in the eyes of the Lord, that it were harder for a rich man to go to heaven than for a beast to pass through the eye of a needle. While we was listening, one man whispered in my ear that Curl was Jack Cade, the captain of Kent, come back from the dead. That scared me, because I know what became of Cade and his followers. I am no rebel nor traitor, Mr Cooper.'

'What then? What happened?'

'Fighting, Mr Cooper. The constable came with the watch by order of the St Botolph parson. They beat us with sticks, but many of Mr Curl's men did fight back. I would not say it was a riot, but it was a bloody affray. Curl's lot made the best of their way out of there with their bruises and cuts. I scarpered the other way and never went back.'

Over the shoulder of the guard, Boltfoot noticed the

approaching figure of William Sarjent, his face contorted with rage. He was accompanied by a pursuivant in hide jerkin, carrying a halberd. The guard shrank back at their approach.

'Where in God's name have you been, Cooper? You were supposed to stay here and keep watch on the traitor Knagg. Now he has run like a hare from greyhounds. Captain-General Norris would have struck off your head for going absent so.'

'But you are not my captain-general, Mr Sarjent. I am answerable to Mr Shakespeare, Sir Robert Cecil and my sovereign.'

'There is treason here, Cooper. Much powder is missing. I have brought in an auditor. All night long his candle has burned as he delved through the ledgers, and they don't add up. There are two to three tons that cannot be accounted for. *Tons*, Mr Cooper, not hundredweight – two or more tons! Five thousand pounds of powder – enough to provision a royal galleon. No one knows where it has gone.'

'Then you have a great deal to contend with here. And I am certain there is no better man to deal with it. For were you not a cavalryman at Sir Philip Sidney's side, a foot soldier beside Norris and a powderman under Mr Quincesmith? I reckon there can be no greater martial man in the land than yourself, Mr Sarjent.' Rarely had Boltfoot spoken so many words at one turn, but he had bile to vent at this braggart and was pleased to have done so.

'Damn you, Cooper. You are a noxious insect of a man and you have no idea what you are getting into.'

'I have business elsewhere.' Boltfoot turned sharply and limped towards his horse. He was about to pull himself up into the saddle when he caught a movement out of the corner of his eye. Sarjent was coming at him, dagger wrenched from his belt and clasped in his fist. Boltfoot thrust out with his right foot – his good foot – and caught the man in the belly. But he unbalanced himself in the process and fell to the ground, hard.

Sarjent stumbled back from the force of the kick, but recovered his composure in moments.

Sarjent lunged forward and fell on the scrabbling figure of Boltfoot. He raised the blade in his right hand. It seemed he would plunge it down into the grizzled face of the old seafarer.

Boltfoot threw a punch. The blow missed, but as he did so he swivelled his head out of the way and the dagger came down away from his face, nicking his right ear, then stabbing harmlessly into the hard earth. Boltfoot wrenched his body the other way, this time throwing Sarjent to the side so that he lost his grip of the dagger's hilt as he tried to maintain his balance.

As he turned, Boltfoot clasped his hands to Sarjent's shoulders and jabbed his head forward with all the force he could muster. His solid forehead smacked hard into the bridge of the other man's nose.

Sarjent squealed in pain. Blood spat from his broken nose. Boltfoot pushed him aside, then staggered to his feet. Blood dripped from his ear where the knife had cut it. Sarjent was sitting on the ground, his hands clutching at his bloody broken nose. Boltfoot pushed his right foot into his chest, knocking him once more to the ground, then walked back towards his horse, dragging his club foot.

This time he made it into the saddle. He glared down at Sarjent, then across to the guard, who was cowering by the entrance to the stockade. The grinning pursuivant leant nonchalantly on his halberd staff. Irritably, Boltfoot kicked his horse into a trot.

Shakespeare sat with Mary, Andrew and Grace, all huddled together on the floor of his solar. He stroked the children's brows and hugged them and tried to soothe their tears. His own would not come.

At last Mary went to sleep and Jane took her away to bed.

Grace was ten and Andrew was twelve, both old enough to comprehend death. Shakespeare talked to them quietly, trying to make sense of an event that made no sense to him. He could not bring himself to say that it was God's will, for that would have been a lie. This was man's doing. All he could say to comfort them was that she was with God now and that she looked over them still and would do so always. He had to let them believe that, even if he was less than certain himself.

By midnight, he had taken them to their beds, said the Lord's Prayer with them and another prayer for Catherine. As he kissed them goodnight, Andrew recoiled from him. He looked in the boy's eyes and saw his own rage reflected. He could find no words of comfort, so left the children, returned to his solar and sat alone. He had a flask of brandy, yet he drank nothing. He did not sleep. In his cold chamber he had found her comb, the teeth entwined with a few strands of her dark hair. He held it and closed his eyes and tried to remember her face. All he could see was bloody remains, severed limbs and disgorged entrails. Joshua Peace had lied to him; there was no escaping this vision. No words, no closing of the eyes, no Bible readings, nothing could wash away the blood and the horror.

At dawn, he left the solar and spoke briefly with Jane, who could not hide the tears that had flowed all day and night and flowed still. He held her hands in his. 'Keep the children busy, Jane,' he said. 'Give them chores, make them do their reading. Tell them they must be strong in honour and remembrance of their mother.'

He strode to the stables and was leading out his grey mare when he caught sight of Jan Sluyterman.

'Mr Shakespeare, I do not have words . . .'

'There are no words, Mr Sluyterman. Do not look for them. How is the girl, Susanna?'

'I believe she was standing behind Mistress Shakespeare, who caught the full force of the blast. She fell to the ground and was knocked insensible. Her arm and leg are broken. She has many cuts.'

'Has there been any more trouble from Topcliffe?'

Sluyterman shook his head.

'What of the servant, Kettle?'

'He has disappeared, thank the Lord.'

Shakespeare was disappointed. He had been certain the man could lead him into dark corners.

'Well, if he returns, let me know straightway, Mr Sluyterman. In the meantime, I would ask you to meet me at the hospital at ten of the clock, for I must talk with the girl and would ask you to interpret for me.'

'Of course. I will be there.'

Shakespeare shook the Dutchman's hand, then clambered into the saddle and rode the mare slowly eastwards through the teeming streets towards the Strand.

Cecil was still eating his morning repast when Shakespeare arrived, but he was immediately ushered in.

'John, I would give you time away to mourn, but I need you.'

'I do not want time away, Sir Robert.'

'Leave the powder inquiry to Francis Mills.'

'Mills, Sir Robert? Forgive me for speaking plain, but he was supposed to be looking after the Morley connection. Now Morley is dead and silenced.'

'I received your message about that, John.'

'Did Mills get the name of the powderman from him?'

'He got nowhere with him. He had returned to me to request authority for the use of other methods of interrogation . . .'

'Torture.'

'I did not permit it.'

'But Morley was scared enough that he took his own life. Or did someone else take it for him?'

'John, that is enough on the subject. There is movement in the powder inquiry. The miller at Bromley-by-Bow has disappeared. A great deal of powder has been misappropriated. I think you can leave this to Francis Mills, your man Cooper and the men from the Royal Armoury. I understand your personal involvement, but there is more vital work for you.'

'Is Boltfoot returned then?'

'No, but Mr Sarjent has reported. I am told he and Boltfoot had a disagreement. Sarjent sports a broken nose.'

'Well, why is Boltfoot not here?'

Cecil gave a brief shrug of the shoulders. 'He will turn up in his own time, as always.'

Shakespeare said nothing. He did not like the sound of this.

Cecil changed the subject. 'Let us talk of Perez and the supposed son of Mary of Scots. Do you believe this Doña Ana?'

'I would believe very little she said, but I did not hear it from her. Everything I told you yesterday came from the old nun's own mouth. I have no doubt that she believed every word she spoke. She was sound of mind and knew exactly what she said.'

'So James the Sixth of Scotland has a younger brother.'

'Yes.'

'A younger brother brought up as a Catholic, with the full weight of Spain and the Vatican behind him.'

'Again, yes.'

'And you believe he is here in England?'

'That is what I am told.'

'Then where is he?'

'I think Perez must know. Or Cabral.'

'Perez knew Cabral was taking you to hear this nun's story. He obviously expects you to return with a large quantity of gold in return for the other half of the information we require: the man's whereabouts. You must go back to them.'

'Do you not think the time has come to bring Perez here to you?'

Cecil sipped at a small beaker of ale. 'Yes, John, I think you are right. Bring him to me. Tell him his demands will be met and that he will be received at court as an honoured guest. I shall talk to Carey and Heneage to make the arrangements. In the meantime, no word is to get out concerning this lost son of the Scots devil. We must not give the story credence.'

Shakespeare understood. The government would never acknowledge such a prince, for if the story came to be heard outside these walls, there would be many Catholics, both in England and Scotland, who would seize on the young pretender as a figurehead for their cause. And there was one other thing . . .

'Sir Robert, I believe that there must also be an implicit danger to King James. His marriage remains barren after more than three years. That means this prince, this brother, will be seen as undisputed heir to his throne – and the Spanish will do all in their power to make him king. Philip of Spain has stooped to assassination many times before. Will he not do so again?'

'I have already sent a messenger to Edinburgh with word of this. The Scots embassy here in London is informed and will cooperate with us. James must be protected at all costs, for I believe him to be the future of England as well as Scotland. My father and I consider him to be the Queen's heir apparent.'

Chapter 18

THE GIRL SLEPT in a plain cot at the ancient Hospital of St Bartholomew. Shakespeare and Sluyterman stood at her bedside watching her. Her fair hair was no longer in plaits, but loose and crinkled, splayed across the pillow. Shakespeare noted the wooden splints strapped tight to her right arm and left leg and the bandages that swathed most of her tall, slender body. Her face had a few scratches but otherwise was mercifully unscathed. The nursing sister stood at the end of the bed in her crisp starched wimple, long apron and smock of white linen.

'Wake her, please. I must talk with her briefly,' Shakespeare said.

The nurse gently shook the girl's shoulders. She stirred but did not wake.

'You must wake her.'

She shook her again, more firmly, and the girl's eyes opened. They were full of fear.

'Explain what we need, Mr Sluyterman.'

Sluyterman nodded, then smiled at the girl reassuringly. He spoke to her in Dutch and she screwed up her eyes and said a few words in a loud voice. The Dutchman turned back to Shakespeare. 'I told Susanna that we must ask her a few questions, but I fear it will be very difficult. The gunpowder blast has deafened her.'

'Can she hear anything?'

'A little. Let us try. What do you wish to know?'

'What she saw before the gunpowder blast.'

Sluyterman said a few more words in Dutch, his voice even louder and deliberately precise. She looked at him as though trying to read the words from his lips. She nodded and spoke back to him.

'She says she saw two men behind the cheese stall. She says she was watching them, for they had a most curious aspect. They had a small wagon or cart, which they parked. It had casks in it. They then did something at the back of the cart, before walking away, laughing.'

'Can she describe these two men?'

'She says they looked like working men, with caps close-fitted about their heads and brows. She was surprised, though, by their attire, for she thought the taller of the two had the aspect of a gentleman.' The Dutch merchant questioned the girl again, then turned back to Shakespeare. 'The other one was shorter with strange amber eyes that seemed to stare right through her. It was his unusual look that caught her attention and made her take note of the men. Both seemed good-humoured, she said. She watched them walk away as Mistress Shakespeare waited to buy some cheese. And then she recalls nothing.'

'You said she thought the taller man a gentleman. How was he attired?'

'She does not recall, except that they wore workmen's clothes. She only remembers their faces and their caps.'

'Very well. If she recalls anything else, please get word to me. And rest assured, I have the word of Sir Robert Cecil that she may return to your household when she is well – and remain there. I must away, Mr Sluyterman.'

*

The shutters were closed at Gaynes Park Hall as Shakespeare trotted up to the house on his grey mare. No guards came out to search him or take away his weapons. He dismounted and rapped his knuckles on the front door.

The retainer who had first opened the door to him two days earlier eventually answered him, a look of mild surprise on his face. The man was no longer dressed in Essex's tangerine livery, nor did he look nervous as he had done before. 'Mr Shakespeare?'

'Has everyone departed?'

'Indeed, sir. They left for Essex House in London before noon. I believe Mr Richard Baines took them on the express orders of my lord of Essex. It is my understanding that Don Antonio is to be received at court. Gaynes Park is now closed, sir.'

Shakespeare cursed silently. How was he to bring Perez to Cecil now? It would be easier for a fingerless man to prise an oyster from its shell than to extract the Spaniard from Essex House under the earl's gaze.

The church of St Boltoph stood less than fifty yards outside the city wall near Aldgate. Boltfoot tethered his horse by a water trough, then walked into the church's bleak confines, stripped of all semblance of joy and beauty by the Protestant destroyers. The church was new-built since the old one fell away into ruin, but only the stones themselves seemed to have any pride and bearing.

A young woman sat in prayer on a plain three-legged stool. He watched her for a while. As she stood to go, he approached her. She averted her gaze and scurried away as if he was a poisonous snake.

Boltfoot walked outside. An old man knelt near a gravestone, cutting the grass and tares with a sickle.

'Good day. I am looking for Mr Curl,' Boltfoot said.

The man looked up at him briefly, then returned to his work.

'I would pay for information.'

The old man looked up again. 'My wife is buried here.'

'I am sorry.' Boltfoot turned disconsolately and walked away. Across the road he saw the sign of a hostelry. The Empty Vessel. He went in and ordered himself a blackjack of ale, then tried to talk with the landlord. 'Do you know anything about the church?'

'What is there to know? It is a church.' He nodded his head to another drinker and set about drawing more ale from a keg.

'Fine kegs you have here,' Boltfoot said.

'Aye, fine kegs, but the beer and ale inside them is better. Kegs never quenched a man's thirst nor took away his pain.'

'Kegs certainly *cause* a man's thirst. The making of them, leastwise. I know it – for I am a cooper by trade.'

'Are you now?' the landlord said, suddenly interested. 'Looking for work, are you? There's always work for a journeyman cooper.'

Boltfoot supped deep of the ale. It was good and refreshing. 'Not work at present, but something else. A place where Englishmen may live among their own kind without the din of strange voices and tongues.'

The landlord looked at him long and hard.

'Would you know of such a place, innkeeper? Of such folk that think like me?'

'That depends how you think. Are you saying you do not like strangers?'

'Do *you*?'

The landlord reached over the bar, removed Boltfoot's half-emptied leather jug and replaced it with the two pennies he had paid. 'Take your money and get out, journeyman cooper. There are too many of your ilk in these parts and I will have none of you on these premises, with or without your threats.'

'How have I offended you?'

'You have offended me because I have a keen sense of smell. You are a dog turd on my shoe. It might please you to know that my goodwife hails from France and you insult her and me with your dirty talk. I won't have it. Begone, master cooper.'

Bolfoot shuffled out. He wished very much to tell the landlord that he was sorry, that he had never intended to insult him or his goodwife, for those were not his opinions, that he was merely searching for one who *did* think like that. But he could not say these things and had to leave feeling like a criminal.

He stood outside the Empty Vessel wondering about his next move. The inn door opened and a man appeared, wiping his dirty sleeve across his mouth. He grinned at Boltfoot. 'Master taverner keeps fine ale and good wine but makes poor company.'

Boltfoot frowned and said nothing.

'I think you might be wanting something altogether stronger, master cooper. I did hear you say you were a cooper, did I not?'

'I am not looking for work.'

'But you are looking for friends, if I am right. *English* friends.'

'Aye, that's true enough. And who are you?'

'I am someone who may be able to help you in your quest. Why not walk with me a while.'

'I wanted to meet Mr Curl. Holy Trinity Curl.'

'Too hot for him around here these days, master cooper.'

Boltfoot looked at the man. He was a grubby weasel of a fellow, who wore a tight-fitting leather cap around his head, though this could not conceal the fact that his ears were both missing. What felony had he committed to warrant such punishment? His face had a single, circular scar that cut across his forehead just above his eyebrows and just below the rim of the cap, and which curved down both cheeks and disappeared into his beard, near his chin, where, Boltfoot imagined, the ends probably met. Someone must have carved that, for it was not a wound gotten in battle nor by order of the courts. Some enemy did that, slowly and with purpose; a former confederate in crime, perhaps – or someone who wanted repayment of loaned moneys.

'First, what is your name?' he demanded, not budging.

'Call me . . . king – Mr King. For we are all kings in the hereafter, are we not?'

'Very well, Mr King. I will follow you.'

Boltfoot left his horse and set off on foot, eastwards along Aldgate street and out into a dark, narrow maze of the poorest housing. These were shabby wood-frame tenements, often six storeys high and so close packed that they blotted out the daylight and seemed to thicken and pollute the very air itself. In every street and alleyway there seemed to be at least one, sometimes two, properties burnt to the ground. Here was a squalor that the wealthy never saw.

'See that pile of dung over there at the corner of the street? That's where they toss the babes no one wants,' King said. 'They are of no more value than the contents of a midden. God bless the Queen's Majesty . . .'

Small, mud-crusted, barefoot children played with sticks and stones in the manure-strewn streets. They looked ill fed and wore tatters. Draggle-tailed women held out hands for alms, though all hope had gone from their eyes. This constantly stirring cauldron, where the meanest of God's creation teemed and thirsted, stood in cruel contrast to the wealth of the nearby merchant city. Boltfoot, limping and weather-worn, and his ragged companion did not stand out. Only the rare nature of

Boltfoot's weapons – his ornate wheel-lock caliver and cutlass – might set him apart from the common horde in such a place and attract a curious glance.

They came to a door so low that even Boltfoot would have to stoop to enter. He hesitated. Was he about to be robbed or killed? His hand fingered the hilt of his dagger.

'Afraid, master cooper?'

'I know nothing about you.'

'You are well armed. You can afford to trust me. Look at these dark houses. Floor built upon floor like anthills. Five families crowded into each floor. The landlord's men come with clubs and bats to take their wages and bread in rent. Or a tallow candle is dropped and the whole place goes up in flames. This is the way English men and women live and die, while the Dutch strangers wrap their wives in New World furs, fuck their English maidservants and drink Gascon wines. You know this to be true, master cooper, for that is why you came to St Botolph.'

Boltfoot nodded. 'Aye, I wished to see Mr Curl. I had heard his name.'

'Then you have heard well. Enter now. Keep your blades and wheel-lock, though you will not need them as yet.'

The man who called himself King ducked through the doorway and Boltfoot followed him. It was surprisingly clean and well lit after the stink and gloom of the street outside. A series of tallow candles lined the walls and a small window added yet more light.

A thin man in a leather apron was standing at a workbench. He looked up and caught Boltfoot's eye, then threw an inquiring glance in the direction of King.

'I have a new friend.' King took his cap from his head and scratched his hair as though it were a breeding ground for lice. 'He is what you want, I am sure of it.'

'Indeed. Well, that is for me to decide.'

Boltfoot noted that Mr King was nervous and ill at ease in the presence of the thin man, who was working on an arqeubus. It was a rusted weapon that looked so old it might have seen service among the pikes and longbows at Flodden Field.

'He is a journeyman cooper, Mr Warboys. You offered me a groat for every man of skill who would support us.' King picked his pock-marked nose and wiped his finger over his grubby jerkin.

'And if he is one such, you shall have your groat,' Warboys said evenly. Suddenly he struck out at King and caught him on the cheek with the blade of his chisel. 'But for all I know, he may be a spy sent by the Cecils, and now you have told him my name . . .'

King clutched at his bleeding face and winced. 'I am sorry, master. I did not think even the Cecils had come so low as to employ cripples—'

'But he's good enough for me, is that it? Begone, before I chisel your head from your mangy body.' He put down his tool and stepped forward, pushing King towards the doorway. 'Go, Sir Dog, back to your kennel. If this is a friend, you shall have a groat. If not, I shall have your nose and tail.' He kicked his breeches and sent him sprawling out into the street, leaving a splattering of his blood on the ground. The thin man, Warboys, turned to Boltfoot. 'You are well armed, cooper. Are you an assassin or do you chase moles and rats for a living?'

Boltfoot got a clearer look at Warboys. His brow was partly covered by a fringe of black hair, raggedly cut like a poorly finished curtain. His eyes were too wide and too high. His nose was long and dominated the thin face unnaturally. His mouth had a permanent scowl. From a lifetime of being despised because of his club foot, Boltfoot was reluctant to turn against a man for being repulsive to look on, yet he felt there was some malevolence in Warboys's ugliness. His instinct was to turn away and leave, but instead he smiled and spoke equably. 'Neither. I am a ship's cooper and fighting man, now laid up in a land I do not recognise as England. I fought to save my country from invasion by Spain and now see it invaded by others who are no better.'

'So you wish to do something about it? Well, you have come to the right place, cooper. If you are what you seem . . .'

'I had heard of a man named Curl. He sounded like such a one as a man might follow.'

Warboys gave Boltfoot a yet harder look. 'Now where, precisely, would you have heard that name, might I ask?'

'In the dockyards.'

'From whom?'

'Men in the taverns. They spoke it quietly to my ear, for they knew my feelings. They said I might find Mr Curl at St Botolph, preaching. Are *you* Holy Trinity Curl?'

The man laughed. 'No, not me. You may call me Warboys, as that blockhead has already given my name – Mr Warboys. But you shall meet HT. I will take you to him. Before then, master cooper, I would ask you to show me your skills. Help me get this old hagbut sound. The stock is rotted and decayed. If you're a cooper, I am sure you could fashion me a new one. We might need it soon. Very soon. When we are done I shall drink a tankard or two of ale with you. And then I shall set you to work making barrels, for we have a great need of barrels – a great need.'

Chapter 19

ON THE RIDE back to London, Shakespeare stopped his grey mare at a crossroads and seriously wondered about taking another turning. Just ride away from all this. Find a small town somewhere with a grammar school where he could teach; send for Mary, Grace and Andrew. Live quietly and anonymously in a place where none would know them or wish them harm. No Topcliffe, no powdermen, no Cecil.

He supped from his flask and looked at the different directions. All roads ran through fields bordered by hedging. Who was to say one route was better than another? Another traveller, a man of fifty or so with grey hair, a neat beard and no hat, approached and reined in at his side.

'Are you lost, sir?' the man said.

Shakespeare looked at him. Something in his manner of speaking and his firm yet kindly face told him that he was clergy of some ilk, though he was dressed in the unremarkable dark woollen doublet of a clerk or scribe. 'In a manner of speaking,' he replied.

'Then the peace of God be with you. He will show you the way.'

'Will he?'

'I am sure of it. I would ride with you a while and talk, but I can see that you wish to be alone.'

'Thank you, Father.' Shakespeare said the words without thinking. Some instinct had told him this was a priest, a Popish priest. Yet if he was such a one, Shakespeare should arrest him, for in law Popish priests who had come to England from the seminaries of France and Rome were guilty of treason.

The man smiled at him strangely, then kicked on. Shakespeare let him go, unhindered, and watched him as he rode into the distance, becoming a speck and vanishing into the afternoon haze. At last he kicked on, too, in the same direction. He would not turn away from this path; there was unfinished business in London town.

Sir Robert Cecil had a visitor when Shakespeare arrived. Ana Cabral, complete with eye patch – this time over her right eye, not her left – was with him, sitting at the long table, sipping fine wine, dressed most decorously.

'Not a moment too soon, John,' Cecil said brightly, as he was ushered in. 'I understand you have had a wasted journey to Gaynes Park.'

Shakespeare bowed. 'Sir Robert.' He nodded to the Spanish woman in acknowledgement of her presence. Doña Ana . . .'

'We have a deal, John. Clarkson is fetching the first sum. Eight hundred pounds in gold, for the information supplied to you by Doña Ana and the old nurse. I know you agreed a lesser sum, but I have increased it as a gesture of goodwill. There will be a further sum of three thousand pounds in the event that she can discover the whereabouts of the said prince and bring the information to us.'

A thought struck Shakespeare: Perez had known all along what Ana Cabral was about – the furtive meeting with the old nurse at dead of night. It was his way of not losing face by being seen to accept a far lower offer. And Perez was political enough to understand that Cecil would pay a great deal more to discover the greater part of the knowledge – where to find their quarry.

'I am pleased to hear it, Sir Robert.'

'In the meantime I shall go to Greenwich to prepare the way for Don Antonio to be received at court. But it will have to be done quietly. The illusion must be kept that he is a guest of the Earl of Essex and not of England. This is no time to poke our enemies in the eye.'

Cecil's retainer, Clarkson, arrived at the doorway with a pouch of gold on a silver platter. Eight hundred pounds – more than a skilled artisan would earn in a lifetime. He bowed low, then presented it before Sir Robert.

'Well, Doña Ana, this is your reward,' Cecil said, pushing the leather bag across the table to the Spanish courtesan. 'Would you like an escort to take you back to Essex House?'

Cabral, smiling and confident, looked towards Shakespeare. 'I think I need one, do I not, Mr Shakespeare? A weak woman alone with a bag of gold. You have cutpurses aplenty in this city, I am told.'

'I am certain you can look after yourself, but in this case, I would agree it would be wise to have guards accompany you.'

'Handsome young guards who can dance the volta, I hope . . .'

Cecil ignored her. 'That is settled. If you would go with Mr Clarkson, he will arrange an escort of six guards for you.'

Cecil and Shakespeare made much of their farewells and expressions of gratitude to Ana, then the old retainer led her from the room, clutching her weighty purse of gold as though it were welded to her small hands. Cecil's light-hearted mask dropped and his manner stiffened.

'You must find this prince, John. I do not trust that woman, nor her master, to bring us the information we need.'

'Do *you* now believe this prince exists, Sir Robert?'

'I would wish it were not so, but . . .'

'But you fear it might be true.'

Cecil shook his head. 'I do not know. But you believed the old nurse, did you not? What I do know is that he *might* exist – in which case we cannot rest until he is found and discredited. The world must be very clear that he is an impostor, part of a Spanish plot.'

'And the gunpowder conspiracy?'

'I told you, John, Mr Mills is—'

Shakespeare's cold grief suddenly exploded into hot fury. 'Yes, but what exactly has he *done*? What has he achieved except to drive Morley to take his own life, or worse? There are leads I must follow, Sir Robert.'

'And have you told Mr Mills these leads of yours?'

Shakespeare glared at his chief. 'You know I have my doubts about him.'

'I sometimes wonder whether you doubt *me*, John.'

'I do believe—' He was about to say that he believed Cecil too often held back intelligence from him, to his detriment, but he stopped himself. 'Sometimes I do not know what to believe, Sir Robert.'

'Which is one of your great strengths.' Cecil picked up the flask of wine and poured a small goblet for Shakespeare. 'A man who knew exactly what to believe – a man who never asked questions – would be useless to me. As to the powder-man, what of your man Cooper? Have you heard aught from him? I am told he has slipped away alone.'

How typical of Boltfoot to go his own way. But nonetheless, Shakespeare was concerned that he had not heard directly from him by now. If this Mr Sarjent had discovered the source of the powder, why had Boltfoot not stayed – or returned to Dowgate with news? He would trust Boltfoot's judgement against any man's. And yet, he was worried, for Boltfoot was not immortal. No man or woman was, as he knew too well.

Topcliffe was at Dowgate when Shakespeare returned home. He was alone, lounging against the door, smoking his pipe, leaning on his blackthorn and perusing a broadsheet.

Shakespeare drew his sword.

Topcliffe took the smoking pipe from his mouth and held it at arm's length. 'Hold fast, Shakespeare, I know of your loss. I am not here to gloat.'

'Get out of my sight.'

'I'm not here for you. I want your maggot of a brother.'

'Go now or I swear by God that I will run you through where you stand.'

'I mean him no harm, though he deserves it. Tell him I need him to help me resolve the Marlowe killing. A little cooperation with me could save him much misery.'

'What do you care about Marlowe's killer, Topcliffe?'

'More than most. I told you – we were as one in our dislike for the filthy strangers corrupting this city.' He tossed his white head in the direction of the Sluytermans' house and beat his cane against his palm.

'What has this to do with my brother?'

'Did he not know Marlowe better than most? He must have some idea who was behind this foul deed. Would he not wish to help Uncle Richard send his friend's killer to Paddington Green with a hempen neckerchief?'

'I do not believe a word you say, Topcliffe. You care not a turd about any man's death, unless you are drawing the blood yourself. Why would a man such as you inquire into Kit Marlowe's murder?'

Topcliffe suddenly laughed. 'Well, *you* are doing nothing to solve it, are you, Shakespeare?'

This was true and it still rankled, for Shakespeare was certain it was murder, not self-defence.

'Where has your wet-arsed brother gone so suddenly? Taken his girl-boy players touring the towns of England, has he? Or perhaps he cowers and shivers in Warwickshire with his Papist father. When you see him, tell him I shall find him soon enough . . . and give him the reward he deserves.'

Shakespeare thrust his sword forward so that its point touched Topcliffe's doublet at the heart. 'If I knew the whereabouts of my brother – or any other honest man – do you think I would tell you?'

Topcliffe stood his ground and met Shakespeare's gaze full on. Their eyes locked for two or three seconds, then Topcliffe turned aside and nonchalantly tossed the broadsheet on to the dust at his feet.

'As you will, you Papist-grovelling milksop. You can put your little sword up. But think on this: stranger or player – one of them killed Marlowe. Nothing else makes sense.' He kicked the sheet of printed paper towards Shakespeare. It blew up in the breeze, then floated down to the ground. 'I had thought you might wish to see that.' With another laugh, the grizzled rackmaster strolled off, pipe in his mouth, fumes billowing behind him.

Shakespeare watched him go, the hilt of his sword tight gripped in his hand. He looked down and noticed he was shaking with rage. He realised then that if Topcliffe had not walked away, he *would* have killed him. At the corner of the street, Topcliffe untethered his horse and climbed up into the saddle. He looked back and called out. 'Whoever did for your grubby Romish dogwife saved me a job. One down . . . you next.' He spat into the dust, dug his spurs into the horse's flanks and rode away hard.

Shakespeare thrust his sword back into its scabbard and

stepped forward towards his door. It was immediately opened by Jane, who must have been watching the exchange from a window. Something made him turn back and pick up the broadsheet that Topcliffe had brought. It was yet another edition of *The London Informer*. He glanced at it, and was about to throw it back down when the words writ across the top stopped him dead. Half in, half out the doorway, he stood and read it with horror and incomprehension. How could Walstan Glebe possibly have garnered this piece of intelligence?

He read it twice, three times. Under the heading 'Pretender to the Thrones of England and Scotland' the broadsheet proceeded to relate the story that the old nun had told him at Gaynes Park – in almost every detail. It ended:

Good readers, I am now in a position to tell you that this selfsame princeling is to be found here in the city of London, harboured and comforted by Popish traitors and conspirators, waiting to snatch the thrones of England and Scotland. We trust that he will be discovered and despatched without delay, for no Spanish pretender must ever be allowed to lay claim to the crown of England.

After the third reading, Shakespeare tucked the broadsheet into his doublet, strode from the house, threw a saddle across the back of the grey mare without waiting for the groom's assistance, then wheeled her out from the stable-yard and rode at a reckless canter through the streets, knocking water sellers, traders and goodwives out of his way. This sheet of paper changed everything. He had to consult Cecil without delay. He had been used by Ana Cabral, perhaps by Perez too. Gold had never been the main issue here; they had simply wanted the information out in the public domain, for how could a man claim a throne if no one had ever heard of him? These were the first shots in a campaign to have their prince recognised by the world as the heir to King James VI of Scotland and to Queen Elizabeth of England.

Secondly, the connection with Walstan Glebe and his *London Informer* raised another possibility, one that he had not even considered until now. How did Glebe have knowledge of both the gunpowder campaign and the supposed lost prince, unless there was some connection? Both conspiracies shared one common intention: the destabilising of the realm. And who would wish that but Spain? There was no time to lose. He had to bring in Glebe and discover all he knew. He was the key to everything.

'It has been too long,' Ana Cabral said, running a finger sensuously down the man's hairless chest to his bare abdomen and moving her open mouth closer to him as she did so. 'I have missed you.'

The man leant forward and kissed the nape of her neck, then laughed. 'Are you addressing me or my prick, señorita?'

'Both of you, sir. I like you both, for between you, you satisfy me body and soul.' She lay back on the sheets, stretched out, abandoned to the erotic moment of warm bodies and cool sheets.

He swung his legs away from her and sat on the edge of the bed. 'Reciprocated. But we have things to talk on. The ship is ready. She stands moored in a remote inlet of the Thames. With dark humour she has been christened the *Sieve* by my Scots friends, but I promise you she is seaworthy enough for any passage. The building of the machine is well under way.'

'When will she be ready?'

'The work is arduous and must be carried out discreetly. A shepherd boy or a fisherman might note something, so great stealth is necessary – and that slows us.'

'Within two days?'

'I hope – yes, I am sure. Though much still depends upon the clocksmith. His device must be perfect.'

Ana lay back on the warm linen, all rumpled and aromatic from their energetic cavortings. 'Can that be a little earlier?'

The man turned her way and clasped his mouth to her young breast. He felt himself stirring once more. He did not really have time for this, but some things were more important than war and religion, and Ana Cabral's remarkable body was one of them.

She pushed his face away. 'Speak to me, sir.' She beat his chest in a sudden squall of fury.

'Maybe two days, more likely three . . . I am not certain. There is much heavy lifting, without benefit of cranes or derricks. We are short of trustworthy men.'

'And the powder? Do you have *all* the powder?'

'It is safely stored and ready. Twelve thousand pounds of finest corned English gunpowder.'

As quickly as her storm rose, it subsided. Ana circled her arms around him and resumed her ministrations. 'Make it twenty. Our masters in Madrid have recalculated. They now say twenty thousand pounds. Enough to make the loudest roar the world has ever known. Enough to make God himself wish he could make thunder as great. Do you understand, Mr Laveroke?'

'Yes, I understand, Doña Ana.'

'Good, then you shall be well paid, for little Robertus Diabolus has provided me with gold. But you must keep your useful Scottish friends about their business. More powder, more powder, more powder.'

Chapter 20

'Who is behind this?' Cecil demanded, slamming the broadsheet down on the table.

Shakespeare had never seen Sir Robert so agitated. 'A villain named Walstan Glebe,' he said. 'I believe I know a way to him.'

'Well, bring him in. Why is such a man at large to disseminate this? If word of this reaches the Queen, her fury will know no bounds. Give your information to Mr Mills.'

'No. I want Glebe alive . . .'

Mills went white. 'Sir Robert, this is a calumny!'

'Morley died under your watch, Frank,' Shakespeare put in. 'I cannot risk another such death.'

'He killed himself! It was none of my doing.'

'Indeed, yet you did not ensure his safety. Nor did you discover the knowledge he would have imparted to me.'

Mills turned to Cecil. 'Sir Robert, this is intolerable—'

Cecil's small, feminine hand rose. 'Stop this. We do not have time for such brabbling. You will work together, not against each other. Do you understand me? God's wounds, we have enough to deal with. What I say is this – if Glebe can print news of gunpowder and a Scots prince, then we are dealing with a conspiracy monstrous in scope and compass. It does not take a great wit to imagine that the powder is the means by which they would put their princeling on the throne of England – or Scotland – or both. Now, Mr Shakespeare, find this Glebe and bring him to Newgate, where we shall question him. If need be, with the rack.'

Shakespeare nodded, his jaw set grimly.

'Whatever your qualms, Mr Shakespeare. Do you understand me?'

Shakespeare looked Cecil in the eye, but said nothing. Cecil turned away and addressed Mills.

'Frank, you will find this clockmaker. If need be, you will bring every clockmaker in London to the Tower. That, surely, cannot be beyond your wit.'

'It is not so simple, Sir Rob—'

'Then make it simple. And John –' he turned back to Shakespeare – 'find out where your man Cooper is and what he has discovered. In the meantime, we shall await word from Perez and his diabolical crew of intrigants. But we shall not wait long. I will have the whereabouts of the pretender prince torn from his mouth. If necessary, along with his tongue . . .'

At times, Beth Evans wondered where life might have taken her had she not broken up with John Shakespeare. Could there have been more to their innocent summer frolic? Might he have married her and given her a family and a home, in place of barrenness and whoredom? Inevitably, she shook her head and smiled wanly to herself, for the answer, always, was no. They would have ended up hating each other. With babes at her feet, he would have resented her for thwarting his ambition.

She laughed at her own musings. The truth was he had not even recognised her. And when he had failed to turn up for their planned meeting to seek out Glebe, he had not even sent word.

Naked, her long fair hair hanging loose, she washed herself, vigorously, squatting over a bowl of cold water with a soap ball in one hand. Her client, an archdeacon from St Paul's, dressed slowly beside the chamber window, gazing out at a grey summer's day. She wished he would hurry up and leave, for he had done his business and she had his shillings. She wanted to erase every trace of him from this room and from her body. Beth could be as accommodating as the next whore – and many men sought her out specially, for the years had treated her well – but when it was done, it was done. She could not bear the ones who wanted to linger and talk, perhaps to assuage their guilt or shame, as though they were engaged in innocent discourse at home with their goodwife.

There was a discreet double knock at the door. It was code from her maid. The hour was up and another client was waiting. If no client was waiting, there would be no knock and she could tarry and dally with the man as long as she wished.

Beth smiled at the archdeacon. 'Duty calls, venerable sir.'

The clergyman caught her eye and nodded gravely. 'Of course, my dear, I was in a dream. For a moment there I quite forgot that you were a working girl.'

'Will I see you next week?'

'Indeed, God willing.'

Still naked, she hustled him out of the chamber as best she could without physically pushing him, smiling inside at the way he invoked the will of God to assist him in his wanton perambulations. As he disappeared down the stairway, Beth's maid appeared. 'You have a visitor, Beth.'

'Who is it this time?'

'Not a client. Your friend Mr Shakespeare.'

Her body stirred like it had once as a girl. She grinned broadly at the maid. 'Then you had better help me dress myself.'

'It is possible he might prefer you as you are, mistress.'

'Oh I think not. No, indeed, I am sure he would not.'

Shakespeare was taut with impatience, waiting in the hall below the gallery. His mind was elsewhere. Cecil had spoken of a monstrous conspiracy – gunpowder to blow a usurper on to the throne – but other thoughts crowded in, too: what was Topcliffe's interest in his brother? Had Will been right in thinking the death of Marlowe was in some way connected to a purge against the theatre world? And was that death really not linked to the events at the Dutch church and in the Dutch market?

He looked up at the tapestry depicting Black Lucy without emotion or wonder. The last time he had been to this whore-house, he had threatened without a great deal of conviction to have all its occupants hauled off to prison. Now, if he did not get an immediate response to his questioning, he was minded to do just that.

At last Beth arrived. He nodded to her stiffly.

'Mistress Evans,' he said. 'I must now have the whereabouts of Walstan Glebe.'

'John, what happened to you? You did not come . . .'

'There were other matters. Now I must get to Glebe.'

'And I shall be happy to take you, for he paid me only half the agreed fee when last I was sent to him.'

Shakespeare ignored her. 'Is your mistress here . . . Mistress Lucy?'

'She is. But John, I must tell you, you look in dire need of rest and food. Your visage, your attire – it is as though you have not eaten nor slept in a week. Forgive me for speaking plain.'

'My appearance is of no consequence. I have ridden hard. Be pleased to fetch Mistress Lucy, and then, within the hour, we must depart to find Glebe. I take it you still know where he is?'

'Yes.' Beth was shaken. This man was in a bad way. She noticed that he was heavily armed: two wheel-lock pistols in his belt, as well as his sword and poniard. 'Please, will you first tarry awhile and partake of victuals. Some meats and wine . . .'

'There is no time. Just do as I say, mistress – Beth.'

'As you will, John. Follow me.'

She took him to the withdrawing room, a chamber of intimate comfort with lustrous drapes, deep cushions, sumptuous settles and tapestries, all finished with red and gold threads. 'Wait here, John. If she is with a client, I will bring her away and return in a few minutes.'

A maid brought him a goblet of sweet wine and he downed it in one gulp. Beth reappeared two minutes later. 'Lucy will be here presently.'

Shakespeare nodded curtly in acknowledgement.

Her eyes went again to the wheel-locks adorning his waist. 'Are you expecting to need those?'

'He gave me the slip once before. It won't happen again. Where is he?'

'Within the city wall by Aldersgate. St Anne's Lane. No more than a mile. I will take you to the very house. You may ride and I will walk at your side.'

'And you are certain he will be there?'

'If not, we will find another way to him. I will not let you down, John.'

Lucy appeared at the doorway. Last time she had worn a gown of gold, now she was in an array of cream linens, which served all the more to accentuate the black sheen of her skin. She held herself erect and proud, her shoulders back. Yet today there was a difference. She was less at ease. She did not smile.

'Mr Shakespeare,' she said, a note of surprise and some disquiet in her voice.

Shakespeare offered no greeting. 'I am going with Beth Evans to find Glebe. Before I go, I wish to talk with you. It is important for you to realise, mistress, quite how precarious is your position, given your refusal to tell me the whereabouts of Glebe. I must tell you that I have already shown the greatest forbearance towards this house. I could have had pursuivants here to tear the place apart and wrench the information from your mouth by force, and the Privy Council would have thanked me for it. I say that to you now not as a threat but as a warning; nothing must come between me and Glebe. The stakes are raised in this game.'

Lucy lowered her eyes. 'I understand.'

'Do you?'

'I do, sir. I will not hinder you in any way. I know about the incident in the Dutch Market . . .'

Shakespeare cut her short. 'You will not talk of that. I have some questions regarding your person. Answer me straight, do not dissemble and do not ask me why I wish to know these things.'

'Very well.'

'Which country are you from?'

If she was puzzled by the nature of the question, she did not show it. 'Africa. My father was an Ethiop, but my brothers and I were taken slave by Mussalman corsairs. They sold me to a great lord of France. I do not know what became of my two brothers.'

'Who was this French lord?'

'The son of Jean de la Fin, Seigneur de Beauvoir-la-Nocle, whom you know as Henri of France's ambassador to the court of Elizabeth.'

'His son is the Vidame de Chartres. Are you saying you were his slave?'

'That is so. Did you not know this?'

'Mistress Lucy, just answer my questions. What were you to him as a slave? A housemaid, a concubine – what?'

'You may ask him that yourself, Mr Shakespeare, for is he not now here in England?'

Shakespeare ignored the question. 'How did you come to England?'

Lucy's eyes shone in the candlelight. 'Yet more corsairs! This time under the English flag. One of Captain Hawkins's fine ships-of-war took me while I was en route to Harfleur. I think the sailors were beguiled by my beauty and brought me to England and freedom rather than sell me on to the Spanish planters in the Indies. So now I am a free Englishwoman and happy to be of service to this proud nation.'

Shakespeare looked at her with a dubious, inquiring eye. 'You do not have slavery here, I believe. I am told that three hundred years of serfdom left a bitter taste and that you do not allow it.'

'But you are not English, and you must know that the Queen believes there are too many men and women of your hue here. She has ordered that Moors and Ethiops be cast out. Do you know anywhere – any friends – with whom you might stay awhile? For your safety.'

Lucy stood to her full height and tilted up her chin. 'I understand what you are saying, sir, but take a look at my face. Do you think it possible to hide such a face anywhere in this land?' She pursed her generous lips, almost in a kiss. She looked to Beth Evans, then back at Shakespeare. 'I think I know enough men of power to protect me.'

'Do you, mistress? Are you not afraid?'

Lucy turned again to Beth. 'What do you say, Beth?'

'I'd take you over a tiger any day, Luce.'

*

As he rode southwards and eastwards towards Aldersgate, thoughts of Catherine intruded. Dark, unholy visions. He saw her bloody remains all dressed in a green velvet gown. He saw her black hair adorning a white-boned, smiling skull, from which stared two piercing blue eyes.

She had not been a saint, and nor had he. Their marriage, more than five years long, had been difficult. She had been stubborn, unyielding in her Papism. At times, in truth, he had resented her for wrecking his career with Walsingham. He might have been a minister of the Crown by now. Many another man would have beaten her for her intransigence, her disobedience and her sullen moods.

He felt Beth Evans's arms around his waist. Sweet, easy Beth. She had laughed the summer long when they were both sixteen in the year '75. She laughed without spite at his seriousness; laughed lewdly when they saw a bull with an enormous prick mount a cow in a field; laughed mockingly when he panicked that he would not get her home before dark in the long, light evenings; laughed with incredulity at his refusal to drink too much strong cider; laughed tenderly at his clumsy moves towards kissing her.

But Catherine, so very different, was the one he loved. In the good times, of which there were many, they soared together. When they talked over a platter of meat and when they drank wine together, they were the best of argumentative friends. It was a love like no other, but it was not one he would have chosen for peace of mind; it had hit him with the force of a flood tide or tempest and had carried him along with it. Like a ship at sea, all he could do was run with the storm. This love had immersed him in its raging passions and thrown him in its wild wind, had done with him what it willed. It was untamed, raw and delirious in its uncontrollable beauty. That was Catherine Shakespeare. He could never have loved Beth like that.

At the city gate, a large draywagon had lost a wheel and collapsed, spilling its load of seasoned building timbers. Even those on foot struggled to get through the blocked thoroughfare. Dozens of carts and wains were backed up for almost a mile to the north along broad Aldersgate Steet, and to the other side, too, deep into the narrow alleyways of the city. Shakespeare was having none of it. He rode on past the crowds and horses, pushing any protesters aside with his cry of 'Queen's business, make way!' At the gate, he and Beth dismounted and they walked the horse across the great oak logs, roundly cursed by the workmen who were trying to hoist them away.

'Down here,' Beth said when they were clear at last. 'This alley on the left.'

They tethered the horse outside a modest and anonymous wood-frame house, the middle of a terrace of three, with jettied floors jutting out exaggeratedly into the dark little street.

Quickly, he loaded and primed both wheel-lock pistols and looped a binding cord around his chest. 'Wait here,' he said to Beth. 'If I'm not out in ten minutes, fetch the constable.'

She watched him go. Just before they left, Lucy had told her that John's wife was dead, killed by the explosion of gunpowder in the Dutch market. She had gone cold with shock. 'Be careful with your friend,' Lucy had said. 'He will want vengeance. Do not get in his way.'

Walstan Glebe pulled the last copy of his new broadsheet from the press and held it up, waving it to help dry the ink. In his mouth he had a pipe of tobacco, which he sucked on like a babe at the teat.

He couldn't keep up with the news. *The London Informer* was selling like saffron cakes on a sunny day at Bartholomew

Fair. First the death of Marlowe, followed almost immediately by the explosion outside the Dutch church. Then this scarce believable story of the secret child of the Scots devil, Mary (even if he didn't quite believe it, the story was one everyone wanted to read). He could hardly acquire enough paper to print the copies he could sell, and the type sorts were wearing so thin that many words were becoming illegible. The press itself had seen better days and seemed unlikely to last the month out. But such problems could soon be put behind him if gold kept filling his coffers the way it did. Soon he would have enough to buy a permanent press, with a new set of type, and secure regular premises. This was the future; London could never get too much news.

The door opened and he turned towards it expecting his girl, Bella, back with the ale and pie he had sent her to fetch. Instead, he saw the tall figure of John Shakespeare, with two wheel-locks pointing straight at him.

Walstan Glebe stood there, as if glued to the floor, a damp sheet of paper in his hand. Shakespeare could see the words across the top of the broadsheet: *Five are blasted to horrible death at Dutch market.* Then the next line: *Her Majesty outraged at strangers' powder plot.*

'Mr Shakespeare—'

'Still lying, Glebe?'

As if suddenly realising what he was holding, Glebe turned the broadsheet and looked at the headlines. He removed the pipe from his mouth. 'This is all true, Mr Shakespeare. I swear it. And my press is licensed.'

Shakespeare gazed past him towards the rickety press, upright against the wall. Nearby was a box of type sorts and piles of broadsheets ready for distribution. How *did* Glebe continually manage to evade the law and find gold enough to replace the presses which the Stationers' Company made it their business to destroy?

'Licensed? If that press is licensed, then I'm the Pope. You've never had a licence in your miserable life, Glebe.' Bitterly, he thought back to the words he had seen printed in Glebe's rag after the church blast. 'Did enough dogs die for your liking this time?'

'Mr Shakespeare, please, I was devastated to hear of your sad loss.'

'Get down flat on the ground, with your hands behind your back. One wrong move and I will discharge both pistols at you.'

'How did you find me?'

Shakespeare said nothing, but moved closer with the pistols.

'Some putrid mangy-arsed whore, I'll wager.'

'Down!'

Glebe let go the sheet of paper and it fluttered to the floor. Slowly, he dropped to his knees, his eyes all the while fixed on Shakespeare's guns.

Shakespeare stuck one of the wheel-locks in his belt and shook the coiled cord from his shoulder. The door creaked. He half turned. A dark-haired girl stood open-mouthed in the doorway with a blackjack of ale and a gold-crusted pie.

It was all the distraction Glebe needed. There was unlikely to be a second chance. He flung himself forward at Shakespeare's legs, knocking him off-balance.

Shakespeare stumbled backwards but maintained his footing. Glebe was faster and launched himself past the girl and through the doorway. The jug fell from her hands, spewing ale across the sawdust-strewn floor. She stood there, mouth agape, pie in hand, as Shakespeare lunged forward after the slippery Glebe, pushing her aside and falling headlong into the street. Glebe was three or four yards ahead of him, running . . .

and then sprawling. Beth Evans had extended her leg and tripped him, sending him hurtling to the ground.

Shakespeare was on his back in an instant, a wheel-lock to his head. He handed the other wheel-lock to Beth, then took the length of cord from his shoulder and tied Glebe's hands tight behind his back.

The thick thatch of hair atop Glebe's head was grey now, but he still wore it in a long fringe to cover the *L* for *Liar* branded on to his forehead by the courts for fraudulently selling odes written by other poets as if they were his own work. Shakespeare wrenched back his hair and leant down to speak in his ear. 'We'll remove your nose this time, Glebe. Try growing your hair to cover that little hole.'

Glebe grunted with the pain of his fall and the wrenching of his head in Shakespeare's powerful fist.

'Get up. I am taking you to the Tower and I promise you will tell me everything I wish to know.'

At last Glebe found his voice. 'You cannot do this. My press is licensed. I have powerful patrons.'

'Well, we'll find out. In Little Ease . . .'

Chapter 21

IN THE CELL known as Little Ease, a man could neither lay his body down fully, nor stand erect. The floor was four foot by four foot and it was no more than four foot in height, like a dice, so that a man of normal height had no room to move, nor rest. He could crouch like a cat or he could kneel or sit against the wall, but he could not stretch his aching limbs or ease the pain in his cruelly bent back by arching it. The very thought of the wretched hole was enough to strike terror and panic into the stoutest heart. The breath came short, the gasping wails of despair rose within the back of the throat. It was a place of madness, a place that would have you pleading for a quick death. After a few days in Little Ease, a man with the strongest of spirits would be fit for nothing but a Bedlam cell or the scaffold.

In his time, Walstan Glebe had suffered the sting of the branding iron and the smell of his own roasting flesh. He had been shackled to the stinking floor of Newgate with scarce enough food to live. He had been whipped for the public's entertainment at Bridewell and had been threatened with the noose on several occasions. Yet none of those memories matched his fear of Little Ease.

'Mr Shakespeare, I beg you, not that,' he whimpered. 'I have done nothing to warrant such punishment.'

It was not long since Shakespeare had dragged Christopher

Morley through the streets towards the Counter prison in Wood Street on a leash linked to his stirrup. It had not been the safest method of taking in a felon, for who could tell when a confederate might dash forward with a razor to slash the cord and free the prisoner. He could take no such chances with Glebe. Instead, he strapped him over the back of his grey mare, his wrists and ankles tied tight by a length of rope stretched under the animal's belly.

Shakespeare turned to Beth Evans. 'Thank you,' he said. 'Take care in returning to the . . .' He stopped, not sure what to say.

Beth laughed as she used to. 'Don't worry about my sensitivities, John. I know what I am – and I am not ashamed.'

'No, of course not.'

Suddenly her smile dissolved. 'I can only imagine your grief. I am desperately sorry for what has happened. I know you loved her.'

He nodded stiffly and turned away, then shook the reins.

The horse walked with the swaggering gait of the fine mare she was. Her powerful hind quarters swayed with every step along the difficult city roads, sometimes cobbled, sometimes mere dirt and potholes. Each step jolted Glebe, crushing his lungs and turning his belly to mush.

'Stop a while for pity's sake. You will shake me to death or make me shit my breeches. I need drink!'

'Do you think anyone cares about your thirst or even your life, Glebe? Do you think Her Majesty is amused by your pernicious little story about the succession and your involvement in the gunpowder conspiracy? Death awaits you.'

'None of it was me! I beg you to listen.'

Glebe was having trouble talking. The taut straps and jogging of the beast continually winded him and loosened his bowels.

Shakespeare stopped the horse. 'So who was it?'

Glebe said nothing for a few moments. Shakespeare shook the rein and the mare walked on.

'Stop. Stop!'

Shakespeare halted again. He looked at the miserable bundle across the back of his horse. Glebe was dressed in good clothes. A well-made brown doublet and breeches, a cambric falling band around his neck. But he was a villainous, untrustworthy creature who scratched a living out of other men's misfortunes. He had crossed Shakespeare's path before and he had not liked him then. He could not bring himself even to read what the worm had written about the blast that killed Catherine. He knew it would dredge up her Papist past and his own failings.

'I will give you a name.'

Shakespeare said nothing.

'Mr Shakespeare, you must let me down from here. I beg you, not the Tower. Not Little Ease. I will tell you everything you wish to know. God's death, I could kill that whore-bitch Beth Evans.' He began coughing uncontrollably.

Shakespeare looked at him in silence.

'Give me at least a chance,' Glebe said when the coughing fit subsided.

'Why?'

'Because I can give you what you want.'

'You will give me what I want in Little Ease, and I will trust your answers more when you are there.'

'I pledge it, by all that is holy. I swear on my life and my mother's soul.'

'Holy? I have heard such words from you before, Glebe. They were as ash and aloes in your mouth.'

They were near Leadenhall, a few minutes' walk from the Tower. Around them, the world passed in a noisy clattering of hooves, creaking of wagons and calling of wares. No one paid them heed. Another felon taken in to face justice – who should care about that?

'Very well. His name is Laveroke. Luke Laveroke.'

'The name means nothing. I have not heard of him. Tell me more.'

'Do you pledge to free me? I have already told you enough to cost my life.'

'Free you? You still fancy yourself the jester, I see.'

'Anywhere but the Tower and I will talk.'

Shakespeare hesitated a few moments, then slapped the mare into a slow walk once more. He leant over to Glebe and whispered in his ear. 'Very well. I have just the hole for you. But if for one moment I do not feel you are cooperating – if I feel you are holding anything back from me – think on this: it will be but a short hurdle ride to Little Ease . . .'

Boltfoot did not fear for his own life, yet he was aware enough to know that he was in a perilous place. Every so often another man, or a pair of men, came into the workshop to converse with Warboys. Their voices and language were guarded and Boltfoot found it difficult to follow what they said. They spoke of deliveries, trainbands and, most confusingly of all, a sieve. But they spoke in low voices and their conversations seemed deliberately to be couched in terms that made their meaning indecipherable. Boltfoot affected to pay them no heed and carried on with his work, chiselling and planing with precision. Warboys, meanwhile, drank pint after pint of strong ale.

On several occasions, men came from other parts of the house and simply nodded in acknowledgement on their way through, or stood awhile, watching, before retreating into the depths of the tenement.

At last Boltfoot was finished and stood back from the workbench. Warboys put down his jar of strong ale and held up the old arquebus in the slanting light from the window. His hands were surprisingly steady, given the amount he had drunk. 'A fair piece of work that, Mr Cooper. A serviceable stock you have crafted there. We do, indeed, need a man like you.'

'Good. That is what I desire. I will help in any wise I can.'

'*Any* wise, Mr Cooper? Do you have no reservations?'

'None.'

'That is good. Faint-hearts do not fare well with us. What do you believe?'

Boltfoot frowned, not comprehending the nature of the question.

'Do you believe in one God? Do you believe in the devil? Do you believe the dead will rise when called on?'

'No, not necromancy, though I had thought I saw things – spirits – in storms at sea. And yes, of course I believe in God.'

'Of course. What man would not . . .' Warboys's nostrils dilated and he spoke with such scorn that Boltfoot gained a clear impression that this man did *not* believe in God. 'And yet, Mr Cooper, though I know that there are many dark things man does not know or understand, I also know that he needs solid things in the here and now – weapons of war. Hagbuts and halberds.'

'What would you have me do?'

'You will find out soon enough, Mr Cooper. Barrels, certainly, but there are other requirements, too . . . Have patience.'

'First, I must attend to certain matters. I will leave you now and be back here soon after dawn.'

Warboys's laugh came from the depths of his throat and would have intimidated a lesser man. There was humour in it, but only the humour of a cat that has a rat with which to amuse itself.

Boltfoot's whole body stiffened. He looked at his cutlass and caliver in the corner of the workroom, on the floor against the wall; they were useless to him in these circumstances. 'I have things to organise, a horse to see fed and stabled.' More than anything, he had to get word to Master Shakespeare.

'You are not going anywhere. You are one of us now, an apostle of the Free English Trainband. We must stay together. You may be a volunteer, Mr Cooper, but I must advise you to consider yourself one of us. Once a man is with us, there is only one way for him to leave.'

There was no point in arguing. He could not appear reluctant. 'I have fought for England before, Mr Warboys, and I will happily venture my life again. But what of my horse? I think he deserves his feed and a stable for the night.'

'Where is he?'

'By St Botolph. If I see to him now, I could be back within an hour or two.'

Warboys clapped him on the back. 'Don't worry, Mr Cooper. We'll see to the nag on our way.'

'Where are we going?'

'You will find out all you need. Now pick up your fine weapons, and let us be gone. Men are waiting for us, each and every one of them with a common complaint – their livelihoods have been stolen from them and they and their families have been left to starve.'

'God's blood, John, this is a terrible pass,' Henbird said.

Shakespeare pushed Glebe down roughly on to a settle. 'I wish you to keep this miserable churl safe, Nicholas. Question him with me, then lock him away. You have a cellar?'

'Beneath a concealed trapdoor. It'll hold this fellow safe enough. And I have information for you.'

'Hold it until we have dispensed with Glebe.'

They were in Nicholas Henbird's pleasant solar room. The sky was dull, but even on such a day, light flooded in through large windows. Glebe, his arms bound behind his back, sat on a settle by a window. He looked as disconsolate as the sky.

Shakespeare glared at Glebe with contempt, then turned back to Henbird. 'He has mentioned a name. Laveroke. Have you heard of him, Nick?'

Henbird shook his head. 'No.'

'Perhaps he is an invention of Glebe's gong-house mind.'

'I swear it, Mr Shakespeare. He is all too real, though I wish I had never met him.'

'Tell us all you know. Who is this man, where did you meet, why is he using your broadsheet?'

'I was approached by him,' Glebe said in a quavering voice. 'In a tavern.'

'Which tavern?'

'The Swan in Gray's Inn Road. I go there often, to listen to the lawyers talk, to garner what news I may. This man, this Laveroke, approached me and asked if I would publish a goodly tale. He said he knew of me from friends. He told me he could give me stories that would sell the *Informer* by the wagonload. Not only that, he said, but he would pay me two pounds in gold for each story I published. How could I refuse such an offer, Mr Shakespeare?'

'So you became *Tamburlaine's Apostle*?'

'No, that was Laveroke. He was the author of the stories: he put that name at the end. And they were good stories, Mr Shakespeare, the news the people wished to read.'

Henbird stood still by his great desk. 'You must have realised you were delving into treacherous waters, Mr Glebe.'

Glebe nodded. 'I was concerned, Mr Henbird, indeed I was. But which publisher would not want such tales? And to be paid gold as well . . .'

'You should have gone straightway to the Privy Council or, at the very least, to Stationers' Hall, and you know it, Glebe,'

Shakespeare said. 'Tell me of this Laveroke. What manner of man is he?'

Glebe sat in sullen resignation. 'What are you going to do with me, Mr Shakespeare?'

'That very much depends on you, Glebe. You have saved yourself from Little Ease thus far. But Sir Robert Cecil wishes you consigned to Newgate, and from there to Tyburn. You would do well to convince me otherwise.'

Glebe sighed heavily. 'In truth, Mr Shakespeare, I thought Laveroke gentry, perhaps even nobility. He had an air about him, sir, an air . . .'

'Explain.'

'I thought him used to command. He was well attired in fine doublet. He had a jewelled dagger at his waist and, though not fat, he looked prosperous.'

'After this first meeting at The Swan, where did you talk? Did he bring the stories to you at the house near Aldersgate?'

'No. There is a tavern where I usually take my evening repast, The Mitre. He would come to me there. I had no idea when he would come. He would arrive with the story written in what I took to be his hand and with two pounds in gold.'

'What was his voice?'

'I cannot say. I could not identify it.'

'Spanish? French? Dutch? English?'

'He spoke perfect English, sir, but beyond that I cannot tell you true what he was, whether of Bristol or Norwich or any other place in this land.'

'Was he bearded?'

'Indeed. A spade beard, I would say, neat and well trimmed, as if he had been attended by a good East Cheap barber. His face was unmarked. He was a fetching man with hair that fell to his shoulder. I noted a heavy gold band on his forefinger and pearls studding the front of his doublet.'

'Where can I find him?'

Glebe lowered his eyes, hunching down into his shoulders. He did not look up. His voice was a mumble, but Shakespeare's hearing was acute. 'I do not know. I never knew. I have never seen him before and wish never to see him again, for it is meeting him that has brought me to this ugly pass.'

'Oh no, Glebe. There is more than that. You have wit enough to know the power of the words you have published. You know well what the Council thinks of such talk. And when it is written, it is a thousand times worse, for it infects others. You know this. Whatever else you are, you are no simpleton.'

Glebe stayed silent.

'Have you heard of one Christopher Morley?'

Glebe shook his head.

'He stayed silent. He is now dead, with a cord wound tight about his neck. That is the price of silence. And Marlowe? Did you know Kit Marlowe or Frizer or Poley or Skeres?'

Glebe hesitated.

'Answer me or be damned to the comfort of Little Ease, Glebe.'

'I have met Poley and Frizer, sir. Not Skeres, I never met him, but Poley and Frizer. They are coney hunters, Mr Shakespeare. They are the sort of men I know. I could not avoid meeting them from time to time . . .'

'Were they involved in the *Tamburlaine's Apostle* story?'

'Not that I know of, sir. That was all Laveroke.'

'You said he handed you the papers written in his own hand. Where are these papers now?'

'Destroyed, Mr Shakespeare. Burnt in the hearth.'

'As you are like to be, Glebe.' Shakespeare had no time to waste. He had to discover this Laveroke.

'Let us consign him to your cellar, Nick. I trust it is dank and dark.'

'Indeed it is, John.'

'Say nothing of this, Nick,' Shakespeare said when they returned to the solar without Glebe. 'I fear there are those that would come after him, for I am not certain Morley took his own life. Keep him alive and keep questioning him. He may know more.'

'About the gunpowder blasts?'

'That and the supposed prince of Scots. There is no difference. Can it be mere coincidence that one man feeds such stories to Glebe?'

'No, it cannot be mere coincidence.' Henbird poured two cups of brandy and handed one to Shakespeare. 'I have some news for you, John.'

'The servant I asked you about, Oliver Kettle? I know he has left the Sluyterman house.'

Henbird settled his corpulent, well-attired frame back into his thronelike chair. 'I had him followed. And where do you think he went? All the way to the Guildhall for the Lord Mayor's banquet, where he served as a waiter.'

'Tell me more, Nick.'

'They take on day staff for the big banquets. Many of those employed on such nights have positions elsewhere in the homes of the city merchants. Your Oliver Kettle was one of those.'

'But now he is missing.'

'Wait, there is more to the story. On the night of the banquet, my man watched Kettle as closely as he could. As you can well imagine, this was not easy, for the watcher was neither a guest, nor a serving man. He is, though, a close acquaintance of the Common Sergeant at the Guildhall and so he enlisted his aid.'

'In return for a turkey cock or two?'

'Or three or four, John. The sergeant is a stout fellow. He and my man were able to observe the evening's proceedings and keep a discreet watch on Kettle. And they discovered something of great interest. Kettle was making a collection. Somewhere between the suckling pig and the swan hearts with syrup of pears, they saw him huddled with a merchant on his way to the house of easement. And then, over the course of an hour, he spoke to others, six in all. And in each case money was passed to him.'

'Which merchants?'

'John, be careful. I cannot abide these merchants in all their ermine-clad satisfaction. They are too pleased with themselves. Yet they are not without power for all their softness of belly; these are some of the richest and mightiest men in the city. They have fortunes that could buy the war chest. In their own way, they wield as much force as a Cecil or a Devereux.'

'Name them.'

'I have been to speak with two of them – Sir Gerald Bookman and Tolly Weaver. They gave me the same story. They laughed it off. They said Kettle told them he was collecting alms for distressed mariners and they gave him a little money. It was a simple story but unbreakable – unless you wish them arrested and tortured for what would appear to be little or no reason. I have not been to the others yet and I do not intend to.'

Shakespeare was silent for a moment. He had come up against the power of wealth before. No, he could not have the men brought in on such evidence; nor would he, anyway. It was no crime to be charitable. The key to this was the man Kettle. Who – or what – was he collecting for?

'My man and the sergeant watched to see more of Kettle's movements – who he approached, where he went . . .'

✝ 197 ✝

'But they lost him.'

Henbird nodded gravely. 'He went to the kitchens and was not seen again. None of the cooks or the other serving men could say where he had gone. They knew him as an occasional worker there, but nothing more about him.'

'What do you think, Nick? What's happening here?'

'There is considerable unrest about the strangers. The placards outside the Dutch church and now the powder outrages . . . There is a fever in the air. I have spoken to some of the poultry traders here. They are wary what they say to me. I think them reluctant to be involved in any way, which is understandable, but one or two have confided that they hear things in the taverns and ordinaries about rabble-rousing. Some speak of a new Wat Tyler or Jack Cade, feeding off the fears of the merchants and the resentment of employed men whose wages have been cut, or whose jobs have been lost. My instinct is that there is something in this, some organisation bubbling up into insurrection. If you asked me to guess, I would say Kettle was collecting for them and that the merchants who gave their gold knew very well what it was for. Distressed mariners be damned. The money is buying gunpowder to blow up Dutchmen.'

'Then this is even bigger than we feared. This is not merely the usual mob of apprentices spoiling for a fight.'

'A great deal bigger, John. That is my honest worry.' He paused. 'Drink your brandy. You have suffered most grievously, and I am sorry . . .'

Shakespeare nodded stiffly, then downed the spirit in one shot. There was, for a moment, silence in the room. At last he spoke. 'Do you think it worth going back to the two merchants, Bookman and Weaver?'

'Possibly.'

'I think you should go. Appeal to their God-fearing natures. Explain that if they don't help you, they could end up in something so deep it will unsettle their comfortable lives. And find Oliver Kettle for me.'

Henbird enjoyed the smooth heat of the brandy slipping down his throat. 'I shall also ask about if anyone has heard of a Laveroke . . .'

'Do that, Nick, do that.' Henbird was right, Shakespeare thought as he refilled his brandy. There *was* a fever in the air. 'Does this all come from the Escorial?' he said, expressing his reflections aloud. 'I know what Mr Secretary would be thinking . . .'

'He would be thinking that we are under attack.'

'And I would have to agree with him.'

It was early evening, a fine evening now that the grey cloud had moved away. The sun was high and the land was warm. No more than a few white clouds drifted on the light breeze.

Boltfoot left his horse at a livery stable, all the time closely watched by Warboys, so that he had no hope of slipping away or getting a groom to take a message for him. Then they doubled back to Brick Lane, where they were joined by eleven other men, all of whom he had seen in the workshop and none of whom were introduced to him. They seemed a strange group, men of different ages and sizes. The only things that united them were the old hagbuts and pikes they brought, their common working men's clothing of leather and wool jerkins, and their obvious deference to Warboys.

Together, they marched north and east, skirting the fields that fringed the urban areas outside the city wall. Now they were in the countryside to the north of Houndsditch.

Boltfoot heard the distant boom of a cannon. As they drew nearer, the intermittent crack of musket-fire grew louder. They were approaching the long brick wall surrounding Artillery Yard, to the west of Spital Field.

'Now we'll try your mettle, Mr Cooper. Now we'll see whether you have the eye of a hawk or the fumbling eye of a mole.'

Boltfoot mumbled in a non-committal way. He knew his worth in the heat of battle. He had staked his life on many an occasion when ships came broadside and the grappling hooks lashed them together for hand-to-hand fighting. He would fear no man in armed close-quarters combat.

There were other trainbands in the area. Hundreds of men were out this day with the militias of the great livery companies. These were the men who would defend London should Spain ever invade. Slightly apart, keeping themselves to themselves as if looking down on the Londoners, were troops raised by the noble families from the shires, all identifiable by their bright tabards and fluttering pennants. Outside the yard, pikemen and halberdiers rehearsed their deadly craft – parry, thrust and chop. Archers, too, reminded those who thought the longbow had had its day that the whisper of an arrow could be every bit as deadly as the bang of a musket-ball. Within the yard, a few artillery men were working on an array of cannons. Also in the yard, a hundred or so arquebusiers stood idly talking, awaiting their turn to step up to the mark, rest their matchlock muskets on notched props and fire half a dozen balls at a range of targets.

There were others here – food sellers with bushel bags of fruit and bread, whores, alemen – all trying to earn a few pence from this ritual, which had become so much a part of London life since King Philip first threatened to send an invasion armada back in the 1580s. All this army of part-time English warriors required was good leadership and cohesion, for they had fighting spirit in great measure and were rapidly acquiring martial skills.

As they arrived in the yard, Warboys nodded to a group of a

dozen men, who came over and mingled with the group he had brought. He turned to Cooper. 'Do you want to show me your skills with a matchlock hagbut or are you content with your caliver?'

'What I would most like, Mr Warboys, is a little more information if I am to hazard my life with you. This is a ragged band. I do not mind fighting for England, but I do not wish to have my belly slit open and my trillibub spilled into the Tyburn dust for a group of worthless vagabonds.'

'All in good time. All will become clear. But I can tell you there is nothing treasonable here. You are risking nothing by training with us. No man who sees us could think us anything but another of the many trainbands honing their aim. What true Englishmen is not out at the targets on such a fine summer's evening? What man would not defend his country from enemies without and enemies within?'

For the next two hours, Boltfoot took his turn to fire at the targets, along with the other men. They did not talk with him much. Finally, Warboys handed him a tankard of ale. 'Here you are, Mr Cooper. You have earned that. Not only are you a good craftsman, but you are a fine shot, too. What else do you know? Have you dealt with ordnance, with powder?'

'Aboard ship, aye, I was proficient enough, but there were plenty of men who knew more than me.'

'Well, go now and sup, then later, you shall make acquaintance with Mr Curl. I think he will like you well. In the meantime, I have other work I must attend to.'

Chapter 22

Cecil's man Clarkson was waiting for Shakespeare at Dowgate. He was on horseback. 'I have never seen Sir Robert so agitated, Mr Shakespeare. He awaits word from the Perez faction and none comes. He says you must go to Essex House and bring the Spaniard forth.'

Shakespeare was incredulous. 'Sir Robert knows well that I cannot go to Essex House. I would not be admitted.'

'He is adamant that you bring Perez to him. I think he does not care how you do it.'

'He demands the impossible.'

Clarkson smiled with resignation. He was one of the Cecils' oldest retainers, having worked for Sir Robert's father, the Lord Treasurer, Burghley, before being taken on by the son. Shakespeare had always liked him and could not be angry with him; he knew he was only relaying a message.

'Well, come in and take a little wine with me, Mr Clarkson. Let us think about this.'

'I fear I must hasten back to Sir Robert to tell him that I have communicated with you.'

'Tell him my reply, if you will. And tell him, too, that I have apprehended Glebe and have him in safe-keeping. He talks of receiving information from a man named Laveroke. Ask Sir Robert if he knows this name, for I do not . . .'

Clarkson bowed, shook the reins and was gone.

Shakespeare watched him go, then stepped inside his house. He stayed just long enough to take sustenance, kiss the children and try to reassure Jane that she would be hearing from Boltfoot soon. Then he rode for the Strand.

Ellington Warboys waited outside the Tower. It was almost ten of the clock and the curfew would start soon. At last the constable, fat and plodding, approached him furtively. He looked about to make sure he was not observed, then stretched out his greedy hand. Warboys placed two angel coins in his palm. 'There's your pound, master constable. Free passage this night.'

'Three angels. It'll cost you three angels. The price is up.'

Warboys had been expecting this. 'You have no men, constable.'

The constable held out his hand for more. 'Three. Or do you wish me to call in the provost-marshal and make search of your supposed brandy barrels?'

For a brief moment, Warboys considered whether it might be wise to cut the constable's throat and be done with him. Instead he formed his scowling mouth into what he intended as a smile. 'Very well, three it is. But be sure of this: the price cannot go up again.'

'Well, now, that's for me to say, ain't it. Strange coves you've got to move your casks. Foreigners are they?'

'Just do what you're paid for and keep your questions to yourself.'

'Aye, well . . . I don't like it.'

'Take the money, constable, for I pledge you this: if I go to the gallows, you'll be there with me.'

The constable grumbled. His hand folded over the three coins that now adorned it. He glared at the thin figure of Warboys, then snorted and ambled off.

It had been like this for a week now. Warboys's workers travelled by night when the tide was with them. There were five of them, and they had a small barge at their disposal. This night, as with every night for many days, they transported barrels from the great warehouse in Crutched Friars and loaded the barge at the east side of the Tower. Night after night, they travelled with their deadly cargo, joined the others to do their construction work, and then returned with the tide in the morning, for the next load.

The barrels weighed between fifty and a hundred pounds each. In all they had three hundred and thirty barrels to move downriver, unseen. As in every other ward of London, the watch and the constables were notorious for their idleness and incompetence. All the same, they could never be taken for granted and needed to be fed garnish. That was Warboys's task. He paid them every evening. In return the constable looked the other way when the carts rolled past with the barrels. Whether or not he believed the casks held brandy or wine from France, it did not matter. So long as he believed this was some kind of smuggling operation, to avoid duty. The garnish had to be generous, for any questioning would quickly reveal the truth of what was going on. Had the constable thought for a moment they held gunpowder, his attitude would have altered sharply.

Warboys returned to the great dusty warehouse. The workers wore dark, sombre gowns. They were Scots and they kept their voices low, for their strong accents would seem out of place in this town. They looked at him apprehensively. He nodded to them and the carts began to trundle. Warboys watched them through his wide, fishlike eyes, and betrayed no emotion. Yet he had worries. This was taking longer than planned. He lifted the flagon he carried at his waist. It had been full of aqua coelestis when he set out. Now there was little more than a mouthful left. He downed it in one.

'I can go no faster with the workers I have,' he had told
Laveroke. 'If I am to make more haste, you must let me
have the use of two or three of the more trustworthy English
lads.'

'No. None of them can be trusted. Even you . . .'

'You know me better than that, sir.'

'Do I?'

So the Scots would have to redouble their work rate, for the
law's forbearance could never be taken for granted. They had to
work with speed as well as stealth. They were willing enough,
for they had a hunger for vengeance in their bellies and their
hearts. Get the work done. Carry the bricks, carry the powder,
carry the iron. Get the *Sieve* ready. 'Work hard for me and you
will be repaid in the only way you desire,' Warboys told them.
'You will have your retribution. You will have justice for those
you loved.'

Francis Mills was unhappy. In his dreams, he honed a butcher's filleting knife and slit the throats of his wife and the grocer
who lifted her skirts and took her every day in the back store-
room of his shop. He woke gasping for breath, certain that
their blood was drowning him. And then, by morning, he was
as irritable and fatigued as if he had not gone to bed at all. How
could he do the work required of him by Sir Robert Cecil when
all his nights were haunted by death and all his days tormented
by visions of their sweat-glistened skins and the dirty sounds of
their fevered moans and piglike grunts?

If he could get away with it, he would kill them both. He
could smell the grocer on her body whenever he was in the
same room as her, smell the man's seed wafting like the salt
stink of the sea up from her cunny. At times he wondered what
he believed in. He was no longer sure what was right and what
was wrong. The Commandments told him not to kill, yet they

also told his wife to commit no adultery. Should the adulterer not face God's wrath?

In front of him on the table he had the ledgers from the Three Mills gunpowder site. His eyes ached from studying them by candlelight. There was no doubt that powder had gone missing. Sarjent insisted that Knagg was the guilty man, but there was nothing here to prove that. All that was certain was that an amount of powder had been produced and a lesser amount had arrived at the Tower. Knagg's disappearance did not look good for him, however.

Shakespeare entered the room that served as Mills's office in Cecil's mansion on the Strand. Mills looked up at him, something close to pity in his gaunt eyes. 'John,' he said, 'I am sorry for the manner in which I spoke to you earlier.'

'It is of no consequence.' Shakespeare gazed at Mills strangely, as if surprised that the man could communicate a normal human emotion. He noted that he was yet more skeletal than usual, his plain, almost Puritan doublet hanging loose about his frame.

'Your wife, John . . . I wish I had words.'

'There are none. Do not say anything.' Shakespeare walked to the window and looked at the teeming street below. Somewhere out there was the man who had killed Catherine. The thought tightened his sinews. He turned back. 'Sir Robert wants me to bring Perez to him, or the Cabral woman – or both. She said she would return with the information we need, but of course she has not. Now they are in Essex House and I cannot get to them.'

'No man's land. Neither of us is welcome at Essex House. We would be dealt with poorly by the sharp end of a pikestaff.'

'If we send a servant, he will be ignored. The message will not even reach Perez. As far as Essex is concerned, Don Antonio is his property. He will wring every last drop of advantage from this Spaniard. He will bring him to court and he will take credit for all the tittle-tattle he can get from him about the royal courts of Spain and France.'

'Which is why I have had another notion. I have spoken with Rick Baines . . .'

Shakespeare put up a hand. 'Baines! He is a villainous rakehell. He is Essex's man. He will do nothing to help us.'

'You are wrong. Baines is no one's man. He will do anything if the price is right. I offered him five marks, he demanded ten. We settled on eight.'

'He will bring Perez to us?'

'No, but he has told me a way to him.'

Shakespeare was doubtful. 'Indeed?'

'Perez will be at the royal races at Greenwich tomorrow. There is to be the celebrated race between Great Henry and this unknown filly Conquistadora. All London talks of it. Essex bruits it about that the Barb will beat the Queen's hobby, and she threatens to box his ears for speaking thus. There is no doubt she will be in a tempestuous rage if her horse loses. To be beaten by any horse would be bad enough, but to be beaten by a filly named Conquistadora would be beyond bearing.'

'How can Baines be certain Perez will be there?'

'Because he has been with him at Essex House.'

Shakespeare was still doubtful. 'They will be expecting us, though. Baines will have mentioned our interest.'

'No matter, you will find a way to Perez. And then there is the clockmaker . . .'

Shakespeare leant forward, suddenly painfully alert. 'Have you found him?'

'It is not as easy as it sounds. The clockmakers are mostly members of the Blacksmiths' Company, yet the names they supply to me are of little use. These men build nothing but the clocks on church towers, working in iron and steel. They tell me we should be looking to the refugees from Holland, France and Germany to build a clock such as the one used in the powder blast, for it had the nature of a household table clock, in which different metals are used. They would be the men experienced in such work, using copper alloys. I am told there are a few in Blackfriars and I shall seek them out. But, in truth, they work quietly and alone.'

There had been a brass wheel among the parts found embedded in Catherine's body. Mills knew this. Shakespeare looked at him a moment, then strode to the door. It was getting late and he was close to exhaustion.

Mills stared desolately at the opening door. 'John, I do not know how to say this, but I wish it had been my wife at the Dutch market.'

Shakespeare wavered, his hand on the latch. He knew all about the infidelities of Mills's wife. It was an open secret in this building. Of a sudden he was struck by the absurd irony of their situations, also by the pathos of Francis Mills, a man who would watch without emotion as a man was racked to the very edge of damnation, yet went home to grovel abjectly before the mocking laughter of his sluttish wife. For all his power and razor wits, he was impotent before her. Shakespeare almost felt sorry for him. He could not find a kind word to say; his spirit was presently too arid to bring comfort to others. Yet he looked across the room and met Mills's gaze. 'You do not have time for these domestic grievances. Bring this clockmaker in. Bring every clockmaker in the realm to Bridewell and search their souls. And find me a man named Laveroke.'

'Laveroke?'

'Luke Laveroke. Glebe said he was the source of his information. Do you know of him?'

'The name means nothing.'

'Well ask about. But mostly, bring me the clockmaker . . .'

'I pledge it.'

Shakespeare shook his head. 'Why do you not find yourself some young maid, Frank? Why do you bother with her?'

Mills emitted a short, hollow laugh. 'Because I love her, John. Because I love the bitch-whore the way a drunkard loves strong ale.'

Chapter 23

THE VIDAME DE Chartres cut an elegant and rather unlikely figure as he reined in his horse in the neat courtyard outside the Vespers bawdy-house in the old convent of St Mary at Clerkenwell. A lantern burned outside the door. He could have brought an escort from the French embassy, where his father held sway; instead he came alone.

He dismounted, tethered his horse and pushed through the unlocked door into the spacious, well-draped and brightly lit interior.

For a moment he stood in the entrance hall taking in his surroundings. He wore no hat and his head was tilted back as he looked about him, his long dark hair swinging as though it had a life of its own. He stood with his shoulders back, a proud man, pleased with himself, afraid of no one. His doublet of sunflower yellow was exceedingly tight, accentuating his slender, muscled body. He enjoyed beauty, a pleasure that extended to his own appearance.

A woman appeared and smiled at him. 'How may we help you, kind sir?'

'I am looking for –' he was about to say Monique, but quickly corrected himself – 'Lucy.'

'Shall I say who wants her?'

'Prégent. Prégent de la Fin.'

'Wait here, master.'

'No. Take me to her.'

'I think she is with someone, sir.'

'I care not.' He took the young woman's upper arm in a firm grip. 'Come, mam'selle, take me to her.'

'Please, sir, I cannot. She will not allow it. You are hurting me, master.'

The vidame released her. 'Well, I shall find her myself.' He strode forward into the great hall and looked about him. Without hesitation, he climbed the stairs.

The unfortunate whore trailed in his wake. 'Sir, it cannot be seemly to barge in on a lady. She may be—'

'This door?' The vidame pushed open a door and peered in. A man knelt over the end of the bed so that his naked arse was exposed. A woman, also naked, was just behind him clutching something that looked very like a parsnip or carrot. The naked man turned at the creak of the door. His eyes met the vidame's in horror and astonishment and he began scrabbling away to cover himself. The vidame laughed and moved on to the next room.

He was about to go in when the whore who followed him put her hands together in supplication. 'Sir, please not that chamber,' she begged.

'Where then?

'Along the way. The great chamber.'

'Very well. You may go, mam'selle. I will not need your assistance.'

He strode to the door indicated and walked straight in. Lucy was stretched out naked, eyes closed. Beside her was a short, fat man with a hairy back. The vidame approached the bed and hauled him up. The man protested volubly, but the vidame ignored him. With little ado, he threw him from the room, tossing a selection of garments after him, and kicked the door shut. He then turned back and stared at Lucy.

Her eyes were open now, shining. She sat up in bed, reclining against a bank of pillows beneath the four-posted canopy, glaring at him.

'Well, Monique,' he said. 'Do you not greet your master?'

'I have no master. But I will say good day to you, Prégent. Good day and goodbye.'

'I have come a long way to fetch you home . . .'

'And I have come a long way to be rid of you. So I say good riddance, Prégent. I do not know how to make myself clearer.'

He stepped forward. She did not shy away. She had no fear of him. She knew he would not hurt her, nor mark her skin.

'Did you not yearn for me, Monique?'

'I expected you, that is for certain.'

'I will have you back, you know. One way or another. You belong to me, body and soul. By the laws of God and man, you are mine, paid for in gold and in passion.'

'You paid for a slave. But this land has no slavery, so I am no slave, nor ever will be again, neither to you nor any other man. I would kill you before that.'

'So you wish your freedom?'

'I have it.'

The vidame gazed upon her dark skin. He knew and adored every inch of it. He knew its value, too, for he had paid a handsome price for her. Eight thousand Venetian ducats, in gold.

'I need you, Monique.'

'Then pay for me, like all the rest. And my name is Lucy, not Monique. Two sovereigns will buy you a night.'

'Can one put a price on love? Do you know how much I paid for you?'

'If it was more than two sovereigns, you are more a fool than ever I thought, Prégent, for that is the price.'

'If I were to free you I would need eight thousand golden ducats.' He looked around the chamber. 'You have a fair property here, but a long way from such a sum. How much is in your coffers?'

'None for you. I *take* money from men, not give it.'

'But you are a whore now, so you are used to striking a bargain. You will pay me or come with me, for this Virgin Queen will hand you to me. She wishes to keep the French and their embassy happy.'

As he spoke, the door opened. Beth Evans entered with two men. They were large and powerfully built and wore the livery of serving men. 'I thought you might need a little assistance, Lucy,' Beth said.

'This man is just leaving. Perhaps you would show him to the door.'

The vidame unsheathed his sword and turned away from the men, unconcerned. He held up the bright, untarnished blade so that it caught the flickering candlelight, and he ran its finely honed edge between his perfectly manicured fingers. 'Do you remember my swordsman's skills, Monique? Would you pit your poor brutes against my blade?'

Lucy looked towards Beth and the two men and shook her head. 'Leave him. He would slice you as fine as bacon before you had even touched him.'

The vidame smiled. 'Fear not. I am leaving now. But think on what I have said, Monique. I would like to say that the choice is yours, but we both know that is really not the case.' Sliding the blade back into its scabbard, he leant across the bed and kissed Lucy on her exquisite black thigh.

Chapter 24

AT THE END of the training the band dispersed into smaller groups and marched back through the dark streets to the house where Boltfoot had carved the new arquebus stock. From the workshop, they herded through towards the back of the building where there was a refectory with two long tables.

One of the men, some sort of lieutenant to Warboys, who had left the group earlier, grasped Boltfoot by the arm. 'You see these men, Cooper. They're a fine-looking bunch, wouldn't you say?'

Boltoot had seen better, but he had seen much worse. He grunted an affirmative.

'They were in poor ways when we found them. Him over there –' he nodded towards a healthy though otherwise unremarkable man of about thirty – 'he was curled up like a stillborn in the mud by the river, just waiting for the tide to take him. Food and training we gave him and now he'll happily die for England. Now get some food for yourself. You've earned it well today.'

Boltfoot counted near forty men in all. At the end of the large room was a table with two steaming pots. The men collected trenchers from a pile and filed past as two solid-looking drabs ladled out generous helpings of a thick mutton broth and a mash of swede or turnip. Each man was also given a tankard of ale, and then took his place at the table benches and began to eat.

So far, Boltfoot had not managed to have much of a conversation with any of these men. He thought them a dour lot, much less cheery than he might have expected to find aboard a ship.

'Good fare,' he said to the fellow on his left.

The man was no taller than Boltfoot and heavy-set with dull eyes. He looked at Boltfoot, said nothing, then returned to his food. Boltfoot shrugged his shoulders and turned to the man at his right. He was of a different cast. His eyes seemed more intelligent than most of those here and he had shared a jest or two out at the Artillery Yard.

'Well,' Boltfoot said, 'leastwise we won't die of hunger.'

'Plenty of other ways to die though, ain't there.'

'I'm Cooper. By name and calling.'

'And my name's my own business, but I'm pleased to meet you, Mr Cooper. You can stand by me in the line of fire any day, for you powder your fine caliver like a proper fighting man and have a good aim.'

'I should say you have a good aim yourself, Mr No-Name.'

The fellow laughed, then put down his wooden spoon and proffered his hand for Boltfoot to shake, which he did.

'Where are you from?' Boltfoot asked at length.

The man looked at him. 'Why would you wish to know that?'

'Just making talk.'

'A man can be too curious, but I think you know that. For what it's worth, I am from these parts, London-born. I was a cobbler, worked for a shoe mercer in the city. Had a shilling a day, which just about kept my wife and six bairns fed and sheltered. When the mercer died, I looked for work elsewhere, but everywhere I went there was Dutch shoemakers setting up and they only employed their own kind. One by one the children died of hunger or ague, all but one daughter, then my goodwife got took by the pest. So now I mend the boots of the men here and know how to handle a matchlock with the best. I'll make a better England for the girl.' He laughed suddenly, with bitter loathing. 'Look around this room, you'll hear this story from half the men or more.'

Just then, Warboys arrived at the head of the room. He stood and looked about, then clapped his hands to call the room to attention. Other men had already drifted in during the course of the meal and the place was now packed out, both standing and sitting. There was a strange light, with half a dozen wall sconces flickering shadows back and forth. The room had the expectant, nervy atmosphere of a crowded dog-fighting pit. Spoons stopped clattering against bowls and the men fell silent.

Boltfoot had seen mutinous men before. There had been times enough aboard the *Golden Hind* with Drake when the crew would happily have slit their captain-general's throat and taken over the ship, excepting they didn't have the knowledge or skill to sail her home without the officers and pilot. But this band here, in this crowded room east of the city, was of a different order. He saw that he was surrounded by men so driven by despair that now they had nothing to lose. They had sunk low, as his copesmate at the table had indicated, but now they were disciplined and determined. And they were well armed.

From the side of the room a small figure appeared. For a moment it seemed he had a halo of gold about his head, but then Boltfoot realised it was his hair that glowed in the candle-light. It was a most unusual colour, like the amber that mariners were wont to pick up from the beaches of the Baltic Sea. His eyes, too, were of a similar hue and shone in the shadowy light.

The man wore workmen's clothes, as did everyone else in this room. Boltfoot knew immediately, from the descriptions given him at the Three Mills and at Godstone, that this was Holy Trinity Curl.

Curl climbed on to a stool so that he overtopped all those present. For a few moments he merely stood there, looking from left to right, surveying his audience, now utterly hushed.

'It is a fine thing to see so many honest English faces,' he said at last. His voice was quiet but strong. His words were met by a thunderous round of applause and banging of jugs and bowls on the table.

Boltfoot saw the reaction and joined in, clapping his hands together with the rest. He studied the gaunt, set faces of the men, illuminated by the unsteady light of the candles.

'We are all here in common cause. We are poor artificers and working men who have seen their fellows and their families starve and die while the strangers who now inhabit this land grow fat and rich.'

Curl's voice began to rise in intensity.

'When this century did begin, no vagabonds were seen abroad in England for every man had work to do and food on his table. Now there are twelve thousand sturdy beggars in London alone – and that be the Lord Mayor's own figure. Sturdy beggars they call them and put them into Bridewell to be shackled and lashed. Sturdy beggars, when all they beg is the chance to do a day's work and feed their children. And who took their work away? You all know who, for it has happened to you. The dirty strangers of France, the Germanys and the Low Countries. A turd in all their mouths!'

The throng roared its anger. Curl cursed the strangers again and vowed to kill them and their wives and children, in their churches and in their beds. His eyes glared into the flickering gloom. He railed at Egyptians and Jews, at France and Belgia.

'Their cut-throat merchants undo us all! They take our trade and raise our rents, while our soldiers are sent abroad to the wars – to *their* wars – to die like dogs for *their* lands. But we'll cut *their* throats. We'll blow *them* to dust. We will spill more blood than was spilled at Paris . . .'

On and on he went, cheered by every man, his voice increasing and becoming hoarse with fury, laying out in painstaking detail all the sins of the foreigners – their importation of foreign goods to undercut the English, their sham religion, their selling of low-priced wares at markets, their secret desire to take over and rule this land.

'And how is this allowed? Who profits in England to permit this secret invasion of our city and country? The nobles. Aye, the nobles. Did I say *noble*? There is nothing noble about the upstart Cecils, nor Heneage, nor Howard of Effingham, nor any of the Council or court, save Her Majesty. These pearl-clad courtiers wound their country and their queen for lucre's sake. Spanish gold and Dutch diamonds, that is what they covet and get from our blood. And yet they had best beware, for our blades are honed and our powder is dry.'

For an hour, he went on, repeating time and again the perceived sins of the strangers, the nobility that allowed them into England, and what would be done against them. At times, his voice calmed and he spoke in measured tones, then it raged like a tempest and his lips were flecked with spit. Finally, he turned to his vision of an England in which all men were landowners and free, where the nobility had been cast down and set to the yoke.

Curl shook his clenched right fist. 'There shall be such an explosion of sentiment in this city that none may withstand it. Tread on a worm and it will turn. I say to stranger and treacherous noble alike, fly! Fly now or die! The time is almost here . . .'

For a full two minutes he stood erect, fist raised, accepting the frenzied applause of his followers. Some men came up to him and kissed his feet, others shook their hagbuts and daggers in the air. Then he stepped down from his stool and shook the hands of those clustered close to him, including Mr Warboys.

Warboys leant close to Curl and seemed to whisper a few words in his ear, at which Curl nodded. Warboys then looked across to Boltfoot and signalled with his hand for him to come over.

Boltfoot pushed through the mass of men towards the front of the room.

'This is Mr Cooper,' Warboys said. 'He says he is eager to serve you.'

Curl smiled gravely and took Boltfoot by the hand, his amber eyes delving deep, as though looking for his soul. 'I want no man to serve me, Mr Cooper,' he said. 'I want these men to serve *England*. Drink a gage of good English booze tonight and prepare to pay the blood price when you are called. Are you with us, Mr Cooper?'

Boltfoot grunted. He would rather eat his own balls than fight alongside this man.

'Mr Warboys tells me you are a skilled woodworker. We have need of such men.'

'It's what I do, Mr Curl, and I don't want to be doing it for no Dutchman.'

'Then we are as one. Now drink ale and get sleep.'

Curl shook Boltfoot's hand again, then turned away.

'There is a dry palliasse for you upstairs, Mr Cooper,' Warboys said. 'With the other men. You will be up at dawn and there will be food for you, then work.'

It occurred to Boltfoot that he was indeed a pressed man, if not a prisoner. He could as well get out of this house as he could have removed himself safely from a ship-of-war in the middle of the Western Ocean. At least at sea, he had a vague notion of where he was headed. Here, in this house, trapped, he had no idea what might be waiting on the morrow.

He picked up his blackjack of ale and drank a deep draught. His eyes over the lip of the jug caught another man's eyes. Their eyes locked. Suddenly a door was opened and a breeze came into the room blowing out half of the candles. Boltfoot's skin crept with dread. The way the man had looked at him. Did he know him? If so, Boltfoot could not place him. He was a cold-faced, unremarkable man, with dark hair, thick as a horse's mane, and a mouth so turned down that it was impossible to believe he had ever in his life smiled. Boltfoot looked away.

Had he seen that face before? Had they once been crewmates under Drake? He struggled to find a memory, but could discover none. He gazed again in the direction of the man to seek some clue in his face, but the man had vanished.

Chapter 25

BOLTFOOT'S DORMITORY WAS near the top of the house. Eight straw palliasses were laid out, taking up most of the floor space. At the end of each mattress was a hopharlot, rolled up to use as bedding.

He did not undress but lay down, his caliver and cutlass at his side. All the men had their arms with them. They did not talk much, but took to their beds. One or two smoked pipes as they lay in the dark, awaiting sleep.

Boltfoot was by the wall beneath the window. Ranged alongside him was the man with whom he had eaten his repast.

'Well, Mr Cooper,' the man said. 'What did you make of Mr Curl?'

'He was as I had thought he would be.'

'A mighty impressive man, would you not say?'

Boltfoot did not reply. He was wondering how high the window was, whether there was any possibility of climbing out this night. He guessed he must be twenty to twenty-five feet above the level of the street outside. A fall from there would do for him.

'Well, good night to you, Mr Cooper.'

Boltfoot said nothing. He was thinking of the face among the crowd of men. The more he thought of it the more he began to fancy that he had seen it before. But where? He needed to remove himself from this place without delay.

Jane was still in her daywear and waiting for Shakespeare at the door. 'Not in bed, Jane? It is near midnight, I believe.'

'You have a visitor, master.'

'Who is it?'

'His name is Mr Bruce. I believe him to be a Scotch gentleman. He invited himself in. He is in your library, sir . . . I could not prevent him.'

Shakespeare's hand hovered by the hilt of his sword. 'Bring us wine, Jane.' Upstairs, he pushed open the library door. A man lay across the settle, his dusty boots crossed and resting on a red velvet cushion. He had his hands behind his head and was staring idly up at the plasterwork. He turned his head on hearing the door open, but made no effort to rise.

'Ah, Shakespeare,' he said. 'You have kept me waiting.'

Shakespeare's hand stayed close to the hilt of the sword. 'Who are you?'

'Bruce. Rabbie Bruce.'

'That tells me nothing. Why are you here?'

Bruce swung his legs from the settle and rose languidly to his feet. He was wearing a clan tartan kilt, wound around his shoulder and down to his knees as a skirt. He had a belt about his waist with an animal-skin purse hanging from it. In his stocking there was the haft of a dagger. 'Take your hand away from your wee sword, Shakespeare. We're on the same side. Did little Cecil not tell you I would be here?'

'I still have no idea who you are . . .'

Bruce raised an eyebrow and looked at Shakespeare as a university tutor might sneer at a doltish student. 'From the Scots embassy. I am an envoy of King James. We are to work together. Do you English not communicate one with the other?'

Jane arrived with a tray of wine. She was clearly unsettled by Bruce and gave him a wide berth. She put the tray down on the table quickly before bowing to her master and hurriedly making her way out. Shakespeare eyed the man. He was an inch or two shorter than Shakespeare was, yet he looked stronger. He was lean and muscular and seemed to be about Shakespeare's age – mid thirties – with an air of relaxed assurance. He was clean-shaven with short brown hair. His eyes were dark and seemed to smile, but closer inspection revealed that there was no smile, just a trick of the lines that had started to gather around his high cheekbones.

'Work together on what, Mr Bruce? Knitting kilts?'

'You are droll, Shakespeare. We are to find this man who claims himself as the King's half-brother. The sooner he is rendered dead, the happier I shall be. For while he is at large, every Popish assassin from here to Rome and Madrid will make it his business to kill James and make their impostor king in his place.'

'It is not my mission to kill any man, Mr Bruce.'

'Is that so? Well, *you* do the boy's work and I shall do the man's. I shall see this princeling skewered, parboiled and spit-roasted.'

Shakespeare moved his hand from the sword. He poured two cups of French wine, sprinkling a little sugar into each measure. He handed the drink to Bruce, who put it down untried.

'No time for wine. Work to be done. I am told you were seeking Glebe, the printer of the broadsheet. Have you found him?'

'Yes.'

'Then let us go to him. Where is he?'

'Under lock and key. But it is midnight, Mr Bruce, and I have already questioned him. We will not go to him now. I am going to kiss my children in their cots, get five hours of slumber, then return to my inquiries.'

'I care not a turd for your sleep, Shakespeare. Tell me where the man is and I shall go to him alone.'

'No, Mr Bruce. Return at dawn and we will discuss a strategy then.'

Bruce showed no sign of taking his leave, nor of letting the matter rest. 'I am going nowhere. I was promised your cooperation, and I shall have it.'

'Indeed you shall. On the morrow. I bid you goodnight. Sleep here on the settle if you wish.' Shakespeare drank his wine and strode from the room, for if he had stayed any longer, he might well have run the Scotsman through.

Boltfoot lay tense beneath the hopharlot, waiting for those around him to drift into sleep. He thought of Jane at home, fearing for him, and he thought of the baby. Never before had he cared much whether he lived or died, for he knew the world would not notice either way. But now . . . now he needed to stay alive for his wife and for little, helpless John Cooper, just eight months old and beginning to crawl about the floor to his father's delight.

Soon he heard the heavy snoring of exhausted men. He got up and stood silently for a few moments. If any challenged him, he would say he needed a piss.

No one stirred. A glimmer of moonlight came in through the unshuttered window. He picked up his cutlass and thrust it in his belt, then slung his caliver over his back. Despite his club foot, he could move with surprising agility and grace when required. He picked his way through the slumbering mass of bodies, step by step. At last he was at the doorway and looked out into the stairwell. It was darker there and he could see almost nothing. But he had memorised the number of steps. Nine between each floor, thirty-six in all. He remembered, too, that most of them creaked like an ungreased church door.

Slowly he lowered his weight from stair to stair. He could not eliminate all the sounds of the aged wood, yet he minimised them. The house was noisy even without his footfalls, for men snored and farted on every floor and the old building groaned as it settled into the night. These sounds muffled his own movements.

He reached the first floor. From behind a door he heard the soft voices of two men. He did not move, straining his ears to hear them. He could not make out the words, but fancied they were Scottish accents. Why would there be Scotsmen here? It was difficult to imagine that the men in this house, so zealous in their desire to rid England of strangers, would welcome the presence of those from north of the border. He pushed the thought to one side. There were more important matters at hand.

Boltfoot carried on down the stairs, even more slowly than before. Now he was on the ground floor, in a small hallway between the workshop at the front of the house and the refectory at the back, where they had taken their victuals and heard the address of Holy Trinity Curl. The doors to both rooms were closed. From beneath the door to the refectory, a thin light danced. Had some fool left a candle alight in there, or was the room still occupied? He had to remain silent. He lifted the latch to the door leading the other way, into the workshop. The latch clicked. It was only a little sound, but to Boltfoot it sounded like a clap of thunder.

He closed his eyes, breathed deeply, then pushed the door open. Immediately, he fell back a step, for he found that this room, too, was lit – and that he was confronted by three men. One lounged against the workbench, another stood with wheel-lock pistol in hand scarcely a yard in front of him. Another loitered in the shadows close to the door to the street.

'Very good, Mr Cooper, very good indeed. If we had not been here waiting for you, I do reckon you might have slipped away into the night, for you were as quiet as a tiny mouse.'

It was Ellington Warboys who spoke. He was the man with the wheel-lock trained full on Boltfoot's heart. The man lounging against the workbench was Curl. He was holding a small penny candle, which was all the light they had. The third, the one near the door now stepped out from the shadows. It was the man whose eyes he had met in the refectory, the man he couldn't place.

'I think he still does not recall me, Mr Curl,' the man said. He looked towards Boltfoot and shook his head. 'But I recall you well enough, Mr Cooper, for I was there when you saved your master, Mr Shakespeare, from Mr Topcliffe at the Sluyterman house, where I was a manservant. My name is Oliver Kettle. Do you not remember me now?'

'If he does not remember you yet, Mr Kettle, we shall give him cause,' Curl said. 'For any friend of Sluyterman's is an enemy of mine.'

'How did you know of us?' Warboys demanded.

'All London knows of you.'

'No, that's not so. Who led you to St Botolph?'

Boltfoot said nothing.

'And how much does Shakespeare know?' Warboys demanded.

Again, Boltfoot said nothing.

'Has he heard of us? Have you told him of us?'

Kettle stepped forward and lashed his forearm across Boltfoot's face. Boltfoot stumbled but did not fall, nor did he cry out.

'Talk!'

'Aye,' Boltfoot said. 'He knows of you. He sent me here and has this place watched.'

'I don't believe him,' Warboys said. 'But we have to be sure.'

'Kill him,' Kettle said.

Warboys shook his head. 'If we kill him, we won't know. And we must know. Give him to me, Mr Curl. I'll soften him so he has no strength left to dissemble.'

'Cut his balls off,' Kettle said. 'That'll make him talk. Then slit his throat.'

Curl pondered a moment. 'I agree with Mr Warboys,' he said finally. 'We need to know this. Take him to Canvey, Mr Warboys. Give him to your fine Scottish friends and let them practise their necromancing on him. It will keep them amused, and they have worked hard. Can a man be dead and buried and talk? They do tell me such a thing can be done, for they have seen it in the churchyards of Tranent. If they be right, then we shall find all we need to know. They say a man who has seen his own death does not know what it is to lie . . .'

Shakespeare woke at dawn as the first of the grey light slipped in the gap between the shutters.

Instinctively, he reached out his hand for Catherine and recoiled at the touch of the cold sheet. He had not dreamed of her. His sleep had been short and empty. He sat up in bed gasping for breath. Another day to get through, another day without her. His eyes felt heavy and his throat was raw.

Rabbie Bruce was already at the table eating meats and yesterday's bread when Shakespeare came through. The children were there, too, seemingly unnerved by this spectre in their midst. Only Andrew had the boldness to ask the stranger in the curious attire who he was.

'Have you heard of Scotland, laddie?'

Andrew nodded.

'Well that's me. From the dark north where witches eat children.' He laughed, then looked up to see Shakespeare standing there. 'I was amusing your bairns, Shakespeare. And I rifled your larder.'

'So I see.' Shakespeare's voice was sharp.

'So you have done with sleeping at last. Good. Time to shift your mangy English arse.'

'I have no intention of going to Glebe this day, and certainly not with you, Mr Bruce. I have more pressing business.'

Bruce glared at him a moment. 'You know, Shakespeare,' he said at last. 'I think you might wish to remove your children from this room before I say what I have to say, lest their tender ears be offended by the lewdness of my language.'

Shakespeare touched Andrew's shoulder lightly. 'Take Grace and Mary to Jane. Tell her I am not to be disturbed for a little while.'

Andrew bridled, as if to say *I'm twelve now, not a small child. You should not dismiss me so.* But he said nothing and took the younger childen away. Shakespeare went to the keg and poured himself a beaker of ale. He drank half of the cup quickly, then wiped his sleeve across his mouth. 'You had something to say, Mr Bruce? Make it sharp.'

'Do you know who you talk to?'

He thought to say *A worm in a plague dog's gut, a weevil, something scraped on to the sole of my shoe.* But he stayed his tongue.

'You have no notion what is at stake here. One day, soon, King James the Sixth of Scotland will be King James the First of England. And I shall be one of his chiefest ministers for the services I do him. You and your little Cecil Crookback will run about like rats, doing *my* bidding. Now, Shakespeare, do you consider it wise to cross your future king and his principal secretary?'

Again, Shakespeare held his tongue, though there was much building up inside him. 'Mr Bruce,' he might have said, 'if you were ever principal secretary of this land, I would be long gone to any other country on the earth, for I would rather live under the Ottomans of Turkey or the savages of the New World than abide a man of such graceless conceit.' But instead of speaking he turned his face away.

'Is that it? Is that the way you intend to go on with me? Do you have nothing to say to me, Shakespeare?'

'I think it is time for you to leave my house. We will meet up at day's end. This evening, at Sir Robert's apartments in Greenwich Palace.'

Bruce ran a hand angrily across his close-cropped hair. He ground his sharp front teeth together like a stoat and his eyes no longer contained even the semblance of a smile. 'Fear not, Shakespeare, I am going. I shall seek out an old friend who will be more obliging. One who will most certainly locate Walstan Glebe for me, and together we shall have much pleasure in making him talk.'

Chapter 26

DOZENS OF ROYAL and noble pennants fluttered in the warm breeze. Canopies of green and harvest gold shone in the sunlight.

John Shakespeare walked through the Greenwich Park crowds and stalls. Here, a pair of oxen roasted over an enormous open fire, their juices dripping and sizzling in the flames; there, a juggler throwing six burning batons of pitch into the air in a constant, circular stream, catching them and twirling them onwards with consummate skill. Everywhere, people and horses milled about, seeking food, drink and amusement from the many open-air cooks and entertainers. Gamesters threw down purses of silver and gold in bets on cards, dice, cockfights and courses. Minstrels plucked and sang for a few pennies. Wrestlers, bare to the waist and glistening with sweat, struggled to exhaust each other in a fight that could only end in surrender or death. A group of whores stood close by, doing all in their power to lure the men by thrusting out dimpled thighs and pulpy breasts. But the men weren't buying today; they found the allure of gaming, of manly sports, of blackened meat and fresh-drawn tankards of beer even greater than the promise of soft female flesh.

He stopped momentarily as a pair of horses thundered past him with whooping riders aboard. It was, evidently, a small private race before the grand main events. They were poor, gypsy animals, with no saddles or stirrups but only cloths about their backs. Yet the riders were powerful and skilled.

Shakespeare looked on these innocent pleasures with unheeding eyes. He was a man apart from this seething mass of humanity, wrapped in a darkness from which there was no escape. All that drove him onwards, like a desperate, blinkered mule at the wheel, was the thought that he must find Catherine's killer.

Before coming here, Shakespeare had spoken with Jane. She was concerned for the children, 'Grace is acting like a little mother to Mary, but it does not feel right, Mr Shakespeare. They are like players, acting out some strange drama between themselves. Andrew is angry. He will scarce look at me nor reply when I ask some straightforward question. He says no more than yes or no. He is a big lad now, and I have no control over him. I had thought he would take a kitchen knife to the Scotch man.'

'I had an inclination to do much the same,' Shakespeare said wryly.

'And yet I have seen him alone, in dark corners, raging and weeping his eyes out. I do not know what to do for the best, Mr Shakespeare, in God's name I do not. How am I to talk to them? They need you.'

He had said nothing, though he knew she was right.

As he reached the main stands, a volley of cannon fire signalled that the royal party was about to depart from Greenwich Palace. Much of London seemed to have migrated downriver today for the pomp and pageantry of these summer races. Thousands of men, women and children lined the half-mile route from the palace to the royal viewing point, all of them hoping for a glimpse of their queen. A score of horsemen on white destriers, all in dazzling armour with sword blades raised in front of them, came first, followed by a series of carriages.

The third carriage carried the Queen herself, resplendent in an Italian dress in cloth of gold, stitched with hundreds of rare jewels. She wore a caul and bonnet after the Italian fashion and cooled herself with a gold-handled fan of white feathers. Every so often she waved to the cheering crowds, seeming to enjoy their enduring love. It was as if, for a day, all was well with her realm; there were no poor, no plague victims, no foreign wars, no threat from Spain.

The Queen was closely followed by ten members of her Privy Council, amongst whom was the Earl of Essex, newly appointed. Essex held his shoulders back and rode tall and proud, adorned in fine white silk and taffeta with buttons of pearl and silver. He sat astride a huge black war stallion caparisoned in the same silk and taffeta as his own attire, a line of pearls ranging down its nose. Beside Essex rode Sir Robert Cecil, small and insignificant, dressed in a modest ruff and black doublet, embroidered with discreet knots of gold. The men, so contrasting in their physique and dress, did not look at each other once.

'A fine sight, is it not, Mr Shakespeare? Almost the equal of Paris or Madrid . . . but not quite.'

Shakespeare turned to find the smiling figure of Ana Cabral at his side. She wore a dazzling gown of black silk, with slashes of lustrous scarlet, sweeping out from her hips with the assistance of a Spanish bell farthingale. It was high-bodiced with a simple, lace ruff that did nothing to conceal but rather drew attention to the erotic smoothness of her throat. The effect of her dress, coupled with her fair and silver hair and black eye patch drew many glances. In her small, black-gloved hand she had a long thin pipe of ebony, which she sucked on now and then, blowing out thin wisps of smoke into the summer air.

'Are you suggesting there is a court anywhere else in the world to match the majesty of Gloriana?'

'Your words, Mr Shakespeare, not mine.'

Shakespeare did not laugh. 'I am glad you have found me, Doña Ana, for I wish to talk with you – and enlist your aid. Sir Robert Cecil is exceedingly anxious to have Don Antonio brought to him. Now that word is out in the broadsheets, it appears all London talks of nothing else but your Scots prince. Sir Robert wishes to have the truth from Don Antonio and will pay exceeding well. Can you arrange it?'

'Of course, if the price is right. For me *and* Don Antonio . . .'

'The price will be as you wish, within reason, Doña Ana. All we need to do is arrange a time. Shall we say this evening, at six of the clock in Greenwich Palace?'

'I am sure we can arrange something suitable.'

'Is Don Antonio here now?'

Ana Cabral waved her fine-gloved hand and carved a stream of smoke with her elegant black pipe. 'He is indisposed. You must know that he suffers from many ailments, which is why he always has his box of remedies at his side.'

Suddenly her smile transformed into an expression of sorrow. She touched his hand with her own gloved fingers. 'I have not expressed my condolences for your great sadness, señor . . .'

Shakespeare stiffened. How free the world was with its sympathy and pity.

Ana sighed. 'I know. There is nothing I can say. Come with me now. Please. Come and meet the vidame and inspect Conquistadora.'

Shakespeare suspected that Perez's indisposition was more likely caused by an excess of opium than by any illness. Or perhaps it was simply a convenient excuse for not coming to the racing. He stayed Ana Cabral. 'You have not given a firm response to my suggestion. Let us fix a time for you to bring Don Antonio to Cecil. Six of the clock, yes?'

She shrugged her narrow shoulders helplessly. 'I am unable to be so definite. He is my master. I can ask him if that is a convenient time – but I certainly cannot hold him to it. You must understand this, sir. No more could you speak for Sir Robert Cecil. But come with me now . . .'

In the makeshift stables area, behind the canopied royal stands, a smell of cooking meat gave way to the aroma of new-dropped horse dung. Inside a large tented barnlike structure containing half a dozen animals, each in their own stall, the Vidame de Chartres was talking with a member of the Queen's equerry. They were beside a black horse that Shakespeare recognised as the Barbary filly he had ridden at Gaynes Park.

Seeing the newcomers, the royal officer bowed and moved away.

The vidame made an extravagant gesture with his hand by way of greeting to Shakespeare. 'Have you come to see Conquistadora, the Barb filly?' He reached out and patted the beast's noble black head.

'Not exactly.'

'Hazard all your worldly goods on her. I will race her against the Queen's stallion Great Henry for the Golden Spur. The gamers offer three sovereigns to the one against the Barb. Take it.'

'Mr Shakespeare does not wish to hear about horses,' Ana said. 'He is at his secret work this day. He wishes me to bring Don Antonio to Sir Robert Cecil.'

'Ana, my dear, I am certain you will work your charms on Don Antonio. But you must also insist that Mr Shakespeare brings forth my prize from the race at Gaynes Park.'

Shakespeare had either forgotten about the favour he was supposed to owe the vidame, or he had deliberately put it out of mind. He took his sword from his belt, laid it across his hands and offered it to the vidame. 'Take it, Monsieur le Vidame. It is all I have to offer, for I do not have the power or inclination to comply with your demand. Under English law, I believe the one you call Monique to be a free woman.'

'But you agreed to the wager and its terms, Mr Shakespeare!'

'Under a certain duress. I said the favour must be legal. How can it be legal to hand a woman into slavery in a land where such bondage is outlawed? Have the sword. It is a poor thing compared to yours, but I have been fond of it. Take it and let that be an end to the matter.'

The vidame did not take the sword. 'No, sir, I will have what is mine. Nothing more, nothing less.'

'I cannot help you.' Shakespeare was curt in his dismissal. He had had enough of these lewd and corrupt hangers-on. While London crumbled before an enemy onslaught, and while a pretender waited to claim the thrones of England and Scotland for Popery and Spain, they twittered of horses and slave girls.

The vidame looked from Ana to Shakespeare and gave a gallic shrug. 'Then nor, I fear, can we help you.' He turned away with a last stroke for Conquistadora, and wandered off.

Shakespeare watched him go, then sheathed his sword and looked to Ana. 'My business here is nothing to do with the vidame. You are the one close to Don Antonio. Bring him to Greenwich Palace this evening, for he must know that Cecil is not the man to cross if he wishes to advance his cause in England.'

Ana brushed a persistent wasp away from her hair. 'Don Antonio's interests do not lie only here. He enjoys the patronage of Henri of France and he is well aware that a word from the vidame or his father could imperil his position at the French court. The vidame is not one to be scorned.'

Shakespeare felt he would explode. 'Then it is up to *you*, Doña Ana. You must come with me to Cecil this evening. He demands more information from you. If you hold anything back, I tell you that this will become a Council matter, and you will not have the immunity that your master enjoys.'

'You do not need to threaten me, Mr Shakespeare. I brought you the secret, did I not? Of course I will be there. It will be my pleasure. I may be Spanish but I am no friend of King Philip.'

Shakespeare looked at her hard, wondering where the truth ended and the lies began. He liked her in a curious way, would find her attractive at a different time of his life, but he did not trust her. And there was another matter to be considered: *The London Informer*. 'It is true that you brought me the secret, Doña Ana, yet if I had waited a few hours I might have read it in a penny broadsheet. How do you explain that – and what do you know of Walstan Glebe and a man known as Laveroke?'

Ana shook her head with a disarming smile. 'I have never heard either name.'

'So how did *The London Informer* hear of the Scots prince – a story, apparently, known only to you, Don Antonio and an old nurse?'

'I was as surprised as you to see that broadsheet, sir. But the story was not had from my lips. I sold you the secret in good faith.'

'I wonder why I do not believe you . . .'

Ana Cabral sighed. 'Oh, my dear Mr Shakespeare, how can I convince you?' She took him by the arm. 'Come with me,' she said soothingly, leading him towards the royal enclosure. Suddenly she stopped and turned, as if she had caught sight of something – or someone.

Shakespeare sensed the change in her; a sudden whisper of

unease. He looked around sharply. There was no one there but a couple of grooms sharing a pipe of sotweed.

'Here is your coffin, Mr Cooper,' Warboys said, running a hand along the smooth wood. 'Do you approve of its fine lines? I crafted it myself, for that is how I earn my daily bread when not doing my duty with the Free English Trainband.'

Boltfoot had no idea where he was. They had mentioned Canvey, but that meant nothing to him. He had been brought here, blindfold and gagged with rags, his arms bound behind his back with thin strips of rawhide. Tossed like a dead deer on the back of a horse-drawn wagon, his journey had been long and painful along potholed tracks. After a while, he had been transferred to some sort of boat and brought across a stretch of water, a journey which seemed to take some hours, then landed and dragged up to this higher ground. The blindfold and gag had been removed and he saw now that he was in a small thicket of stunted trees, surrounded by tangles of brambles and bracken-bushes. He could hear seabirds. Beyond the spinney, he could make out an endless bleak landscape of tufted grass, dried mud and dark, still pools of water. A few more low trees hugged the skyline. The coffin of good elm lay before him, close to a half-dug hole in the earth. There were four men. Warboys and three others garbed in black, with cowls, who were busy digging into the earth with spades.

'And there,' Warboys continued, pointing to the hole they were making, 'will be your grave.'

There were no beaten tracks here, no way for a man to discover where he was. Why, he wondered incongruously, would they provide a coffin for his body? Why even bother digging a grave, rather than simply throwing his carcass into a creek or leaving it for the birds and wild animals to gnaw on?

Warboys put his mouth close to Boltfoot's ear. 'I wish to

know what Cecil and your master know. These Scottish sorcerers wish to make merry, and we must keep them happy. Sadly for you, Mr Cooper, *you* are their entertainment. And as they go about their business, I am assured they will discover the secrets of your soul.'

Boltfoot noted that Warboys's speech was slurred from drink, but he was not listening to the words. With the blindfold off, he was becoming accustomed to the drear, cloudy light, and was trying to take in all he might about this place and these men, his captors.

Warboys took a swig from his flagon and gasped with pleasure. He put the flagon to Boltfoot's lips. 'Drink, Mr Cooper, for it is the last liquid you will have.' Boltfoot gulped at the raw brandy. It did nothing to quench his thirst. Warboys patted his shoulder, as though taking leave of an old crewmate at the end of a voyage. 'I must bid you farewell, Mr Cooper, for there is much to be done. But our Scottish friends will weave their spells and summon the truth from your lips. As you lie in your coffin ask yourself this: how do you determine whether a man tells the truth? If I were to pull out your fingernails and ask you a question, you would straightway say whatever I wanted you to say. But would it be the truth? This way, we *will* have the truth. This way you will tell us exactly what you and your masters know of us, even though you know you will die for saying it. You will beg for sweet death to take you.'

As Warboys strode off, Boltfoot gazed without emotion at the three men in black. They had finished their hole and were busy starting a fire of twigs and dried dead-wood. They said nothing to him. He was bound and they were armed with skenes and firearms. He could see that they had his own caliver and cutlass, too.

With the fire under way, two of the black-robed men strode across. Boltfoot watched, powerless and motionless, as they dragged the coffin into the hole in the ground. It was a shallow hole, and the top of the coffin was no more than twelve inches below the surface. He did not try to struggle against his bonds, for it would merely use up valuable energy; he must stay as still as stone. Without ado, they lifted him up and dropped him with a bone-jarring thud into the coffin, then hammered down the lid with iron nails. Boltfoot was on his back, his face close to the lid. His arms, tied behind him, were pressed agonisingly into the small of his back. The weight of his body drove his wrists hard into the ungiving elm.

There was a grey speck of daylight, a breathing hole, otherwise darkness. A tube of metal was suddenly pushed down into the breathing space, then he could hear the sound of earth being thrown on to the casket above him. After a few minutes, there was silence. He was alone and buried. He could not move. All he could do was struggle for breath through the tube. Or scream. And he had no intention of screaming.

Two members of the royal guard beat a drum roll, then the herald in his royal tabard trumpeted a fanfare and called order. Standing beside him, the Master of the Revels, Edmund Tilney, grey and stooped, rose to his full height on his rostrum in the royal stand. 'The horses are at the start!'

The Queen, still fanning herself, for the day was warm and close, sat between Essex and old Thomas Heneage, her ever-faithful friend. She paid no heed to Tilney and continued to talk confidentially to those near her.

Shakespeare watched them from a distance of some thirty yards. If Essex saw him, it did not register on his face.

'If the Barb filly wins the Golden Spur,' Ana Cabral whispered into Shakespeare's ear, 'it will not matter a half-penny apple what little Cecil says. The Queen has a private wager with Essex and if her hobby loses to Conquistadora she has vowed to admit Don Antonio to the presence-chamber. If her Great Henry wins, then she will boot Antonio across the narrow sea to France. I believe she is torn, for I am told she enjoys the company of charming, indiscreet men – and that is Don Antonio. I am told, too, that she calls him traitor and would have none of him – and yet she is intrigued by him and delights to hear tales of all his doings.'

'We shall soon find out.'

The Queen was so close now it occurred to Shakespeare that Ana could stride towards her from the crowd and shoot her through the throat or heart with a wheel-lock pistol before any guards had a chance to stop her. How many conspiracies and attempts had there been on her life in the thirty-five years she had reigned? He had lost count, and yet still she presented herself to her people as though she had not a care for her safety. Shakespeare could not help but admire her courage. Nor could he help wondering about the motives of Ana Cabral. He turned to look at her and saw her gazing at the Queen.

'She looks very vulnerable, do you not think, Doña Ana?'

'*Hmm?*' Ana appeared lost in a dream.

'The Queen. She is in her sixtieth year. I have not seen her in many months. She seems smaller, more frail.'

'If you say so, sir.'

'What do you wish from us, Doña Ana? What is your purpose in coming to England?'

She smiled and frowned at the same time. 'Why, pleasure, sir, of course. I am a daughter of Spain. I want music and strong limbs, rich wines and little deaths. What else would I wish? I fear I do not understand the question, though, for you know that I am here merely as consort to Don Antonio.'

He thought back to the room at Gaynes Park where she lay with Perez's insolent secretary. Their eyes had met when he opened the door. She had seemed unconcerned by his prying gaze, had even seemed to enjoy his looking upon her coupling; likewise, she had seemed unconcerned that her lover Perez took peasants for bedmates and spent much of his days in an opium haze.

'*Are you an assassin, Doña Ana? Would you kill our Queen?*' Shakespeare suddenly realised he had spoken his thoughts out aloud.

She looked at him, puzzled, then laughed. 'What a strange, forward man you are, Mr Shakespeare. I am a pleasure seeker, nothing more. If Don Antonio's interests lie elsewhere, I will seek gratification where I may.' She smiled at him, reached out and squeezed his hand.

He recoiled from her touch, as if bitten by an adder.

Chapter 27

IT WAS WRONG to have the warm hand of a living woman touch him. Shakespeare looked at his hand as though it were on fire.

Ana looked at him with questioning in her eye, then looked away, back at the track.

The horses had started at a strong pace. There were six in the race. They had two miles to go, two laps of a prepared circuit. The vidame, dazzling in purple silks, was easily distinguishable from this distance. The Barb's black coat shone as she settled in the middle of the small pack. The rider of the hobby, Great Henry, was the Queen's finest jockey from her stables at Eltham. He was small and light, yet exceedingly strong, with such power in his forearms that in a driving finish few ever bettered him. He took Great Henry straight to the front and galloped on by a couple of lengths; it was the only way the horse knew to run; go to the front and stay there. At six years of age, he had never been beaten, and had won the Golden Spur twice before. Most of the crowd's money was on him. They knew him and loved him and he had been trained with this, the premier race of the year, in mind. He had already beaten the other four English horses, which meant the Barb should be the only threat to his dominance. How could an unknown three-year-old filly from France, even one so well bred and conformed as Conquistadora, have Great Henry's measure?

The horses were into the home straight. Great Henry was a length to the good, galloping with power and resolve, hugging the inside track. The vidame, purple silks billowing, had not moved a muscle nor raised his whip on Conquistadora. The other four horses were trailing in their wake. Now, they came within a furlong of the finishing post. Great Henry was thundering home like a champion. But then, with a sudden kick of the vidame's spurs in the barrel of the black Barb, Conquistadora surged forward and was past the Queen's hobby in three strides. The crowd's roar died and a gasp went up in its place. The vidame's young filly had beaten the Queen's champion.

Shakespeare did not see it. Had he looked, he would have seen Essex bowing deeply to his sovereign and kissing her hand with fervour while she affected to sulk. But Shakespeare had already turned to walk away, nodding coldly to Ana as he went. This was all vanity. No concern of his. There was no more for him here. He strode off, down towards the river.

The day was bright, but he was lost in a fog. He thought of all he had to do. Get Antonio Perez or Ana Cabral or both of them to Cecil. Find the prince of Scots, if he was there to be found. Find the powderman. Somewhere there was a clockmaker who had colluded in terror and murder. Find the clockmaker.

The water-stairs were crowded with tilt-boat oarsmen touting for business. They had brought hundreds of Londoners here to Greenwich and were waiting for fares back again at the end of the races. Shakespeare stepped into the first boat in line and settled back beneath the awning, unaware that the man who had followed him all the way here was about to step into the boat immediately behind his.

*

The magnificent southern facade of Essex House, with its high square turret and tall windows, dominated the Thames just before the river curved in a graceful arc upstream towards Westminster. Shakespeare paid the watermen and stepped ashore on the Earl of Essex's private landing stage. He glanced up at the turret. Inside the room at the top lay the hub of the earl's own intelligence network.

Shakespeare was immediately confronted by two halberdiers barring his way with long axe-pick staffs.

'I am John Shakespeare, an officer of Sir Robert Cecil. I am here to see Don Antonio Perez.'

Beyond the pleasant riverbank stood an eight-foot high wall. The water-stairs led directly to a narrow, arched gateway that gave on to the earl's beautifully tended gardens. The gateway was the only way in.

'I do believe you are not to be allowed admittance, master,' one of the guards said. 'I will look at the list of proscribed names, but it is my recollection that you are at the top.'

'This is nothing to do with my lord of Essex. This is a Privy Council matter involving Sir Robert Cecil and Don Antonio and there must be no delay. If you do not let me pass, you may expect the full force of Her Majesty's law to descend upon you.'

The guards looked at one another doubtfully. The one who had spoken before lowered his halberd. 'Wait here, Mr Shakespeare. I shall seek advice.' A minute later he returned with Edward Wilton, the chief of guards from Gaynes Park Hall. Wilton eyed Shakespeare with distaste.

'Keep turning up where you are not wanted, don't you, Mr Shakespeare.'

'This is Council business, Wilton. I must confer with Don Antonio. Bring him to me here if you will not admit me to the house.'

'You can write him a letter. I will deliver it for you person-ally. An ardent letter writer, the Spaniard. I am sure he will like to have one from you.'

'Bring me quill, ink and paper.'

'Come with me . . .'

Wilton walked Shakespeare through the gardens towards the guard room, which was at the side of the house. A dozen or so guards were lounging around, playing cards. They rose to attention at the sight of Wilton, but paid Shakespeare no heed.

'Here you are, Mr Shakespeare,' Wilton said pushing a paper and quill to him across a table. 'Write away.'

Shakespeare wrote a simple note: *Sir Robert Cecil would see you with utmost urgency at Greenwich Palace this evening at six of the clock. It will be to your great advantage to be there.* He considered adding that a failure to attend would be viewed with utmost disfavour, but decided against it. He folded the paper and handed it to Wilton.

'I will await a reply.'

'Not in here you won't.'

'I will be by the river. Do not fail me, Mr Wilton. You are not above the law of the land.'

As he strode back through the garden with Wilton two steps behind him, clutching the letter, Shakespeare caught sight of a familiar figure, the Earl of Essex's beautiful sister Penelope Rich. She saw him at the same time and walked towards him. She had a posy of new-cut flowers in one hand and a small pair of garden scissors in the other.

'Good day, Mr Shakespeare.'

He bowed. 'Lady Rich.'

'I heard—'

He met her black eyes. 'Please, my lady.'

'Indeed. I am sorry. Truly sorry, whatever our differences.'

He said nothing.

'Yet I am surprised to find you here. I had not thought that you would dare come to Essex House again.'

'I must speak with Don Antonio.'

'Ah, yes, of course. I understand. My charming little Spaniard is much in demand suddenly.'

'Would *you* bring him to me?'

'I am not certain my brother would like that, Mr Shakespeare. He does not have a good opinion of you.'

'I have come here openly, on a matter of great import to the realm.'

She looked at him a moment. He recalled a time when he had looked into those dark eyes and wondered whether she might lead him to betray Catherine. He felt none of the stirring now that he had felt then.

She was dressed in a summer gown of light worsted, with an exquisite mulberry bodice and sleeves of yellow gold – a colour which perfectly complemented her abundant fair curls. Even cutting flowers, at home in the garden, she looked a match for any woman in the land. At last she nodded to him and smiled. 'I will speak with him. Wait here. Mr Wilton, have a footman bring refreshment to Mr Shakespeare.'

Wilton was clearly put out. As Penelope departed indoors, he handed the letter back to Shakespeare. 'Won't be needing this. What refreshment would you like? Spirit of monkshood? Henbane beer?'

'I would not wish to deprive you, Mr Wilton. Common ale will suffice.'

Shakespeare sat in the sun on a garden bench. Within a few minutes, Penelope Rich reappeared. 'He will be with you presently, Mr Shakespeare. I think it best that you meet here in the garden.'

'As you wish, my lady.'

She smiled. 'Though the circumstances are full of sorrow,

it has been a pleasure to meet you again.' She extended her hand.

Shakespeare took her elegant fingers and bowed to kiss them, then watched as she disappeared into the house. He sat and drank the ale that had been brought to him. It was half an hour before Perez finally appeared at the doorway. He stood for a moment on the steps leading down to the garden, blinking like a creature that has been deprived of light suddenly emerging from its hole. He looked small and much reduced. In his tremulous hands, he clutched his gold box, close to his chest. Once again, Shakespeare found it difficult to think that this feeble, insignificant thing had been the most powerful man in the world. He rose from the bench and walked towards the Spaniard.

'Don Antonio, thank you for coming to me,' he said slipping more easily into the Spanish tongue than he had at Gaynes Park.

'Did Prégent's little Barb filly win her race?'

'I fear I do not know,' he said truthfully.

'No matter. I shall discover soon enough. So, am I correct in thinking Sir Robert has the gold ready for me?'

'Indeed. I am sure Doña Ana has explained the details to you. But Sir Robert is eager to meet you in person. He will recommend to the Queen that you be received by her in the presence-chamber, without delay.'

'That is good. Good. But to think I am come to this, begging for a few ducats of gold when once I controlled the treasure fleets from Peru.'

'I believe it is more than a few ducats, Don Antonio.'

'But I need riches, Mr Shakespeare. I am not a well man. I ail.'

Shakespeare could not pretend to be either concerned or amused. 'Can I take you now, perhaps, to Greenwich Palace?'

His voice was brittle. 'Sir Robert will be there this evening. It is but a short journey by tiltboat.'

'I am not well enough for such a voyage. Can Sir Robert not come to me?'

'No you must go to him. He has promised you the gold. He will keep his word.'

Perez hesitated. At last he sighed. 'You are a man of honour, Mr Shakespeare. If Sir Robert has agreed to pay me the gold, then I must believe he will pay. I shall reveal my secret to you now, and you will bring me my reward. Come.' He lowered himself on to a bench at the top of the steps and patted the space beside him with his soft white hand. 'Let us sit here in the glorious sun and I shall tell you a tale of such intrigue that your astounded heart will beat like the sails of a windmill.'

Shakespeare frowned. Perez must surely know that he was already in possession of the secret. All he needed was the whereabouts of the prince. Shakespeare said nothing. Let Perez tell it in his own way, in his own language. The vital thing was that he should offer up the one missing detail.

'As I have intimated,' Perez continued, 'this tale goes back more than twenty years. The events of long ago haunt us still . . .'

Perez shot Shakespeare a warm smile. 'Have you heard of Montigny? What I am about to tell you is a state secret of Spain, Mr Shakespeare. A secret so close guarded that none but four outside this garden have ever heard of it – and two of them are now dead. King Philip would hide away with shame were he to hear that I have told you.'

The day was ticking on. Yet Shakespeare was at this man's mercy. Perez would tell this as he wished, at his own speed.

'I ask again, do you know of Montigny?'

Montigny? The name registered in some distant recess of his memory, but meant little.

'From the days of Alba's tribunal, Mr Shakespeare – the Council of Blood, as it was known in Protestant circles. Montigny was one of the Flemish nobles sentenced to death.'

Ah yes, that was it. Shakespeare's brow creased deeper. 'That is ancient history, Don Antonio. What bearing can such an event have on your great secret?'

'Drink your ale and listen, Mr Shakespeare, and then you will understand. If you convey this to the Basilisk, she will clap her wrinkled, mottled hands and order you to bring me to her. Of that I am sure. But before I go to her, you must be certain to instruct me in her tastes and desires, for I know she will have heard of the wonders I can offer a woman and will wish to sample them.'

Shakespeare was trying to conjure up all he knew of Montigny. Everything had changed since those long-gone days. Back in the late sixties, in a futile attempt to put down the rebellion in the Spanish Netherlands, Philip's then governor, the Duke of Alba, had set up a notorious court that had become known as the Council of Blood. It had sentenced hundreds, perhaps thousands, of rebels to death. The most infamous executions had been those of the counts Egmont and Hoorn in 1568. Montigny – or, to give him his full title, Floris van Montmorency, Baron of Montigny – was Hoorn's younger brother. In 1567, he had been sent as an envoy to Spain to plead for reform in the Netherlands and to beg that the Inquisition be kept away. Instead of a royal hearing, he got a cell in a castle dungeon where he later died, largely forgotten, of an ague. So what had any of this to do with Mary, Queen of Scots and a baby born at Lochleven castle?

'I believe you are sceptical, Mr Shakespeare, but hear me out. This is Philip's great stain, the sin that will consign him to perdition.'

'As you will.'

'In 1570, Montigny is still alive, held in the castle of Simancas to the north of Madrid, about a hundred miles from Philip's great monastic palace, the Escorial. This is the year that King Philip takes the last of his four brides, Anne of Austria, his niece.

'By this time, King Philip has determined that Montigny must be executed. But then fate intervenes. While Anne of Austria is en route to Spain to become Philip's queen, she stops at Antwerp and there meets Montigny's mother, the dowager Countess of Hoorn. The countess has already lost her elder son to the Council of Blood and now she goes down on her knees as a supplicant, begging Anne to intercede on behalf of her imprisoned younger son. Anne is touched by the plea and promises that her first act on arrival at Philip's court in Spain will be to solicit mercy for Montigny. She is certain that such a request will not be denied to his new queen for she knows she is a beautiful woman and has the wiles to gain whatever favour she wishes from a man.'

Shakespeare was about to interrupt, but Perez held up his soft, mottled hand.

'Be patient, Mr Shakespeare. All will become clear. Now, before Anne departs on the long last leg of her journey, the Duke of Alba hears of her vow to the Countess of Hoorn and is alarmed. He knows the King's will, which accords with his own; all such rebels must die, especially the Flemish noblemen such as Montigny, whom they see as ringleaders. Without delay, Alba sends a messenger ahead to the Escorial to warn Philip of the plea that his young bride intends to make.

'Philip is horrified. He feels compromised. If he orders the execution now, it will be clear to Anne what has happened. That would not be a good start to a marriage. And so he determines that Montigny must die by other means. It must be quiet and secret and be made to look like some illness.'

'So Philip determines to murder Montigny. I still do not understand . . .'

Perez was not to be stopped. 'A letter signed by Philip is sent to the governor of Simancas castle, ordering the killing and giving details of how it is to be concealed. I have seen this letter. It specifies that word is to be put out that the prisoner is seriously ill. Every day for a week a physician is to be admitted to the castle with remedies for Montigny's supposed ailments. The governor of the castle follows his instructions faithfully. The physician is brought in very publicly day by day so that his presence is noted. Then comes the day of death. Imagine, if you will, the dark-shadowed stone walls of this remote castle. At midnight the brutish executioner arrives with his garotte concealed beneath his black cape. He is welcomed with wine by the governor. They speak in whispers. No one must know what is happening.

'Some time between two and three of the clock, when the castle sleeps, the governor and his squat, strong-armed guest walk silently through the dungeons to the cell where Montigny slumbers. He wakes in a panic to find the governor and a masked man staring down at him. The governor tells him that the King has granted him a special dispensation. He will not, after all, be executed publicly in the manner of commoners, but will die quietly here in his cell in a style befitting his noble status. He is telling Montigny that he is to be murdered, here and now, and that he should be thankful for the favour! But first he must write a last letter to his wife, as if composed on his sickbed, to prove that he has died naturally. It will bring her comfort, he is told, to believe that he has not suffered a violent death. He is left with no option; with a heavy heart he writes his last will and testament and sends his love and blessings to his family, revealing nothing about the true nature of his impending doom. There is no priest to administer the last rites but he is told he may pray. He falls to his knees and is about to commend his soul to God when the assassin strikes from behind, looping the garotte about his neck and twisting the rope and rod with his blacksmith's muscles, choking the life from his victim in silence.

'The executioner slips away into the night and the governor sends a letter to Philip to tell of the sad death of the prisoner from fever. The people of Simancas and the officers of the castle believe this, for they saw the physician day by day. They do not see the body, nor the purplish weal on the neck, for Montigny is already in his winding sheet, ready for interment. The king affects sorrow, and the world thinks no more of Floris van Montmorency, Baron of Montigny. If Anne of Austria and Montigny's mother have suspicions, what can they say? What can they prove?'

At last, Perez paused for effect. He looked at Shakespeare and shrugged his shoulders lightly as if all should now be clear to him. 'And there you have it. That is the kind of man we have as king of half the world. That is Philip the Second of Spain. A man who would kill without honour and hide behind the skirts of women. What do you say to *that*, Mr Shakespeare? Will this tale not bring me to court? Is it not worth Cecil's gold?'

Shakespeare struggled for something to say. Yes, this was of great interest, but nothing more. The Queen would listen to it avidly and clap her hands with glee and horror. Yes, it *would* cause a sensation at court. It could be used against Philip. It would stiffen the resolve of Protestants and cause consternation among Catholics. In its way, it had value. But in the greater scheme of international politicking, it was a trifle. And at home, it was of no significance to the safety of the realm and no relevance to the succession. Compared to the story told by the old nun, it was as nothing.

'It is a hideous story, Don Antonio. But what has this to do with Mary, Queen of Scots and the secret of her son by Bothwell?'

Perez, exhausted by the telling of his story, had opened the lid to his box and was sifting through the glass vials. At last he plucked one out, removed its little cork stopper and tipped the contents down his throat. He closed his eyes and reclined on the bench, the hazy sun full on his pallid, mottled face.

'Don Antonio?'

'I do not know what you are saying, Mr Shakespeare. There, you have the great secret. My life is worth nothing now. Philip has tried to kill me these many years for fear that I would disclose it. Now, he will divert every assassin in his armoury towards me.'

'Don Antonio, we were led to believe you had information of the son born to Mary of Scots in the castle of Lochleven.'

Perez breathed deeply, luxuriating in the warmth of the opium spirit as it spread through his body. 'You are talking in riddles, Mr Shakespeare . . . What we need is a coalition against this murderous Philip and his empire of death. We must bring in the Dutch, the French, the Portingales and the Mussalmans of Turkey . . .'

'You sent a message to Sir Robert Cecil that you had a secret to sell, one pertaining to the royal succession. The tale of Montigny has no bearing on the English Crown. How could it?'

'I said I had a great secret to sell. I said nothing of succession.'

Shakespeare looked at him hard. A cloud passed across the face of the sun. No. Of course he had said no such thing, for it was not Perez who had given the message to Cecil that there was a secret for sale. That task would have been given to his secretary, who would most certainly have listened to Ana Cabral. Perez was nothing to do with any of this. He was a bystander, a convenience. This was all about Ana Cabral and the old nun. Perez could propose his grand schemes for the overthrow of Philip, yet all the while his mistress was busy with the real plot. Perez had been no more than a ticket of passage to England. Without knowing it, every action he took was abetting the very regime he wished to destroy. Shakespeare stood up. He could not wait here a moment longer.

'I remember such a tale, Mr Shakespeare,' Perez said languidly, eyes now closed. 'In the late sixties, it was whispered in court circles that a child had been brought from Scotland to Spain, but I paid such tittle-tattle no heed . . .'

Shakespeare was not listening. He had already bowed curtly to Don Antonio and was now running through the garden towards the water-stairs. He needed to bring in the Cabral woman without delay.

Chapter 28

THE OARSMAN BROUGHT the tilt-boat smoothly alongside the little pier beside Essex's private water-stairs.

'Greenwich,' Shakespeare said brusquely. The boat rocked and the water lapped at its bows as he settled into the seat at the back. 'Why are there not two of you? I'm in a hurry.'

'My copesmate ails, master. The bloody flux. But the tide is with us . . .'

'Put muscle into it and you shall have an extra groat.'

Boltfoot felt that death must come soon and that it would be a kindness. He could scarce struggle for breath now. The pain in his back and neck and bound arms had turned into an agonising numbness, where feeling seemed to be slipping into everlasting non-feeling.

What little fetid air he could snatch through the metal pipe went to his lungs in short rasps. He could not have screamed even if he wished to. Was he conscious any more? He was not certain. He no longer wondered what was happening. His only thought was Jane and little John, his baby son. They were what kept him alive, they were his only reason to survive.

Occasionally, he opened his eyes. A tiny spot of light came through the tube, but all it offered was a charcoal dimness instead of utter black. He had no way of knowing how many hours he had been here, but thought it must still be daylight outside.

There was a noise above him. A scraping sound. He gasped at the stale air. The tube was pulled out from above and a spray of dry earth fell through the hole into the coffin. It dusted down across his face, spreading into his eyes, up his nostrils and into his mouth. He tried to spit it out, but more came in, so he closed his lips. Now he could not breathe at all. The gritty earth was at the back of his throat. He began to retch uncontrollably and his chest heaved.

From above, the scraping continued. He vaguely realised that someone was clearing the earth from the coffin. It seemed they were digging him up, but his life hung like the last ember buried in the ashes of a fire that has been left untended overnight.

Suddenly the lid of the coffin was levered off. Boltfoot spat and coughed out as much soil as he could. He tried to open his eyes, but they were thick with dust and the brilliance of the light was unbearable. He felt his body being lifted by a number of hands.

'He has risen from the dead.'

The voice was Scottish, high-pitched and coarse.

'Why, I do declare it a miracle.'

Without ceremony, he was flung to the ground. He blinked open his eyes. He could see now that he was close to a fragrant fire of sticks and branches. With an effort, he turned to one side and saw the three black-robed men. They were standing in a semicircle, looking down at him with curiosity, as if wondering what to do next with their prize.

Then he noticed something else about them, something he had not been able to discern before his entombment. Only one of these three Scots was a man. The other two were young, fair-haired women with brutish faces. From the similarity of their faces and masculine build, he took them to be sisters and thought them barely out of their teen years.

'Do we have a little potion to revive him, sister Agnes?'

'I think we do, sister Gellie.'

'Look at him. Do you not think him wide-eyed beneath the soot and soil? Maybe he is surprised to be alive . . .'

'And to be welcomed by two such lovely sisters and their fine brother, with the cooper's image all prepared in wax with his hair.'

'Give him the remedy, sister Agnes. Is it mixed well? Give it to him and let him wonder at our craft as we cut him and pass him over the fire nine times. Let us call on Dog to help us in this and we shall kiss his red buttocks and stroke his red tail. Then we shall see how this cooper do sweat and whether he waste away and melt as his wax image do . . .'

The waterman struck just beyond the bridge. They were in mid-stream. The river was crowded with many different boats and sailing vessels. A barge pulled by a boat with a dozen strong oarsmen had just passed, creating a heavy swell in its wake. The tilt-boat rocked madly. The waterman stumbled back beneath the canopy, as if trying to regain his balance.

Shakespeare held out his arms to steady him, but found himself instead being dragged forward and, in one deft move-ment, flung over the side into the grey, swelling depths of the river.

He sank into the dark water, frantically kicking and pulling with his arms to find the surface. But he was disoriented, dragged by the tide and his encumbrances – sword, pistols, boots, clothes. He could not discern whether he was going down or up. Suddenly, he broke surface and gulped in air. The first thing he saw was the blade of the oar descending towards his head. He tried to duck back beneath the surface, but he was not fast enough. The hard, heavy wood hit the crown of his head like a hammer.

The blow knocked him sideways through the water. He floundered, flailing with his arms, but did not lose consciousness. The oar was coming at him again. This time he dived down before it hit. He tried to swim away from the boat, fighting against the current. The water was murky, and he could not see. At last, he came up again. He was no more than four yards from the boat. The oarsman had a pistol. He was pressing a single, heavy ball, wrapped in cartridge paper, into its muzzle. Shakespeare dived again, but this time he headed back towards the boat. Its shape loomed above him, narrow and dark against the surface light.

Shakespeare and the tilt-boat were both being dragged downstream through the teeming shipping lane, past the Tower. With an immense push of both arms, Shakespeare thrust upwards on one side of the boat, trying to upturn it. It swayed slightly, but it was far too heavy to capsize.

The waterman looked down at him. He had the pistol loaded and primed. Their eyes were barely three feet apart. Shock registered as Shakespeare saw the face of the man trying to kill him. It was a face he had not registered when he hired this boat, for whoever looked at a waterman's face? The face broke into a grin as he pulled the trigger.

The blast of powder rent the air and the ball spat harmlessly into the water. The waterman peered into the smoke. He must have hit Shakespeare, but he could see nothing through the powder-fug. Then he looked back. Shakespeare had somehow contrived to emerge twenty yards behind him and was rapidly receding.

Shakespeare clung to the chain of the buoy and gazed at the tilt-boat disappearing downstream. One moment he had been about to die, the next the buoy had hit him and he had thrown his arms about it and held on.

He was not far from the southern bank of the Thames, just east of Horsey Down. But in this ebb tide, he had no chance of swimming ashore. If he let go of this buoy he would be swept downriver until death took him.

A small wherry was approaching. Shakespeare waved at it. With great skill, the two oarsmen came alongside and threw a mooring rope around the wooden buoy.

'We saw that,' one of the young oarsmen said as they hauled Shakespeare aboard. 'You're lucky to be alive; he was trying to do for you.'

Shakespeare nodded. He knew he had been most fortunate. But why, he wondered, as he slumped, drenched, into the oarsman's arms, had Richard Baines been trying to kill him?

The three black-clad Scots had a long, three-inch thick branch of ash. It was strong young wood. They thrust it between Boltfoot's bindings – arms and legs – so he was like a whole pig ready to be spit-roasted over the fire.

On one side of the fire, which was low in flame but scorching in intensity, they had driven a stake into the ground. At the top there was a deep notch. They lifted Boltfoot and put one end of the ash branch into the notch. The man and one of the women gripped the other end, close to Boltfoot's head and began to chant as the other woman danced around the fire playing a Jew's harp.

Boltfoot was breathing more easily now. He felt like laughing out loud at these preposterous people, but he was not at all sure that was wise given his precarious position at their mercy.

Suddenly the woman with the Jew's harp shuddered, fell to her knees and threw up her gown to display her naked arse, like an animal in rut. It was like a cue at the playhouse for the other two to chant louder and begin to bring Boltfoot around across the fire. They held him there, slung low so that his back was no more than a few inches above the red, fiery heat. Involuntarily he tried to arch his back away from the unbearable burning pain, but to no avail. He was held there for ten seconds that felt like ten minutes, his teeth clenched against the scream that his throat and very being longed to utter.

They moved him on, to the other side of the fire. The fire had caused agony such as he had never felt before. And he knew that it would come again. Nine times across the fire, they had said. Nine times. He exhaled a long, straggling breath. In front of him the woman with the Jew's harp was on all fours on the ground, her gown clutched up around her waist so that her pink nakedness was exposed. It seemed to him that her grunting and panting was the hunger of a bitch in heat. She was offering herself up, to some unseen presence. Begging to be taken by the devil himself.

Shakespeare was still soaked through when the wherrymen landed him at Greenwich. He wondered, vaguely, whether the involuntary drinking of the putrid Thames water might do for him. For the present, however, he had more pressing concerns.

The races were all done with. If Baines was here, there was no sign of him. As for the Queen and her courtiers, they had long since departed back to the confines of the palace. Only the common folk were still in the park, eating, drinking and enjoying the entertainments in the late afternoon sunshine.

Shakespeare found the Vidame de Chartres near the palace stables. The French nobleman was ensuring that Conquistadora was well looked after for her journey back to the stables at Wanstead, where she was now to be housed. The vidame held up the golden spur he had won for his victory. 'Given me by your Queen's own fair hand. I told you the horse was no nag, sir.'

'I am looking for Doña Ana.'

'I have not seen her since the race, Monsieur Shakespeare. But I imagine she will be at Essex House this evening. There is to be feasting in honour of a famous victory. Come – and bring my woman with you.'

'You have heard all I will say on that matter.'

'Her Majesty the Queen has other ideas. She agrees Monique is my property and has granted me her return.'

'I believe the courts will not accede to your demands. Certainly, I will not. Slavery is repugnant to God and humanity.'

'Have you told that to Mr Hawkins, your great slaver?'

Shakespeare said no more. He went to the servants' quarters at the palace, where he stripped naked so that his clothes could be hung up to dry in front of an open fire. As he waited, he sent a messenger to request a meeting with Sir Robert Cecil.

Chapter 29

T HE PRICKLES ROSE on Shakespeare's neck. He was in Sir
Robert Cecil's richly appointed apartments, at a table
with Francis Mills and the kilted Rabbie Bruce. Cecil was cold
with anger.

'How will we beat Spain if we cannot work together?' he
demanded.

'Blame him,' Bruce said, jabbing a finger at Shakespeare.
'He has kept the man Glebe from me. Give Glebe to me and I
will twist the truth from his miserable English mouth within
the hour.'

'Is this true, John?'

'He means he would kill him, Sir Robert. How many more
witnesses do you wish to lose?'

'This is the problem of which I speak. There must be
common cause here. It is in no one's interest for this prince of
Scots to remain undiscovered. If he is in England, he has been
brought here with but one purpose in mind – to usurp a
throne. Now, John, I told you to take Glebe to Newgate, but
Mr Bruce says he is not there. So where is he?'

'Safe, and being questioned, though I believe I have all the
information he has to give.'

'Then speak it here and now to Mr Bruce and Mr Mills. But
be clear on your aim. You are to find this Scots prince. The

court talks of nothing else and the Queen . . . well, let us just say that I have never seen her so angry. And I am one of those who saw her tempestuous rage when Ralegh married Bess Throckmorton. It took all my powers of persuasion to get her to the courses this day. The calm that the world saw turned once more to wrath when she returned here. Do I make myself plain?'

Shakespeare and Mills nodded.

'Good. Then I will leave you, gentlemen. You will sit around this table and devise a plan by which to proceed. I care not what you think of one another – personal difficulties will be set aside.' He nodded brusquely, then departed before any of them had a chance to speak.

Bruce leant back, feet on the table. 'He thinks to include me with you two flunkeys. One day, he will be *my* servant.'

Shakespeare fought to calm himself down. He could see the truth in what Cecil said. This inquiry was proceeding slower than a twenty-year-old mule. He took a deep breath and rested his forearms on the table. 'Very well, I will detail all that I have uncovered. Firstly, this is nothing to do with Perez. He never had the secret. It all came from the woman, Ana Cabral, the old nurse and, perhaps, Perez's secretary. But the Cabral woman is now missing. She has slipped us.'

'The Spanish slattern?' Bruce said. 'She may have slipped you, Shakespeare, but not me. You won't find her because I have her.'

Shakespeare's calm did not last. He eyed Bruce as if he would happily murder him. 'What do you mean, Mr Bruce – how can you *have* Ana Cabral?'

'I took her. Had her arrested by honest English pursuivants as she left the courses. She now resides with my friend.'

'Where?'

'Somewhere safe, Shakespeare. Somewhere you can't get

your tender, milk-fed little hands on her. Unless, of course, you wish to do some sort of trade for Glebe . . .'

Shakespeare turned to Mills. 'Do you know about this, Frank?'

Mills shook his head, but a little too slowly.

'Frank?'

Mills sighed heavily. 'She is a guest of Topcliffe at Westminster.'

'Topcliffe! God's blood, what has Topcliffe to do with any of this? He is more unclean than the lice of Limbo.'

'Oh aye,' Bruce put in. 'He speaks most highly of you, too. Calls you a Papist-swiving, stranger-hugging sheep turd.'

Shakespeare ignored Bruce and looked directly at the thin, spidery figure of Mills, who seemed to sag ever deeper into his bony shoulders. 'Frank, does Cecil know of this?'

Mills's eyes swivelled to Bruce and back to Shakespeare. He said nothing.

Shakespeare turned to the Scotsman. 'Well?'

'Do you think I give a fishwife's piss what Robert Cecil knows or doesn't know? I am answerable to the King of Scots, not to an English cripple.'

'Mr Bruce, Ana Cabral may hold the key to the riddle of this Scots prince. But she is also a guest of this realm, here with the train of Don Antonio Perez and under the protection of the Vidame de Chartres and his father, all of them envoys from Henri of France. She cannot be lifted off the streets and consigned to Topcliffe's torture chamber without order of the Privy Council. Do you think Her Majesty would thank us for starting a war with France?'

Bruce leant forward in his chair. The generous cloak of his kilt flopped low across his chest. 'Well, Shakespeare, *you* get her out of there – if you can.'

Shakespeare rose from his chair, knocking it to the floor, and strode for the door.

Mills was up instantly. He grabbed Shakespeare by the arms to hold him back. 'Wait, John, there are other matters we must talk on. We must work together.'

Shakespeare shrugged off his restraining hands. He was shaking with rage.

Mills unfolded himself to his full height. 'John, listen to me. Cecil is right: we have a common enemy. We cannot afford this hostility between us.'

'Do we have a common enemy?' He jerked his chin in the direction of Rabbie Bruce. '*He* seems like the enemy.'

Bruce was stone-faced. 'Is that so, Shakespeare? The world blows apart, an assassin stalks my sovereign and you retire to your bedchamber. Should I wait on *your* pleasure in this?'

Reluctantly, Shakespeare took his seat again. Behind his anger, he knew they had to sort this out. Mills and Cecil were right. Mr Secretary Walsingham had said it so often that his words were imprinted on Shakespeare's brain like the royal seal: *The farm that is riven will fall into disarray, its crops will fail and its beasts sicken and die. We fight a common enemy. We have no time to fight one another.*

'The question we must answer,' Mills said firmly, 'is what this conspiracy is about. Topcliffe knows he cannot apply the rack or gyves to the woman, but he can scare her well enough – and that is what he is presently engaged on. Let us see what she reveals.'

Bruce had his dirk in his hands, flipping and spinning it. It was a mean weapon with an eighteen-inch double-sided blade and a hilt of deer horn. To Shakespeare it looked more like a short sword than a dagger. Bruce idly ran his finger along its keen edge and brought forth a thin line of blood, which he put to his mouth. 'One thing is certain,' he said. 'There is a death plot here. She and her conspirators will try to kill King James. His death is the key to both kingdoms.'

'But there is more than that. There is the powder . . . the attack on the strangers.'

Mills looked doubtful. 'I am not certain there is a connection, John.'

'Of course there is a connection. Cecil accepts it. Glebe is the link. One day he publishes seditious discourses against the strangers, the next he has the tale of the Scots prince. This can be no coincidence. And who is this Laveroke who brought him these tales?'

Bruce suddenly sat up straight. 'Did you say Laveroke?'

'Have you heard the name before?'

'Oh aye, we know Luke Laveroke well enough.' He thrust his dirk hard into the table. It stood there, embedded and quivering. 'He is a man I would happily slice to dog meat with my little blade. There was a time he pretended to work for us, but all the time he has worked for the scarlet whore and his friends in Spain. You must know him well, for he has spent much time in England.'

'I have never heard the name before.'

'No? How about Baines? Richard Baines. That's one of his aliases. In Rheims or Rome, they'll know him as Father Benedictus, ordained priest. Changes his name, changes his appearance. A great player, he is. You never know who he is today, or who he'll be tomorrow. Most recently, he was the middleman for Errol and Angus, carrying sedition between Edinburgh and Spain. We heard the truth about Laveroke from his servant, under torture. But by then he had gone. So now he's in England, is he?'

'Baines tried to kill me not two hours since. I thought he was working for Essex.' Shakespeare looked at Mills in disbelief. 'Did *you* know he was Laveroke?'

Mills seemed as stunned as Shakespeare. He shook his head, his jaw tight shut.

'Mr Bruce,' Shakespeare said. 'Are you certain of this? How is it that the Scots have never mentioned the connection to us before?'

Bruce laughed. 'Do you tell us all *your* secrets, Shakespeare?'

'But Baines has been consistently anti-Papist. He tried to poison the well at Rheims while posing as a Roman Catholic exile. They even slung him in gaol for a twelvemonth.'

'And did he succeed in poisoning any of the fathers? I think not. A fine ruse that was, then. Take it from me, Shakespeare. Baines is Laveroke and he's a greased priest.'

'And he was the one that said Marlowe's mouth should be stopped. What in the name of God is his connection to Marlowe in all this?'

Bruce gave an indifferent shrug of his shoulders. 'I know nothing of that, nor care. What I want to know is where he is now. Glebe must know. Take me to him and you can have the woman.'

Suddenly, Shakespeare remembered something – the stench of Baines when he arrived at Gaynes Park following his ride from London. That had been no ordinary stink of sweat and dirt, but the smell of rotting cabbage – the smell of brimstone, otherwise known as sulfur, an ingredient of gunpowder.

The door to the room opened. Sir Robert Cecil had returned. A slight, dark presence. He nodded to the three men assembled around the table. 'Gentlemen, do we have progress? Can I tell Her Majesty that this pretender will be found, seized and brought to trial as an impostor without delay?'

'Baines is Laveroke, the man who brought the stories to Glebe,' Shakespeare said. 'The Scots know him as a Papist spy.'

'Well, that is news, but I am not sure that it surprises me.' Cecil's expression did not alter. 'My father had doubts about

Baines before, said he had never been certain of his loyalties. We were considering bringing him to Star Chamber for questioning on certain matters – letters passed to Spain through the French embassy which the code-breaker believed might have been in his hand. But he was under Essex's protection – and then he wrote that denunciation of Marlowe and that seemed to prove his trustworthiness. I fear we took our eye off him.' Cecil turned to Rabbie Bruce. 'I suggest you bring him in, Mr Bruce. Have we any idea where he might be?'

'Essex House, perchance?' Mills suggested.

'He just tried to kill me, on the river.' Shakespeare ran a hand across the swelling on the crown of his head.

Cecil smiled thinly. 'Well, I am pleased to see he failed. Let us pray he fails at all else he attempts.' He paused a moment. 'But I bring you back to the main point. Put this talk of a Scots prince to rest. That is your task. Your *only* task.'

'We were discussing whether there might be a link with the powder outrages. And the name Baines must bring us back to Marlowe . . .'

'Mr Shakespeare, you are like a hound with a dead fox. You have done enough. Unclench your teeth. There is no link to Marlowe.'

'You seem very certain, Sir Robert.'

'I am. I grant you, however, that a connection to the powder conspiracy is most likely. It has all the bitter tang of Spanish intrigue. I am told that Knagg, the powder-master of Three Mills, is still missing. As is five thousand pounds or more of powder. What I would like to know is what they are planning to do – an attack with such an amount placed well could cause much consternation. Have you heard yet from Mr Cooper?'

The name chilled Shakespeare like an icicle sliding down the neck of his shirt. He had been so preoccupied with thoughts of

Catherine, he had scarce given a thought to his faithful assistant. Shakespeare looked at Cecil blankly, but said nothing.

'John, there is something I believe I should now tell you about William Sarjent, the man sent to accompany your man. He is not quite what he seems.'

The cold began to freeze the blood in Shakespeare's veins.

'He is not a common Tower powder-master but an intelligencer in my father's service. I did not tell you before now, for you know that I would only ever reveal one of my spies as a last resort. But I think it only fair to set your mind at rest by telling you that he has served us for many years, both here and in the Low Countries, keeping a close watch on the movements of gunpowder. He is a good man. Mr Cooper could not be aligned to a better.'

A pistol shot rent the air. Boltfoot opened his eyes. He lay by the fire in desperate pain. His back and arms had been scorched by the flames like meat on a spit. The hair on the back of his head was singed away. He had been passed nine times across the fire. Each time had been more agonising than the last, searing into his flesh and turning his clothes to blackened shreds.

He looked up. So did the two women and the man who held him prisoner. They had been copulating shamelessly before him, like wild animals, squealing and screaming, calling on the devil to join them. Now, of a sudden, they were silent.

Boltfoot twisted his body to try to see where the shot had come from. He managed to turn and edge further away from the fire. William Sarjent was standing there, smoking wheel-lock in hand. His nose was bruised and swollen and his eyes yellow-blue from Boltfoot's vicious head-butt at the Three Mills powder plant. Sarjent thrust the pistol into his belt and removed another gun, which he pointed at the three rutting Scots. *What were they*, Boltfoot had found himself wondering as he drifted in and out of consciousness, *satanists, anabaptists, witches, what?* They had been singing or chanting. Strange words that held no meaning for him: '*Kimmer, go before, kimmer go. If you will not go before, kimmer let me . . .*'

The three froze at the discharge of the gun. They looked like startled hares. Their black gowns were up about their waists and they were naked below, in rude obscenity. As if suddenly realising their shameful discovery, they disengaged their parts from one another and began scrabbling away, first on all fours in the dust and grass, gathering their skirts about them, then up and running, running, running, sliding down a bank of dusty earth through the copse until he could see them no more.

Boltfoot heard William Sarjent laugh. Unhurriedly, he sauntered over to Boltfoot, put down his gun, took a dagger from his belt and began to saw through the ropes that bound the prisoner.

'I think it fair to say I gave them the devil of a scare, Mr Cooper,' he said. 'The devil of a scare!' He roared with laughter at his own jest. 'Now then, sir, let me have a look at you.' As he freed Boltfoot from the ropes and sat him up, he shook his head. 'You are in a mighty poor way, Mr Cooper. I think I arrived just in time to save your hide, for you do seem cooked to a turn.'

Sarjent lifted Boltfoot with astonishing gentleness and strength and carried him out of the woods. Boltfoot could see more clearly now where he was. They were on the side of a small hill that rose from the estuary plain of the Thames. He knew this stretch of the great river, not far from where the Thames met the North Sea, having sailed it under Drake. From the low sun to his right, he deduced they were on the northern, Essex bank. In the distance, across the water, lay the county of Kent. There were no people here. This bleak land was given over to wild birds and rabbits. The low sun sparkled on the water and highlighted the billowing sails of dozens of ships of many different shapes and sizes, sailing with the wind or tacking against it.

Boltfoot winced even at the light touch of the man's hands on his back, so severe were his burns. Sarjent carried him up to the brow of the hill, which was not far, and then Boltfoot saw the ghostly remains of an ancient castle. He also saw, in a creek below, a sea vessel, leaning at an angle and stuck fast in the low-water mud. From this distance he guessed it to be a pinnace or bark, perhaps for fishing, though it was large enough for trading. A group of men, ten or so, were working on it, perhaps careening her. Who were they, fishermen?

'Well, Mr Cooper, I think this ruin will do for shelter.'

'Just get me home, Mr Sarjent.' Boltfoot's voice was weak, no more than a whisper.

'I fear you are in no condition to journey. You need food and rest. I have seen men with burns on the field of battle. You will need lotions – oils and the like – to soothe you so that your body may repair itself. The old tower will at least give you protection while you regain strength.'

'Give me water to drink. I can ride. I must get to Mr Shakespeare.'

'Take it easy, Mr Cooper. We must restore you to health.'

'My weapons . . . where are my caliver and cutlass?'

Sarjent carried Boltfoot through the litter of old ragstone blocks and brought him into the remains of what must, once, have been the south tower of a fortress intended to defend the gaping mouth of the Thames.

The tower was broken open on its eastern flank, so that a man might step in and look up through its echoing emptiness to the sky above. The floor was mere dirt. With exquisite tenderness, Sarjent lay Boltfoot down by the stone wall, so placing him that his back was not touching anything. He looked down at him. 'You may be only a mariner but, by God, you bear your pain with fortitude. And I forgive you my broken nose.'

'My weapons . . .'

'I do believe they are near by, for I saw some stores and armaments as I approached the thicket. I will fetch them and bring you food.' He nodded in salute, then left.

Boltfoot closed his eyes. He breathed deeply; just the movement involved in filling his lungs was excruciating, yet he had enough presence of mind to know that, whatever his agony, this could not be a safe place to stay for long. His captors, wherever they were now, might well return and he knew they had well-armed comrades. Boltfoot was also alert enough to wonder how Sarjent had found him here, and he was not at all sure that he liked the answer.

He turned on his hands and knees and began to pull himself up, inch by painful inch.

Chapter 30

Richard Topcliffe had a pipe of tobacco in his mouth and, in his right hand, a branding iron which he was heating in the coals of a cresset.

Ana Cabral had her eyes closed as though asleep.

Topcliffe always enjoyed having guests in this strong room in his home by St Margaret's churchyard in Westminster. He was proud of his rack, which he had helped design and had paid for from his own purse. Another of his favourites was the pair of high rings against the wall, where a priest might be hung from iron gyves in such pain that he would recant his faith. But today Richard Topcliffe was unsettled. Though he was sixty years of age, his brain was still sharp enough to realise that the presence of this woman meant trouble. He owed much to Mr Bruce for the information he had brought him over the years concerning the location and movements of certain Jesuits and seminary priests, but this could be an unhealthy and expensive way of repaying him.

Topcliffe's assistant Nick Jones paced the room in hungry anticipation, like a dog awaiting a haunch of prime meat to be thrown by its master. He came closer to the cresset and warmed his hands, then leered at the prisoner.

'Which instrument shall we use first, Mr Topcliffe?'

Topcliffe looked at Jones with a cold, grim expression as if he was unsure whether to make a merry remark by way of answer or punch him for speaking out of turn. Instead, he did neither, but flicked the branding iron. 'Always a pleasure to sear a pretty young body.'

Ana was chained to a ring on the floor, her gown splayed about her as though she had just descended in a curtsy. She still wore her eye patch. Without looking at either Topcliffe or Jones, she said, 'If you touch me with that, I swear I will bring this house down about you. You do not know who you deal with here.'

The problem for Topcliffe was that he was, in truth, painfully aware with whom he dealt. He knew that he could not touch this woman without risking the wrath of the one person in the world he feared – Elizabeth herself. He had told Bruce as much. Bruce had other ideas. 'Just threaten her, Mr Topcliffe. The woman will tell you everything you need to know before the iron even gets close to her pale flesh.' Topcliffe was not so sure. The woman seemed less anxious than anyone he had ever brought here, as though she knew very well how powerless he was. She sat on the floor, strangely beautiful with her silver-streaked fair hair, her eye patch and her vigorous, well-formed body. Here, in his strong room, she seemed more like a carefree lady of breeding awaiting a maid to dress her hair than a prisoner fearing the sting of the torturer's tools. As Topcliffe gazed at her, she opened her uncovered eye and smiled at him.

Topcliffe went cold in sudden realisation that there was only one way for this to end. He turned to Jones.

'Release her. Unlock her chains.' The order was harsh-spoken.

Jones, heavy-set, thin-bearded and slick-haired, was taken aback. 'Mr Topcliffe?'

Topcliffe lashed out with the branding iron, catching Jones

on the side of the head. The blow stunned him and knocked him sideways, clutching at his bloody, seared face. Topcliffe moved forwards and grabbed the front of the younger man's jerkin and brought his smoky breath to within an inch of his nose. 'Do it. Now. Take my fine guest to the withdrawing room and bring her my best canary wine. Have you no manners to treat this gentlewoman so?'

Jones dabbed a kerchief to his face and scrabbled about for the keys to unchain Ana Cabral. With trembling hands, he knelt before her and thrust the keys into the locks.

'My lady Cabral, I can only apologise for the poor hospitality offered you by this wretched youth. He will be whipped this day for the way he has treated you. My humble apologies. I will do all in my power to make amends to your gracious person.'

'Why, think nothing of it, Mr Topcliffe,' Ana said as her feet were finally freed of the chains and she stood to her full, magnificent height. 'Your delightful chamber is quite palatial. Quite charming . . .'

Shakespeare beat at Topcliffe's door. Behind him stood a squadron of six heavily armed palace guards, supplied by Cecil, who had gone pale with anger when apprised of the abduction of Ana Cabral. 'Get her out of there, Mr Shakespeare – and bring her to me.'

The door was answered by a woman of middle years wearing the clothes of a serving drab. Shakespeare pushed past her, followed by five of the guards, while one remained outside, sword in hand.

'Mr Topcliffe told me not to admit anyone,' the serving woman said helplessly as Shakespeare and his men drove on through the dark hallway.

'Bring him to me.'

Shakespeare knew where the strong room was. He had been

in this house of malevolence before, as a prisoner. He pushed onwards, through its myriad rooms of gloomy, dark-stained panelling. Topcliffe emerged as they reached the entrance to the torture chamber. The door was sturdy, fortified with thick straps of beaten iron.

'Open the door, Topcliffe.'

'I am the Queen's servant!'

Shakespeare nodded to the soldier nearest him. 'Open it, sergeant.'

Topcliffe moved forward and tried to bar the door. The powerfully built sergeant, his body protected by a studded leather cuirass, brushed him aside and pushed it wide open.

'Queen's servant, Shakespeare! Injure me and you injure the body of the Queen!'

Shakespeare strode in. The room smelt of stale sweat, smoke and old, dried blood. He shuddered at the thought of all the men and women who had suffered here, their agonies licensed by the Privy Council with the full backing of Elizabeth. It was the dreadful paradox at the heart of all Shakespeare's work. Though he could not abide the use of torture, he was well aware that he was the instrument of a power that employed it. His only comfort? The thought that the enemy, Spain, with its dread Inquisition, was infinitely worse.

'Search the place,' he ordered the sergeant. 'Send your men elsewhere in the house. Tell them to break down any doors that are barred. Use whatever force is necessary.'

The sergeant-at-arms barked an order at his men, then busied himself in the torture chamber, immediately spotting the cresset in which the coals were still hot. 'Someone has been here, Mr Shakespeare.'

Shakespeare joined him and kicked over the cresset, sending the coals flying across the straw-strewn floor. He indicated with his head to another door. 'There is a smaller room through there, a cell.'

Topcliffe put out an arm to try to stay the soldier. 'Do you know who I am, sergeant? I am the Queen's servant.'

The sergeant ignored him and pushed open the cell door. The room was empty.

From outside, they could hear shouting. Nicholas Jones, hand still clasped to his burnt and injured face, arrived breathless. 'They are breaking up your house, Mr Topcliffe. Your tables, your settles, even the panelling.'

Topcliffe turned on Shakespeare. He swung at him with his blackthorn cane, but Shakespeare easily parried the blow with his sword. Topcliffe's face was as white as his hair. His teeth were bared and his voice was a feral growl. 'You will pay dearly for this. The Queen will hear what you do here this day.'

'Save your threats for someone else. Your mind is diseased. How can you live with such instruments of evil in your home? The place stinks, like you. You are an obscene old man. Now produce her for me, for until you do, this search will continue.'

'Produce who?'

'You know who: Doña Ana.'

'Why, Mr Shakespeare, you should have said. You have no need to break up my humble home to find my honoured guest.'

Shakespeare touched the point of his sword to Topcliffe's chest. 'Take me to her.'

'But she has gone, Mr Shakespeare. I gave her fine wine and sweetmeats and we conversed politely in my withdrawing room, but she has now departed.'

Shakespeare's sword point hovered. He raised it a few inches so that it was close to Topcliffe's throat. His hand was itchy. He could thrust forward now, rid the world of this malign presence for good.

One of the soldiers returned and saluted his sergeant. 'There is no sign of any Spanish woman. Five servants and that creature.' He indicated Jones, who skulked behind his master. 'That's all.'

'Where have you taken her, Topcliffe?'

'I have told you all I know. She left of her own free will.'

'Keep these two here, in this strong room, sergeant. I will talk with the servants.'

As Shakespeare left the room, he caught sight of Topcliffe from the corner of his eye, whispering close to the soldier's ear. 'Queen's servant, sergeant. I shall have your entrails in my blazing cresset for what you have done this day.'

The sergeant whispered back with equal venom. 'We're all Queen's servants here, Mr Topcliffe. Now stow you unless you want my sword up your arse.'

Shakespeare found himself smiling.

Half an hour later, convinced by the servants that Ana Cabral had, indeed, left Topcliffe's house, Shakespeare despatched the guard back to Greenwich Palace with a message for Cecil. He left one of their number outside Topcliffe's door.

Shakespeare mounted his grey mare and headed for the city. He felt a bitter satisfaction at the damage and humiliation he had inflicted on Topcliffe. It had been good to see the defiant courage of the sergeant, uncowed by Topcliffe's threats, where others trembled merely at the mention of his name.

It was almost dark as Shakespeare rode, but he needed to see Henbird.

He found him in bed at his fine home in St Nicholas Shambles, nursing two yellowing black eyes and a mass of other bruises about his face and body.

Shakespeare looked at him aghast. 'What happened, Nick?'

'A Mr Bruce, a noxious Scotsman, came here, said he was a

friend of yours ... asked me the whereabouts of Walstan Glebe.'

'What did you say?'

'I told him nothing. He seemed most discontented. He said he had heard from certain intelligencers that I had him. I rather felt Mr Bruce might have killed me, here in my own home, had my servants not intervened.'

'I am sorry, Nick. I feared he might be led to you. Where is Glebe now?'

'Safe in my cellar still, locked beneath the trapdoor. Is that why you're here?'

'No – unless he has told you more.'

'He has said nothing. I suspect he has nothing more to tell, for you have wrought great fear in him. I am sure he would squeal like a piglet if he had aught to squeal about.'

'I'll deal with him in good time. It's Baines I want for the moment. Do you have a way to him? I must tell you, he is not what he seems.'

Henbird attempted to laugh, but winced and thought better of it. 'Who *is* what they seem in this world we inhabit, John? Here.' He tried to rise from his bed. 'Help me up. I need more brandy.' With Shakespeare's assistance, Henbird struggled up from his sickbed and waddled to the door, where he bellowed for liquor. With great effort he went across to his table and sat down beside it on the bench, which creaked beneath his weight. 'So, what have you discovered about Rick Baines?'

'He's also known as Laveroke.'

'Ah, the man you mentioned before. The one who spoke with Glebe about this prince of Scots. Was that really Rick Baines?'

'He took us all for gulls, and we fell for it.'

'Baines always had a talent for being someone else. Who told you this, John?'

'Our Scots friend, Rabbie Bruce. I would not trust him on much, but I believe him on this. I have reason enough . . .' He grimaced, thinking back to the deep, turbid waters of the Thames, the gulping in of foul river water as Baines, or Laveroke, tried to drown him. He shook his head to dispel the memory. 'The question now is – how do we get to him?'

'The only way is to put word out on to the street.'

'Do it. Let it be known you must have his whereabouts – without his knowledge. Offer ten pounds. I will find the money from Cecil.'

'As you will, John. There is no harm in trying.'

The servant brought brandy. He poured a large measure for Henbird and, at his own insistence, a far smaller one for his guest. Shakespeare looked out the window. It was late. Night had fallen. 'There is also the matter of the merchants and Oliver Kettle. Did you discover more?'

'Nothing. I told you. They are rich, powerful men. They close up like English footmen on the field of battle. There is nothing there and will be nothing unless you have them all arrested and brought to the Tower for questioning. Would Sir Robert like that?'

Shakespeare knew the answer to that well enough. This realm was dependent on trade; no minister would get away with such a move against the great merchants.

'We could have them followed, find out with whom they deal.'

'John, they are mere money men, they have no part in any of this. If they were more than that, they would not be handing over a few shillings at a public banquet. They were giving silver to this man because they liked what he said, not because they were actively engaged in insurrection. Their gift was of little more consequence to them than your gift of a farthing to a beggar.'

'And Kettle?'

'No sign.'

Shakespeare sipped his brandy. He said nothing. All avenues were closing down. Mills had got nowhere with his search for a clockmaker, Ana Cabral was missing, probably ensconced in the safety of Essex House with Perez – and where was Boltfoot?

Other names crowded in: Topcliffe and his curious connection with the Scotsman, Bruce; the men in Ellie Bull's room in Deptford – Poley, Frizer, Skeres – there had been no word of them since the inquest, nor any clue as to their motive.

Shakespeare felt he was in the middle of some teeming hell. A picture came into his mind, a diabolical painting he had once seen while travelling in Brabant on a secret errand for Mr Secretary back in the early eighties. He recalled the name of the artist, Mijnheer Bosch. He had never seen the like of this strange picture. It was full of demons, iniquity and punishment; men and women consigned to damnation. Now, as he thought of it, Catherine was there at its centre, her beautiful face so faint he could scarce make out its features. He shook the unbearable vision from his mind.

'Nick, this is bleak. We fear an attack is imminent, an onslaught far worse than anything yet ventured . . . and yet I make no progress.'

'Tell me more, John. Confide in me.'

Shakespeare gazed at him. His battered face looked like a windfall apple that had been kicked by boys and was turning to mush. Henbird could be trusted; his face told its own tale. 'It is true, I need your help. Our enemies attack on all sides. I fear I am missing something. We must find him.'

'The prince of Scots?'

'The tale is bruited all around court.'

'The city, too. People in the ordinaries and taverns speak of little else. I have heard it said that certain great nobles of the

Romish faith are plotting how they may proclaim him King of England.'

'Do you have names?'

'The usual. Southampton, Lord Strange, Northumberland, the imprisoned Arundel . . .'

'This is all conjecture, yes? Mere tittle-tattle.'

'Perhaps, but it does amaze me how quick such talk spreads. Suddenly a word said in jest turns to established fact. One ember will start a forest fire.'

Shakespeare sighed heavily. 'And do the gossips talk of a link between this pretender prince and the powder outrages?'

'How could they not?'

Shakespeare paused. He had to trust Henbird. He needed him. 'I can tell you, Nick, that five thousand pounds of gunpowder is missing. Five thousand pounds to spark the flame. Perhaps more than that. What will they do with such an amount?'

Henbird's eyes widened. Such an amount could wreak havoc. 'Have you discovered anything from the first two outrages, John?'

Only that I no longer have a wife, he almost said. Instead he nodded grimly. 'Joshua Peace found some metal fragments. He believes they came from a clock, that the powder in the second blast was lit by a timing device. Frank Mills is supposed to be finding the artificer.'

'Did the first blast have such a device?'

'Not that is known.'

'Perhaps they were experimenting in the second blast.'

'It had occurred to me. It had also occurred to me that there must be few enough clockmakers capable of designing and constructing such a thing. Frank Mills is instructed to find the clockmaker but is making painfully slow progress. Do *you* know clockmakers, Nick?'

As if a key had clicked into a lock, Henbird's attitude suddenly changed. 'John, I have had a worrying thought.'

Shakespeare caught his friend's shift in mood. 'Does this mean something to you, Nick?'

'Yes, I fear it does. My mind goes to the hellburners of Antwerp . . .'

Chapter 31

BOLTFOOT DID NOT make it beyond the castle boundary before collapsing. William Sarjent found him slumped forward across a broken block of ragstone and helped him back into the tower. Now darkness had fallen and Sarjent was gnawing at a hunk of bread, washing it down with ale. He gave a little meat and ale to Boltfoot, but Boltfoot could not take much before the bile rose in his throat.

Sarjent's eyes were fixed on Boltfoot, who sat in silence inside the desolate and derelict castle. 'I think it only fair to tell you something, Mr Cooper,' Sarjent said slowly. 'I am an intelligencer working directly to Lord Burghley. I have been operating in secret, investigating the disappearance of gunpowder for some weeks. I had penetrated the secret militia of Mr Holy Trinity Curl and his treacherous band of malcontents long before you blundered in with your club foot. You should have told me what you were engaged on when you rode off from Three Mills. I could have saved you much pain. More importantly, I could have saved my inquiry. They are now alerted. You have done much harm.'

And you should have kept me informed, Boltfoot felt like saying to William Sarjent. But argument used up energy, and he had little enough of that to spare this night. What he did manage to say was, 'How did you find me?'

'I knew of this place already from my investigations. They train out here with powder. It is safe for them, for none come here but seabirds, a few stray sheep and foxes. I came here to spy on them – and found you instead.'

'If you knew of Curl and his band, why have they not been broken up by pursuivants or the royal guard?'

'Mr Cooper, you have been in this business long enough to know the answer to that: I had to find the source of the powder and I had to identify their chiefest man. Lord Burghley fears that powerful merchants, even men of nobility, are involved in this conspiracy. Knagg of Three Mills was supplying Curl with powder, but that hole has been plugged. Who are the puppet masters, though? How shall I find them now? My work is ruined by your bungling.'

Sarjent's words had reason. Yet, even in his present weak state, Boltfoot's instinct was strong. He did not like any of this, nor did he like Sarjent and his swaggering ways.

'The Scots sorcerers, what have they to do with Curl and his band?'

'Ah, the witches. They are not the common rump of Mr Curl's rebellious band. I know something of them. They have another purpose.' Sarjent took a swig from a flagon and passed it to Boltfoot. 'I fear they have treated you most cruelly, Mr Cooper. Did you tell them aught?'

Boltfoot looked at him with mild contempt but said nothing.

'Good. That is good. Then let us pool our knowledge and bring what we know to the Cecils, for I have reason to believe an attack of some nature, some insurrection, is coming, and soon.'

Boltfoot tried vainly to struggle to his feet. 'Let us requisition a boat and make our way to London . . . we must make haste.'

'We will, Mr Cooper. But surely you had already got word to Mr Shakespeare before you were brought here?'

'Yes,' Boltfoot lied without hesitation, as he had told the same lie to Warboys and Curl before being brought to this place. 'Yes, Mr Shakespeare knows all about Curl and his band. And he will be mighty concerned about me by now.'

'Well, you are safe.'

'And he will be most grateful to you, Mr Sarjent, for saving me from certain death. As am I . . .'

Sarjent was silent for a moment. It had not escaped Boltfoot's notice as he spoke that Sarjent's hand was close to his belt where he kept his wheel-lock and his dagger. The hand hovered there, like a kestrel fluttering the tips of its wings, as if deciding whether to swoop on a shrew or move on to tastier prey. The hand moved on and took the flagon back from Boltfoot. 'That is good, very good,' Sarjent said at last. 'It is fortunate that I was able to help, as I once saved Captain-General Norris on the field of blood. Did I ever tell you of that day?'

'No, Mr Sarjent, I do not believe you did. Perhaps you would tell it to me now, while I drift off to sleep, for I need rest.' There was another question that Boltfoot wished answered, but he would not ask it. He wanted to know why, if there was an imminent threat of insurrection, did they not simply descend this hill to the creek below and enlist the aid of some passing fishermen to get them to London without delay. He did not ask him because he knew the answer. He smiled wanly at his companion. 'I trust you will understand that I need to sleep, Mr Sarjent. If you must go, leave me here to rest. Otherwise stay and let us move from this place at dawn.'

Shakespeare felt a cloud of fear descend. The hellburners of Antwerp. He knew of them. 'Nick, this is terrifying to think on . . .'

'But it could make sense. You say they have five thousand pounds or more powder. That could be used for a series of attacks like the Dutch market outrage, or one so huge that it would shake England to its very foundations. If Philip wanted vengeance for Antwerp and for the Armada, if he wanted to sow discord and create havoc, what better weapon?'

'Maybe more than five thousand pounds. How much powder was used in the hellburners?'

'Seven thousand pounds in each, all topped up with slabs of stone, ploughshares, scythes, sickles, rusting iron and nails, sharpened staves. It was the most deadly weapon ever conceived. A thousand or more Spaniards died in a single blast. The roar was heard fifty miles away. They were still finding the scattered bodies many months later.'

'God's blood. If that is what they have planned for us . . .'

'It is only surmise . . .'

'But as you say, Nick, it makes sense.'

Henbird wiped his nightshirt sleeve across his mouth. The aroma of brandy hung heavy in this fine chamber. A servant arrived with cold cuts of various fowl, slices of manchet bread, some cold beef and kidney pudding. Shakespeare had lost his hunger, but he accepted a platter with good grace.

'Eat, John, eat. You need strength. Do you know of Federigo Giambelli?'

'I know of him. We have never met.'

'But you know he is in England, yes?'

Shakespeare nodded. Giambelli was the engineer from Lombardy who had devised the infernal hellburner machine for the Dutch defenders of Antwerp. He was now in the pay of the English, engaged on various defensive works around London and the south coast. 'But where – here in London?'

'Sometimes. I believe he is presently on the Isle of Wight, completing the Carisbrooke earthworks. I am pleased to count him a friend. But more importantly than that, I know with whom he deals. In particular I know a clockmaker who has worked with him and will certainly understand the workings of such a device as was used at Antwerp and, more recently, at the Dutch market. After you were dismissed from Walsingham's service, Giambelli and this clockmaker were engaged by Mr Secretary to design and build a series of defensive hellburners. Nothing ever came of the plan, for the Queen refused to outlay the money needed, and then Mr Secretary died. But if anyone will know about timing devices, this clockmaker will be the man. His name is Peter Gulden – Gulden of Gutter Lane. That is but a few streets from here. We can go to him at first light.'

Shakespeare understood. As he picked at the food, he summoned up his recollections of the Hellburners, or *Hellebranders* as the Dutch knew them. In the spring of 1585, messages from the Low Countries to Walsingham's intelligence network in London had been hot with news of them. They had come into existence at a time when the Duke of Parma, general of the Spanish armies in the Low Countries, was besieging Antwerp and had built a barrier of ships across the river Scheldt to stop supplies reaching the city.

Federigo Giambelli was there. He was an ambitious military engineer from Mantua who had tried to sell his expertise to King Philip, but had been rebuffed. Now he offered his services to the city of Antwerp, believing he had a way to break through this impenetrable siege barrier. Ordinary fireships – ships piled high with firewood and set ablaze – would be too easily doused by the Spanish soldiers guarding the barricade. Giambelli's hellburners would be a different proposition. And the city fathers of Antwerp agreed to his plan.

Two seventy-ton ships, the *Fortune* and the *Hope*, were appropriated for the purpose. Giambelli had these vessels stripped down, then built enormous chambers deep in their holds. Shakespeare tried to imagine how they looked. He had heard that the chambers were like funnels, built of brick and stone – forty feet long and three feet in diameter. The chambers were packed solid with good corned gunpowder. More stone slabs and old scrap metal were piled high above the chambers to compact the powder and maximise the blast. False decks were then built above the huge bombs so that the Spanish would not know them from the far less dangerous fireships they had encountered in the past.

As Shakespeare recalled it, the last problem Giambelli faced was how to light the powder. In one of the ships, the *Fortune*, he used a slow-burning taper. He saved his masterstroke for the other vessel, the *Hope*. For this one, he enlisted the aid of a local clockmaker, who designed a timing device that would bring down a lever at a given time, soon after the ship had drifted into the Spanish barricade. This lever would turn a ser-rated steel wheel – much like a wheel-lock pistol – sending a shower of sparks into the powder.

When the ships were ready, the Dutch sent ordinary fire-ships towards the barricade, as a decoy. These were easily extinguished by the Spanish, who were much amused by the feeble efforts of the Dutch. Then came the hellburners, dis-guised as fireships by the burning of a few smoke-belching twigs and branches on their decks. The *Fortune* drifted into the riverbank and its fuse fizzled out. The *Hope*, however, reached its target. The unsuspecting Spanish swarmed all over it with their pails of water. And then the clock lever dropped, steel span against flint and sparks flew into powder . . .

'One thousand dead?'

'Possibly more, John. But some believe the effects were far greater than that. Signor Giambelli insists that his hellburners gave England victory over the Spanish Armada.'

'Surely no hellburners were involved?'

'No, but the Spanish did not know that. When the English sent commonplace fireships towards the Armada near Calais, the Spanish convinced themselves they must be hellburners. They were in utter terror – panic ensued. The Spanish dispersed and were never able to regroup in good order. That, asserts Signor Giambelli, is how the battle was won for Drake and England.'

'Let us go to clockmaker Gulden now. We cannot afford to wait.'

'It is mere conjecture, John,' Henbird replied, 'but you are right, of course.'

Shakespeare gazed on Henbird's black-bruised face. 'I will go, Nick. You stay here. Return to your sickbed.'

The watchman, lantern in hand, called the hour of eleven and eyed Shakespeare with suspicion. 'Where are you going after curfew, master? Only whores and thieves are abroad at this time of night.'

'Queen's business,' Shakespeare said sharply. 'You can light my way.'

The watchman, a stocky fellow of middle years, grumbled, suddenly unsure of himself. 'Find your own way,' he said and turned away.

Shakespeare grabbed him by the collar of his thick woollen jerkin. 'No, you light my way. Take me to Gutter Lane.'

The watchman, half a foot shorter than Shakespeare and ten years older, considered for a moment whether to summon other members of the watch for assistance. Instead, grudgingly, he shuffled forward as ordered. It was only a few hundred yards eastward and took them little more than ten minutes. The house was in darkness. Shakespeare banged his dagger haft at the door and kept banging until it was answered by a nervous-looking serving girl in her nightgown and cap.

'I am here to talk with Peter Gulden.'

The girl stood well back from them. 'He sleeps, master.'

'Wake him. This is Queen's business.'

She scuttled off into the house. Shakespeare dismissed the watchman, then stepped into the hall. It was a large, well-appointed room. Clockmaker Gulden was clearly a wealthy man.

He appeared shortly, pulling on a doublet over a hastily applied shirt and breeches. The clockmaker was a tall, weak-built man with high cheekbones and almost no hair on his pate. He wore a beard, trimmed short, but no moustache. He looked as if he had spent too many long hours stooped over a workbench, eye fixed to a magnifying glass, working at his intricate springs, pallets and toothed wheels.

'Peter Gulden?'

'Yes,' he said slowly. 'But who are you, sir?'

'My name is John Shakespeare. I am an officer with Sir Robert Cecil. I apologise for waking you at such an hour, but I have important business with you.'

Gulden clearly had been in the depths of sleep for he rubbed his eyes and stretched his aching back. He had a good-humoured but worried face, with blue eyes that might have twinkled had he not been so sleepy. 'What sort of business could Sir Robert have with me, Mr Shakespeare? I am a clockmaker.' His brow creased in bemusement.

'I am told you worked with Signor Giambelli on a project to build English hellburners.'

Gulden nodded. 'That is true, yes. In the late eighties. But it came to nothing.'

'You were working on the timing devices?'

'I was.'

'I can tell you, sir – though it is not to be repeated – that the recent gunpowder blast in the Dutch market involved a timing device.'

'That is deeply shocking, Mr Shakespeare. I had no idea.'

'Are you Dutch, sir?'

'I am, yes, but I have been here for years.'

'You must know most of the clockmakers of London.'

'Indeed, I am sure I know them all. There are no more than twelve of us to my knowledge.'

'Could any of them have made a timing device such as the one used in the market?'

'Why, all of them would be capable, I am sure. With patience, such a thing would not be demanding for one versed in the clockmaker's art, certainly not one experienced in constructing domestic table clocks. The hardest part would be making the timing device accurate enough to operate within a minute or so of the required time. Too quick and the attacker might be blown up, too slow and the device could be discovered and disabled.'

'Give me a name, Mr Gulden. Of the dozen clockmakers you know, who might do such a thing? Who would attack your people?'

'Oh, Mr Shakespeare, what a question!'

'But one that must be answered.'

'It is not something I have ever considered.'

'Consider it now.'

'Well, I suppose none of the Dutch. There are four of us, all *refugies* from the endless war. Nor the Huguenot, Sieur Josselin. Never was there a more kindly man. One of the English, I suppose, for was it not an attack on strangers?'

'What are their names?'

Gulden suddenly put his hand to his mouth. 'You know, Mr Shakespeare, I have just had a terrible thought. I believe I may know the man you want.'

'Yes?' Shakespeare was impatient now.

'He is a man I have had much trouble with over the years.

He has accused me of taking his trade, for when I first came to London my premises were within two doors of his in Goldsmiths Row. He has insulted me in the street in the worst, most ungodly language and has had his apprentices throw stones through my windows and at my servants. I think he resents all strangers, perhaps because his clocks are so poor in comparison to ours. He has never built other than church-tower clocks of iron and steel, but wishes to learn our ways with finer machines . . .'

'But you believe this man has the skill necessary to make a timing device?'

'Oh yes, most certainly. He has learned enough.'

'His name, Mr Gulden, give me his name and where I may find him.'

'His name is Walter Stacker. Like me, he has moved from Goldsmiths Row. You will find him near St Paul's in Knightrider Street, to the east of the Doctors Commons. It is a poor house. You will know it by the clock on its wall. The time is always wrong.'

Chapter 32

SHAKESPEARE WAITED IN the dark shadows on the other side of the road from the house, observing it, waiting. He was neither tired nor hungry, but alert and expectant. For the first time in days, he felt he was moving, that he might be drawing close, that he would find a way to the men who had killed Catherine.

The occasional flicker of light through the drapes showed that the house was not asleep. Something was happening. Something would happen soon. He could feel it in his blood and in his tingling flesh. He was suffused with energy and a dreadful rage.

The street was almost deserted, save for the occasional night animal, crying for a mate. A pair of late-night revellers in the gowns of lawyers traipsed by but did not see him in the darkness. He was as still as stone, his eyes fixed. At last he saw a light by the window closest to the front door, then the door opened and a figure stepped out. The figure was that of a man. The man hesitated, looked up and down the street, then set off eastwards. Shakespeare followed him, softly, keeping his distance.

He could take the man at any time, but he wanted to see where he was going.

*

The rented warehouse by the glassworks in Crutched Friars was empty now, save for a drying heap of dung and the two people who stood by the great double door. Laveroke, also known as Baines and by a dozen other names, held a pitch torch and looked about him. All the gunpowder was gone. The air was thick with dust.

'How many barrels in the end, Mr Laveroke?'

'Two hundred and ten. Each of a hundred pounds. That must be more than twenty thousand pounds, Doña Ana.'

Ana looked at Laveroke's handsome face. His teeth shone white. When would she see him again? Another month, another year, five years? It was always pleasant when their paths crossed. He was full of energy, clever, merciless. She was the chief and the thinker, Laveroke the foot soldier and killer.

'And is it now packed tight in the vessel?

Laveroke laughed. 'As tight as a bull in a cow. There are no holes in this *Sieve*.'

Ana did not laugh. 'We need to be clear now,' she said. 'We need to be precise on our roles. Timing is everything. No one must fail. It is a simple plan: an assassination in Scotland, a powder blast, an uprising in London. If each of these three parts succeeds, this tinder-dry island will blaze like a dead oak . . . and fall.'

The two of them stood in silence a moment. Ana said this was simple, but they both knew the plan had been long in the devising. These two people were the only ones outside the Escorial who understood it in its entirety. Its success depended on no one else understanding it.

Neither Curl and his band of English malcontents, nor the Scots, understood what they were engaged on. Curl and his men believed they were staging a commoners' revolt, rising up against the hated foreigners and their noble sponsors. The

Scots believed they were taking revenge against James for the roasting of their kin. They were all dupes.

'How fares our Prince Francis Philip?'

Ana Cabral drew a short draught of smoke through her ebony pipe. 'He is . . . as well as can be expected. His every need is catered to, as befits a prince of the royal blood of Scotland, England and France.'

'And yet?'

Ana shrugged her shoulders. 'What can I say? He is not like other men.'

'Would it not be better to move him to Scotland now?'

'No. He must stay here. We will do nothing but build up his name. Let his legend grow while the fires rage. The prince's hand must remain clean, unstained by blood. The moment will become clear. When blood and fire rain down on Scotland and when England's Roman Catholic faithful take arms against the dog-spittle Cecils. That is when the prince will step forward as saviour.'

'If ever I settle down to a quiet life farming some orange grove in Castile, I think you would make a perfect wife, Doña Ana.'

Ana smiled and performed a light curtsy. 'I am flattered, Mr Laveroke, though I fear I will never be the marrying kind. Now, sir, let us kneel and pray for God's benediction on our enterprise, done in His name. Then you must ride. By the time the *Sieve* blows its hole you should be halfway to Edinburgh, for I believe you have an appointment with the King that you must not miss.'

It seemed to Boltfoot that William Sarjent slept. He had been watching him through narrowed eyes for the best part of half an hour and had seen no movement. Sarjent had done with his incessant tales of his own heroism in battle, but was he really sleeping?

Boltfoot ached in every bone and sinew. The skin on his back was on fire with pain from the burning, yet he had to move, and move with stealth. Now. There might be no other time.

He rose to his feet. It was dark save for a guttering tallow candle. He was a little stronger now. He looked down at the still figure of William Sarjent, and his eyes immediately went to the man's wheel-lock and dagger. He looked about at his surroundings. There was nothing here to hold him in, yet could he move soundlessly enough to escape? If Sarjent awoke, Boltfoot would never outrun him. Sarjent had the weapons. Boltfoot had to take control before he could get away. He took a pace forward. He was within three feet of the man. If he could prise the dagger from the belt, he would have Sarjent at his mercy.

Sarjent exhaled, then drew in a deep breath that rattled in the back of his throat. He was snoring. He must be asleep. Boltfoot went down on one knee and reached out for the hilt of the dagger. Sarjent's hand flashed out like the head of a snake; his fingers clasped on Boltfoot's hand, like hissing jaws.

With his other hand, Sarjent took the wheel-lock from his belt, and pushed its muzzle into the centre of Boltfoot's face.

'Dear me, Mr Cooper. I told you mariners were no match for a soldier. Sit yourself down, if you would.'

Boltfoot gritted his teeth in frustration and sank back in his place close to the tower's wall of stone blocks.

'Now where was I? Ah, yes, I was telling you about the Scottish lads and lassies. They were witches, you see, Mr Cooper. Mighty riled by their king, I do believe. Do you not know the tale of the witches of North Berwick?'

Boltfoot said nothing.

'It is a tale of much dancing, cannibalism and fornicating with the devil. But let us start at the beginning. Three years ago, King James of Scotland sailed home from Copenhagen with his new young bride, Anne of Denmark. And a mighty anxious time he had of it, by all accounts, for a great storm blew up, sinking one of his fleet and endangering his own life. It was said that his ship was the most badly buffeted save the one that perished. No one could explain this strange, unexpected weather, for the sea had been calm. What you may ask, Mr Cooper, had this to do with witches? All became clear a year later. A coven was uncovered by a lord's bailiff in a village near Edinburgh.'

Sarjent quaffed some ale and offered the flagon to Boltfoot. He took it and drank, for his throat was as arid as a stone.

'It came about like this. The bailiff had a pretty young maidservant named Gellie Duncan, who claimed some magical skill at the curing of illnesses and the healing of wounds. The bailiff suspected her of witchcraft to have such powers. With the help of others, he questioned the wretched girl with the help of a thumbscrew and other means, but she confessed to nothing.

'But then a mark was spotted upon her throat, the mark of Satan. Again she was tortured, and this time she confessed that she was, indeed, a bride of the devil and that all her cures were done by witchcraft. Once her mouth was open, there was no stopping her. The names of all the rest of her coven came tripping from her tongue – men and women, goodwives of Edinburgh, even a schoolmaster. In all, she accused thirty or more people of being witches with her.

'Among them was a midwife named Agnes Sampson, who at first denied any dealings with the devil. But when she was tortured and a mark of Satan found upon her, she confessed to all that pretty maid Gellie had confessed. And she told yet more of their doings, the most notorious being a meeting of two hundred witches in the church of North Berwick on the eve of All

Hallows.' Sarjent wiped his sleeve across his ale-soaked beard. 'Are you following me, Mr Cooper?'

Boltfoot growled sullenly.

'It was said this church meeting was organised by the school-master, Dr John Fian, a man with powers, who was as nimble as the devil. He used this skill for the collecting of cats for Satan, to help him raise storms. His purpose in bringing all the black-clad coven to this church was to meet the devil himself. Well, old Lucifer did turn up, baring his fangs and scaring them with his claws, no doubt. And he told them he had a little mission for them: he wanted them to go to sea and sink King James's ship, for he did not like his Christian ways.'

None of this made sense to Boltfoot. He had other matters on his mind. Yet he found himself curiously beguiled by the tale.

'Without ado, the witches set to sea in sieves, carrying with them a cat that had been drawn nine times across a fire, one of the beasts captured by the catlike Dr Fian.

'When they saw what they believed to be the King's ship, the devil ordered Dr Fian to hurl the cat into the sea – a satanic version of baptism, I am told by those who know about these things – which he did. This caused the seas to rage and the wind to howl up into a tempest that nearly sank the King's ship and *did* sink another. The devil's fleet then returned to North Berwick in their sieves. Upon reaching shore, the happy witches marched to the church. Gellie Duncan was at the front playing the Jew's harp.

'The church door was locked, so Dr Fian blew through the keyhole and it burst open. The church was in darkness, so the cunning schoolmaster blew on the dead candles and they came alight. The devil was already there, waiting for them, standing in the pulpit with his long tail hanging over the edge. He made all the witches kiss his arse, then out they trooped into the churchyard and feasted on dead bodies from the graves. The evening ended with another dance, Gellie Duncan on her Jew's harp once more, playing a little satanic ballad called "Kimmer, go you before, kimmer go you".' Sarjent smiled evenly at Boltfoot. 'I trust I am not making you queasy, Mr Cooper?'

'I have not heard such gibberish in all my life.'

'Nor I, Mr Cooper, nor I. But there's many as did believe it, including the King of Scotland himself. All this was told at the trial of the witches, an event attended by King James in person, for he has a keen interest in witchcraft. He was also present at much of the torture of the unfortunate souls who were accused, and even had Agnes Sampson brought to him at the palace of Holyrood House so that he might examine her in person. While there, she implicated Lord Francis Hepburn, saying he was the leader of the witches and had been the chief conspirator.

'This earl, you may know, Mr Cooper, is the cousin of the King and would inherit his crown if he died without leaving children of his own. The King was loath to believe all this wild talk by Agnes, but then she asked him to draw near and whispered in his ear something that he had said to his bride on their wedding night, and which only they could know. James was so struck by this that he had the earl arrested. It didn't help poor foolish Agnes Sampson, though. She, Gellie Duncan, Dr Fian and many others were all burned to death on Castle Hill in Edinburgh, on the King's orders, for he proclaimed that witchcraft was a crime so abominable that it was God's law they should be so destroyed.

'As for the earl, he escaped and is still at large. But the thing is, you see, Mr Cooper, this all caused much resentment among those who loved the ones burned as witches. For each one burned at the stake, another ten wished harm upon their king. That was bad news for James, but a fine opportunity for a muster-master to raise an army of insurrection. Sons and daughters, brothers and sisters, nephews and nieces, mothers and fathers – all came flocking to our cause when they heard we had work to be done against this Scottish king and his English cousin. Do you understand a little now?'

Boltfoot made the occasional noise to make Sarjent think he was interested. All his thoughts were on finding a way to escape this place. He was feeling stronger, but Sarjent was a seasoned fighting man and would not let down his guard. He leant against the stone, hands never far from his sword, dagger and pistol, and talked incessantly by the tallow light.

'But what are we to do with you, Mr Cooper?' he said at last, as though he had finally come to the moment of truth. He shook his head. 'I had thought our dark-clad friends would so weaken you that when I rescued you, there would be a little gratitude and that I would discover exactly what your master has been told. But I now know you to be made of sterner stuff, that you will reveal nothing to me even to the point of death.' His voice turned harsh. 'There is no more to be learnt from you . . .'

Suddenly there was a noise outside. The three Scots stood there, three dark shadows against the dark sky. At that moment, a cloud slipped past and the moon cast a weak glimmer so that he could see their blank, cold faces and the dust and dirt stains on their black gowns. Boltfoot looked at his caliver in vain, for it was not loaded. And then he noticed another man behind them. Quincesmith. Jeremiah Quincesmith, the master of Rotherhithe Powdermill, where he had first encountered Sarjent. It could mean but one thing: they were confederates, misappropriating gunpowder together for God knew what purpose. He found himself thinking of Mr Knagg of Three Mills, hunted by pursuivants on Sarjent's orders. Please God he had not been taken. He gritted his teeth; there was nothing to be done about that now.

Sarjent grinned broadly. 'Why, Mr Cooper, talk of the devil. It appears our friends have come back for you. And my good friend Mr Quincesmith has arrived, too. They have all had a long day's toil. And I do believe they wish to hurl you into the sea like a cat and bring forth another tempest . . .'

Chapter 33

SOMEWHERE IN THE maze of houses that made up the poorest part of London, east of the city, Shakespeare stopped. His quarry was outside a house, looking up at its dark windows. Tentatively, the man knocked at the closed door, but there was no reply. He lifted the latch and the door opened. The man went in.

It had taken half an hour to reach this point. Shakespeare had followed the man through the dark streets with practised stealth. Now, he moved a little closer so that he could try to see inside the building into which the man had disappeared. There was no light except from a segment of moon, dipping in and out of the clouds. He heard his quarry calling softly inside the building, seeking someone. Still there was no reply. He heard his footsteps on creaking boards, moving deeper into the house. Shakespeare stepped through the doorway after him and found himself in a small empty hall. He could smell fresh wood, as though a carpenter had been at work. He waited in the gloom by the front door, unseen.

The man he had been following was walking up a flight of stairs, for he heard ancient boards bending under feet and a diminishing of the sound as he went higher up through the old building. All the time, there was the same soft calling, but no response. The footfalls began to get louder once more. The man was coming down again. Shakespeare tensed and waited, his poniard in his right hand.

He saw a vague shape. The man was in the front room, not three yards away. He had stopped. Shakespeare's heart beat faster. He heard a sniff, as though the man was smelling the air. Did he sense his presence? Shakespeare did not wait to find out. He lunged at the shape, knocking him to the ground, hard. The man let out a low moan as the air was beaten from his lungs by the fall. Shakespeare brought his left forearm down hard into the side of the man's head.

The man grunted with pain and tried to wriggle aside, but Shakespeare had him now, kneeling astride him, pinning him down at the shoulders and upper arms. With his left hand, he grabbed the man's hair and slammed his head down on to the floor and held it there. The tip of his poniard found the man's throat and pricked the skin, just enough to let him know that his life was forefeit if he tried anything. He moved his face down to the man's ear and whispered hoarsely. 'Mr Gulden, you have one slender chance of avoiding the butcher's filleting knife at Tyburn. You will tell me all you know. There will be no second chance.'

Peter Gulden was tall, probably as tall as Shakespeare, but he was soft and did not have the strength to resist.

'I cannot breathe!'

'If you can speak, you can breathe. And if you wish to continue to breathe, you will speak – and speak plain.'

'Let me up. I will talk. I will tell you everything, I swear it. I wanted none of this.'

Shakespeare increased the pressure on Gulden's head. 'Who were you expecting to find in this house?' he rasped.

'I don't know, please.'

The knife nicked the skin of his throat, a little flick of flesh cut away by the poniard's fine razor point. Blood ran along the blade and into the hot palm of Shakespeare's hand.

'Curl, maybe Curl . . . Laveroke. I came to find Laveroke.'

'And they were here?'

'Yes, in the past. With many others. I thought they would be here, but they are all gone.'

'Who is Curl?'

'Holy Trinity Curl.' Gulden spoke in a rush, his voice high-pitched with panic, as though he could not divulge his secrets fast enough. 'Curl and Laveroke. Mr Shakespeare, I am sorry about your wife. I beg your forgiveness, sir. I did not know they would do such a thing. They threaten my own family. My wife, my children—'

'Where are they?'

'In Spanish hands, in the Low Countries.'

'Not your family, Gulden. Laveroke and this Curl. If they are not here, where are they? You have built them another clock, I know it. Where is it?'

'I will take you there, Mr Shakespeare. Only spare me, sir. I beg you, spare my life.'

'Where?'

'Many miles from here – I do not know the name of the place, but I can take you.'

'Hellburners, yes?' The knifepoint again digging into his throat.

'One – one *hellebrander.*'

Shakespeare dragged Gulden to his feet and held him against the wall, the poniard close and sharp, his hand so tense it could rip Gulden's throat out with a single jerk. 'How far? East, west, north, south?'

'Eastward, Mr Shakespeare. Please, the dagger – I know it was eastward, perhaps forty miles – I was always taken there.'

'There must be stables near here. We need horses.'

'No, we must go by boat, downriver, Mr Shakespeare. An island in the Thames. The estuary.'

Shakespeare could feel the man's fear as his blood trickled through his fingers. He knew he had him, that he was a broken, terrified man. He took the poniard from Gulden's throat, wiped the blade on the man's sleeve, then thrust it in his own belt. He pulled him by the arm and pushed him hard out of the door. 'Then let us find a boat, Mr Gulden.'

It was no more than a quarter of a mile to the river. Shakespeare walked at a fast pace. Gulden stumbled ahead, saying nothing but clutching his nicked throat as he was pushed along. Shakespeare estimated they were some way east of St Katherine's Hospital, towards Thames pool. Ahead of them was a wharf. This was what he wanted. He saw a landing stage where fishermen had lanterns lit and were working on their nets. Two men were bringing their catch ashore from a moored, single-masted fishing boat, rigged fore and aft, which he guessed to be a skiff or small smack. He strode up to them.

'A good catch?'

'Aye master, fair enough.' The elder of the two men eyed Shakespeare cautiously, his eyes flicking to Gulden, who was clearly under duress.

'What will you make from it?'

'This little lot? I reckon there's four stone of good herring and salmon there. Got a couple of eels, too. But if you're buying, you're out of luck. It's all spoken for at Billingsgate.'

'I want to buy your services. One of you take the fish to market – the other sail us downriver. I'll pay you twice the price of the fish you have there, in gold.'

'We'll get a pound for this lot.'

Shakespeare didn't believe him, but he wasn't going to haggle. 'Two pounds, then. Here.' He spilt coins from his purse into the man's palm. 'Take it.'

The elder fisherman looked at the money in amazement, then glared into Shakespeare's eyes. 'What's this about?'

'Queen's business. I am in a hurry and have no time to explain. You must take us down the river . . . to one of the islands.'

The old fisherman hesitated, then laughed. 'Yes, master, I'll take your gold.' He winked at his companion. 'Robert, you get that fish to market and get them nets mended. I'll sail these gentry coves wherever they want. Go to the New World for that kind of gold, if so they please.'

Within two minutes the remainder of the catch was landed and Shakespeare and Gulden were in the sailing boat with the fisher, tacking out to mid-stream, where they caught the best of the ebb tide and began the race downstream. 'We'll make more'n ten knots an hour with this tide, master. But then it'll turn and we'll be like a sea snail. Now tell me, which of the islands is it you want?'

'Well?' he said to Gulden.

'I do not know its name. I wish I did. It is nothing but mud-flats and creeks, beyond Gravesend, well beyond it – towards the northern shore of the river.'

'Sounds like Canvey or Two Tree Island,' the fisher said.

'I'll know it when we see it,' said Gulden.

'How?' Shakespeare demanded. 'There is nothing to be seen in this darkness.'

The only light was the lantern the fisher kept by the tiller. There were few lights from the riverbank, yet he steered a course with the confidence that only a man who has been out on this stretch of water night after night all his life could have done. 'It will be light soon enough,' he said, addressing Shakespeare. 'If I'm sailing into danger, master, you might tell me what to expect.'

It occurred to Shakespeare that he might need the fisher's assistance before this day was done, so he explained briefly.

The fisher laughed. 'Should have asked for four pounds, not two.'

Shakespeare settled back towards the rear of the boat. The water became increasingly choppy as the river broadened. He had his sword across his lap, in case Gulden suddenly learnt courage. They travelled an hour or more in silence, all soaked through by the constant spray. The only sounds were the slapping of the waves and the occasional barking of a dog from somewhere on land, to the south or north. 'Well, Mr Gulden,' he said at last. 'It's time to hear your sorry tale.'

'How did you know?'

'That you were the clockmaker I sought? Instinct, Mr Gulden. Instinct is a powerful force. It is what Sir Robert Cecil pays me for. The ability to spot a deceiver. I suggest you try telling me some truths.'

Gulden was desperate to tell his tale. He had been at Antwerp in '85, had helped the clockmaker who set the timing device for the *Hope*. 'When Parma captured the city I fled, thinking the Spanish would hear of my part in the deaths of so many of their soldiers. My wife and children remained and I told them I would send for them. I had thought they would be safe, for Parma had pledged free passage to all Protestants. That was a terrible error on my part, for I fell into the hands of two English soldiers – soldiers who had already sold their honour to Spain.'

Shakespeare could see, even in this poor lantern light, that tears were streaming down the Dutchman's face. 'My wife and children were taken hostage and I was told to seek refuge in England. I would have to perform certain tasks for the Spanish and my family would be safe. If I did as I was told, I would, in time, be reunited with them. And so I came here and met up again with Signor Giambelli and worked with him on the English hellburners plan, all the while giving details of our progress to the Spanish. I must say that Giambelli knew nothing of my double-dealing. I kept begging the Spanish to let my wife and children join me, but to no avail. And now . . . now I have destroyed your family, Mr Shakespeare, with my infernal clocks, and I fear I will soon have aided and abetted in a plan to kill many, many more. I would take my life, hurl myself into this river. I have thought of such a course of action often enough, but I do nothing. I am a coward.'

'You spoke of two English soldiers?'

'Yes.'

'What became of them?'

'They are here in England. They were my contacts. They are the ones who gave me my orders and made me work for Laveroke and Curl.'

'Their names?'

'William Sarjent and Jeremiah Quincesmith. In the Low Countries, they were armourers and gunpowder men with Captain-General Norris and the Earl of Leicester. But they dealt treacherously, communicating secrets to Parma and others on the Spanish side. I always believed their motive was gold, not religion.'

'Did you say Sarjent?'

Gulden nodded grimly and wiped a sleeve across his bloody, tear-stained face. In the distance, directly ahead of them, Shakespeare caught the first glint of the rising sun. He felt a cold knotting in his entrails. Sarjent – the man the Cecils believed to be their intelligencer. Boltfoot had been handed to him, like a tethered sacrifice in an arena of lions.

Chapter 34

A FLOCK OF seabirds, waking with the dawn, drifted across the bows. The dirty, off-white canvas of the sail billowed in the following breeze. The cloud had gone, and it was becoming a bright, sun-filled morning.

The river narrowed as they passed the ferry port and shipyard of Gravesend, bustling with dozens of great vessels. Tall cranes of oak and elm reached out their arms across the wharves. Dominating it all were the battlements of Gravesend fort, built earlier in the century by Elizabeth's father, to deter any enemy who might think of attacking London from the Thames. Then the river broadened out again and the signs of humanity ashore diminished, though the waterway was still decorated by the slow-changing scape of dozens of sails. On another day, a man might have found himself captivated by the raw beauty of this wild stretch.

Shakespeare saw none of it and wished to hear no more of Peter Gulden's treachery. He turned to the fisher. 'How far have we come?'

'Twenty-five miles, but the tide is turning.'

'Do you recognise any landmarks, Mr Gulden?'

'Only the Gravesend docks. I have been this way twice before. I would say there is an hour to go if this current holds, perhaps less.'

'No, we have had the best of the tide,' the fisher said. 'It'll be slow going now.'

The Thames began to curve northwards in the last great bend of the river before its gaping mouth opened into the North Sea. The waters were becoming rougher as the tide turned. A swell of waves pushed hard against the bows of the fishing boat. The turbulence and the stench of fish began to turn Shakespeare's stomach, but he refused to submit to nausea, unlike Gulden, who puked over the side. The fisher had to use all his experience and knowledge of the wind to keep the craft on its downriver course.

'There will be islands soon,' the fisher said. 'Canvey, Two Tree and Incular to the north, in Essex. A few others, too. Then Grain and Sheppey to the south, in Kent. Bleak, inhospitable places all of them, fit for nothing but sheep and outlaws.'

A high-masted square-rigger rode the tide past them, on its way upriver. From the poor state of its sails and rigging, a man might have deduced it was returning from a voyage halfway around the world.

'There,' Gulden said tersely, pointing northwards as the vessel finally straightened out eastward once more. 'The tree.'

Shakespeare scanned the northern bank. He saw a few squat trees dotted along the land a mile or so up ahead, but none that stood out in any way. 'Mr Gulden?'

'The dead tree. It has the shape of a bull's head. The two branches stick up like horns. I noted it before. That is the island.'

'Canvey,' the fisher said.

'There is a series of creeks on its northern shore. The hell-burner is moored in one of them. At low tide it will be stranded in the mud; but with this tide coming in it won't be long before she floats.'

'When were you last here?'

'Two days since. It was not fully prepared; they were still loading the powder. They had men working on it, Scottish men. Carting aboard bricks and slabs of stone and rusted iron tools. It must be near completion. My work on the clock is finished. It is my best work . . . I was told its success would bring my family to me. Now I pray you will destroy it before more harm is done.'

'What are they planning for it?'

Gulden seemed about to speak, but then shook his head. 'I do not know.'

'You were about to say something, Mr Gulden. I suggest you say it before I spill your blood in the Thames.'

'I did hear something . . . something I do not think I was meant to hear.'

'Yes?'

'Laveroke was with Sarjent. I heard them talk of a bridge. That is all. I straightway thought of the great London bridge . . .'

London Bridge. What better target for an enemy of England. Shakespeare shuddered. If a hellburner had killed a thousand men aboard a boom of wooden ships across the Scheldt, what might one of similar size do to this bridge, the greatest such structure in the world? Countless numbers would die and it would blow London in two, cutting the city off from Southwark for months or years to come. If true, it was a plot of nightmares.

London Bridge. The glory of England, a spectacle that men and women travelled from the far corners of the globe to set eyes on. Less a bridge than a small town. Many of the city's greatest houses, some seven storeys high, were supported by its nineteen stone arches. More than a hundred and thirty of the finest shops lined its nine-hundred-foot span. It had once even had its own church, the chapel of St Thomas Becket, standing atop the central section, but the Protestants had closed it and turned it into a fine dwelling for a merchant. And at the southern end, the gatehouse with its piked heads of traitors, a symbol of unforgiving power to all who harboured treasonous thoughts about their monarch. The irony of that was not lost on Shakespeare.

London Bridge. Above all, it was a thoroughfare that carried the lifeblood of the city, the beating heart of England. Constantly in use, throughout the day. At its busiest times, it might bear the weight of two to three thousand people, along with their wagons, horses and driven farm beasts. How many men, women and children would die if a hellburner wrought its malign work there, blowing them to pieces or sweeping them into the river's flood? It was enough to make any man quake with fear and anger.

As they tacked into an inlet to the east of the island, Shakespeare was thinking fast. He had little idea what to expect at this place. Gulden said there had been men here when last he came. But who would be here this day, and how would they be armed? He had two wheel-lock pistols and a pouch of a dozen balls and a horn of powder. Apart from that, he had his sword and poniard. It was little enough.

'See that tower over there?' said Gulden, pointing to a ruin. 'We are not far off now.'

'Moor here, Master fisher,' Shakespeare said.

'This place is naught but mud and sheep, master.'

'I would dearly wish it so.'

The fisher brought the boat in close to shore. Shakespeare jumped out and found himself sinking in thick clay up to his ankles. The incoming waves lapped around his legs. He pulled Gulden out after him, by his collar. Stumbling, Gulden toppled headlong into the turbid surf. Shakespeare left him to struggle to his feet and turned to the fisher. 'I would ask you to stay here. You already have my gold . . .'

'I'll be here, master. I have ears. I heard what was said.'

'Good man. I need one more thing from you – rope.'

The fisher gave Shakespeare a coil of mooring cord, which he curled around his shoulder. Then he primed and loaded a pistol and pushed its muzzle into Gulden's dripping face. 'Which direction?'

'We follow the shoreline a little north, then westward, in the lea of this hillock. I sailed there before. That castle –' he nodded towards the ruined tower, at the top of the incline – 'that was used by them as a storage space and shelter.'

'Walk.'

They trudged for quarter of an hour across the flat, desolate land. Even in this dry summer, the earth was boggy and the two men walked around dark pools, seeing nothing but sea-birds. Gulden walked ahead, his back arched, knowing all the while that Shakespeare's wheel-lock was pointed at him. To their right, the tower of the castle loomed. There was no sign of any human life. Suddenly Gulden stopped and pointed. 'There.'

Shakespeare followed Gulden's finger. He could see the tip of a mast about two furlongs off. He thrust the pistol into his belt. 'Lie down, on your face. Hands behind you.'

Without ceremony, he uncurled the rope and bound Gulden, hands and feet. He wrenched the rope tight, painfully tight, then knelt beside him in the marshy grass. 'If I survive, so might you. If I die, then you will waste and perish here. And no one will mourn you, Mr Gulden. The wind will blow through your bones for evermore, and no one will know that you are here, nor care. Not a soul on earth, nor God in heaven for what you have done . . .'

'Forgive me, Mr Shakespeare.'

Shakespeare said nothing. He could no more forgive Gulden than he could forgive the man who had taken the casks of powder to the Dutch market. For a moment, he thought of gagging Gulden, but that would have been a cruelty too far and would have likely brought death. Anyway, he wasn't going to cry out.

Shakespeare moved forward more cautiously. A little way off, to the left of the castle, he saw a copse of stunted trees and, from within it, a thin trail of smoke drifting skyward. Moving at a crouch now, he ran towards the thicket, a wheel-lock once again in his hand. From here he had a better view of the landscape. He could see the ship clearly. There were men moving about its decks. One or two others were ashore. The vessel was almost afloat with the rising of the tide.

He found the ashes of a fire in a clearing in the middle of the spinney. The earth was greatly disturbed. He shuddered at the sight of an empty, mud-thick coffin and a hole that looked like a grave. What in God's name had been happening here? There was more evidence that someone had been here recently: a hunk of bread, an empty flagon, tatters of charred clothing, sticks of burnt wood.

Coming out of the woods, he made his way to the ruin of the castle, keeping behind the brow of the hill as far as possible so that he would not be observed from below. He approached the ruins at a crouch. There was an old flagon. A rat was gnawing at some discarded food and ignored his approach.

Shakespeare gasped involuntarily. Boltfoot Cooper's caliver and cutlass were there. So Boltfoot had been here. He would not have left of his own accord without these weapons. Shakespeare picked them up. He had to do something, and fast.

He descended the incline towards the ship. If anyone looked up, he must be visible now. Close to the creek, he dropped to his belly, crawling forward to the raised bank of the creek. Looking over the grassy lip, he could see the mudflats sloping away down to the dark channel of water where the vessel rode. The ship was larger than he had expected. The *Hope* at Antwerp had been seventy tons, but from his knowledge he guessed this ship to be a bark displacing perhaps a hundred and twenty tons. Small enough at about sixty feet to negotiate these narrow waters, but large enough to carry many tons of gunpowder. It was afloat, but its painters were still secured. One plank from the gangway stretched down to a makeshift quay of old wooden struts driven into the mud.

Two men stood on the decking at the landward end of the plank. They were deep in conversation. From this distance, perhaps a hundred yards, he could make out their features clearly but did not recognise either of them. One was tall with a black beard, thin eyes and a military bearing. He had a scabbed nose. Shakespeare had heard of Sarjent suffering such an injury at the hands of Boltfoot. The other man was larger of body, with an enormous barrel chest, though not as tall as his companion. Shakespeare stared at them a few moments, buried as well as he could be in the tufts of grass. From the descriptions given him by Peter Gulden, it seemed entirely possible that the men were Sarjent and Quincesmith. His gaze drifted to the ship. Emblazoned on its prow was the word *Sieve*. Amidships he saw shapes, figures moving about. Eight or nine men, strangely attired in black. What could he do against such a band?

The creek was swelling rapidly with the incoming tide and the mooring lines were tightening as the ship rose. Soon, very soon, there would be enough depth to allow the vessel to bear room from this place. The shrouds were flapping in the wind. Would it sail this morning? Was this the day of reckoning? Surely, this was why these men were here. There was no loading, no construction. Their dread weapon was ready.

The two men who had been talking looked around.

Shakespeare ducked lower in the tufty grass, so that his face would not be visible. The larger of the two clapped the other man on his back and they both began striding up the plank to the ship.

Shakespeare rose to his feet. He held out the first pistol at arm's length, aimed it at the big man's back, and fired. The recoil of the weapon knocked him backwards. Through the billowing powder smoke he saw that the two men had stopped at the head of the gangway and were looking back in his direction, unharmed.

The bull-chested one cupped his hands to his mouth. 'You're a little late.' Then he laughed and kicked the boarding plank away from the vessel. He took a dagger from his belt and strode around the bulwarks, slashing at the mooring ropes, cutting the vessel adrift.

Shakespeare was reloading the wheel-lock, keeping his hands as steady as he could as he poured in the powder. From the corner of his eye, he saw that there was much activity aboard the vessel. A bundle was hanging in nets from the bowsprit and one of the men in black was clambering, like a monkey, along this spar at the front of the ship. The one he assumed was Quincesmith had a long-barrelled musket. He had climbed a companion ladder to the poop deck and now rested the muzzle of the weapon on the bulwark. He lit the match, blew on it so that it glowed, then fired.

The ball spat past Shakespeare and slapped into the mud a foot to his side.

Shakespeare dived to his left. He was an open target and his pistols were impotent against such a long-range weapon.

The ship was drifting out into mid-stream. Six of the figures in black were climbing the rigging, unfurling sails.

'I know not who you are,' the man with the musket called. 'But if you want the man Cooper, you will be pleased to learn that he hangs from the bowsprit. Our Scots friends couldn't find a cat, but they are satisfied that he will do as well in the casting of spells.' He bellowed a laugh that made his barrel chest quake.

Shakespeare's eyes drifted back to the bows. The black-gowned man was sawing at the rope that held the bundle. As Shakespeare watched, the bundle twisted from the severed netting, then fell like a stone into the dark waters of the creek.

For a moment it sank, then bobbed back to the surface, drifting beside the vessel on the side nearest the shore. Shakespeare tried to make sense of what had just happened. Was that really Boltfoot wrapped up like a dead mariner in a canvas shroud and tossed overboard? Was he alive or dead?

The ship's sails were catching the wind and she was gathering a little speed. Shakespeare hesitated no more than a few seconds. He divested himself of his weapons and doublet and dived into the mud-churned water.

William Sarjent had taken the whipstaff, the lever that swung the tiller, and was steering a course away from the creek. He felt a rush of irritation that this man had somehow got so close to them. He seemed to be alone, though. Better to finish him now, before setting sail. They could not afford to miss this tide, so it had to be a well-aimed musket-ball.

At the side of the vessel, Jeremiah Quincesmith reloaded the matchlock and fired downwards at the swimming man. The weapon was accurate enough when fired horizontally with the support of a stand, but firing downwards from a moving vessel was near to hopeless. The balls slapped silently into the grey water, one after the other as Quincesmith loaded and reloaded. He cursed the Scots for their maddening super-stition. Why hadn't they merely put a dagger up beneath the cooper's ribcage?

*

Shakespeare swam with all his strength. He was a strong swimmer, but he was encumbered by his clothing and held back by the tidal current that swept in and kept him from the bundle he had to reach.

'Boltfoot!' he roared above the waves, and choked on a mouthful of salt water for his pains.

He redoubled his stroke power. But the distance did not seem to shrink. On and on he drove himself, his muscles cramping, his lungs in agony. Suddenly he was there. He grasped hold of the canvas-wrapped weight. From his belt he took his dagger and slashed and slashed at the ropes and canvas that bound the limp parcel.

Desperately paddling his legs beneath the surface, he clawed at the bundle, ripping, shredding, hacking with no plan other than to free whatever was inside it.

Piece by piece, the canvas and ropes came away. And there was Boltfoot Cooper, motionless in his arms. Shakespeare slapped his face for a response but there was nothing, just cold blue flesh. Regardless, he lay back and stretched Boltfoot's limp body atop his, clasping him beneath the armpits and kicking out with his feet to draw him, inch by inch, to shore and away from the musket-fire.

Chapter 35

S HAKESPEARE FELL BACK into the mud, his feet in the water. He panted for breath. Boltfoot lay beside him, still as death. He had been far lighter to carry here through the waves than Shakespeare would have imagined. It was no effort at all, but now all his energy was expended.

Had he really lost Catherine and Boltfoot within the space of a week? The two people, apart from his children, that he loved best in the world. He could not let it happen. With a force born of rage, he struggled to his knees, then turned Boltfoot on his side.

'You are going to live, Mr Cooper,' he said. 'I order you to live.'

He pulled back his right hand, full swing, and slammed it into Boltfoot's back as if he were a midwife determined that an uncrying newborn should utter its first wail and take its first breath. The back arched at the blow and a terrible scream broke forth from somewhere inside. Boltfoot spewed out water, then retched and howled again.

'Boltfoot!'

Shakespeare tried to turn Boltfoot over, but he fought against it, spluttering, gasping for breath, coughing up water.

'Help me, Boltfoot,' Shakespeare ordered, once again trying to turn him over.

Boltfoot let out a yell of pain, the noise of a dying animal, the scream he had refused to emit even when he lay long hours in the coffin and when he was passed across the fire. Now it came from him, as if from the ravines of hell.

Shakespeare stopped trying to move Boltfoot and he flopped forward, taking in great aching breaths.

'I thought you were dead.'

'Blood of Christ, Mr Shakespeare! My back . . .'

Shakespeare examined Boltfoot's back and saw the tatters and flaming crust of red blisters. He looked out across the creek. The bark was just disappearing around the low headland, its sails unfurled and billowing with the breeze that came up the Thames from the North Sea. He tried to gauge whether it would head up the river towards the bridge or down to the open sea, but could not tell from here.

'Boltfoot, I see your terrible injuries, but we have little time. Are you able to walk?'

Boltfoot turned on to his front, on all fours. Slowly, he rose to his knees. Shakespeare got up and stood before him. He reached out and took his hands, lifting him to his feet. 'What has happened to your back? What did they do?'

'Those madpike Scotch witches roasted me like a suckling pig. Nine times they held me over the fire.' Boltfoot winced as he spoke.

'I say again, can you walk, or shall I leave you here and go for assistance?'

'I'm coming, master. I wish to drown those black-clad drabs as they tried to do for me.'

Shakespeare was about to turn away, inland, when the fishing boat hove into view, drifting in on the tide.

'I think assistance has arrived, Boltfoot.'

*

'Did you see the bark, master fisher?'

'Indeed, sir. Driving upriver with the tide, and with the wind for the moment. But it will soon change against her and she will have to tack, even though the tide's swell will give her a ride. She did look a mighty cumbersome vessel, lumbering low in the water.'

'She carries a heavy burden of death. Can we catch her?'

'Given time, aye. But then what will you do? I don't believe a broadside from your pistols will cause them much consternation.'

'We'll fetch Gulden, then head for Gravesend.'

Shakespeare settled back beside the fisher. Boltfoot sat with his back over the low bulwark, his burns soothed by the wind. Shakespeare had inspected the scorching and realised there was nothing he could do but get him to an apothecary. 'You smell like roast pork, Boltfoot, but I fear you will survive.'

Boltfoot tried to smile, glad of Master Shakespeare's disrespectful jesting. The last thing he wanted was sympathy.

Gulden lay, bound, in the bottom of the hull, soaking in fish-stinking bilge-water. Shakespeare had tossed him there, saying he would serve as ballast.

In the distance, as they rounded the cape of Blythe Sands, they could make out the sails of a bark, three miles distant. Was that the *Sieve*?

The harbour-master at Gravesend was a straight-backed former mariner named Winch. He looked at the fishing smack and its occupants with undisguised scorn.

'Look what the tide brought in today, Mr Adam,' he said to the man at his side on the dock. 'Never have I seen such miserable flotsam.'

'I'd throw them back, Mr Finch.' James Adam was about

forty. He was a man of middling height, with the weathered forehead of a mariner, though the cut of his clothes suggested he was a ship's officer rather than an ordinary seaman.

'We need help,' Shakespeare said, stepping unsteadily from the boat. 'This is Queen's business.'

'And I'm the King of France,' Winch said.

'A plague of toads, I know that dismal face,' Adam said suddenly. 'I'd recognise that face and that excuse for a foot anywhere. Why, it's Boltfoot Cooper!'

'Mr Adam,' Boltfoot said grimly.

'Aye, Cooper, I'm your master. Finest ship's master you ever served under. How in England's name have you landed here? Are you shipwrecked?'

'Something like that.'

'I will explain,' Shakespeare said, taking Adam's arm and holding it unnecessarily tight, 'if you will be silent a minute or two . . .'

Chapter 36

Luke Laveroke's hired horse clattered into the cobbled stable-yard behind the Waggoner's Arms, a post inn a little way south of Derby. He had beaten the horse mercilessly. Its sides were blood-streaked from his sharp-wheeled spurs and it was flecked with sweat. Quickly he dismounted and handed the reins to the ostler.

'Have a fresh horse saddled for me in three hours,' he ordered, affecting a French accent.

The ostler looked at the post-horse in dismay. 'You'll have no horse from here if you treat him like that, master.'

Laveroke tossed him a gold sovereign. 'Three hours.' He strode through into the inn's taproom and demanded a room with food: roast capon with pickled cabbage and Levant raisins. 'And half a flagon of good Gascon wine, unsweetened.'

The chamber was on the first floor with a four-poster bed. He removed his dusty boots and lay back on the sheets, his doublet loosened. He would eat quickly, rest without sleeping, then resume his journey. Riding post, he believed he could make Edinburgh in three days. When the *Sieve* blew, he would be well away from London. No man would outride him to Scotland. The King of Scots would have no knowledge of events in England; his guard would be down and he would be content to meet an envoy – an old friend – from France.

Their meeting would be in the presence-chamber, alone, for he would say he had possession of a secret missive from Henri of Navarre. Laveroke had met James twice before, under another, French name, and he had charmed the monarch with much flattery, extravagant gifts of gold and tales of the French court's debauchery. The King would welcome him again, but this time Laveroke's long-bladed dagger would be in his sleeve. It would slide down into his right hand, then sink into James's soft, unsuspecting belly and drive upwards into his heart. All the while, Laveroke's left hand would be at the King's weakling mouth, stifling his cries, holding him close and silent until death. Speed was all. *Unhurried* speed. Kill, then walk away. Nod to the guards, smile at the courtiers, touch them lightly on the shoulder and bow extravagantly to their ladies, walk without haste, but depart. Then ride eastward like the furies, for North Berwick where the kin of Agnes Sampson and Gellie Duncan would smuggle him aboard a collier-ship to safety.

A girl of seventeen or so arrived with his food and wine. He watched her closely as she lay the tray down upon a table near the window. She looked like any one of the peasant girls he had supplied for Don Antonio. They were all the same to him, all available at the right price, all disposable. He smiled at her and held up a shilling coin for her to take.

Her blue eyes opened wide. A shilling was a week's wages in this part of England. 'Thank you, sir.' She took the coin in her small hand.

'My pleasure, mam'selle.'

She giggled at the strange tone of his words and the healthy sheen of his handsome face and hair.

'Will you pour me a cup of wine?'

She bowed again and did so, then brought the cup to him where he lay, reclining on the pillows beneath the bed's canopy.

'And a cup for you, mam'selle.'

She reddened. 'I shouldn't, sir.'

'But you will – for me, yes.' His hand touched her pale arm and she did not move away.

A shy smile crossed her lips. 'If you wish.'

'I do.'

'But there is only one cup, sir.'

'Then you will have to drink from mine. Here.' He held it to her rich lips as if she were a communicant. 'Do you like it?'

She nodded.

'Sit with me here.' His arm circled her slender waist and brought her down so that she sat on the edge of the bed.

'Where are you from, sir? You have a most curious voice.'

'You do not like it?'

'No, no, sir, I like it very much.'

'Today I think I am a sultan from Turkey, and I should like you in my seraglio.' He held up another coin, a small gold one. 'This for a kiss, mam'selle.'

'You do not need to pay me, sir.' She leaned over and kissed him, quickly, on his bristled cheek.

'Take the money, please, for I am a wealthy man and you are a beautiful girl.' *Oh, you want the money,* he thought, *you just do not like the connotation. But you will take the money. I will make it easy for you.* 'It is worth a sovereign just to gaze upon your face. From the Russias to Peru, from the Moluccas to Africa, I swear I never set eyes on such beauty.'

No one had ever called the girl beautiful before. In truth, she had only once seen her face in a looking-glass and had wondered whether she might be fair. Her skin was clear and her eyes were bright. Many men passed this way and sojourned here on their ride north or south, yet she had never met one such as this. She accepted the compliment and, glowing inside from his words, she accepted the coin too.

*

Rabbie Bruce ate his supper alone in a booth of the Waggoner's Arms taproom. The young capon was excellent, with crispy, blackened skin and juice running from the flesh. He had seen Laveroke enter the hostelry and had smiled to himself. This was going to be easier than he had expected. He would not have to make the long journey to Edinburgh after all. He carved a slice of breast flesh with his dagger. It was a good knife, crafted from hard steel and bone. He had killed with it before and it would serve its purpose again.

In the back room of The Pelican, sometimes known as the Devil's Tavern, close by Wapping, to the east of the Tower, Holy Trinity Curl rattled a pair of wheel-lock pistols in the air. 'Will you die like dogs or fight like men?' he bellowed.

'We'll fight!' the powerfully armed men roared back. There were thirty-eight of them in the room, too few to fill it. There should have been seventy or more, fifty at the very least. Warboys had even suggested there could be more than a hundred.

'Where are the others?' Curl had whispered to his lieutenant, Oliver Kettle, a few minutes earlier.

'Slipped away, scared, the mangy-arsed maggots.'

'And Warboys? Why is he not here? He's not scared. Never, not Warboys.'

'Tom says Warboys is sick with the flux. But I reckon he's cup-shot in a gutter somewhere. He's always been one for the strong ale and aqua coelestis when things got rough. Maybe he'll turn up.'

'Well, the devil's puke on them all. We'll stand and fight, Mr Kettle.'

'Aye, that we will.'

'The poor will join us for they have nothing to lose, the prentices will fight with us for they hate the strangers, and the merchants will do nothing to stop us for they want their trade back. Our only foes are the Cecils and their council of traitors. Who could fear Little Crookback or Old Whitebeard? Wait until the *Sieve* blows, then we will strike. Then the people will join our apostle band and tear down the walls of the palaces. It will be as if Bedlam had opened wide its doors. Do the men all know their separate duties?'

'They do. Eight to the Dutch church with me, with honed blades and sharp axes; twenty on the street with you to march on the bridge and gather men as you go; those remaining – the ones who should have been under Mr Warboys's command – will cross the river with Mr Foal instead, there to meet Mr Sarjent, Mr Quincesmith and the Scots contingent when they disembark. Together, they will march on Greenwich. All will stand firm. There is not a craven spirit in this room.'

Curl had his doubts. He surveyed the men ranged before him; they were hard enough now, but how would they be when the firing began? He banged the butts of his wheel-locks on the table, repeatedly, like a drumroll. The men roared back their approval, and Curl's misgivings began to evaporate into the smoke-filled room.

'Will you cut their Dutch throats, in their temple praying?' he bellowed.

'Aye,' the men called back, 'we will cut their throats.'

Curl's mouth tightened, his lips turned down; he banged the butts of his pistols down on the table once more. 'Then stand with me, brothers-in-arms. Our swords shall play the orators for us. Be bold, be resolute – and this day you shall see a victory for England as great as Agincourt or Crécy!'

The *Swiftsure*, a royal ship of three hundred tons with thirty-four guns, cruised upstream with elegant majesty. As a fighting ship against the Armada, she had carried a complement of one hundred and eighty men, but James Adam had been able to muster no more than thirty, which was enough to get the ship under way and man the cannon.

They had departed from Gravesend with great speed. She was well scrubbed, having recently been refitted and armed in preparation for a tour of duty patrolling the narrow sea.

'Well, Mr Cooper,' Adam said as they rode the churning flood past Dartford, 'it seems we are shipmates once more. I had heard you were now a scurvy freshwater mariner.'

Boltfoot ignored his old master's insult. They had been together before Drake's circumnavigation. Adam had always been fair enough, but he had been hard, too.

'Catch her, Mr Adam,' Shakespeare said. 'That is all I demand of you – catch this wretched vessel.'

'If the *Swiftsure* cannot, nothing can. I reckon her the fleetest galleon in the Navy Royal, sir. With the wind and tide behind us, we'll make ten knots. Your floundering bark will not make half that speed.'

'How do we do this? Can we board the *Sieve*? Gulden insists he is able to disarm the clock.'

'I trust you are making jest with me, Mr Shakespeare.' Adam glanced at the Dutchman who stood with them on the poop, his brow creased in fear. 'If it was my decision, I would string the man up from the yard-arm here and now.' He turned back to Shakespeare. 'There is but one thing to do – blow her out of the water, and all in her.'

Shakespeare had feared this was what he would say. It was not an option that brought him joy. Cecil might be pleased to learn that they had saved London Bridge, but he would not be happy with a thunderous blast breaking the peace of Her Majesty.

'Now then, Mr Shakespeare,' Adam said, 'pray tell me, what do you think that ship is, ahead one mile? Does that bark look like your *Sieve*?'

Shakespeare shrugged his shoulders. One vessel looked like another to him. From this distance there was no way of knowing. 'We will need to close on her to tell.'

'Close to four cables,' Adam ordered his helmsman. He turned back to Shakespeare. 'Eight hundred yards. Nearer than that would be insanity. I am not firing cannon at a ship packed with ten thousand or more pounds of powder when I'm broadside to her, sir, for she would blast us all to heaven.'

Boltfoot nodded grimly. 'That's her. I'd recognise the bastardly bark from ten miles, let alone one.'

'Helm,' Adam called. 'Bark ahead, mid-stream. Master gunner, prepare to fire starboard sakers, four cables. Helmsman, maintain course, then turn about on order.'

Shakespeare grasped James Adam's sleeve. 'God's blood, you cannot fire on her. Look about her, sir. The river teems with ships and boats.'

Adam shook his arm free from Shakespeare's grip. 'Would you have us wait until we are outside Greenwich Palace, or the Tower? Or why not let her sail merrily into the bridge itself, which is, you say, their plan? Do you think there will be fewer vessels as we approach the great wharves and dockyards? The Thames is the busiest waterway on the face of the earth, Mr Shakespeare. There is no safe place to do this. I will attempt to take her as she passes the Erith marshes, then all we can do is pray.'

He sighed in resignation. 'Fire at will, Mr Adam.'

James Adam grinned. 'Our figurehead is a tiger, Mr Shakespeare. Let me show you how we open our jaws and bite . . .'

*

The first volley fell fifty yards short of the *Sieve*. 'Come about, helmsman,' Adam called. 'Master gunner, prepare for a second salvo, larboard sakers, range plus fifty yards.'

From the poop of the *Swiftsure*, Shakespeare could see frantic activity aboard the target ship. He felt the tight knot of fear. If the *Sieve* got through to London Bridge, it would be slaughter on a scale never known.

'Fire all guns!'

The second volley roared forth and the *Swiftsure* reverberated with the recoil, throwing up a great wash of water.

'A hit!' the master gunner cried out.

They had all seen the ball smash into the sterncastle of the bark. They saw, too, the mad racing of those aboard the *Sieve*, crowding to the back of the ship to see whence the attack had come.

'Come about again, master gunner. Starboard sakers, three and a half cables.'

Shakespeare squinted through the fug of gunpowder smoke that belched from the saker cannons, medium-sized guns that could hurl a five-pound ball a mile or more. He tried to peer closer; one of those on the *Sieve* was climbing down a rope ladder to a cockboat.

'Fire!'

The sakers boomed again. The *Swiftsure* rocked violently. Smoke billowed up. Time seemed to stand still.

And then it happened . . .

Chapter 37

AT FIRST THEY saw a plume of flame shoot up, fifty, a hundred feet in the air, perhaps more. A whoosh of fire, as if the earth itself spewed forth its entrails. So monstrous, so malevolent, it towered over the world and grew so that a man might think it would develop horns, hooves and a flashing red tail.

Almost simultaneously there was a great cloud of smoke, littered with a mass of wood splinters, iron, stones, bodies; all hurled upwards and outwards with uncontainable, venomous energy. Then the sound, a blast of such ear-splitting ferocity that the brain could scarcely register it, and the shock – a sudden wind with the power to knock a man off his feet, senseless.

The *Swiftsure* pitched over to the larboard at such an angle that all those aboard, all the cannon, all the stores, were hurled down. One saker drove two gunners into the sea, another crushed the master gunner's left leg.

Shakespeare fell hard into the bulwark, which saved him from going over the side. Boltfoot smacked into him, winding them both.

As the vessel righted itself, then heeled back over, they saw Mr Adam and the helmsman sliding across the deck like a pair of children sliding down a slope of snow on wooden boards.

Shakespeare clung on to a rope, and Boltfoot clung on to Shakespeare's waist.

At last the *Swiftsure* steadied. Shakespeare jumped up. He looked over the bulwark and saw two men in the sea. 'Men overboard!' he shouted, and dived in without thinking what he was going to do.

The water was churning foam. For the second time that day Shakespeare pushed out with an overarm stroke to try to save life. Then he saw the ship's boat, broken loose from its line to the *Swiftsure*, just two yards away. He lunged for it, grabbed the side and clambered in. There were two oars aboard. He started rowing towards the two seamen, one of whom was floundering, the other seeming unconscious.

Up on the ship's deck, Boltfoot looked upriver to a patch of water and floating debris where once a hundred-ton bark had been. Now it was no more than a hulk, alight and belching forth hot steam and smoke and surrounded by flotsam. No one within a hundred yards of the *Sieve* could have survived. Boltfoot looked at his hand. It was shaking. His hand had never shaken before, even in the hottest exchange of fire. He tried to imagine what such a blast would have done to London Bridge. It would have reduced its nine-hundred-foot span to rubble.

James Adam struggled to his feet and came across the wet, slippery deck to where Boltfoot stood. He put an arm around his shoulders. For a moment, Boltfoot forgot the pain of his scorched back and welcomed the touch of another human being.

'God's teeth, Mr Cooper, but my ears are ringing like Bow bells. I think it fair to say we hit the correct vessel, don't you?'

Boltfoot found himself laughing for the first time in many days. 'Aye, that I do, Mr Adam,' he said, shouting against the din of his own ringing ears. *Plenty of holes in that Sieve now*, he thought, but declined to say it.

Debris started to rain down on them – wood, ash, fluttering shreds of sail, blood.

'Time to haul Mr Shakespeare aboard and look to the injured,' Adam shouted back.

The damage to the *Swiftsure* was not great. A broken spar, cracks in the bulwarks and gunports where the sakers had rolled. The whipstaff and bilge-pump would need repairs, but they were minor faults, easily remedied.

The harm to the men was greater. The master gunner's shin and thigh were broken and one of the sailors Shakespeare had brought in had concussion from a head injury. As the officers fought to bring order out of chaos, Shakespeare suddenly realised that Peter Gulden, the clockmaker, was missing.

'I saw him jump,' Boltfoot said. 'Just before the hellburner went up.'

They all peered over the bulwarks into the water.

'No sign of him,' Shakespeare said.

'Better dead than what he had coming had he lived,' Adam said.

'Wait – I think I see him there, amid the wreckage.'

There was a body, floating face down. They could tell from the man's rich attire and bald head that it was Gulden. From this distance, it seemed almost certain that he was dead. A pair of sailors were despatched to bring the body aboard.

Shakespeare said nothing. It would have been better if he had taken his life before ever he designed so foul a device, but Gulden had found his courage at last. He had been weak, not evil.

The *Swiftsure* was making way slowly. All along the route, they saw the anxious, news-greedy faces of spectators lining the banks. None knew what had happened and no one aboard the ship was about to tell them.

The officers and crew kept a look-out to see whether any other shipping or fisher boats needed assistance. The damage wrought seemed mercifully slight. Shakespeare looked over the poop bulwark at the remains of the *Sieve*. He saw the bodies of three of the black-clad Scots, floating face down. He could not tell whether they were men or women. Boltfoot had told him a little of their strange rituals. Doubtless other bodies would appear in the days to come, for none could have survived.

'Sister Agnes and Sister Gellie, you say?'

'They were kin of witches by that name, Mr Shakespeare,' Boltfoot said gloomily. 'Burned by James for setting to sea in sieves with intent to sink his ship.'

Shakespeare shook his head in bewilderment. Scots or English, heathen or Christian, he was certain of one thing: they were pawns in a bigger game. This was a Spanish conspiracy; Gulden the clockmaker had confirmed it. Everything had come from Madrid and from the Spanish regime in the Low Countries, and it was far from done. 'We cannot rest, Boltfoot. We must find this prince of Scots.'

At the time of the explosion, horses had reared and whinnied, men and women had stopped their work as far away as Chelsea and had looked at each other with questioning, unbelieving eyes. Was this the second coming, or had a powdermill exploded? London was rife with rumour and fear. At Greenwich Palace, Sir Robert Cecil had closed his keen eyes and murmured a prayer of supplication. He knew he would be summoned by the Queen for an explanation, so he immediately sent out messengers to gather information and to order the palace guard doubled, before making his way to the presence-chamber.

Across the river, Holy Trinity Curl had felt a surge of pride and satisfaction. It was all coming together. He would have his vengeance. The Dutch would die in their hundreds. He would make a special diversion to the Sluyterman household and do for them, every one. That would be the greatest pleasure. *Sluyterman.* The very name stank of foreign treachery and usury.

Oliver Kettle's brow furrowed at the sound of the blast. 'Mr Curl,' he said. 'This is three or more hours early. And the direction of the sound is not right. I would swear that blast was in the east, not the west.'

'Sound plays tricks, Mr Kettle. It will echo and distort. That was our hellburner, there can be no doubt. Glory be, the wind must have carried it sooner than we could have hoped. Have you ever heard a more thunderous or wondrous sound?' He turned to the gathering. 'This is our time, men. Have courage. File from here in good order and follow your commanders with the mettle of true Englishmen. When they see what damage is wrought, the prentices and journeymen will rise up in their hundreds, then their thousands. The stout hearts of London will join you, this I pledge.'

The *Swiftsure* picked up a group of six men whose fishing boat had been turned over and who were clinging to the upturned hull. They also went to the assistance of a fisher who had been struck by flying debris.

In the early afternoon, Adam ordered the ship to drop anchor off Greenwich to await the turn of the tide, which would not be long. Shakespeare and Boltfoot disembarked with the injured gunnery crew and the fishermen.

Cecil was on the quayside, standing apart from a group of courtiers. He was clutching a crystal goblet of red wine. Shakespeare hurriedly despatched Boltfoot and the seamen to be treated for their injuries, then bowed low to Cecil. The privy councillor was more tense than he had ever seen him.

'You heard the blast, Sir Robert?'

'Of course I heard the blast. They must have heard it in France!'

'It was a hellburner, greater even than the one used at Antwerp. Thanks to God's will and fine English gunnery, we were able to destroy it off Erith marshes. They had meant to blow the bridge and bring slaughter and mayhem to London. It was a conspiracy of terrible proportions involving many men. Even your father's intelligencer William Sarjent. There is much to be told.'

'Sarjent? God's faith, John, I am sorry . . .'

'He and Quincesmith have been double-dealing for years, since their time in the Low Countries. I suspect they took many tons of powder from Rotherhithe. They were in league with Baines and a rabble-rouser called Curl – and they nearly did for poor Boltfoot.'

'My father will be mortified. He never suspected Sarjent. If such a man betrays us, then who is to be trusted?' He shook his head gravely. 'Much has happened, John. The palace has been in uproar. The royal guard has been engaged in a skirmish with a band of renegades within this past hour. Seven of them, all now dead. They came upon Greenwich with stealth, thinking to storm through the palace unhindered. The guard was ready and killed them like dogs.'

'They must have been Curl's men.'

'Indeed. And a man identified as this same Curl tried to march through the city to the bridge. I am told his militia stopped in its tracks, open-mouthed with horror when they came close to the bridge, as if they had seen a spectre. Clearly, they had expected to see it destroyed and hoped to garner support among the people of London. Little did they realise what affection our London folk hold for Her Royal Majesty. When no one joined their band, they seemed unsure of what to do next. They were milling about like lost sheep when a detachment from the Tower found them and engaged them. Most of Curl's men tried to turn tail. Two or three escaped, but the others were either killed or captured. That is not all: there was another disturbance, at the Dutch church. But it was already heavily guarded and the rebels were driven off, excepting two dead, one of them their ringleader, a Mr Kettle.'

'What of Curl? Was he taken?'

Cecil shook his head briskly. 'No. He was recognised in the skirmish but escaped. What I want to know, Mr Shakespeare, is what in God's name is going on? Do we have a civil war on our hands?'

'It seems we have quelled the first wave, Sir Robert.'

'But?'

'But there is still this prince of Scots. Somewhere. We must find Baines and the Spanish woman. They hold the keys to this.'

Cecil looked grim. His hand tightened around his crystal cup of wine. 'This is not over – will never be over – while the Papists of this realm believe such a prince exists. Get to him before it is too late.'

Chapter 38

SHAKESPEARE TROD THROUGH the acrid dungeons of Newgate gaol. At his side, struggling to keep up, was the keeper, a stout fellow with a red beard and well-fed belly, whom he knew well.

'Tell me, master keeper, who brought him here?'

'The constable of Westminster, Mr Shakespeare, sent by the sheriff.'

'Where was he found?'

'He had sought refuge with the Member of Parliament, Mr Topcliffe, sir, but was immediately arrested by that gentleman and handed over to the constable.'

Shakespeare laughed bitterly. 'Mr Topcliffe was always good at protecting his back.'

'Indeed, master.'

They found Holy Trinity Curl sullen and silent in Limbo, Newgate's deepest pit. What little air was to be had in this lightless hole was putrid with stench and disease. This was a waiting-room for death, the place men came when the only journey left was the ride to the scaffold.

Shakespeare held a candle in his hand and looked at the miserable figure without compassion. 'I have some questions for you, Mr Curl. You are about to meet your maker. I cannot promise this, but you may think it possible you will receive a less hostile reception in the hereafter if you cooperate with the forces of the law in the here and now.'

Curl said nothing.

Shakespeare could see that the man had been injured. He had an untreated gash on his temple and blood caked his strange amber hair and beard.

'You have nothing to lose by talking, and I can make your last hours easier by having food and ale brought to you. Tell me this, at least. You knew one Christopher Marlowe, yes?'

'Tell him, Curl.' The voice of another condemned man came from the darkness. 'If you don't want ale, there's others here that do.'

Shakespeare looked into the shadows at the man who had just spoken and felt a sudden surge of pity for him. This cell was filled with humankind brought to its lowest ebb. There were twenty men here waiting the noose for various crimes. He determined to send them ale, whatever the outcome of his talk with Curl.

'Well, Mr Curl? Talk.'

'I knew of Marlowe. Who didn't?' Curl spoke with a surprisingly firm voice.

'And you sought his death?'

'No. Why should I?'

'So you did not have him killed by Poley and Frizer in Ellie Bull's house in Deptford.'

Curl shook his head. 'I heard of that death, but that was nothing to do with me. He was nothing to us.'

'But you signed your poster *Tamburlaine*. And you had Glebe write broadsheets signed *Tamburlaine's Apostle* . . .'

'I never knew what that was about.'

'Who suggested it? Baines?'

Curl looked genuinely puzzled. 'Never heard the name.'

'How about Laveroke?'

Curl nodded.

'They are one and the same. Laveroke is Richard Baines, a notorious intelligencer.'

'So? Many people use different names. Many more earn a crust of bread selling secrets to men like you.'

'And would it surprise you to learn that Mr Laveroke, alias Baines, is an ordained priest and that he was working for Spain?'

Curl blanched. He seemed to gasp and almost shrink. He was silent a moment, then he struggled angrily against his fetters. 'You lie!'

'No, Mr Curl, I do not lie. He worked for Spain – as did you, though you never knew it. Had you succeeded in your designs against the strangers of the Low Countries and against the Crown, you would have brought strangers here of an altogether different cast: the steel morion and blade of the Spaniard. You would have opened the floodgate to Philip's murderous yoke and the Pope's Inquisition.'

'No.'

'Yes, Mr Curl. They thought you a convenient tool. I see you as nothing more than an inconvenient fool. Tomorrow, I will bury my wife because of your unholy deeds. It is as much as I can do not to cut your throat here, but I will let the law run its course.'

'Your wife was an accident. We wanted to kill the Dutch . . .'

'It was no accident. It was murder. But there is still one thing that puzzles me: who were those Scots, the ones in the black gowns? What was your cause to them?'

Curl laughed. 'A strange lot. They were Laveroke's. He brought them down. They were kin of the witches burned by King James. Laveroke promised them vengeance and death to the King in return for building and manning the hellburner.'

'Why not use Englishmen?'

'Because we knew there would be spies among the English – spies like your little friend Cooper. There would be no such spies among the Scots. We could not afford to have word get out about the hellburner, so they were the ones that carried the powder there and fashioned her.'

Shakespeare nodded. It showed the diabolical range and extent of this conspiracy. Whether any other than Baines understood it to be a Spanish plot, they might never know. But where was he now? Clearly Curl would not know.

'And where is this Scots prince?'

'That's nothing to do with us. That's just broadsheet tittle-tattle. Why would we care about a Scots prince?'

'Indeed.' Shakespeare nodded his head slowly. This man really had no idea what he had been engaged in. 'One last question, Mr Curl, and I will send you ale. Why did you seek sanctuary at Topcliffe's house?'

Curl laughed again. 'Because I thought he was on our side. Now I know that he is on no one's side but his own.'

John Shakespeare walked to the church of St John in Walbrook, holding the hands of Mary and Grace. Andrew walked at their side. A few paces behind them came Boltfoot Cooper with Jane, who carried their baby.

A few chosen friends were there to pay their respects. Catherine's brother was down from Cambridge, as were her old friend Berthe Haan, the Sluyterman family and Susanna, on her first day out of hospital. There were no more than twenty mourners. Sir Robert Cecil was not there, and Shakespeare understood why. Catherine would wish her requiem mass to be said in the Romish way and Cecil could not be seen to condone such a thing.

'There will be no repercussions, John. Find a seminary priest to say the mass and I vow he will have free passage on this day. Take one from Bridewell or the Marshalsea. But I ask only this: keep the church door closed while the mass is said, so that the people of London do not hear of it. Keep the sad occasion small in scale and private.'

Many tears were shed, though not by John Shakespeare. The tears that, throughout his life, had habitually pricked his eyes with the onset of emotion, were dry in the face of such overwhelming grief.

After the burial, he asked Boltfoot and Jane to take the children home without him, so that he might be alone at the graveside. The day was bright and the sky was blue. It should have been black with clouds and a constant rain.

He spoke to her, head bowed, as though she were there. 'I should have been a better husband to you. I should have understood more. Thank you, Catherine, for our days together. Thank you for the children.'

A man came and stood beside him. Shakespeare turned and looked into his eyes. He knew that face, that grey hair and that well-cut beard, but could not recall where he had seen them.

'We met at a crossroads,' the man said. 'You seemed lost. Did you find the way to go?'

Shakespeare shook his head. 'I found a way. But I do not know if it is the right way.'

The man put his arm around Shakespeare's shoulders. 'God gave us free will, yet we pray to him to show us the way. Can a man have a guide and yet choose his own path?'

Shakespeare hung his head. He could not move from this man's arms. The tears were flowing now, washing down his face. He uttered great choking sobs, weeping in a way he had not done since childhood.

'And yet He is with us, John. He is with you . . .'

*

The quiet unnerved Shakespeare. His ears still rang from the deafening blast of the hellburner, yet all else descended into silence. Cecil had sent messages to Scotland, but no word was received back of any attempt on the King's life. Luke Laveroke, alias Richard Baines, seemed to have disappeared into the ether, as had Rabbie Bruce. Nor was there any sign of Doña Ana.

While Boltfoot lay, face down, on his bed, his back slathered with ointments brought from the apothecary, Shakespeare followed what leads he could muster. He went again to Henbird and together they stepped down to his cellar to talk with Walstan Glebe. Shakespeare came to realise there was some value in the man. 'Work for me, Mr Glebe,' he said of a sudden. 'And I will ensure your press is licensed. But I vow that if ever you do a trade of the sort you did with Laveroke, I will personally drive the tumbrel that carries you to the gallows. Everything you hear, you will pass to me, however small. Do you understand?'

Glebe, happy to be alive and pleased at the chance of release from his piss-acrid cell, accepted the offer. Shakespeare knew he could never be trusted, yet he knew, too, that he could not function without the services of such doubtful men.

'What I most want from you, Glebe, is any word on the whereabouts of this prince of Scots.'

'Thank you, Mr Shakespeare. I pledge I will keep my ears open.'

'Good, for if you do not, they shall surely be sliced off by order of the court. And in the meantime, I will have a little task for you to perform with your confounded press. There is a matter that needs to be set straight.'

In Privy Council, Sir Robert Cecil demanded information from the Earl of Essex. 'You know whom we seek, my lord, where is this woman? I ask this, for it is known that she was at your house.'

Essex, irritated at being asked such a question in a way that seemed to accuse him of collusion with Ana Cabral, bridled. 'I do not know what you mean, Sir Robert . . .' But he did know what he meant, and he knew, too, that Cecil had the Queen's backing in asking it. He tilted his proud chin and gazed down his nose at his little rival. 'All I can tell you is that I have not seen the wretched whore since the day of the Golden Spur. Nor has Don Antonio, who resides with me still. In truth, I believe him glad to be rid of her.'

On Cecil's orders, the trials of those captured in the skirmishes around the city were heard with little ado and at speed. Six men were found guilty of insurrection and riot and were sentenced to be hanged at the places they had been taken: three by the bridge, two by the Dutch church and one, Curl, in Westminster. Cecil insisted they be spared the *godly butchery* of drawing and quartering, 'For the Queen will not have martyrs made of these so-called apostles.'

On the day of execution, Shakespeare rose at dawn and went to the refectory. Jane followed soon after, with Mary and Grace, and set about preparing food and drink for their breakfasts.

Shakespeare did not feel like eating, but he sipped some small ale. He was surprised that Andrew was absent. 'Is he still abed, Jane?'

'I shall go and fetch him, master.'

'No, no. Leave the boy. He needs sleep.'

After a few minutes, Shakespeare went to Andrew's room. The boy was not there.

Andrew Woode fought his way through the heaving crowd close to the Gatehouse at Westminster. At twelve years of age, he was nimble enough to duck under people's arms but tall and strong enough not to be easily elbowed aside. He had the fair hair of his long-dead mother, and something of her solemn aspect. He could not remember her. All he knew of her was her portrait, in which she wore a black gown, a white coif about her hair and a cross at her slender neck. In truth, Catherine had become more of a mother to him.

The morning was bright. There was a carnival air. Street sellers shouted their wares. 'Saffron cakes!' 'Kent strawberries!' 'Broadsheets here!'

The boy found a place at the front of the throng, with a clear view of the scaffold, not fifteen yards away. His heart pounded like the beat of a war-drum.

At seven of the clock, just as the bells of St Margaret's began to chime, a cart came into view. In the back, arms bound tight, Andrew could see the pathetic creature who had come here to die. He was a man with amber hair, amber freckles and amber eyes; strange, piercing eyes that flickered here and there through the crowd of onlookers as though seeking someone he knew, some help or comfort in these last minutes on earth. For a moment, Andrew felt the man's eyes meet his, then they turned away.

'Do you have anything to say?' the hangman demanded.

'I beg forgiveness of Her Majesty, to whom I never meant any harm. All I did, I did for England. And if there is a God, I pray for His mercy.'

'That's enough.' Without ceremony, the hangman tried to thrust a hood over the man's head, but the condemned man shied away from it. 'No, not the hood.' The hangman shrugged carelessly, put the hood aside and went straight to the noose. He looped the rough hemp cord about the man's neck, then tightened it and stepped down from the cart. For a few moments, the condemned man stood on the cart, staring ahead with terror in his eyes, then the hangman lashed the horse away.

Holy Trinity Curl swung violently. He kicked and choked. His death dance lasted twelve minutes. No one stepped forward to pull his legs and hasten death.

The crowd drifted away, bored. They had hoped for more of a speech, perhaps a jest or two from the condemned man. All London had heard of his paltry attempt at insurrection and considered it laughable. Had he really thought they would take up arms and join him? The apprentices could organise better riots at Bartholomew Fair. The real talk of the city was the hellburner. That had been some bang, some thunder.

Andrew stayed and gazed at the grotesque tableau. The distended tongue lolled out. The amber eyes, open and bulging, stared without sight. Blood from the ears streaked the beard. A dark patch on the breeches betrayed the last humiliation, pissing himself in public. Andrew breathed deeply to prevent the bile rising in his throat, then turned away. The frantic beating of his heart had calmed. The killer of the woman he loved as a mother was dead.

'You look as if you need food and drink,' Shakespeare said when Andrew arrived home.

'I have no appetite, sir.'

'No. Nor would I. But at least sup a little ale. Here.' He handed him his own cup.

Andrew took a few sips, then thirstily downed the whole half-pint.

'Better?'

The boy shook his head. Suddenly, he looked old beyond his years. 'No. Not better. Empty. I had expected some kind of elation, but there was none. My hatred seeped away into nothingness.'

Shakespeare held the boy to him. 'You are a man now,' he said. 'A good man. We will talk of your future, soon.' As he spoke, there was a knock at the door, and he heard Jane's soft-shod feet scuttling through the hall to answer it.

'Will, it is good to see you.'

'I would have come sooner. There were . . . difficulties.'

'Well, you are here now. Welcome.'

'I am lost for words.'

Shakespeare smiled. 'There is a first time for everything, Will. Say nothing. It has all been said.' He embraced his brother, whose clothes were dusty and stained.

'In truth, John, as well as bringing my condolences, I come with another purpose. I fear I was not wholly open with you the last time we met. I knew more about the death of Kit Marlowe than I told you. I thought it safer to avoid London for a while. I believe I am still in grave danger.'

Shakespeare stood back from his brother and looked into his eyes inquiringly. 'You are safe here, Will. Come to my solar. Let us talk in comfort. You look as if you have been dragged here from Stratford. Jane will bring us refreshments.'

In the quiet of Shakespeare's sunlit room, his brother unburdened himself.

'John, I am sure you must know of the arrest and torture of Thomas Kyd before Marlowe's death.'

'Of course. He was one of those believed to be this *Tamburlaine* who wrote the attack on the strangers, which was posted outside the Dutch church. But I did not believe it for one moment. It was Francis Mills who ordered his arrest and hard questioning. Mills has a taste for torture, I fear. Perhaps it is revenge for the ill-treatment he has at the hands of his sluttish wife.' Shakespeare could not help noticing that his brother's hands were trembling and that his brow was deeply furrowed with concern.

'You will know, too, John, that Tom Kyd had shared lodgings with Kit Marlowe.'

'Yes, of course. It was much discussed.'

'So when Kyd was arrested and the pursuivants searched his rooms, what were they looking for?'

'Why, evidence linking him to the Dutch church tract. All they found, though, was some discourse on atheism, which is offence enough in the eyes of many. I believe he said it was not his paper, but Marlowe's.' Shakespeare snorted, without humour. He was bemused. 'But Will, this was just one of many lines of inquiry into the Dutch church posters. A reward of a hundred marks was offered for information, and torture was sanctioned by the Privy Council. Few believed, however, that Marlowe was behind the posters, for why would he have named himself so clearly, knowing the penalty for such sedition?'

'Perhaps the searchers were looking for something else when they tore apart Tom Kyd's room and broke his body on the Bridewell engines of torment. Perhaps Poley, Frizer and Skeres were seeking the same thing when they took Kit Marlowe to a room in Deptford and killed him.'

'What else could they have been looking for?'

'I cannot tell you for the present. Suffice it to say that I know of it. I could add that there are some who do believe Poley, Frizer and Skeres were not the only ones present in that room when the killing occurred.'

'Who else?'

'I cannot tell you.'

'Why did you not mention any of this before?'

'You would have been compromised. It would have been your duty to seek out whatever Poley and the others were after, and then destroy it.'

'You must at least tell me what manner of thing you mean. Is it written matter, some sedition?'

'Not now. You will know soon enough.'

'Coining, perhaps? Marlowe had much trouble with his counterfeiting activites when he was in Flushing. It was a weakness of his. Had he treasure hidden, false money, that they sought?'

'Be patient.'

Shakespeare poured brandy for his brother from the jug left by Jane. 'Will, beloved brother, if Marlowe was involved in counterfeiting the Queen's coin or writing something of a seditious nature and you know what it is, you are already in peril. Nothing you can tell me will make your position more dangerous. You say they tortured Kyd and killed Marlowe because of it. Why would they stop there? The slightest suspicion that you know of its whereabouts could lead to your arrest, and worse.'

'That is why I left London so hurriedly after the inquest. I had only stayed as long as I did to discover what came out in the testimony of Poley, Skeres and Frizer. I went home to Stratford, but I soon realised I could not stay there; I had to face up to this matter. These past days I have been in Shoreditch, for I had much to organise. I fear I did not hear of Catherine's terrible death until now. My coming here to your home has had to be most quiet, and I must keep it that way.'

'Someone is after you?'

'It is possible.'

'And is there some link to Catherine's death?'

'No, none that I know. John, come with me on the morrow and you shall discover all that I know.'

'This disturbs me greatly.'

'Yes, but I must ask you to trust me on this.'

Chapter 39

THE KEEPER OF the Marshalsea shook his head and rubbed his long, grease-streaked beard. 'I am sorry, Mr Shakespeare. Ingram Frizer is no longer here. Got his pardon from the Queen yesterday and so I had to let him out.'

Shakespeare uttered a low oath. 'Where did he go?'

'I have his place of abode. I did write it in the black book. You are welcome to consult it, though whether he went there I could not say.'

The keys on the keeper's belt clanged with every step through the echoing halls of the old prison as he led Shakespeare to his little room. 'Here we are, master,' he said at last as he opened the door, letting Shakespeare in first.

Shakespeare held a kerchief to his nose in disgust. There was a foul smell in here of cooking fat, which added a nauseous quality to the common gaol scents of ordure and sweat.

The keeper brought down the black book and opened it flat on the crooked table, where, judging from the stains, scraps and crumbs, he took his daily food.

'There we go, sir. Admitted the second of June, killed a man in self-defence. Following inquest, to be held on remand awaiting decision of court in Chancery. Now he has had his formal pardon. Let me see, where did he abide?' The keeper scratched his dirty, fat forefinger across the page. 'Ah, there it is – not far from here, master. By the river, St Augustine Inn, my old father always knew it as. Now, though it is called Sentlegar House. Tenement building. Many of the worst sort live there, sir. You will find it hard by the Bridge House.'

'Thank you.'

'And I wish you fortune of Mr Frizer, sir, for I cannot say I liked him much. A sly fellow, I would say. Not one to turn your back on, lest you wish a poniard in the kidney.'

Shakespeare was relieved to step out into the comparatively fresh air of Southwark. The streets were thronged with stalls selling goods from the world over, brought back by the great trading carracks. Spanish gold and fruits could be had here, wine from France, printed books from the German lands, furs from the Russias and spices from the Moluccas. Looking down Long Southwark to the bridge, he saw nothing but people, wains and farm beasts, packed tight in an endless stream. He shuddered at the thought of what might have been, had the hellburner done its foul work.

St Augustine Inn was less than a furlong from the gaol. Shakespeare walked straight in, for the door was open. A family of ten huddled in the first room he saw, a drab band of whores in the next. He asked after Ingram Frizer. No one would admit to knowing him. He looked in all the tenements. There were only poor families, whores and rats. Not a clue as to his whereabouts.

The windows were shuttered at Robert Poley's splendid, timbered townhouse in Birchin Lane, just north of Lombard Street. Yet it was not entirely empty, for a housekeeper answered the door to Shakespeare.

'I would speak with Mr Poley,' Shakespeare demanded.

'I fear he is not here, master,' the woman said. She was an honest-looking woman in her thirties. Shakespeare looked at her questioningly and wondered why any decent goodwife would wish to work for a villain such as Poley.

'When will he be back?'

'He has left for the summer, master. Gone to the country to escape the pestilence. I just come here to dust and look out for the place while he's away.'

'Did he say which part of the country?'

'Norfolk, I do believe. He said he would be travelling for a few weeks and that he might go to the Low Countries for a while. He has a friend with him, sir, one Nicholas Skeres.'

Shakespeare looked at the woman's eyes yet more closely and could see no dissembling in them. So Poley and Skeres had left town, and Frizer was gone, too. Well, that was most convenient for them. Shakespeare cursed beneath his breath, then smiled at the woman and thanked her for her assistance. There was only one more place to try: Deptford.

It was a journey of no more than half an hour by tilt-boat. Shakespeare paid the watermen, then strode across the green to the fine house of Ellie Bull. He hammered at the door, with more than a hint of impatience. He was well aware that Cecil would be in a fury if he had any idea what he was about and would damn him for not devoting his time to the Scots prince or the Spanish woman. But since the arrival of his brother, there was this matter of Marlowe again, this *murder*; he was convinced of it. It had lain unquestioned too long.

Mrs Bull eyed him warily. 'Yes, master, how may I help you?'

'I am John Shakespeare, an officer of Sir Robert Cecil.'

'Yes, sir, I know that.'

'You are well informed, mistress.'

'You were here at the inquest on poor Mr Marlowe, here in my humble house.'

Shakespeare looked up at the facade of the building. There was nothing at all humble about it. Ellie Bull had clearly been left a widow of some means, for the house had a large frontage, all in a single wood frame, and a pleasant aspect with views across Deptford Green and the river. It was well away from all the other housing in the village.

'I would come in and talk with you.'

'And why would that be, sir?' Ellie Bull stood her ground and crossed her plump arms across her ample bosom. She would have been a comely girl in her younger days, and still had an attractive blush to her cheeks. But there was a hint of hardness about her, too, the hardness of a woman of business who liked gold and would not give an inch in the getting and keeping of it. 'I have no knowledge of the sad events in my house. I had let the room to the gentlemen for their afternoon of gaming and drinking, and the next thing I knew, there was a brabble and an accidental death. That is all I know or can tell you, Mr Shakespeare.'

'Did you hear the fight?'

Mrs Bull hesitated.

'It is a simple enough question, mistress. There was a violent quarrel. You must have heard something, for you were in the house, bringing them refreshments of ale and sweetmeats from time to time. Yes?'

'I may have heard something . . . but I paid it no heed. Young gentlemen will fight and brawl now and then. It is their nature. No concern of mine.'

'But you heard something?'

'I suppose I did. Yes, now that I come to think of it.'

'What time was that?'

'As I recall, the inquest was told it was six of the clock.'

'That is not what I asked, mistress.'

'If the inquest said six, then six it was.'

'Who was in the room that day? Did men come and go?'

Mrs Bull began ticking off names on her fingers. 'Well, there was Mr Marlowe, of course, and Mr Poley. Oh, and the poor lad who killed him in the terrible accident, Mr Frizer. And I believe there was one other, a jolly, red-bearded fat fellow – that's him, Nicholas Skeres. Fine gentlemen all.'

'Do you know where they are now? Where is Frizer?'

'The only one I know of is Mr Frizer. I do believe him to be in the Marshalsea.'

'No, he has had his pardon.'

'Well, then, I am mighty pleased for the lad, for he did not deserve to be incarcerated for defending himself. Any man must have the right of self-defence.'

'Where might he have gone?'

'Home?'

'No. He is not there.'

'Well, he is certain not here, so I could not say.'

'What of the fifth man? There was a fifth man in the room.'

Mrs Bull looked puzzled and began counting off names on her fingers again, then shook her head. 'No, sir, four was the number.'

'What manner of house is this, Mrs Bull? For it is surely no tavern, nor inn – yet these men – these five men – treated it as a taproom that day. Or if not a taproom, they had some other purpose. So I say again, what manner of house is this?'

'It is my dwelling-house, sir, and respectable. My late hus-band and I did bring up twelve children within these walls, though none survived, God rest their poor little souls.'

'If it is nothing but a dwelling, why were Poley, Marlowe and the others here that day?'

'It was a favour, sir, a favour for a friend. Now, if you have learned all you require, I must be about my chores.'

'I am not finished with you. This matter is Council business, ordered by Sir Robert Cecil. I will have answers from you, for I believe there were five men here that day and that Marlowe died earlier, more like three or four of the clock, and that one man had to slip away unobserved. I believe you all conspired to lie about the time of death in case anyone in the vicinity saw this fifth man leave. It would not have done to link him with the death.'

The warm cheeks of Ellie Bull suddenly took on the sharp-edged aspect of the business woman that she was. 'You can name your names, Mr Shakespeare, and speak of Sir Robert Cecil and the Council, but I tell you this – I am kin of Cecil and old Burghley and I will not be intimidated by you, nor have words put in my mouth. The tale was told at the inquest, and that is that. The matter is at an end. Good day.' She stepped back into the spacious innards of the house, and slammed the door shut in Shakespeare's face.

'If you were going to murder a man, Joshua, why go to the bother of luring him to a house in daylight? Why share a few cups of ale and then stab him through the eye? Why not, instead, wear a cowl, slide up to your intended victim in a side-street by night and cut his throat? Or run the man through with a sword?'

Joshua Peace was examining the lacerated tongue of a woman found dead, probably murdered, near the archbishop's palace in Lambeth. 'You have a very good point, John.'

'Which means that Poley and the others did not take Marlowe to Widow Bull's house to murder him. Why, then, was he there? If they had wanted to play at cards and take ale together, why not go to a tavern or inn? There are plenty of those in Deptford.'

'Perhaps the widow offered them a good price for ale . . . or a fair sirloin of beef?'

'The widow Bull does not need the money. There is something else: she is well connected, claiming some kinship to the Cecils.'

'Hold this, John.' Peace handed Shakespeare a steel implement for the widening of orifices. 'The Cecils, you say? You are entering dangerous territory there, I think.'

Shakespeare took the tool absent-mindedly. His thoughts were not here in this chilly crypt beneath St Paul's, but in the room where he had seen the corpse of Christopher Marlowe. 'I think it a distant thing, through marriage. I cannot pay such things heed.'

Peace said nothing. He had his nose close to the dead woman's mouth, sniffing.

'But I have developed a theory, Joshua, one not entirely based on wild surmise. It is this: Marlowe was taken there to be tortured. They wanted to obtain some information from him. It was the perfect place for that. Widow Bull's house stands apart. A man's screams might be muffled there. You recall the injury to his hand? You speculated that it could have been caused by some sharp edge of iron. Could that injury have been caused by an attempt to apply a thumbscrew?'

'Yes, it could.'

'You noted, too, that he stank of ale. One could not miss it. It seems to me possible that they might have plied him with drink elsewhere, so that they could lure him, drunk, to the widow's house with promises of more ale or other pleasures. I believe that would explain their presence there. But then things went wrong. He was a strong man. They overestimated his inebriation. And when they tried to bind him and apply the instrument of torture, he fought back with great force. In the fracas, he was killed, perhaps with his own knife, perhaps with Frizer's. It doesn't matter which.'

Peace put out his hand and Shakespeare returned the

implement to him. 'Everything you say fits, John. Except one thing: why would anyone wish to torture a fellow like Marlowe? What could he possibly have that Poley and his friends would want?'

'I am not sure, Joshua. But I am hoping that I will soon find out.'

'John, before you go, there was the other body you sent me, one Christopher Morley, found hanged in Wood Street Counter.'

'What did you discover?'

Peace shrugged his lean shoulders. 'That he died by hanging, nothing more. I think you know he had weals about his wrists, as though tied, but you had bound him yourself, I believe. There was nothing to say he was hanged by others. On balance I would say it was self-destruction, for most men set upon in such a way would put up a fight and suffer injuries to their hands and nails. But I am afraid there is no certainty in my judgement.'

Shakespeare nodded. Perhaps they would never know. 'There was one other thing, Joshua. There were letters writ in blood on the dungeon floor. *RB* or *RP* I could not discern which.'

'That is something I cannot help you with.'

'No. But I find myself believing it was *RB* – Rick Baines. And there were two other lines, which could have been *LL* Morley was trying to tell me that Luke Laveroke was Baines. He left that message because he knew he was going to die. He was certainly afraid.'

'Then that is for you to discover. I wish you well, John.'

Chapter 40

'WHERE ARE YOU taking me, brother?'
'To a place of agreeable entertainment and good beer.'

'The playhouses are all closed while the plague persists, Will.'

'Well then we cannot go to the playhouse. Patience, John.'

They were mounted, walking their horses slowly through the evening streets northwards along Bishop's Gate Street. Arriving at the gate, Will halted and looked about. 'Are we being followed? You have better eyes.'

Shakespeare hesitated. Were they safe? Normally he had an instinct for such things; the shadow that lingered too long against the wall, the man who moved against the flow and stopped too frequently. But in this teeming throng, nothing was clear. And his thoughts had not entirely been occupied with the ride. 'I have no reason to believe so,' was all he could say.

'Then let us rein in across the road at yonder inn, have water brought to our parched horses and share a jug of beer together.'

'Very well.'

They trotted into the stable-yard adjoining the Dolphin Inn, just north of the Bishop's Gate. From the outside, it seemed a poor sort of place, with daub breaking away from the walls.

The sign of an arched dolphin was in sad repair and needed repainting. Shakespeare wondered why his brother should have brought him to such a hostelry, for it would not have been his first choice of tavern or inn for a pleasant summer's evening drink.

The two watchers nodded to each other. One turned his horse's head, then peeled away and rode south. The other dismounted and found a tethering post for his mare.

The taproom was gloomy and almost full of drinkers. Will signalled to a serving girl to bring them beer.

As Shakespeare's eyes grew accustomed to the dim light, he spotted a somewhat soulful face that he knew: Richard Burbage, the acclaimed player who had been with Will in Deptford at the time of the Marlowe inquest. He nudged his brother to point him out. Will simply nodded in acknowledgement. And then Shakespeare noticed that Burbage was talking with the poet and playmaker George Peele, who had also been there at Deptford. Suddenly, he realised that everyone in this room was a player or manager or somehow involved in the playhouses of London and beyond. Ambitious young Thomas Dekker, Philip Henslowe the money man, good Edward Alleyn, Marlowe's old friend and collaborator George Chapman. Even Will Kempe was there, smiling again, jesting with his friends and fellows. Most surprising of all was the presence of Thomas Walsingham, nephew of the late Sir Francis, patron of Marlowe and sometime acquaintance of the three men in the room with him when he died.

'Will, what is this? Some sort of convention or council of players and playmakers?'

'Each and every one, John. All here knew and admired Kit Marlowe's work, though it would be false to suggest that all liked him. You will find men of all the great players' companies here – the Admiral's Men, Pembroke's Men, Lord Strange's Men and others. Some have come away from their tours for this evening's entertainment.'

In the corner, Shakespeare spotted Thomas Kyd, hunched forward on a straight-backed chair.

Will caught his brother's eye. 'He cannot walk. His body is broken by the tortures, but he demanded to be here. His friends carried him here in a cart, most painfully.'

Shakespeare was unnerved by his brother's talk. Whatever their motive for being here, this was a secret convocation, a meeting that Edmund Tilney, Master of the Revels, would be happy to break up with sword, hagbut and mace. And he would doubtless have the full backing of the city aldermen and some of the more Puritan-minded men on the Privy Council. 'I say again, Will, what is this?'

'You fret, John. Come and talk with Kyd. Discover what has been done to him.'

'No. I will not talk with him. He has lately been in Bridewell, hard-questioned over certain seditious papers. I cannot say hale fellow to him.'

'Very well. But I must say to you that I have made a pledge to every one of these men here gathered that you will not tell a soul who you have seen here this day. You may tell the world what you see and we will thank you for it, but not the names. If you cannot abide by such a pledge, then leave now. If, however, you wish to understand why Kit Marlowe was killed, then stay.

Shakespeare breathed deeply. His mouth was set. What in God's name had his brother got into? Whatever it was, he could not leave him here to take the consequences alone. 'Very well, I will stay. But do not try me too hard, Will.'

Will smiled. 'Come with me, and I shall show you to your

seat in the yard. The performance will be starting very soon.'

The backyard of the hostelry was bounded by a high wall, along which a low stage had been erected with screens to either side. Before it, there was one stool.

'There, John, is your seat. You are about to watch a play called *The White Dog*. It was the last thing ever written by Christopher Marlowe. It may never be seen again after this evening, but all gathered here believe it must be performed, if only this once. Please, John, take your seat.'

'This performance is all for *my* benefit?'

'No. It benefits all. The whole world of playmaking. All who believe in virtue and civility.'

'And will we all lose our heads?'

'All the men here know the risks they run. They merely have to gaze on the fractured body of Tom Kyd and consider the fate of Kit himself to know what ills may befall them. But I think we will not lose our heads. Not if we stand together. For without us, who would entertain the royal court?'

Shakespeare laughed. It was true enough. The Queen would not allow anything to come between her and the pleasure she took from plays and masques, however indignant such things might make the Puritans. 'And if I am sitting here, alone, where will you be, Will?'

'I am the chorus, I will provide the prologue. Sit. Drink your beer. And allow us a few errors, for we have had no rehearsal.'

Shakespeare sat down. Despite the obvious peril, he felt light in the head, as though he had not slept enough or had had too much strong liquor. What could worry him? It was a pleasant summer's evening and he was here to watch a play by the estimable Christopher Marlowe. Accompanied by Catherine, he had in the past taken pleasure in Mr Marlowe's *Tamburlaine*. What care could he have now, on such a balmy evening, with such a good company of men and the scent of summer flowers in the evening air? What fear should he have for his own life, with Catherine gone?

For five minutes he sat and drank his beer, aware of the bustle and hum of players about the screens. He found himself thinking of Baines's betrayal of Marlowe. It seemed probable to him now that Baines, alias Laveroke, had used Marlowe to divert attention away from himself. In writing his vile note of all Marlowe's alleged blasphemies and seditions, he was shifting suspicion to another. He could not afford to be brought in for questioning when he had a conspiracy to organise, and when the plot was at such a critical stage. He had gone to great lengths to implicate Marlowe, signing the Dutch church posters *Tamburlaine* and writing in *The London Informer* as *Tamburlaine's Apostle*. The ploy had worked for Baines. But why had it cost Marlowe's life? That was still not clear. Perhaps this play would shed light into the dark crevice that was Ellie Bull's room of pleasures.

At last there was a hush and Will appeared, alone, in centre stage. He bowed to his brother, then spoke in a firm voice with no book of lines or paper to aid him.

'The White Dog,' he announced, 'a play in two acts, by Christopher Marlowe.' He stared at his brother gravely, but with a lightness of tone in his voice as though addressing a packed audience in the Rose.

'Two realms within one border, one stained by blood and savage brutishness, the other exulting life, beauty and nature. Two realms, intertwined like a briar, full of bloody thorns, yet perfumed by the wild rose. Two realms, one of dark, one of light, and ruled by one sovereign.

'In this land a feral dog runs free. Its maw drips pain, its teeth are as poisonous as any adder's. When it is near, slavering through the streets, honest householders cower behind locked doors, for this dread cur has the mark of death all about its chill white fur.

'Rabid, lethal, cruel, unspeakable, it is fit for nothing but the slaughter knife. Yet none dare destroy it, for this selfsame monarch of the twin realms claims ownership of the baleful mastiff, loves it like a child, and will hear no ill of it.

'The dog has manlike appearance, metamorphosed as Apuleius's golden ass reversed. It stands on two legs not four, nor has it tail. But be not deceived, for this beast is not a man. Though it take human form on this our humble stage, yet it *is* a dog, as you shall determine from its fangs as sharp as any wolf, its bark as wretched as any plague animal. This is our scene, this roundel the realm entire. Forgive us our poor bowl, but travel in your fancy, if you will, to a dungeon in the city of Nodnol. Enter, the white dog . . .'

As Will bowed low and retreated towards one of the screens, a squat man dressed all in black, yet with a shock of white hair, appeared from the side, dragging chains. He had a pipe in his mouth that belched forth tobacco fumes, and at his side, hunched and unctuous was a boy with slimed hair, rubbing his hands.

'Where is this cat, Nick? Has it yet purred?'

'It is racked, master, racked. It will not purr, though I stretch it into a leopard.'

From the other side of the stage, two men carried a young man, prostrate upon a wooden door, his arms above him with ties bound to nails, his feet likewise bound to the other end of the door.

The white-haired man looked at it closely. 'You are certain it is a cat, Nick?'

'Aye, master, for it has whiskers.'

'Yet it will not admit it is a cat? Then tighten the rollers, stretch it yet more.'

'I fear it may be dead, master.'

'Then beat it!'

Shakespeare understood. This was about Topcliffe. The white dog dragging his chains was the torturer himself. The boy Nick at his side was his vicious young assistant Nicholas Jones. The cat on the rack was every poor Popish priest or playmaker such as Thomas Kyd or any other innocent who had ever crossed his path and ended up in his stinking chamber of torment. It was a play written as a comedy, but the humour to anyone who knew of Topcliffe was as black as a moonless night. Shakespeare sat, immovable, as if clamped in a pillory.

And then the dark humour vanished and only brutality remained. The story told was so grotesque as to make *Tamburlaine* and his conquests seem a light, sugared confection by comparison.

The White Dog was a tale of a brute so grown in pride and arrogance that he took sovereign powers unto himself. As *Tamburlaine* had been a tale of conquest after conquest, so this was a story of horror after horror. It was, too, a damning indictment of all who let the white dog go about his blood-lusting business unchecked.

Here in the cast, all too recognisable, was Heneage, there Cecil and his father Burghley. And Essex and Effingham and Ralegh and Francis Walsingham and Buckhurst and Whitgift and long-dead Leicester. No one in power escaped Marlowe's savage satire. For these men stood aside and watched, muttering at the side of the stage, as the white dog disembowelled a tailor for making a doublet for a priest. They covered their eyes and ears and mouths with their hands as the white dog – Topcliffe – accepted payment to torture a family to death so that their kin might inherit their estates. They giggled and jested among themselves as the slavering beast raped a poor girl and demanded lands from her family. They washed their hands in water as he washed his in blood.

Yet the most bitter denunciation of all was saved for the monarch of these twin realms of good and evil. Though the sovereign was not named, nor even made clear whether it was king or queen, yet all who had eyes to see and ears to hear would know that it was Elizabeth, and that it was she that allowed the white dog its freedom, revelling in the tales of all its sordid doings.

Shakespeare sat and watched it all. He was bathed in sweat, not from the warmth of the evening but from the sheer sickening horror and force of the drama. He felt physically ill. His throat was parched, though he had drunk three pints, and his eyes were sore from not blinking.

And then, as the drama drew to its heart-stopping conclusion, with the crucifixion of the priest Robert Southwell – a notorious poet and Jesuit languishing in the Tower – the white dog himself arrived.

Chapter 41

TOPCLIFFE RAGED IN with unstoppable might. His men – thirty leather-clad pursuivants – beat down the door to the inn with a battering log, then crashed through the taproom, sweeping bottles, tankards and kegs across the sawdust-strewn floor.

All of those with him were made in his own image, hard-faced men with heavy weapons and a taste for brutality. They wore the Queen's escutcheon to show in whose name they came. It gave them an authority which they did not have in other parts of their lives, as minor courtiers, apprentices or, in some case, prisoners of the Crown, released specifically to do Topcliffe's brutal work.

Two men shouldered down the door leading to the yard. Had they bothered to try the latch, they would have discovered that it was neither locked nor bolted. And then they were standing there: thirty men with swords and pistols, ready to kill any who stood in their path.

Topcliffe was among the first through. He stood surveying the scene, legs astride in his aggressive, feral-dog pose. His pipe was in his mouth, his blackthorn stick in his hand, slapping down into the palm of the other. Without removing the pipe from his teeth, he blew forth a cloud of tobacco smoke.

'What a nest of vermin have I uncovered here beneath this stone,' he growled from the corners of his mouth.

And yet there was no play in progress. All those present were milling about the yard, drinking beer, talking of this and that, laughing without a care, ignoring him.

There had been no stage properties to hide, no costumes apart from the white wig worn by the player of Topcliffe, and that was easily concealed in his doublet. The stage had a few kegs ranged along it, so that it seemed just like a raised platform where such things were normally stored. The screens were quickly furled up and leant against the back of the inn. There was no evidence here that this was anything other than a group of men drinking and conversing on a summer's evening.

Shakespeare ambled up to him. 'What is this, Topcliffe? By what right do you intrude on this private gathering?'

'By mine own authority, Shakespeare. For I am the Queen's servant and there is treason here.'

Shakespeare frowned. 'Here are gathered old friends, enjoying a pleasant evening of converse and beer. Where is the treason in that?'

'There is a book here, a play – you know there is such a one. And there has been said such a play that will spill the blood of all those here present into the Tyburn soil.'

'You rave and drivel, old man. You are in second childhood. Get back to your hearth with your pipe and rattle, lest you soil yourself in public.'

'Search them all,' Topcliffe ordered Newall, his chief lieutenant. 'Search every inch of this yard. No one is to leave until it is found, for I do know it is here and has been spoken this evening.' He prodded Shakespeare with the tip of his blackthorn. 'My Nick was without the wall and heard it, so I *know* it is here.'

'Heard what?'

'A play. A calumny. You know what it is. You are in so deep this time, Shakespeare, that no amount of crawling to Sir Robert Cripple will save you.'

Shakespeare turned to his brother. 'Do you know what he is gibbering about, Will?'

'Would that I did, John, would that I did. For I think it might make a play to amuse a good throng of groundlings when this pestilence is done. We could call it *The Mad Dog*. No, I think *The White Dog* a better name. What say you, Topcliffe? Shall I write a play and called it *The White Dog*?'

Topcliffe ground his teeth. 'Both of you Shakespeares, both you Papist-loving traitors, I will have both your heads.'

The pursuivants were elbowing their way through the crowd of players and playmakers, trying to search them. But they had little idea what they were looking for, and no cooperation from those they would search. The players merely continued to converse and laugh among themselves and drink their beer and wine.

'Take care with that poniard,' Henslowe said to one sullen pursuivant who was trying to cut his way into his doublet. 'That's Venetian silk. Ten gold crowns. I'll have you in court for the price if you so much as cut a thread.'

Suddenly Shakespeare noticed that Edmund Tilney, Master of the Revels, had arrived with Topcliffe and his grim band. Tilney, old and arched, was hanging back in the shadows as though he did not wish to be seen. Shakespeare touched Will's sleeve and pointed him out. Will walked away and whispered in the ears of both Philip Henslowe and Edward Alleyn, who both nodded and, together, marched towards Tilney.

Topcliffe looked confused. He had removed his pipe and was baring his yellow-brown teeth so that he did, indeed, look like a dog.

'What were you hoping by bringing Mr Tilney here,

Topcliffe? Did you think he would take your part against the players and, thus, deny our performances to Her Majesty? Are they not her greatest pleasure? There is nothing here, Topcliffe. Nothing to be found. Why do you not turn your tail now and leave and save yourself from further humiliation?'

Topcliffe's eye twitched with rage and frustration. The more he fought to control the spasm, the more pronounced it became. 'I have had enough,' he bellowed. 'I am arresting you all. Men, shoulder-clap these sodomite girl-players and take them into custody. Bring them bound to my chamber at Westminster and let them piss themselves in fear.'

Edmund Tilney stepped forward. He was an elegant, unruffled man with a voice that was soft when he was not performing as master of ceremonies at some royal event. And yet it was a voice that, for all its calm, commanded attention. 'I am afraid you cannot do that, Mr Topcliffe,' he said. 'You have found nothing and from the demeanour of those here present I would venture to suggest that you *will* find nothing. Much as I would like to see some of these scoundrels racked, we do need a little evidence before we can start arresting so many of Her Majesty's most favoured players and playmakers. We should both lose our ears at the very least, and possibly our heads.' Tilney had not survived and thrived these twenty-five years in royal service without understanding the wisdom or foolishness of certain courses of action. 'Admit it, Mr Topcliffe, you have been bested, sir. These men are too cunning for you.'

The yard had gone quiet as Tilney made his gentle little speech. There was a pause after he finished, then suddenly everyone roared with laughter. Even some of the pursuivants were seen to smirk at Topcliffe's discomfort. Topcliffe looked at Tilney as though he would run him through.

'So that's that, Topcliffe,' Shakespeare said, chuckling, with a broad smile creasing his face. 'I would offer you a gage of ale before you go, but I am not certain that anyone here can stand your murderous stink a moment longer. Begone, and take your rag-tag band of brutes with you.'

The actor who had played the white dog now came up to him. He had replaced his white wig on his head so that it was as if Topcliffe were looking at himself in a glass. The actor had his chains and shook them at the torturer. 'Boo!' he said.

Topcliffe did not move. He stood, rigid, fixed to the spot, legs astride. But his men *did* move. The words of Edmund Tilney carried weight, for they knew in what esteem he was held by the highest in the land. They knew this game was done and they were not about to risk their ears or necks for Topcliffe.

Slowly, they began to trickle out, heads bowed, avoiding Topcliffe's glare as they went. One of the last to leave was a slime-haired, thick-set young man who was well known to Shakespeare. Jones. Nicholas Jones. The torturer's apprentice. The sight of him was like a candle being lit in Shakespeare's brain. Of course. Poley would have needed an expert in the application of pain at Deptford, one who could report back directly to his master, Topcliffe. Shakespeare understood it all now. He stayed Jones with his hand, gripping his leather-clad upper arm. Jones was taken aback at being restrained so. His bloodshot eyes opened wide in panic.

'Jones,' Shakespeare said, 'I was talking earlier this day with Mistress Bull. She told me you were there at her dwelling the day Marlowe was knifed. Why did you not mention this at the inquest? Do you not know it is a crime to withhold evidence?'

Jones, his face still seared red, looked startled, then he mumbled, 'It was of no consequence, that was why. I left hours before the killing. What's it to you?'

Shakespeare grinned. 'I see. So you *were* there?'

Jones's face reddened yet deeper. He looked to his left and

saw Topcliffe glowering at him. 'No,' he spluttered. 'I misunderstood you. I was not there . . . not that day.'

'Now we know all we need to know, don't we, Topcliffe?'

Topcliffe spat at him. The spit landed in the dust at his own feet. 'That's what I know, Shakespeare. What will you do? Produce the play at the Rose? Or perhaps you will perform it to Her Majesty at her birthday revels. See how long your bowels stay in their housing then!'

Shakespeare turned away. He clapped his arm around his brother's back. 'Come, Will, come home with me and let us sup together and talk. I have had enough entertainment for one night.'

Neither of them turned back to see Topcliffe pummelling Jones to the ground with the heavy, club end of his blackthorn.

As they rode home, Shakespeare thought of all the suspicions he had harboured and how wrong he had been. He could admit it to himself now. He had feared Cecil had been involved in the death of Marlowe. But Marlowe had died for one reason only, the same reason Kyd had been tortured. Topcliffe had to find and destroy the play that laid bare the horrific truth of his crimes. One man had died and another brought to the brink of death to save the white dog's shame.

But where was the book of this play, the last work of Christopher Marlowe? The actors had spoken from memory, their lines learned. There had been no sign of a book-holder to prompt them with cues. He knew that Will would never tell him, so he did not ask. Some things were better left unknown.

'You can never perform it again, Will, and it were best the thing were destroyed. Best for you, best for all.'

'If I knew where it was, do you think I would destroy such a thing, John?'

Shakespeare knew the answer to that and said nothing. Yet

he could not help but muse. How could Will have come to hear of it? There was only one man: it had to be Thomas Kyd. Even in the worst agonies of torture he must have kept silent about it because he realised he would die if he revealed its whereabouts to Topcliffe. Instead, he had thrown them scraps of information to gnaw on, little titbits about Marlowe's atheism. Bad enough in their own way, but as nothing compared to *The White Dog*, a play so seditious it amounted to accusing the Queen of England of complicity in murder and unwarranted torture.

There was one more nagging doubt in Shakespeare's mind: even if Cecil was not involved in the death of Marlowe, it must certainly have suited him to have this play suppressed, for it showed him and others on the Privy Council in almost as bad a light as the Queen. It was not a possibility Shakespeare wished to think on this evening. He wished, rather, to drink a great deal too much fine wine with his brother and sink into blessed oblivion for a few hours.

His wish did not come true, not this night. A surprise was waiting for him at home, one that shook him right back into the unpleasant present.

Chapter 42

BETH EVANS WAS mighty agitated. Her dark brown eyes were etched with dark lines of concern. She immediately clasped Shakespeare's hands in hers. 'John, please, I beg you to help us.'

They were in the refectory at his home in Dowgate. Jane was bringing ale and bread. Will expressed surprise at seeing his brother's old sweetheart, but greeted her with good grace before immediately seeing that this was no place for him tonight. 'I will take my leave of you, John.'

'Yes, another evening, Will. But walk this city with care. And the same advice to all your friends. The dog may be cornered, but he still has a bite.' He turned back to Beth. 'Now what is this?' he said, his voice softening.

'They've taken Lucy. Snatched her away. That Frenchie, the one who came before, marched in with two other men and took her, bound and gagged, off into the night. I saw it, John. I saw it and could do nothing.'

'You say a Frenchman came before?'

'Yes, very fine and elegant. A nobleman. Claimed Lucy as his slave.'

'The Vidame de Chartres, Prégent de la Fin.'

'Lucy told me all about him.'

'Do you know where he has taken her?'

'No.' Her full, plump lips closed then parted, as if she would say something else, but then she closed them again and shook her head.

'Beth? Tell me all you know.'

She sighed. 'I did not want to come here, John. You have suffered grievously enough without hearing the concerns of others. But I did not know which way to turn. The constable would have laughed and said he could find plenty of trugs to take her place. The justice would have ordered me whipped at Bridewell for whoring.'

He squeezed her hands, then released them. 'You did right to come to me. This is not to be tolerated in a free land. If the vidame has taken her, then I think he will try to remove her from England as quickly as he can. We must move with speed.'

Francis Mills could not sleep. He sat on a stone bench in his small back yard, drinking brandy and listening to the sounds of the summer night. Every so often his head slumped forward, hanging before him like the miserable vulture-bird encaged at the Tower aviary. He could not bear the thought of going indoors to his empty chamber. His wife was not home. She was with the grocer. The dream of the filleting knife and the slitting of their throats came in his waking hours now, not just in sleep.

Shakespeare's hammering at the front door to his modest home was a welcome relief from the reverie.

'Forgive me for the lateness of the hour, Frank, but I need your help.'

Mills allowed Shakespeare the benefit of a haunted smile. His face became more cadaverous by the day. 'It is my pleasure, John,' he said. 'I was not going to sleep this night, not until *she* returns.'

Shakespeare did not need to ask who *she* was, nor did he wish to engage in talk of Mills's blighted marriage bed. 'I have come to find whether you have intelligence on the whereabouts of the Vidame de Chartres. Is he still at Essex House? Or is he with his father at the embassy?'

'Neither, John. The French have acquired a country property in Surrey and he has fled there with his horses. Whores, too, I am sure. We have kept a close eye on this Frenchman in recent days . . .'

Shakespeare was tempted to say, *Well I am glad you have been doing something of value, Frank*, but instead merely nodded his head. 'Good.'

'A fair-sized old hall by the village of Molesey, a little way south of the Thames, not far from Hampton Court Palace. His father, the ambassador, has visited and Don Antonio Perez has travelled there also, but I know that he has now departed. No one else of note.'

'Is this hall watched?'

'Indeed, night and day. Sir Robert Cecil insists on it. Sawyer and Shoe are the men.'

'And what activity has been noted apart from the arrival and departure of Perez and the Seigneur de Beauvoir-la-Nocle?'

'Nothing but the comings and goings of everyday tradesmen.'

'Thank you, Frank.'

'We are on the same side, you know, John.'

'So I am told.'

Shakespeare rode through the quiet early hours. Against his initial judgement he had Beth Evans with him. They talked little. The road was poor and pitted and the night was dark; they could demand no more of their mounts than a cautious walk. A twenty-mile journey that might have been completed in two to three hours in daylight took them six hours, so that they arrived at the village of Molesey soon after dawn.

He had taken Beth because it made sense. 'How will you gain entry to the hall, John?' she had said. 'If it is a property of the French embassy, you will not be able to march up to the front door and demand that Lucy be produced. I could be of assistance. My . . . profession. I know how to coax a man with guile and caresses.'

'What? You will go the the hall and offer your services? Come now, Beth.'

She had smiled the smile that had once won his heart in the meadows of Warwickshire. 'Do not mock, sir. There may be ways. You have nothing to lose by taking me.'

It had been true enough. An uninvited intrusion into the house would be resented as much as an invasion of France. And what harm could there be in taking her? She could ride a farm horse well enough in the old days; she could probably manage a night's ride now. *She'll have the thighs for it*, he found himself thinking, and straightway reproached himself for the unkindness of the thought.

From the village, Shakespeare and Beth rode out westwards in the bright early morning light. In the distance, to the north, they saw the towers of Hampton Court, the palace built by Wolsey and purloined from him by Great Henry.

The Old Hall at Molesey was more modest but a goodly house nonetheless. Shakespeare reined in his mount half a mile away and considered his options. This had to be done with stealth. There would be guards here, as at the French embassy in Hackney. After a minute or two observing the house, he wheeled his horse's head and they rode back to the village.

At the Silver Stag inn, Shakespeare ordered breakfast for Beth and himself: boiled eggs, gammon slices and small ale. He also asked for a loaf of manchet but had to make do with heavy black ryebread. They sat in a partitioned booth, at a table that still stank of last night's ale.

As they ate, he asked her why she lived the life she did with all its perils. 'Why do you not return to Warwickshire?'

'I don't care a pail of slurry for them and their parish ways, John. What would I do? Work my backbone bent over a loom or milking cows. If I had never come to London, I would never have tasted fine spices or sipped French wine.'

'But you won't be able to carry on this life many more years.'

Beth smiled that sweet smile that had once captured him. 'Am I losing my looks, sir? Is that a way to speak to a lady?'

She could make him laugh still, which was something in this dark, empty time when it seemed his soul had been torn from his chest.

After eating, he left her and went in search of Jonas Shoe. He found him, asleep with a whore, in a small first-storey room of the inn. Shakespeare shook him awake.

'Get up, Mr Shoe. You have slept long enough.'

The man was groggy, but managed to swing his thin, hairy legs from beneath the bedcovers. The woman at his side snored on unawares.

Shoe was one of Mills's hirelings, a foot soldier willing to do anything demanded of him so long as he got booze, beef and a shilling a day. He was short, bald and undistinguished. You would not note him in the crowd at the bear-baiting or among a field full of harvesters, a fine attribute in a man whose work involved following others unseen.

'I have done my hours of work, Mr Shakespeare. Sawyer's been out on the late shift, watching since two in the morning.'

'I don't want Sawyer. I want you. Have you seen a black woman out at the Old Hall?'

'A blackamoor? In Surrey?' Shoe laughed, then coughed as though his lungs would come up through his windpipe. He reached for his pipe and tobacco.

'Well, Mr Shoe, *could* such a woman have been taken there?'

'No. Impossible. We have seen nothing and our watch is constant, night and day.'

'But you are *here*, Mr Shoe. How can your watch be constant?'

'Because Mr Sawyer is *there*.'

'Can he watch back and front at the same time?'

'There is but one approach road to the hall, a half-mile avenue to the front of the house. Anyone visiting the property comes that way.'

'Are you saying that at night, when there is only one of you watching, that it would be impossible to smuggle someone in unseen through a postern door?'

Shoe looked uneasy. He was trying and failing to strike a light with his tinderbox. He shook his head. 'No, Mr Shakespeare, I am not saying that, for you are right. It *would* be possible to smuggle a person in unseen by night, if they approached the back of the house by way of the woodland path. Mr Sawyer and I would not see them under such circumstances. But we have not been looking for such a thing. Our charge was to note all visitors, not to besiege the hall.'

'I understand, Mr Shoe. You have performed your duty well, I am certain, but we have established that the woman could be there. In which case, I come on to my next question: what are my chances of gaining access to the hall? Unseen.'

'Poor. There are guards. Frenchies.'

'How many?'

'Outside, there are six. They work three on, three off. Day and night, like us. But I am sure there are more indoors.'

'And do they know about you and Sawyer?'

'Of course. They expect it. Even if they never saw us, they'd know we were there. But they do see us. It's a game, Mr Shakespeare. Same at the embassy itself, where I have passed many a long hour. They know we dare not intrude on their property, for it would spark a brabble between nations. So their guards are always lax; they know they have nothing to fear. Sometimes, we have even been known to share a drink or two, here at the inn.'

'So what do you suggest? How do I get in?'

At last Shoe succeeded in firing a spark into the tinder. He blew on the smoking glow and managed to light a taper. Shakespeare looked at him impatiently.

'Well, Mr Shoe?'

'I'm contemplating, Mr Shakespeare, contemplating . . .' He lit his pipe of tobacco and drew deeply of the pungent smoke. 'That's better,' he said, and promptly resumed his coughing. He smacked himself on his chest, then sat back on the edge of the rank, over-used bed, satisfied that his morning ritual was done. 'You know what I'd do, sir? I'd walk straight in. Do it in broad daylight. Don't wait for nightfall, that's when they *would* be alert for intruders. In daytime, though, people come and go all the while to a big hall like that – traders bringing wares, gardeners, estate hands, builders.'

'How do you suggest I do it?'

'You need to dress yourself as a tradesman, Mr Shakespeare. Ride up, slow as you like, pulling a cart behind you, with produce. Sort of delicate stuff Frenchies like.'

Shakespeare looked at him as if he were mad. 'You have just told me that they have three guards on duty all the time, Shoe. Why would they not stop me, and then either throw me off the land or call in the sheriff's men to have me arrested?'

'Because you will have created a diversion, Mr Shakespeare. Some manner of distraction that will make the sight of a common trader with his cart the last thing on their minds.'

'A diversion? What diversion?'

'Ah well, sir, that's for you to think on, isn't it. That's why I earn but a shilling a day and you live in a grand house by the river.'

At Shoe's side, the whore stirred and turned over. A soft, unwashed aroma wafted Shakespeare's way from her body, and he suddenly smiled. That was how to do it. The oldest trick there was.

Chapter 43

SHAKESPEARE STOOD IN the woods with Jonas Shoe and watched. It was mid afternoon and the guard had changed. The three pickets who had been there protecting the Old Hall in the morning had gone off to sleep or drink or eat.

The new watch took up their posts. Two were at the main gate, the other one at the front entrance to the house. They were good positions from which to observe and stop any newcomer. The guards had Swiss pikestaffs, as well as swords. Their role was not exactly ceremonial, but nor was it arduous or dangerous. No one really expected an attack on French embassy property. They were there to let the English observers know that they, too, were watched. Also to greet visitors and to deter poachers.

'The vidame will be taking his afternoon ride soon,' Shoe said. 'Always goes out alone after his midday repast. I pity the horses because he rides like he is pursued by a demon. Lashes the beasts to the bone.'

Shakespeare said nothing. He knew the vidame's liking for speed, but knew, too, that he had a great affection for his horses and would do nothing to cause them harm.

'Here they come, Mr Shakespeare.'

Three women were trudging through the woods, not fifty yards from them. They were moving in a strange way, as though they were trying to be stealthy, but instead they merely seemed to stumble and giggle. Their dress was awry and they carried flagons.

Shakespeare's eyes shifted to the two guards at the gate. Their eyes were following the women, too. They grinned at each other, glanced around furtively, then one of them began walking, quickstep, in the direction of the three women. As he neared the woods he gestured with his hand to the guard at the house, who immediately leant his pike against a wall and walked with purpose to join his comrade.

The new sentries had enjoyed a good midday break at the Silver Stag. It was, Shoe told Shakespeare, the place they always went for their daytime meals. They had a weakness for English ale and seemed to have an eye for the local girls, whom they flattered and courted with a singular lack of success. Until today. This had been their lucky day. Three willing wenches had been there at the inn. Happy-go-lucky peasant girls who had accepted the Frenchmen's wine and fumblings with enthusiasm.

The girls had suggested a walk in the meadows, where the men would be rewarded with whatever they desired, for it was a fine summer's day and who could not wish for a roll in the grass on such a splendid afternoon. But the three French guards had run out of time. They had to be at their posts by two of the clock.

Beth Evans had perched herself on the lap of the eldest of the three watchmen, a prematurely grey man in his thirties, who had consumed twice the amount of wine he normally drank. She whispered in his ear, then nibbled at the lobe. Beth had the sort of open, cheerful face and womanly body that always promised bliss and joy. She knew the way to draw any man from the righteous path, and today she was using every ploy she knew. The other two girls – Shoe's companion of the night and a friend of hers – were performing their own tasks well, too, for Shoe and Shakespeare had offered them a silver pound apiece and had coached them in what was required. The three Frenchmen were in their thrall. They would have sold the King of France to have their way with these three women.

And now here they were, in the woods. Hands caressed breeches. Smocks rode up thighs to reveal flesh. Mouths kissed and moaned.

It was time for Shakespeare to make his move.

Shakespeare bent forward as though he were a man of sixty as he pushed the rickety barrow up to the front gate.

The solitary guard glanced at him, then his hungry gaze returned to the woods where his two companions were swiving with delirious, drunken abandon. The lone guard could not take his eyes away. Why did Jacques and Michel not hurry up? It was his turn. There were three women there; one was for him.

Shakespeare let the legs of the barrow come to rest on the ground and stood up, rubbing his back as if it ached from long hours of work. 'Songbirds and sweetmeats, master.'

'*Quoi?*'

'Delivery of songbirds, fresh berries and sweetmeats. To the kitchens.'

The guard threw up his chin with indifference and waved him through. Slowly, Shakespeare wheeled the cart up the avenue towards the house. He kept his eyes in front, ignoring what was happening away in the woods and trying not to attract the attention of anyone who might glance from a window.

The house was large and wide-fronted, built of brick and stone with high, ornate chimney stacks. Shakespeare skirted the west wing, following a well-worn path that Shoe had assured him went to the kitchens by way of a walled garden.

The door to the garden was shut. Shakespeare hesitated, then lifted the latch and pushed it ajar. He peered in through the gap and his eyes instantly met the startled eyes of Ana Cabral. He tensed, his hand on the latch. Then he opened the door further and stepped through to the walled garden, leaving the barrow behind.

'Mr Shakespeare,' she said, quickly regaining her composure. 'You seem to be on private French property. Are you invited?' Her eyes, without the black patch, seemed to sparkle with good humour, but Shakespeare sensed an undertow that was far from humorous.

'I have been looking for you.'

'Indeed. And why would you want me? I am nothing to you.'

Suddenly, Shakespeare realised there were others in this garden. A trestle table was laden with meats and wines, much of which had already been consumed. There were armed guards, four of them, with hands at the hilts of their swords. And there was an old woman and a young man at the table, staring at him. The old woman was the nun from Gaynes Park Hall. The young man was quite beautiful. His skin was flawless and almost translucent. His eyes were dark and distant. He had the aspect of someone Shakespeare had seen before, but he could not think where or who. The young man stared at Shakespeare without expression as a tiny child might look at a butterfly, with interest but little understanding.

The old half-blind nun rose from the bench. Her gnarled left hand clasped the knob of her walking stick. On the knuckle of the ring finger, sunlight reflected from a gold and diamond band. In her other hand, she gripped the rosary he had seen before. She gazed at him as if through gauze, with haughty loathing. She tapped her stick on the ground impatiently.

'Do you not genuflect in the presence of royalty, Mr Shakespeare?'

And then he understood where he had seen the face before. The young man was the son of Mary, Queen of Scots. He had her looks in every detail. Shakespeare had seen her once, at Tutbury Castle in 1585, while delivering a message to her keeper from Sir Francis Walsingham. This was her flesh and blood, and yet more striking, more beautiful than his mother, whose beauty was marred by her sharp nose, her too close eyes and her dark soul. There could be no doubt in any mind that this perfect boy (Shakespeare could scarce find it in him to think of him as a man, even though he must be twenty-five years) was the Prince of Scots.

'You seem to be rather outnumbered and outgunned, Mr Shakespeare,' Ana Cabral said. 'I am not at all sure what we should do with you.'

'Kill him,' the old nun said instantly. 'We cannot afford sentiment. Guards, kill him!'

They drew their swords but did not move forward.

Ana smiled. 'Sister Madeleine, you must not become over-wrought. These guards are French, they are not ours to order. And we cannot just kill Mr Shakespeare.'

'That is the prince, yes?'

'Could anyone have any doubt? Every man or woman in this country and Scotland will know the truth merely by gazing on his lovely face.'

'He looks at me as though he does not see me. Is he blind?'

'No, Mr Shakespeare. He is physically without defect. A divine prince among mortal men.'

Shakespeare stepped further into the walled garden. There were intricate patterns of herbs, lavender and other flowers.

Against the walls were espaliered fruit trees. Bees buzzed from flower to flower in the afternoon's hazy heat. He had a sense of unreality, as though he had entered some supernatural arbour where faeries danced and communed. Time hung. He knew he had to get this young man, this prince, away from this place and bring him to Cecil; the others here knew that he could not be allowed to leave.

'You know, Doña Ana, this young man was not the reason I came here today.'

'Indeed? Did you then hope to be asked to stay and eat with us? I must say you are dressed most unusually for a secretary to Sir Robert Cecil. Why, if I did not know better, I should say you were a costermonger or a farm hand.'

'I am looking for a woman called Lucy. I think you know of her, for the vidame spoke of her at Gaynes Park. She has now been abducted by him against the laws of this land. Is she here?'

Ana Cabral laughed out loud. 'No, she is not here!'

'Am I so amusing?'

'Indeed you are, Mr Shakespeare. You come looking for Prégent's blackamoor slave and instead you find the person little Robertus Diabolus would truly wish you to find. Is there not some strange irony in that? The sad thing is, I do not see how we can possibly allow you to leave this place. It pains me greatly to say such a thing, for I fear we have already wrought grievous harm on you and your children, and I vow that I never intended such hurt.'

Shakespeare moved forward. He grasped the prince's arm. 'You are coming with me.' He turned to the guards, who were within a few feet of him, swords raised, standing side on, as if at fencing, points poised to strike at Shakespeare's throat and puncture him like a joint of meat, from four sides, if they so decided. He growled at them in French. 'As for you men. Do not even consider harming me or trying to stop me, or you will die on the scaffold at Tyburn and your king will seek retribution against your families in France. *C'est compris?*'

Their blades wavered with indecision, but were not withdrawn.

Shakespeare ignored the swords and pulled the prince from his chair. He did not resist. There seemed to be no power in him. His body was loose like a baby's. He stood unsteadily and allowed himself to be cajoled along, as if it was something that happened every day of his life. His gait was slow and awkward and his left leg trembled. Shakespeare stopped and turned to Ana.

'What is the matter with him?'

'Leave my brother be, Mr Shakespeare. He will become distressed.'

'Your *brother*?'

Ana shook her head. 'I always thought of him thus. I love him as my own. He was brought up as part of my family, in my father's *casa de campo* outside Seville. We are of an age. I cared for him as if he were my brother or my child. Have you ever seen a more lovely face?'

'But there is something wrong with him . . .'

'A palsy at birth. He is wholly innocent of life.'

The old nun cracked her stick down on the table. 'Do not talk of him like this! He is a prince of the royal blood. He is the holy martyr's son. He will be King of Scots!'

'Not on my watch he won't.' All turned at the words. It was Rabbie Bruce's voice. He had appeared like a spectre at the little doorway to the garden, standing there, swathed in his kilt. In his hands he had a pair of wheel-lock pistols.

Before anyone had a chance to comprehend what was happening, let alone react, he took three steps forward, pointed the muzzle of one of the guns at the young prince's heart, and pulled the trigger.

Chapter 44

FRANCIS PHILIP BOTHWELL Stuart, Prince of Scots, crumpled and fell. His head cracked against the trestle table as he tumbled, but he was already dead from the shot to the heart.

Smoke billowed all around his assailant. The guards, who were used to the sound of musket-fire and the sight of death from the long civil wars of France, immediately closed on Bruce. But he had his second wheel-lock primed and trained on them. 'Stay back!' he ordered. 'All of you, stay back.'

Ana Cabral and Sister Madeleine ignored him and fell to their knees at the side of their prince. His face was still unblemished. His pink lips – fuller than his mother's thin and disdainful mouth – were slightly parted. His eyes were open but unseeing. The old nun began to wail. Ana Cabral clutched at his poor, lifeless hand and caressed it as if by so doing she could spark the flame of life back into his body.

For a second or two, Shakespeare was shocked speechless. Then he was seized by an ungovernable fury. He lunged forward, but Bruce stepped back. 'Don't think I won't kill you if needs be, Shakespeare. One death, two deaths, a hundred, I shall still sleep the same at night.'

Shakespeare breathed deeply. He looked at the Scotsman with diamond-hard contempt. 'That was murder, Mr Bruce.

Simple, calculated murder of an innocent boy. Is that what your king pays you for?'

'What would you have done, Shakespeare? Lock him up in Tutbury, Chartley and Fotheringhay for twenty years like his mother? Then chop off his head when the plots surrounding him began to press? This is not just what my king wanted, this is what your Cecils wanted, too.'

Shakespeare was about to rage and argue, but the words he wished to say stuck in his gullet, for he knew that Rabbie Bruce spoke the unpalatable truth. Oh yes, the Cecils wanted this princeling dead. That had been their objective and desire all along. They would be happy at the events of this day.

He looked down once more at the corpse. Perhaps the young man was better off dead. He would never have under-stood the politics and warfare that would have swirled around him all his life. The hellburner on the Thames was none of his doing, yet it was done in his name. How many hundreds, thousands, would have died in the struggle to put him on the thrones of Scotland and England? For the Spanish and their Catholic supporters in England and Scotland, he would have been the perfect puppet king; utterly pliable, a man to wave to the crowds when commanded to do so, and leave the decision making to others.

Ana Cabral looked up at the man with the smoking gun. 'I shall see you pay for this, Mr Bruce.'

He shook his head. 'You will do nothing, señorita, except return to Spain. This is over. All done for.'

Sir Robert Cecil sat at his desk at his home in the Strand, just outside the city walls of London. The minutes passed in silence, except for the scratching of his quill as he deftly dipped the cut nib in ink and wrote at speed in his elegant, sloping hand. At his side stood John Shakespeare. Facing them were Jean de la

Fin, Seigneur de Beauvoir-la-Nocle, King Henri IV's ambassador to the court of Queen Elizabeth, and his son, Prégent de la Fin, Vidame de Chartres. The father stood stiffly, shoulders back, lips tight, bracing himself for this unpleasant encounter. The son was nonchalant, as if he would rather be anywhere else.

At last Cecil looked up from his writing. He addressed himself to the senior of the two Frenchmen. 'I must now pass on to you the outcome of the deliberations of Her Majesty's Privy Council. The councillors are, in a word, appalled. You have assisted a power hostile to England at a time when relations between your country and mine are, to say the least, exceeding delicate. Does your king know of what has passed on embassy property?'

'No, Sir Robert, he does not. This was all our – my son's – doing. I can do nothing but offer my sincere and humble apologies.' As he spoke, in excellent English, he never once looked at the vidame, his son.

'Do you think King Henri would be pleased to hear that his embassy has been implicated in a Spanish plot?'

'He would have my head, Sir Robert.'

Cecil leaned back in his chair. The flicker of a smile passed his eyes and mouth, then vanished. 'I have always liked you, Jean. I have thought that we saw eye to eye on many things.'

'That is true, Sir Robert. I feel shame that my name –' and now he *did* look sideways at his son – 'should be connected to such a conspiracy.'

'Good. Then we can proceed. I have here written the terms which you must accept, without demur.' He turned the sheet of paper so that the Frenchmen could read it.

'Firstly, the vidame will return to France. You, Jean, will stay as ambassador. Secondly, you will make it your business to discredit all stories of this Scots prince. As far as you are concerned, as far as we are concerned, the man never existed. It was all a tale put about by the Escorial to sow the seeds of unrest in England. To that end, there will be no trial of the Cabral woman. She will be deported forthwith. Her plot very nearly succeeded. I do not know whether your son had any knowledge of the plan to destroy the bridge, but it is certain that he has dealt dangerously and treacherously. And so there is a third condition: the vidame will return the woman known as Black Lucy to her home in Clerkenwell, unharmed.'

'*Non!*' At last the vidame erupted. 'No. I will not have it. The woman is mine. My property!'

Cecil's voice stayed icily calm. 'No, she is not yours. If you listen further, you will understand what is to happen. Mr Shakespeare, you know a little about horses and women, please explain to the vidame what we are offering.'

Shakespeare smiled. He had been looking forward to this. 'You have a horse, a black Barbary filly named Conquistadora. You and your family also have extraordinary debts because Henri pays you nothing but promises, and you must fund your lavish embassy from your own depleted coffers. We will pay you a thousand sovereigns for the horse on condition that the woman is returned to us.'

'The horse is worth twice that! And the Queen herself has pledged that I may have Monique back. As I kissed her hand and received the Golden Spur from her, she gave me her word that I could ask anything.'

'Would you like me to tell Her Majesty what the French embassy has been involved in?'

The vidame turned his head aside contemptuously. 'Then why do you not just make me an offer for the whore and leave me the horse?'

'Because, monsieur, we do not buy and sell human flesh. A thousand sovereigns will buy you a stable full of fine horses in

France. And a whore every night for ten years should you wish it. Take it. You have no option.'

The vidame's face was suffused with rage. He glared at his father. 'Are you party to this, Papa?'

'There is no other solution, Prégent. This is not a matter for negotiation. If we do not accept, the English will inform Henri of your foolish collusion with these Spaniards and we will lose our heads. It is as simple as that.'

Cecil offered the quill to the two Frenchmen. 'So, messieurs, if you will just make your mark on the paper, I believe we will have a contract.'

After the Frenchmen had gone, Shakespeare stayed. 'I confess, Sir Robert, that I am much troubled. The role of the Scotsman, Mr Bruce. He was nothing more than a hired assassin.'

'And yet you understand why King James thought it necessary to employ him?'

'Was he, then, employed by James?'

'The English paid him nothing. He was out of our control.'

'But you allowed him leeway to operate on our land as he saw fit.'

'We winked at it, nothing more.'

'And what of Baines – or Laveroke?'

'He has disappeared. It was believed he was heading for Scotland with a plan to murder James. Nothing has been heard of him since. Perchance, he was set upon by bandits.'

Shakespeare looked askance at his master.

'This is a war, John. Men die in wars.'

'I understand the heat of battle, Sir Robert. But there are times—'

Cecil put up a hand. 'Leave it, John. Mourn your wife, do not grieve for some unknown palsied prince, now buried in an unmarked grave. Do not grieve for a murderer like Baines who, if God be just, now lies feeding the crows in some woodland ditch.'

'And what of Marlowe? I know what happened to him.'

'Do you? Then you know more than I do, and more than I wish to know. Whatever you believe you know, I do not wish to hear it from your lips and you do not wish to tell me, for I believe that to do so would heap much trouble on you and yours and many others. Suffice it to say that whatever the reason Marlowe was in that room, he was not taken there to be killed. It was unpleasant, tragic even, but it was not a premeditated murder. We both know that. The inquest decided it. Let it rest.'

'And Topcliffe?'

'Do you have some evidence against him that would be listened to in court?'

Shakespeare shook his head slowly. Not an ounce of evidence. Nothing to prove his guilt in attempting to extract information from Marlowe by illicit torture. Nothing but a play called *The White Dog*, and who knew where that was? All he had was the partial confession of Nicholas Jones. 'I have words spoken by his apprentice, admitting he was there in the room at the time when the Searcher of the Dead says the killing took place.'

'And will this apprentice testify as much in court?'

'No.'

'Then all you have is hearsay.' Cecil closed his mouth and looked Shakespeare square in the eye. There was nothing more to be said on the matter and both men knew it.

'One day—' Shakespeare began.

Cecil reached out his small, neat hand and stayed Shakespeare with a light touch on the forearm. 'Let us talk of this horse, this Conquistadora. I had thought to give it to Her Majesty. I think such a gesture would lift her spirits and help us ease Don

Antonio Perez's progress to her presence-chamber. Do you not agree?'

Cecil had changed the subject. Shakespeare sighed. No more delving into murky waters, for to do so could only harm Will, Kyd and all the others from the Dolphin Inn. 'Yes, Sir Robert, I agree. Her Royal Majesty would be most pleased with such a present.' At last he managed a faint smile. 'And I confess I am delighted to be depriving the vidame of his most prized possessions. Perhaps he will collect silver treasures and fine paintings, not slaves, to satisfy his quest for beauty.'

'Indeed so. Her Majesty shall have the horse. I am not certain, however, that she would appreciate the animal's name.'

'It is a little bit . . . *Spanish*.'

'Then let us change the filly's name . . . to Gloriana. That will please her very well, I do believe.'

Chapter 45

THE RAIN CAME down like mare's piss, soaking Shakespeare through to the skin as he strode from Dowgate to Wood Street.

At the Counter gaol, the ancient, grey-bearded keeper did not look pleased to see him. Mr Shakespeare had brought nothing but trouble on his previous visits. 'Good day, kind sir, good day,' he said, but the tone of his voiced betrayed his true feelings.

Shakespeare stared at him with icy dispassion. 'Who takes command of the gaol when you are not here, master keeper?'

The old man scratched his beard and crumbs and lice sprinkled out down his jerkin. He hesitated before answering, unsure what was for the best.

'It is a simple enough question. I cannot believe you spend twenty-four hours of every day and seven days of every week here.'

'Indeed not, Mr Shakespeare, sir. Why, the chief turnkey is my deputy.'

'The one I demanded be shackled?'

'Yes, sir. Or one of the other turnkeys when he is not available.'

'Bring me to him.'

The keeper shifted uneasily. 'I cannot, sir.'

'He is in irons, is he not? I ordered it.'

'No, sir, I had to unlock him. He was ill with the ague. I had the fetters removed so that he might receive care of his good-wife.'

'So you disobeyed me? You do realise what this means for your position here?'

'Indeed, sir, I do, and I am most fearful. It was with a heavy heart that I made the decision to free the turnkey. But what choice did I have? Had I not done so, I know it would have cost his life. He would have wasted and perished, though he had not been convicted of any crime. I would have consulted you, master, but I knew of no way to get word to you.'

'Where is he now?'

'Gone, sir.'

'Home?'

'No, gone altogether, sir, to his maker. Hanged. By the Dutch church. He was among those arrested following the recent disturbances in the city, Mr Shakespeare, after the ship blew up on the river, sir.'

Shakespeare breathed in deeply. So the turnkey had been one of the rebel band of Baines and Curl. He must, surely, have been responsible for Morley's death. Well, he had had the self-same fate meted out to him: hanged by the neck until dead.

'Thank you, master keeper. That is all. Take better care when you employ a replacement for the man.' Shakespeare turned and left, stepping through the great studded door out into the bustle of Wood Street and the pelting rain. He had not even bothered to ask the name of the hanged turnkey. What did it matter? A gnat of a man, he had thought him. Well, he had now proved himself of no significance. No one would remember him save, perhaps, his wife and children, and they would do well to forget all about him as soon as they could.

*

Lucy was delivered to Shakespeare's door by two horsemen in tangerine tabards. She had been a guest at Essex House, waiting to be carried aboard a French packet-boat to Calais. She was unharmed.

'They told me I was there with the Queen's express permission,' she said as they sipped wine in his refectory. 'I confess my time in the earl's house was well spent, though. I do believe I have acquired new clients of great wealth. Yet, I must thank you, Mr Shakespeare, for I have some inkling of all you have done to rescue me.'

Shakespeare thought she looked magnificent, yet vulnerable and, perhaps, a little afraid. Her hair was soaked from the rain and her black skin glistened. The vidame had thought her a jewel to be added to his collection, but she was a human being, a frail woman leading a life of debauchery that all too often ended in disease, violence, the ravages of liquor and early death. Perhaps this woman could rise above it all, but she would not be the first to have tried and failed.

'I think it is Beth Evans who most deserves your gratitude,' he said.

'I know that very well. She is a fine woman. My right arm. You must come and see her all you wish. No fees will be levied . . .'

Shakespeare laughed out loud and shook his head. 'No, Lucy, I think not. Her charms belong to a time long gone. Long, long ago. No, I will not be coming to your trugging-house.'

The rain stopped and the sun came out again and burned the city dry. The exodus of the wealthy and powerful gathered pace. All feared that a hot summer would bring more disease.

'I confess that I, too, am going to leave, Mr Shakespeare,'

Jan Sluyterman said. 'It is too dangerous to keep young children here. They are always the first to die when King Pest arrives.'

Shakespeare had no argument with the Dutchman's decision. He, too, was planning a departure. He would take Andrew, Grace and Mary to Stratford for the summer. Boltfoot, Jane and their baby, too. Cecil had suggested it. 'You must have time with them. And you must find yourself a woman to help you. No man can raise three children alone.'

'I have my servant Jane to help,' Shakespeare had said shortly. He wanted no woman to replace Catherine. But, yes, he did wish time with the children. They were growing fast and they did not know Stratford, where he had been born and brought up. It would be good to take them there, while his parents yet lived.

Now, here, in the Sluytermans' garden, he nodded in agreement with his host. 'Yes, I will do the same.'

The garden was cool, with good shade from an array of well-tended trees: birch and young oak, hornbeam and ash. Shakespeare and Boltfoot were sipping Dutch brandy with Sluyterman. Boltfoot looked ill at ease. His back was still scorched. The mere touch of the cloth of his shirt could make him wince. Further down the garden, the young Sluytermans were playing with Shakespeare's three children. It was Sunday and morning prayers were done.

Shakespeare's eyes followed the servant girl, Susanna, as she carried a jug of cordial to the children.

'She is well, Mr Shakespeare,' Sluyterman said. 'We are pleased to have her once again in our home. There has been too much suffering. I owe you a great deal for all your help. More than I can ever repay, I fear.'

'I believe you had some knowledge of Curl?'

'That Curl, yes, I recall him well. I had hoped never to hear his name or see him again when we parted company two years since. Was ever a man so ill-named? Holy Trinity . . . *ha*!'

'You believe he deliberately put the servant Kettle into your home?'

'I do, Mr Shakespeare, I do, indeed. He wished to find an excuse for calling in Mr Topcliffe and the pursuivants. It was all done in vengeance for some perceived ill done him. Yet *he*, Curl, was the faithless servant.'

'What were your dealings with him?'

'He was a wool factor, but he had little success. He asked to work for me as an agent, saying he could supply good grease wool in great quantities. I was uncertain at first, but then he brought me samples and I agreed to his terms, for wool is difficult to come by for export. I knew I could sell it for good profit in the Low Countries, where there is a great demand. Their home supply has been much disrupted by the wars. This worked well for both of us for two months, no more. Then I realised he was cheating me. He took me for a gull. I did not know it at first, but the wool he shipped was mostly of poorer quality than he had first shown me, and I received complaints from my buyers. I found, too, that he had been charging me for greater quantities than he supplied, so I severed my links with Mr Curl. He was angry with me, but what could I do?'

Shakespeare said nothing. It was a lamentable story which, through a cruel twist of fate, had caused Catherine to be in the Dutch market with Susanna at the very moment that a cask of gunpowder exploded.

Jan Sluyterman shook his head mournfully and repeated, 'What could I do?'

Suddenly, Shakespeare realised that Boltfoot was looking at him curiously, as though he had something to say. 'Boltfoot?'

Boltfoot looked away, then took a hefty swig of the brandy. 'Eases the pain, master.'

'I thought for a moment you wished to say something.'

'Just that.'

'What was that, Boltfoot, that look you gave me?' Shakespeare asked quietly as they walked the short distance home a little later.

'Master?'

'I know you well enough, Boltfoot. That look wasn't pain. There was something else – something you wished to say.'

'I do not wish to speak out of order.'

'God's blood, Boltfoot, speak your mind.'

Boltfoot shifted uneasily, looking down at his club foot. 'I do not know at all whether I should be saying this, for it do sound bad, and I know Mr Sluyterman to be a good man, or at least I believe I do. But I did hear another version of that story of him and Holy Trinity Curl.'

Shakespeare stopped. He stood in the middle of the dusty road and tried in vain to look Boltfoot in the eye. 'And from whom did you hear this story?'

'From Curl himself, after they had discovered me. I couldn't stop him, no man could. The tale came out of his mouth in every last detail. He foamed at the mouth with venom as he told me what he thought of Mr Sluyterman and said what he had supposedly done to him.'

'Tell me.'

At last, Boltfoot looked up and met his master's gaze. 'The way Curl told it, he was a successful wool merchant when along comes Sluyterman and suggests they join forces. Curl is to supply the English wool, just as Sluyterman said just now, and Mr Sluyterman will sell it on. But that's where the similarity in the tale ends. For Curl said he was not Sluyterman's servant at that time, but an equal partner, and he says that bit by bit he was cheated out of his share of the concern and was left impoverished. In the end, he had to go a-begging for work to Mr Sluyterman . . .'

'And?'

'He was given a job in the counting house, as a ledger clerk, dealing with bills of lading at twelve pence a day. That was scarce enough for him and his wife and two young children, but at least they ate. But that was not the end of it. He said Mr Sluyterman dismissed him in the winter of '90, claiming he had made misrepresentations in the ledger, though as Curl tells it he had always been honest. After that, Curl could find no work and was brought to such a turn of poverty that he and his family lost the roof over their heads. The children, cold and hungry, took sick and died. His wife cut her own throat. Curl heard later that his job of work in the counting house had been given to a nephew of Sluyterman newly arrived from the Low Countries, which he believed to be the real reason he was dismissed. Now I have no way of knowing whether any of that is true, Mr Shakespeare, but I tell you this: I did believe it at the time of being told.'

Shakespeare did not know what to say. Had he been so wrong about Sluyterman? It was an uncomfortable, troubling thought, and one that was difficult to accept. Yet it would undoubtedly explain why Curl was so fervent in his loathing of the Dutch strangers. He stood there in the street. Above him, swallows swooped and soared. The fragrance of summer flowers drowned the foul city hum, yet his mouth had a bitter taste of rising bile. He wanted to return to Sluyterman's house and put it to him directly.

It was Boltfoot who stayed him. 'There is nothing to be gained, master. That is why I said nothing.'

Was that it? Was no one honest in this city of thieves and whores? He nodded briskly to Boltfoot. 'You are right.' He turned back and strode the last few paces to his own open door.

Ahead of him the children were laughing and skipping, full of the delights of their afternoon at play. He shut the door behind him and enclosed himself in his own world. At least there was beauty and decency here.

KING PHILIP AND A PRINCELY LIE

✥ ✥ ✥ ✥

Fair reader, while London suffers the darkness of Satan's foul pestilence, secure in the faith that the Lord's light will prevail, we have at last a sunbeam of news. Sooth to say, it is news of no news, but it is a fine thing for all that. We have learned on the greatest authority that the recent scurrilous report of some Scottish prince is naught but perfidy, wrought by our enemies in Spain.

This fanciful princeling was but the fevered reverie of Señor Felipe and his cringing, timorous lickspittles. Their wish was to sow discord and unrest in England, but this enterprise, like the Armada before it, has failed in every degree. This imagined son of the devil Mary and her viperous partner in murder, Bothwell, is as substantial as the air itself. That is, no substance at all. He does not exist and never has. This prince was a fantasme, designed to stir the disaffected, be they Romish or atheistic, to insurrection. Puff, he is gone.

Of greater concern, dear readers, is the plague that daily weaves its evil amongst us. The aldermen of the twenty-six wards tell us that King Pest is spread through the air by cats and dogs, and that they must be destroyed. It is *The London Informer*'s duty to spur the aldermen, the Lord

Mayor and his marshals to action, for word has reached us of a rabid white dog that does spread his vile poison around the city. Is it not time to toss this white dog's carcass into the Hounds Ditch, that honest men and women may sleep sound at night without fear of his savage bite?

God Save the Queen.

Walstan Glebe, publisher

Acknowledgements

I AM INDEBTED to many people for their support and help. They include:

Dave Sim of the Royal Gunpowder Mills at Waltham Abbey, Essex, for taking me around the mills and explaining in great detail how gunpowder is made. Any mistakes in the book are mine, not his. I would recommend the mills as a superb family day out (see www.royalgunpowdermills.com for details). Alex Crossley, for her care and attention to detail in helping me with the Dutch language. Andrea Nollent, for giving me the germ of an idea. As always, my wife Naomi, editor Kate Parkin and agent Teresa Chris, for their valiant efforts on my behalf.

Books that have been especially helpful include: *Antonio Pérez* by Gregorio Marañon; *The Dutch Revolt* by Geoffrey Parker; *The History of Horse Racing* by Roger Longrigg; *Christopher Marlowe and Richard Baines* by Roy Kendall; *Elizabeth's Spy Master* by Robert Hutchinson; *I Spy Blue* by Donald Rumbelow; *My Heart is My Own* by John Guy; *The Defeat of The Spanish Armada* by Garrett Mattingly; *The Confident Hope of a Miracle* by Neil Hanson; *The World of Christopher Marlowe* by David Riggs; *The Reckoning* by Charles Nicholl; *The Cradle King* by Alan Stewart; *The Gunpowder Industry* by Glenys Crocker; *The Witches of Warboys* by Philip C. Almond; *Sir John Norreys and the Elizabethan Military*

World by John S. Nolan; *The Pursuit of Stability* by Ian W. Archer; *The Second Cecil* by P. M. Handover; *A Spaniard in Elizabethan England: The Correspondence of Antonio Pérez's Exile* edited by Gustav Ungerer.

Historical Notes

Hellburners and the Spanish Armada

Hellburners – exploding fireships packed with gunpowder – were first used on the night of 4 April 1585, at Antwerp.

In the long-running Dutch revolt against Spanish rule in the Low Countries, the mainly Protestant city was besieged by the Duke of Parma's Catholic armies. To enforce their iron grip, the Spanish had blocked the vital river Scheldt – Antwerp's main supply route from the sea – with a half-mile bridge built on piles seventy-five feet deep and, in the middle section, secured by a pontoon of ships and longboats linked by massive chains. It was covered from both shores by forts with two-hundred-gun batteries of heavy artillery and was patrolled by an army of battle-hardened soldiers. With food running short, the suffering people of Antwerp were desperate to break this seemingly impenetrable barrier.

Help was at hand. An ambitious young Italian military engineer named Federigo Giambelli was in the city. He had already offered his services to the Spanish, but had been spurned. It was a decision that would cost Spain dear, for Giambelli was now working for the Dutch instead. He had a design for a floating bomb which, he claimed, would blow the river barrier apart and allow food and munitions to be brought into Antwerp under cover of darkness.

The burghers of Antwerp had nothing to lose, so they accepted his plan. They gave him two seventy-ton ships, the *Hope* and the *Fortune*. These were stripped down to their hulls. The holds were then lined with long funnels of brick and stone, thirty-six feet long and three feet in diameter, and each packed with more than three tons of high-quality gunpowder. To make the huge bombs even more devastating, a mass of iron implements and rocks – anything sharp and hard which they could find – was added to the deadly mix. The devices were then topped off with sheets of lead and more stones, including flagstones and graveyard headstones.

The final, brilliant, innovation was to add a timing device to one of the bombs, the one aboard the *Hope*. An Antwerp clockmaker built a machine, based on the wheel-lock pistol, in which, at a set time, a lever would fall, spinning a steel wheel against flint and sending a shower of sparks into the gunpowder.

To lower the Spanish guard, a number of traditional fireships were first sent with the ebb tide downriver against the barrier. These were piled with firewood and burning pitch. The Spanish troops, unperturbed by the smoke-belching vessels, boarded them and doused them before any damage could be done to their own ship-bridge. Finally, the *Hope* and the *Fortune* were let loose to run with the current. To make them look like normal fireships, small fires had been started on the decks – as camouflage for what lay beneath.

The *Fortune*, which had a normal fuse, drifted into the riverbank and fizzled out harmlessly. The *Hope*, however, arrived at its target. Spanish troops swarmed aboard with pails of water, laughing scornfully at the pathetic attempts of the Dutch to break the siege. And then the time-bomb went off.

The blast was heard fifty miles away, and the slaughter was on a scale never before known. Up to a thousand people were killed and many more were injured – even by twenty-first-century standards, a huge number for a single, non-nuclear weapon. The Duke of Parma himself was knocked off his feet by a flying stave. The pageboy at his side was killed, as were several of his senior officers. Bodies – and parts of bodies – were still being found many months later.

A hole of more than fifty metres was blown in the barrier. But there was confusion among the Dutch and the relief fleet did not manage to get through the gap before the shaken Spanish army repaired the damage.

Antwerp was not saved. The defenders (around a third of whom were Catholic) held out for a further four months before surrendering in August 1585. But the psychological impact of the hellburners was longer-lasting; the memory of that bloody night came back to haunt Spain three years later during England's decisive battle against the Armada in the summer of 1588.

The Armada had been harried by the English fleet all the way up the Channel but had remained largely intact. Now the Spanish ships were anchored off Calais, awaiting their chance to embark Parma's troops from the Low Countries for the planned invasion of England.

In desperation, the English decided to send fireships against them. In the past they had not been effective weapons; usually they were easily evaded or steered away by ships' boats with grappling irons. But this was different.

The Duke of Medina-Sidonia, admiral of the Spanish fleet, and his captains were all painfully aware that the architect of the hellburners, Federigo Giambelli, had gone to England to work for Queen Elizabeth. They naturally assumed that Giambelli was building hellburners once more. In fact, he was at that time vainly attempting to build a defensive boom across the Thames, but Medina-Sidonia had no way of knowing this.

When the Spanish look-outs spotted several harmless supply barges approaching the English fleet from the north, their worst fears seemed to be confirmed; surely these must be Giambelli's hellburners.

That night eight large English fireships were sent against the moored Spanish ships. Their decks and sails ablaze, they were pushed by strong winds directly towards the heart of the enemy fleet. As their loaded cannons exploded, the Armada captains' jitters turned to outright panic. In 'shameful confusion', utterly convinced they were about to be blown apart, most of them cut their anchor lines and ran for safety.

The Armada, previously so tight and disciplined as it sailed up the Channel, was now in total disarray, battered by howling winds and churning seas. Having lost their anchors, they were never able to regroup successfully. The threat to England was all but gone.

The hellburners may not have saved Antwerp, but they had helped save England. What is not recorded is whether Sir Francis Drake and the other English admirals understood in advance why their fireships – which did not set fire to a single Spanish vessel – would prove so effective.

King James and the Scottish witch trials
The Scottish witch trials were a sensation of the 1590s. Dozens of people were burned at the stake for a variety of crimes such as communing with Satan and plotting to kill King James VI.

The most prominent witch-persecutor was James himself. He was both horrified and obsessed by the cult and wrote a treatise, *Demonologie*, in which he clamoured for all sorcerers and devil-worshippers to be executed. His interest in the subject started in 1589, when he went to Oslo to marry Anne of Denmark. During the celebrations, he met the demonologist Niels Hemmingsen and was fascinated by his opinions.

Witchcraft trials were common in Scandinavia at that time. Returning to Scotland with Anne, the young King was almost shipwrecked by a storm – an event blamed on witchcraft.

Meanwhile, a few miles east of Edinburgh in the town of Tranent, a young serving girl named Gellie Duncan had aroused the suspicions of her employer, David Seton, who was bailie – or sheriff – for the area. Gellie was known locally as a healer. Seton decided her powers must emanate from the dark side, and interrogated her. Unhappy with her responses, he had her tortured with thumbscrews and other devices.

When she still denied being a witch, her body was examined and a 'mark of satan' was found on her. This was a nipple-like patch of skin which, when pricked, neither bled nor caused pain. It was supposed to be used to suckle demons. Gellie now made a full confession. She said her healing powers came from the devil.

Then she went further – and implicated thirty other people as witches. Most of them were women, including seemingly respectable wives of the Edinburgh middle classes. They included a midwife named Agnes Sampson and a high-born woman named Barbara Napier, lady-in-waiting to the Countess of Angus. All were arrested and held in prison. Scottish society was rocked to its foundations but there was more to come. All the accused were tortured and their bodies searched for the mark of the devil. King James attended some of these torture sessions and personally interrogated the accused.

Agnes Sampson now confessed that there were more than two hundred witches in the coven – and she said they had conspired with the devil to kill King James and his bride by sinking their ship on its voyage home to Scotland. Their plan was devised at a meeting with the devil in the church at North Berwick, a coastal port not far from both Tranent and Edinburgh. Among the two hundred witches present were a schoolteacher known as Dr John Fian or Feane and an old man named Graymeale.

Satan ordered them to take a cat, pass it nine times across a fire, then put to sea in sieves. They were to cast the cat into the sea, a sort of demonic baptism. This would raise a storm to sink the King's ship. Their plan did not, of course, succeed.

On their return to land, they marched back to the church, led by Gellie Duncan, who played a reel on her Jew's harp – a small, lyre-shaped instrument played against the teeth. They walked three times around the church, against the passage of the sun, then Dr Fian blew into the locked keyhole of the church and the door burst open. The church was in darkness, so he blew on the candles and they immediately lit.

The devil was waiting for them. He conducted a satanic service, then put his tail over the pulpit and made the witches kiss his buttocks. His followers then went outside where they feasted on dead bodies from the graveyard, before having a last dance, accompanied again by Gellie, who sang *'Kimmer, go you before, kimmer go you. If you will not go before, kimmer let me.'*

At their trials, the alleged witches were accused of a number of crimes, including plotting against the King, burning his wax effigy, foretelling deaths, casting revenge spells against neighbours, being transported by the devil to foreign lands, keeping moles' feet as charms, and dismembering the corpses of unbaptised children.

King James was particularly interested in the fates of Gellie Duncan, Agnes Sampson and Barbara Napier. He had Gellie brought to his palace of Holyrood House and made her play the tune which she had performed for the witches. He also had Agnes brought to him and questioned her at length.

At first he did not believe her tale, but then she asked to be allowed to approach him. She whispered in his ear words which had passed between him and his new queen on their wedding night in Oslo, when they were alone. The King was convinced by what he heard, 'and swore by the living God that he believed all the devils in hell could not have discovered the same'.

He was in no mood for forgiveness. Over the winter and spring of 1590–1, Gellie and Dr Fian and many others were taken to Castle Hill in Edinburgh and burned at the stake. Then in April 1591, another highly political element entered the reckoning. Agnes Sampson accused the King's heir – his cousin, the Earl of Bothwell – of sanctioning the assassination plot and of being linked to the accused witch Barbara Napier. Bothwell was arrested, but escaped and continued to cause James problems for many years to come before going into exile. Barbara Napier's fate is less certain. She claimed to be pregnant to avoid the death penalty. James was incensed. He ordered his Lord Chancellor, John Maitland, to have her examined by physicians to see whether she was telling the truth or not. 'Take no delaying answer,' he demanded. 'If you find she be not [pregnant], to the fire with her presently.' He also insisted she be publicly disembowelled.

The jury had other ideas – and refused to have her sentenced to death. It was a small act of humanity, but the terror was far from over. Witchcraft trials and burnings in Scotland would last for many more years.

A modern audience can sometimes find it difficult to relate to a world where ordinary women – and they were mostly women – should be tortured and then killed in the most horrible way for what seems to be an imaginary crime. But to most Elizabethans (though not all, for plenty of people were sceptical), the crime was all too real.

In *The Book of English Magic* (2009), authors Philip Carr-Gomm and Richard Heygate estimate that up to 2,500 witches were burnt at the stake in Scotland between the fifteenth and seventeenth centuries. Up to five hundred were hanged in England during the same period.

The most high profile case in England during Elizabeth's reign was the Witches of Warboys saga (Warboys is a fenland village in Huntingdonshire). An old woman named Alice Samuel, her husband John and their daughter Agnes were convicted of killing Lady Susan Cromwell (grandmother of Oliver Cromwell of Civil War fame) by enchantment and casting a spell to harm the children of local Huntingdonshire landowner Robert Throckmorton. All three members of the Samuel family were hanged in April 1593. They had been condemned to death under the Witchraft Act of 1562, which made sorcery a capital felony.

Even if witch-finding fervour never reached the same heights in England as in Scotland, the public was still fascinated – and terrified – by the subject, a fact not lost on Will Shakespeare. He would have heard lurid tales of the Scottish trials and would have known of King James's keen interest in witchcraft. In *Macbeth*, which was performed before James (by then, King James I of England) the first witch says, 'in a sieve I'll thither sail' – a line clearly inspired by Agnes Sampson's confession of putting to sea in sieves to sink the King's ship.

A Who's Who of Elizabethan Theatre

PLAYHOUSES IN THE late sixteenth century boasted a wealth of talent apart from Christopher Marlowe and William Shakespeare. Some of the other big names have minor roles in this book.

The Actor Manager: Edward Alleyn (1566–1626)

Alleyn started as an actor at seventeen and went on to make a fortune from his theatre and bear-baiting enterprises. His lucky break was to marry Joan, the stepdaughter of Philip Henslowe. The two men went into partnership, successfully running the Rose Theatre. Known for his powerful voice and commanding stage presence, Alleyn's starring roles included Marlowe's Tamburlaine and Dr Faustus. His greatest legacy is perhaps Dulwich College, which he founded, and which would bring forth many renowned writers including Raymond Chandler and P. G. Wodehouse.

The Star Player: Richard Burbage (1568–1619)

A much-loved actor, he was a good friend of William Shakespeare and was one of only three theatre colleagues named in the bard's will (he was left money to buy a 'mourning ring', a common practice of the day). Burbage, son of the theatre impresario James Burbage (builder of The Theatre, the first permanent playhouse), starred in many of Shakespeare's plays, including *Hamlet*, *Othello* and *King Lear*. A famous anecdote by John Manningham implies that Burbage and Shakespeare were both womanisers who, on one occasion, competed for the favours of the same lady. Shakespeare won, and boasted that 'William the Conqueror was before Richard the Third'.

The Impresario: Philip Henslowe (1555–1616)

A courtier to both Queen Elizabeth and James I, Henslowe had immense influence and wealth. He was the moneyman behind many plays and playhouses, including the Rose and the Fortune. When his stepdaughter married Edward Alleyn, the two men forged the most formidable partnership of the age, with Henslowe seeing himself as a father as well as a friend to the younger man. Henslowe was a hard-nosed businessman who made sure he wrung every last farthing out of the players and their productions. He owned much rental property around Southwark (where he lived) and had a reputation as a tough landlord. His other main source of income was as an owner of Southwark stews – brothels.

The Clown: Will Kempe (birth date unknown–1602)

The most celebrated comedy actor of the late Elizabethan age, Kempe was a tousle-haired, immensely fit performer who could hold an audience rapt with wonderment and laughter at his acrobatics and clowning. He had parts in plays by Christopher Marlowe, Thomas Kyd and, later, William Shakespeare, playing most of his famous comic parts, including Falstaff and Bottom. Always a free spirit, he quit the stage in 1600 to morris dance from London to Norwich, a journey of more than a hundred miles, which he called his 'Nine Days Wonder'. The Mayor of Norwich was so impressed he gave him a pension of £2. It has been suggested that Kempe's athleticism was not confined to tumbling, but extended to bedroom antics too.

The Popular Playmaker: Thomas Kyd (1558–94)

Kyd's *Spanish Tragedy* was probably the most popular stage play of the 1590s, being performed over many years both at the Rose Theatre in Southwark and, in translation, on the Continent. The play is a so-called revenge tragedy in which much blood is shed. But Kyd's success did not save him from a tragic clash with authority. In 1593 he was arrested on suspicion of being involved in the writing of virulent anti-foreigner tracts found outside the Dutch and French churches in London. Tortured, he claimed that heretical papers found in his room belonged to Christopher Marlowe, with whom he had lodged. Kyd was released from prison but his body had been broken by the ill-treatment meted out, and he died a year later. Like Shakespeare, he had been scorned by the university wits for being a mere grammar-school boy.

The Censor: Edmund Tilney (1536–1610)

Tilney, Master of the Revels to Queen Elizabeth, was born into trouble. His mother, Malyn, was a confidante of Catherine Howard, the second of Henry VIII's wives to be executed. Implicated in the events surrounding Catherine's fall from grace, Malyn was sentenced to life in prison, though she was soon freed. Her son Edmund spent much of the rest of his life avoiding trouble and currying favour with the highest in the land. He was Master of the Revels from 1578 until his death, his main duty being to organise entertainment for the court – bringing William Shakespeare and the top players of the day before his sovereign. He would watch rehearsals, lending props and costumes from the royal wardrobes when necessary and overseeing the building of elaborate stage sets. While he censored any work that might offend those in power, he also did much to protect and promote the London playhouses and acting companies.

The Patron: Sir Thomas Walsingham (1560–1630)

Thomas Walsingham was a cousin of Elizabeth's spymaster and chief minister Sir Francis Walsingham, for whom he worked in his younger days as an intelligencer, hunting Catholic priests. He was a patron of the theatre and of Marlowe in particular. Marlowe was a guest at Thomas's house in Chislehurst, Kent, in the days before his death. Curiously, Thomas was also linked to his killer, Ingram Frizer, and the other men known to have been in the room when he died, Robert Poley and Nicholas Skeres. Though some have wondered whether he had a role in the killing, Thomas was a mourner at Marlowe's funeral and seems to have been a true friend and benefactor. The American writer Calvin Hoffman suggested that Thomas and Marlowe were homosexual lovers. Hoffman left all his money to fund an annual prize for contributions to the debate.